WINNER OF THE G

LONGLISTED FOR **THE**
PRIZE 2023–24

A 2023 BOOK OF THE YEAR FOR *THE TIMES,*
SUNDAY TIMES, TELEGRAPH **AND THE**
NEW STATESMAN

'A dizzyingly inventive retelling of St Cuthbert's life' *Telegraph*,
Books of the Year

'[A] bold, experimental novel' *Sunday Times*, Best historical
fiction novels of 2023

'A bold story about faith and nationhood that upends
preconceptions of the "historical novel"' *New Statesman*, 20 best
books of 2023

'A book of remarkable range, virtuosity and creative daring ... A
millennia-spanning epic told in a multitude of perfectly realised
voices, this visionary story of St Cuthbert and the cathedral
built in his honour echoes through the ages' Tom Lee, Chair of
Judges, Goldsmiths Prize

'Part poetry, part electricity, this story carries relics between the
ephemeral and the eternal with all the disarming vitality of a
truly illuminated text' Helen Oyeyemi

'A bold novel that whirls us through a dizzying range of
poetic and prosaic styles' *Daily Telegraph*, The 75 best books for
summer 2023

'The work is alliterative and emotive. Strangely, I found it quite haunting. Wonderfully written' *Belfast Telegraph*

'Brave, bold and brilliantly alive, *Cuddy* calls forth the voices and the places of the north in a kaleidoscopic portrait through time. Myers at his best: dark, sharp, earthy and superbly funny. *Cuddy* isn't a novel, it's an invocation' Rob Cowen, author of *Common Ground*

'A work of art. Ben Myers has pulled off a kind of magic trick ... Daring, expansive and deeply satisfying, *Cuddy* is a truly original piece of writing which weaves a special kind of magic. I was left completely spellbound. I loved every minute of this dazzling and deeply original novel' Clover Stroud, author of *The Red of My Blood*

'Once again Ben Myers has built another time machine in words ... Most of all I appreciated how Myers explores faith and belief without the usual eyeroll and cynicism of our excessively secular age – I feel St Cuthbert's monks and masons looking down through history with a certain sense of pride' Luke Turner, author of *Out of the Woods*

'To be able to move from the Dark Ages, to the Middle Ages, to the Victorian Era to Modern Times and so ably capture the zeitgeist of each is a rare feat of imagination' Gabrielle Drake

'Incorporates poetry, prose, play, diary and real historical accounts to create a novel like no other' *Northern Life*

'Myers employs competing voices and different literary styles to pull together an ephemeral yet somehow tangible narrative that is both sweeping in its history and arresting in its style' *Yorkshire Life*

BENJAMIN MYERS was born in Durham in 1976. He is the author of ten books, including *The Offing*, which was an international bestseller and selected for the Radio 2 Book Club; *The Gallows Pole*, which won the Walter Scott Prize for historical fiction and has been adapted as a BBC series by Shane Meadows; *Beastings*, which was awarded the Portico Prize for Literature, and *Pig Iron*, which won the inaugural Gordon Burn Prize. He has also published non-fiction, poetry and crime novels and his journalism has appeared in publications including the *Guardian*, *New Statesman, TLS, Caught by the River* and many more. He lives in the Upper Calder Valley, West Yorkshire.

CUDDY

BENJAMIN MYERS

BLOOMSBURY

BLOOMSBURY PUBLISHING

LONDON · OXFORD · NEW YORK · NEW DELHI · SYDNEY

BLOOMSBURY PUBLISHING
Bloomsbury Publishing Plc
50 Bedford Square, London, WC1B 3DP, UK
29 Earlsfort Terrace, Dublin 2, Ireland

BLOOMSBURY, BLOOMSBURY PUBLISHING and the Diana logo
are trademarks of Bloomsbury Publishing Plc

First published in Great Britain 2023
This edition published 2024

A catalogue record for this book is available from the British Library

ISBN: HB: 978-1-5266-3150-3; TPB: 978-1-5266-3148-0; PB: 978-1-5266-3146-6;
WATERSTONES SIGNED EDITION: 978-1-5266-6337-5;
EBOOK: 978-1-5266-3149-7; EPDF: 978-1-5266-6070-1

2 4 6 8 10 9 7 5 3

Typeset by Integra Software Services Pvt. Ltd.

Printed and bound in Great Britain by CPI Group (UK) Ltd, Croydon CR0 4YY

To find out more about our authors and books visit www.bloomsbury.com
and sign up for our newsletters

For David Atkinson and Anna Barker.
And Cliff, canine co-pilot.

Contents

Introduction

Cuthbert was born circa 634 in Dunbar in the Kingdom of Northumbria (now in Scotland). After experiencing a vision while working as a shepherd he entered the monastery in Melrose aged seventeen and became prior there in 661.

He soon became widely known for his humble character, piety, love of the natural world, and for travelling great distances to preach in remote communities.

In 665 he was made prior of Lindisfarne, a North Sea island off the coast of Northumbria, accessible from the mainland via a causeway at low tide. There he spent many years in service.

Seeking a quieter life, Cuthbert retired to a smaller island off Lindisfarne in 676, then shortly afterwards moved to a simple stone structure on the even more remote island of Inner Farne.

A popular and respected figure affectionately known as Cuddy, in 685 he was persuaded to come out of retirement and was consecrated as Bishop of Lindisfarne, but soon returned to his small cell on Inner Farne. After a painful illness he died there on 20 March 687.

Over a decade later Cuthbert's body was believed to have been found to be intact, and he was declared a saint.

Under attack from Viking invaders, the monks of Lindisfarne fled the island in 793, taking with them the exhumed coffin containing the corpse of Cuthbert and various sacred relics. A long period of wandering then followed, during which a community of acolytes and devotees protected their saint.

His body was moved between various locations, though never found a permanent home. In 995 the 'Cuthbert community' finally settled in Durham, where they built the first of a series of churches and then, later, a vast cathedral to house him and his relics. Though his corpse has been exhumed on five more occasions over 1,200 years, and the cathedral the location of much tumult throughout the ages, his shrine remains there today and is a popular destination of international pilgrimage, with St Cuthbert widely recognised as the unofficial patron saint of the north of England.

Prologue

Inner Farne. AD 687.

March 20th. A Sunday.

A rheumy slit glued shut.
   My eye.
A gate against eternity.
   I open it.
All is as was; stone, sea and sky
   pouring in.

The other stays locked
lest the eternal world be rent asunder,
torn in two,
   split down the middle
   like a mackerel for the smokehouse rack.

And for a long soft moment
one part of me dwells in darkness,
the other in light.
   For a moment a part of me lives
   in death and the other dies in life.

✝

Limbo silence
then that silence is broken.

A seagull shrieks –
　　a pubbled white thing of feathers and beak
　　flung sideways on an unseen western gust,
　　one of His comic details.

But.
　　But it cannot be put off any longer. It is time to open the
other eye.
　　To raise the cullis, open the gate. Prise it.
　　I do.
　　And I die.

✝

Now here I lie,
something tickling at my elbow.
    It is a large   spider
    climbing the waxy incline of my cold and lifeless limb.

    Even here in death I feel it.
    Even here in death I serve a purpose as all things living
serve you
                    o lord.

I think: what I would like now more than anything is to be licked
about the face by dogs or nipped at the toes by Coldingham
crabs or nuzzled at the earlobes by seals or otters who waddle
over low-tide banks, trail-dragging patterns from seabed to
skyline, tresses of kelp draped across the head of one or two as
if in anticipation of a gaudy performance, others barking with
throaty delight, black eyes as black as peat clods, sea-swollen
bodies shifting on the hissing sand. The sun over the land.
    Strange the way the dead mind works.
    Such curious cravings.
               Such
                    queer notions.

Otherwise, as I say, all is as was, save for the tones of the brothers
who now talk as if I am somehow suddenly blind to their busy-
ness, deaf to their quibbles and squabbles, impervious to their
bird-fowl clucking just because I've finally passed over.
    The Bishop, it's the Bishop, Cuddy.

Daresay I detect a competitive edge to their sudden mourning too.
        He is dead.
        O lord he is dead.
        O lord he is dead and now we are dead with him.
        O lord he is dead and now we are dead with him, deliver us
        as one to your kingdom of heaven. Guide us, praise be. Christ
        receive him.

Their voices overlapping in a chorus of lament, each outdoing
the last.

      o! Cuddy this and *o! Cuddy* that

On and on
and on and
on.

And not for the
first time
I drift
of
f.

✝

Now see how they rush about the rock with their oils and their
bandages,
  their tinctures and their amulets and their wailing:
  o woe o woe
  wool cassocks flapping like the skirts of fisherwomen in a gale –
  see how they sob as they stumble in prayer, hear how they
wail like harpies,
  their words lost on the wind like tallow wick flames snuffed
by the night.
  O Lord
  o lord
  o.

I mean. What a performance. What rot.
  And the din
  the din
  echoing round the priory walls
  like the cries of purgatory itself –
  boom voice and sorry spittle
  flooding the halls,
  bouncing from stone to stone
  and out across the water,
  where the first boats
  have already docked,
  double-tied on a
  choppy tide,
  here to take
  me home.

✝

Death is a surprise party you knew all
along was to be thrown in your honour.

✝

Well now.
    You should have been here a candle or two ago.
    The scenes of despair amongst the monks at my final days of
retreat
       to this bluff in the foaming ocean was quite the picture.

Granted, death comes only once,
    and they are alarmed,
    but I'm glad you're here now, dear friend,
    to join me in the amber of the moment,
    holding my cracked and callused hand as
    we stride forth into the fevered hinterland.

And though my palms may be
    weathered and withered,
they are safe

as I straddle chasms,
    walk across the burning plain.
Spew flames.

    I am sun and moon and rain.

    Tomorrow's skeleton swathed in silk.

But you.
    You
    can call me
    Cuddy.

✝

BOOK I

Saint Cuddy

Dunholme. AD 995.

'*A furore Normannorum libera nos, Domine.*
From the fury of the Northmen, O Lord deliver us.'

Eighth-century prayer

I

'Medcaut, the "Island of the Tides", the Angles' name for Lindisfarne.'

> *Vanished Kingdoms: The History of Half-Forgotten Europe* by Norman Davies

'A vast prospect of sands, mud–flats and sea, stretching away south and east into a great bight and north and west to a far whiteness of breakers rolling in on an endless front from the North Sea; and in the middle distance of sands and flats a long low island.'

> *A Naturalist on Lindisfarne* by Richard Perry

'Twice every twenty-four hours the sea throws a glimmering girdle around its sandy perimeter. It takes five hours to complete the cycle of rising and falling tides.'

> *Lindisfarne Landscapes* by Sheila Mackay

'The name Lindisfarne is said to come from the Old English "lindon", meaning water, and "faron", meaning island – though no one is certain. Druids lived on the island before Christians.'

> *100 Days on Holy Island: A Writer's Exile* by Peter Mortimer

'The island took its name from the *Lindis*, a brook not more than two feet in breadth, which emptied itself into the sea from the opposite shore. Farne is the Celtic *Fahren*, a place of retreat.'

Saint Cuthbert, with an Account of the State in which his Remains were found upon the opening of his Tomb in Durham Cathedral by James Raine

'In the first centuries after the Romans left Britain, political and cultural dominance was established by the Northumbrian centres around Jarrow and Lindisfarne.'

The Anglo-Saxon Chronicles (Introduction) translated and collated by Anne Savage

'Lindisfarne, or Holy Island, in Northumberland was founded in 635 ... this event marked the beginning of remarkable monastic developments in Northumbria, the influence of which spread south over much of England and eventually beyond, to the continent of Europe.'

Monasteries in the Landscape by Mick Aston

'The new monasteries were deliberately built on islands or the coast as sanctuaries of learning.'

The Anglo-Saxon Chronicles (Introduction) translated and collated by Anne Savage

'The [original] Priory would have been sheltered below and behind a great ridge of volcanic rock to the south, the Heugh, which lies between it and the sea.'

Monasteries in the Landscape by Mick Aston

'He was carried by ship to our island, but first his whole body was washed, his head wrapped in a head cloth and an obley placed upon his holy breast. He was robed in his priestly garments, wearing his shoes in readiness to meet Christ.'

Two Lives of St Cuthbert by Anonymous Monk of Lindisfarne

'We placed the body of our venerable father in the boat and bore it across to Lindisfarne, where it was received by choirs of singers and a great crowd that had turned out to meet it.'

Herefrith of Lindisfarne

'If necessity compels you to choose between two evils, I would much rather that you take my bones from their tomb and carry them away with you to whatever place of rest God may decree, rather than to iniquity and put your necks under the yokes of schismatics.'

Cuthbert, from *Life of Cuthbert* by Bede

'Contrary to his wishes, Cuthbert was buried in a stone coffin.'
Lindisfarne Priory: English Heritage Guidebook

'The seventh-century coffin was a work of great art that showed how Cuthbert and his contemporaries imagined their Gods, angels, the apostles and God's mother… it was almost certainly painted and made even more vivid, even more of a rich focus for devotion.'

To the Island of Tides: A Journey to Lindisfarne by Alistair Moffat

'They were not willing to lose the fame and honour which would accrue to the place where his body was laid. He charged them, however, that if ever they had to flee the island, they should take his body with them.'

St Aidan and St Cuthbert by Henry Kelsey

'There had been no significant attacks from the sea for over two hundred years, and none were expected.'

The Anglo-Saxon Chronicles (Introduction) translated and collated by Anne Savage

'Dire forewarning came over the land of the Northumbrians, and miserably terrified the people: there were excessive whirlwinds and lightnings, and fiery dragons were seen flying in the air.'

The Anglo-Saxon Chronicle

'The monks dismantled the timbers of their first church and packed them onto carts; they lugged their ancient stone cross out of the ground and added it to the load. They dug up and disinterred the bones of their founder… Finally they prepared a great chest, a travelling coffin covered in hides to guard against the elements. This would transport the now antique coffin-reliquary, concealed within whose angelic, apostolic carvings lay the community's most precious and revered essence: the miracle-working, sanctuary-granting, divine portal that was the incorrupt corpse of St Cuthbert.'

St Cuthbert's Corpse: A Life After Death by David Willem

'Other important treasures were placed in the wooden coffin: the head of King Oswald, the bones of Aidan and the bones of Eate of Melrose.'

St Cuthbert of Durham by Philip Nixon

'His splendid burial deposit, including silk vestments, a gold and garnet pectoral cross, an ivory comb, a small gospel book and a silver-plated portable reliquary suggests his was an opulent milieu.'

The New Cambridge Medieval History I c.500–c.700 ed. Paul Fouracre

'It was because St Cuthbert was so passionately venerated that, in 793, before the men called "the wolfcoats" and "the berserks" could do his remains any harm, the Lindisfarne monks, knowing that precious shrines were a favourite target of the Viking sea-raiders, took his body from Lindisfarne and spent seven years wandering with it, looking for a safe place of refuge.'

A History of Britain: 1 by Simon Schama

'So great a blast of trial beat upon the church that many of the brethren chose to depart from the place than be in the midst of such danger.'

Bede

'They left Lindisfarne to flee from the barbarians.'

The Historical Works of Symeon of Durham

'Sea-raiders from Scandinavia roared onto the scene.'

Vanished Kingdoms: The History of Half-Forgotten Europe by Norman Davies

'The Danes came, burning and ravaging.'
   St Aidan and St Cuthbert by Henry Kelsey

'The sudden appearance of the Vikings was violent. Lindisfarne and the monastery were sacked.'
   The Anglo-Saxon Chronicles

'The pagans from the Northern region came with a naval armament to Britain, like stinging hornets, and overran the county in all directions, like fierce wolves, plundering, tearing, and killing not only sheep and oxen, but priests and Levites, and choirs of monks and nuns ...'
   The Historical Works of Symeon of Durham

'The ravaging of heathen men destroyed God's church at Lindisfarne through brutal robbery and slaughter.'
   Alcuin of York writing to King Ethelred of Northumbria

'... some of the brethren they killed; some they carried off in chains; many they cast out, naked and loaded with insults; some they drowned in the sea.'
   The Historical Works of Symeon of Durham

'Never before has terror appeared in Britain such as we have now suffered from a pagan race.'
   Alcuin of York writing to King Ethelred of Northumbria

'Pouring down the coast they destroyed Lindisfarne.'
   Vanished Kingdoms: The History of Half-Forgotten Europe by Norman Davies

'The raiders were out for plunder and to show their power to conquer. The island was chosen carefully as easy pickings and as an example. They took any silver and gold that had been left, smashed altars and broke down the high cross placed there.'
   Fire of the North: The Life of St Cuthbert by David Adam

'How could it not be thought that a blood price was coming down to the people from the north?'

The Edge of the World: How the North Sea Made Us Who We Are by Michael Pye

'Behold, the church of Cuthbert spattered with the blood of the priests of God, despoiled of all ornaments. The place more vulnerable than all in Britain is given to pagan people to plunder.'

Alcuin of York writing to King Ethelred of Northumbria

'On every road lay the corpses of clergy and laity, noblemen and commoners, women, youngsters and babies. Indeed there was no village or highway where the dead did not lie.'

Journal of Ecclesiastical History by S. Coupland

'The heathen defiled God's holy places and spilled the blood of saints all around the altar, destroyed the houses of our hopes. They trod on the bodies of the saints in God's temple like they were treading on shit in the open street.'

Alcuin of York writing to King Ethelred of Northumbria

'We can be confident that the psychological damage was immense – the most sacred centre of Northumbria had been violated.'

From Holy Island to Durham: The Contexts and Meanings of the Lindisfarne Gospels by Richard Gameson

'A man could no more forget the Vikings than his own bloody image in the mirror.'

The Edge of the World: How the North Sea Made Us Who We Are by Michael Pye

'A terrible famine gripped the land, caused mainly by the cease-less ravages of the Vikings.'

St Cuthbert of Durham by Philip Nixon

'Most of the already – severely – depopulated community were carried off by plague; the short incumbency of Cuthbert as

Bishop of Lindisfarne was itself troubled by disunity, and the interregnum that followed.'

> *From Holy Island to Durham: The Contexts and Meanings of the Lindisfarne Gospels* by Richard Gameson

'Even on the remote monastery island of Lindisfarne, sickness persisted for a year and almost every man died; even Lindisfarne was in the world.'

> *The Edge of the World: How the North Sea Made Us Who We Are* by Michael Pye

'Nourished by Continental connections and culture (not to mention codices), so Lindisfarne waned, still struggling to achieve stability and find a new identity in the changed ecclesiastical landscape.'

> *From Holy Island to Durham: The Contexts and Meanings of the Lindisfarne Gospels* by Richard Gameson

'Though checked from time to time by temporary defeats, the menace of the Danes remained in being.'

> *A Naturalist on Lindisfarne* by Richard Perry

'When the rude Dane burned their pile,
The monks fled forth from Holy Isle,
O'er northern mountain, marsh and moor,
From sea to sea, from shore to shore,
Seven years Saint Cuthbert's corpse they bore.'

> *Marmion* by Walter Scott

'Throughout this time of privation and danger the coffin of the saint was carefully protected. No outsider was allowed to touch the bier on which it was carried by seven carefully chosen men.'

> *St Cuthbert of Durham* by Philip Nixon

'The porters included Hunred, Stitheard, Edmund and Franco. On their journeys they must have encountered all weathers in

all seasons – all endured as an expression of their loyalty and devotion to St Cuthbert.'
Building St Cuthbert's Shrine by Lionel Green

'They managed to travel the length and breadth of Northumbria without being captured. Obviously this was often due to the devotion and help of others. Wherever they went they were met by the faithful.'
Fire of the North: The Life of St Cuthbert by David Adam

'Wherever the company went their precious burden attracted great respect and affection and indeed many gifts poured in – money, garments, cloths of finest silk and wool, magnificent fleeces, and donations from poorer folk.'
St Cuthbert of Durham by Philip Nixon

'They were given gifts of gold, fine garments, even land.'
Fire of the North: The Life of St Cuthbert by David Adam

'For seven years they were a peripatetic community, crossing to Cumbria and Galloway before recrossing the Pennines to North Yorkshire and eventually travelling north of Chester-le-Street in 882. Here, in a new church dedicated to St Mary and Cuthbert, the body rested for more than a hundred years.'
St Cuthbert and Durham Cathedral: A Celebration ed. Douglas Pocock

'Here, Cuthbert had shown himself more than capable of defending his own. Those who failed to treat him with due respect were struck with madness and a loathsome stench.'
Æthelstan: The Making of England by Tom Holland

'For some time the inhabitants on the estates of St Cuthbert between the Tyne and the Tees had been known as "haliwerfolc".'
St Cuthbert and Durham Cathedral: A Celebration ed. Douglas Pocock

'*Haliwerfolc* – the "folk of the holy man". County Durham seems narrowly to have escaped being called Haliwerfolc, rather like Norfolk or Suffolk.'

'The Wanderings of Saint Cuthbert' by D. W. Rollason
(from *Cuthbert: Saint and Patron* ed. D. W. Rollason)

'Cuthbert's community kept a book – they called it "The Book of Life" – in which were the names of all the benefactors for whom they prayed…The cult of Cuthbert symbolized a region's identity.'

The Oxford Illustrated History of Medieval England ed. Nigel Saul

'The Cuthbert cult spread throughout the land.'
Fire of the North: The Life of St Cuthbert by David Adam

'Men who had touched with their hands the incorruptible body of Saint Cuthbert, had explored it with their stead-fast eyes, had lifted it up and sustained it with their clasping arms, and they had learnt every secret concerning him.'

Reginald of Durham

'The body was the visible symbol of authority over men: over the *haliwerfolc*, the people of the saint.'

'The Wanderings of Saint Cuthbert' by D. W. Rollason

'Know and remember that, if of two evils you are compelled to choose one, I would rather that you should take up my bones, and leave these places, to reside wherever God may send you.'

Cuthbert, recorded by Bede

✝

II

Somewhere. AD 995.

I say this way.

Which way?

This way.

This way?

Yes.

This way here?

Yes. That way there.

Into the wood?

Yes.

This wood?

Into this wood indeed.

Are you sure?

Into a wood, out of a wood, sure or unsure. What difference does it make?

What difference does it make? he says. *What difference does it make?*

Saying it twice doesn't make it right.

Still but.

Still but what?

Still but I'm right to wonder. Praise the lord.

To wonder what? Praise the lord.

To wonder whether you might guide us blindly into eggy bog or flame-scorched black pit of hell, over looming scarp or 'neath swinging polearms of a Norseman's ambush?

No Norse here, brother.

How can you be certain?

God guides us away from the devil Dane.

It is true He sees all. Amen.
Well then. Amen.
Still but.
Still but what, dear brother?
Still but I'm right to wonder.
I do wish you would stop saying that.
Which way then?
I say this way. Praise the lord.
Which way? Praise the lord.
This way. Praise be St Cuddy.
This way? Praise be St Cuddy.
Yes.
This way here.
Yes. That way there. O lord give me the strength to endure the
perpetual torture of the foolish. Amen.
Amen.
Both together: *Amen.*

On
    and on
    they go:

    this way, that way,
    day upon day,
    just two voices *amening*
    amongst the many

in this colourful caravan of committed Cuddy acolytes
    this coffin-carrying cult, forever on the flit,
    forever making camp and breaking camp,
    consulting maps drawn only
    in northlands dirt with crooked sticks
    and no shortage of uncertainty,
    all the while
    bearing the ultimate burden:
    the bandage-bound body of the
    bier-mounted saint himself.

He formerly the most earnest and humble
Cuthbert of Melrose and Dunbar

from up there at the Firth of Forth, then later a wandering herder
of lost souls and man of great visions and miracles
and more latterly first Bishopric of Lindisfarne

then hermit on a large rock
then hermit on a small rock
then a corpse in a stone box.

Cuddy.

✝

I hoist the pack from my back and set it down.
    It is fashioned quite cleverly from a lobster creel
    and is over half my bodily length.

I am the smallest of those they call the *haliwerfolc* – that is,
the wandering folk of the holy man, the only female also,
but not once has another shared my breathless burden.

Such conversations as the one I have just documented
I have grown quite accustomed to.   Along
every lonnen we have stramped   beside
each cold and dreary black lough   always
the same.   Men
of cloth and scabrous of pate.   Pious
men.   The cast might change
but the arguments   remain   the same.

Often I think of this community as like rainwater on a
rock, forever reshaping itself into new configurations
though unlike rainwater rarely does it find the path of
least resistance. The inanity of monks is the only certainty.
The other thing that causes more consternation than which
direction to take
and for what reason,
and which prompts
the greatest competition,
is piety. That is: who is the
most pious brother in their
devotion to he who lies in repose
at the centre of our rag-tag menagerie
of wandering souls. I'm talking about the
bones of the sainted Cuddy, our one constant.

So while they bicker it out
I sit and watch and wait.
And in my mind I speak to him.

✝

o Cuddy tell
me about
your passing,
I say.

If that is what you want Ediva, then I shall tell you
how death finally folded over me like a breaking wave.

Two seasons before the slow drama of my bodily demise,
I retreated to that rock after several years away
fulfilling my duties to Him in service.

Seeking silence and solitude I returned
to a carillon of kittiwakes
at this outcrop in the moiling
broth of turbid brine.

The brothers would simply not leave me in peace,
just as I was soon to see them fussing about my corpse
(swift with their swaddling and lavish with their ointments,
they had already dug a coffin hole for me the very day I passed

and twice two squabbled over a spade,
or fell to their knees in the wet dirt
to scratch at earth,
as if mourning were a treasure hunt
and piety the prize).

They are nothing if diligent, these lads:
the boats were prepared for my short passage from the rock,
though I fancy I'd sooner be left out there as food for the gulls,
to be pecked apart, stripped and lifted,
sustenance for my old friends
the kitti
as lowered into the soil.

My monks —
they thought me unaware
that the priory's finest craftsman
had been carving sigils
and runic inscriptions
onto my casket since Epiphany:
Matthew, Mark, Luke *and* John
carefully cut with the finest scorper.

      I smelled, you see, Ediva, the beeswax
      he rubbed into those new notches.

o Cuddy, I reply.
I will find
a true home
for you.

✝

I stretch my back and arms. Swig from my flask.
    My young bones creak old, and many sore patches of skin
    yuke in places
    so private
    I could not hope to scratch them until sundown.

    And I fear
    I have put
    on weight.

These brothers of the brethren need to squabble it out until one
of them cedes or receives a sign or gets too hungry to continue,
but often this can take hours, days even.

    Once we waited
    at a fork in a track
    by an abandoned byre
    for fourteen moons
    as reasonings raged,
    though I'd wager the delay
    had much to do with the nearby farming family
    whose father had sired seven fine strong daughters
    – seven, of course, being a holy number –
    and the butterballs they brought down
    from their squat croft of sod and peatsmoke.
    Buckets of them, bobbing in the beastings.

    My cooking pots and tools rattle a little
    when I set my creel in the long grass
    that fringes this little used ride, and only the
    good Lord knows if I have walked it before,
    for in my short life I must have carved a trail
    into the land all the way from Coldingham to

Carlisle and from Cartmel to Chester-le-Street
and then on to hell itself on certain winter days.

Now the *haliwerfolc* is all I have known
since they said I was sold in for service
for half a hog and a few bricks of salt,
the opening of my sorry story: unknown.

I am the cook if cooking is what you can call it for often it is
barely food that I conjure from little. A slop of pap. A pap of
slop. At the very least it is always hot.

Yet still the brothers remark that
I have gained in girth and weight.
Certainly I feel different, perhaps
it is the spring season changing around me.

So I sit and sip and wait, then say a silent prayer:
      o Lord o God o Jesus
      o Cuddy sainted soul
      cast across these barren
      lands, not for the first time
      I ask not for a sign but for
      plugs of wax that my ears
      might become deaf to the
      infernal clucking of these
      wandering monks who
      I introduce to you now:

                Edmund
                Hunred
                Stitheard
                Franco
                Chad
                Eadmer
                the Bishop Aldhun

and a nameless boy a little older than me who joined us
most recently and who I have taken to quietly calling

Owl Eyes.

✝

The mission of the men is holy,
their cargo precious.

Each brother is made of shadows
into which the light of Cuddy shines.

So they shoulder the bones of a man
made great through miracles

and protect those parts the crows
would otherwise peck as carrion.

They say Cuddy does not rot but
all I see is a stone box

in search of a plot.
And we all walk on.

✝

The Bishop Aldhun remains, to me at least, something of a mystery, for in his attempts to at all times appear a figure of authority over those they call the folk of the holy man, he has made himself aloof, always one step ahead or one step behind the party. At each kirk or farmstead or home to which we arrive – and only recently have I learned that the island priory from which these monks have descended is a diocese in possession of no small amount of land stretching all the way down from the Tweed to the Tees, which might explain why often we can wander with impunity – he presents himself. And at each he is more often than not greeted cordially for he is a bishop, though it is never with the reverence shown towards that of our precious coffin containing the body of a man also once a bishop, but now elevated to a place high above, that of the sainted one, untouchable soul of eternity.

I don't know. Perhaps the Bishop Aldhun feels the burden of responsibility over Cuddy. With the devil Dane still prone to raiding this exposed coast and burning his way across these barren shores, inland woodlands and upland moors through which we wander, we are never truly safe, for even when seeking sanctuary in consecrated grounds the hogback coffin of Cuddy remains exposed. The devil Dane is a heathen you see, and to him our holiness and piety and devotion and goodness matters not one bit. In fact, possibly it vexes him all the more. We seek safety in our small number.

And we each carry Cuthbert within us.

✝

o Cuddy tell me more
about the joy of dying.

> *I will, child.*
> *I will.*

> *So: five days and nights I sat in silence,*
> *the divine storm raging around me.*

> *The wind whistling through my roof of straw: hear it.*

o Cuddy
I can hear it
I can hear it
now.

> *Twice it tried to lift the latch of my window but it was held*
> *fast: see it.*
> *Smoke from the snuffed candles swirled and dissipated: smell it.*

o Cuddy
I can smell it
I can smell it
now.

> *The swell kept all boats at bay and when I stood and shuf-*
> *fled to the latrine, limbs stiff with stasis as I clambered over the*
> *raised bank of dirt and rock, the dark sea was seen as nothing*
> *but furrow upon furrow, stacked shadows, slick mountains, and I*
> *thought of the bare-backed curves of a great grey serpent whose*
> *head dives deep beneath islands such as this, and whose tail*
> *flicks towards the shores of the godless Dane. And I prayed hard*
> *through the pain.*

I knew my brothers were afrit
at my ailing plight spent in hermetic reflection,
and those changes that my imminent passing
might bring to end their cossetted lives there,

and I knew too that the most stone-headed
or foolhardy brother would fill the oarlocks
and cast off at the first sign of the squall's settling,
that he might tear his arm sockets to see me,
but for now, in those final days
of preparation,
a sense of perfection

                      prevailed.

                      I feel it again now.
                      I feel
                      it.

o death
Cuddy?

                      o death
                      indeed.

As if made from the marriage of a feathered father and a blood-moon mother, the boy I call Owl Eyes is a curious lad, his story a mystery as my own past is to me.

He too the brothers picked up along the way, another scrawny orphan unearthed, or perhaps it was the call of Cuddy that he heeded.

Had he flown down from a branch to join us in the night I would not have been surprised for he has the silent, stealthy demeanour of a solitary hunter, but also a look of the hunted about him too. Nothing escapes his wet black all-seeing, unblinking eyes. Also, he is as perfectly self-contained and miraculous as a tiny bird held in the branch bowl of a nesting mother but – I am led to believe – as fragile too.

He understands horses. He has a way with them that goes beyond words and which makes him an asset to the monks. He handles them. He knows them. Loves them, even. And they too respond to Owl Eyes in a way quite unlike any other.

We all have our roles and this is his. The feeding and the watering. The whispering and the coaxing. The cleaning and clipping of their hooves.

He shows little interest in becoming a monk and the brothers have long since ceased to press the notion upon him despite their efforts. Better his time is spent with the beasts than lost in prayer; someone has to ensure the Cuddy community keeps moving, and between his handling and my cooking we have more than repaid the welcome afforded us by these coffin-bearing men of the cloth.

The horses pull the cart, you see, the cart that carries the stone casket, the cherished crate, the precious sarcophagus in which there lies a body corrupted neither by time nor maggots, and whose safety is our mission. We will not rest until we have received a sign that tells of a final resting place free from molestation from the devilish Dane, a place of pilgrimage, somewhere under soil and stone. A great mountain sculpted in visions into a place of wonder as befits a beatified soul.

So Owl Eyes plays his part, and I play my part, and we are rewarded with food and learning and what protection the brothers can offer, which is a lot, for their armour is faith in God and as two outsiders drawn into their strange congregation, there is an unspoken kinship between us, the two lost children of the blood-soaked northlands.

✝

All that I own:
flint and tinder box
two smocks.

Seeds of flax
corn dolly plaits.
Nubs of wax.

Kindling cord
toy sword
button hoard.

Wishing bone.
Blue river stone.
Fossil cone.

All that I own.

✝

Lightning heat and bolt flash. Blue fork. Skull clang and sulphur. Mud flame and fire stone. Great towers of it, rising. Bellowing. Roaring. The upthrust. And then this night from the thick wet soil it sprouts again, not for the first time, a mountain of stone like an oak pushed from an acorn. Surge of stone, a burst cave turned inside out. Needles of rock reaching upwards, shoots of stone as sharp as sickles or adze blades, others blunted, carved, curved, sensual. The great mass of stone stretched and sculpted into towers, the stone blasted and shaped into being. Hammered and chipped and rain-lashed into the shape of something emerging from hill top bedrock. A barrow of trees surrounding it, a looping oxbow creating the idea of an island. River as moat, moat as a serpent slow-sliding through the woodlands, carving a wooded gorge of jutting cliffs. Bone blast and shatter. Angels aflame, behold the burning trumpets. Christ on his cross beaming with joy as from the ashes grow great shoots of stone. Stone tendrils tangling and intertwining as one. Grit gash and hammer. Stone dreams and dreams of stone. Summoned by a saint, envisioned by woman, built by man, by hand. A cathedral, as big as heaven. Looming large over the wooded Wear that echoes with the cuckoo's call and the gouk's song singing still out across the holme, as the mountain unfurls, creates corners of itself. The shape becomes something howled out, hollowed out, a thou-sand churches inflated to greatness, a carved cavernous place of worship the size of the sky. Shrine and sanctuary, fold and temple, stone scooped out to house the pilgrims of the world. The sordid and the saved, the sick and the savage. This place. Made so ornate as to silence all who climb the hill to cast awestruck eyes upon windows that tell stories and shatter the day into stunning rainbows. Balustrades as high as clouds and stairwells stretched and spiralling like augers. Steps that wind to dizzy heights. Up and up and up and then out, out onto the celestial plane, a platform from which to whisper into His ear and to comb the hair of angels. Heat flash and white sheets. Blue fork and screaming eyes. The scent of stone, spicy. A thunderclap into further visions of high-vaulted transepts and stone-trapped silence so deafening. Galleries and shad-ows and shrines and incense and naves and arcades and undercrofts and dormitories and claustral adjuncts and great carved doors depicting beasts and foliage and paint-ings and friezes and chapels and ornaments and sturdy columns. Dozens of columns, carved with chevrons and lozenges and fluting in detail so fine, and a refectory and a clerestory and a presbytery with adjoining apses, and kitchens and libraries and dorters and chapter houses, and everywhere slabs of stone sliced sideways and laid like the pages of a book unpicked and placed carefully. Flames of the vision raging inside. The cathedral realised. Growing. Bellowing. Roaring. Scenes of shrines, so many shrines, but none more holy than that of St Cuthbert, our bishop, our saint, Cuddy of Melrose, Cuddy of Lindisfarne. Cuddy of these visions. Cuddy of the ducks and otters and birds and seals and sand dunes. Cuddy of the rock in the foaming sea. Cuddy of the marram grass, humble Cuddy, sweet Cuddy. Guiding light, beacon of the wandering folk of the holy man. Cuddy of these visions. Cuddy of the church, Cuddy of the kirk. Cuddy of the north, Cuddy of England. Cuddy of these visions. Shepherd, bishop, brother, friend, monk. Cuddy the creator of this stone mountain in the deep green dene that carries the river and the gorge and all the wild creatures that stalk the waterways and roam the quiet clearings and burrow deep down into the cellar of the island, his perfectly preserved corpse forever held in the cool embrace of the sunning mountain that man shall see fit to take and turn into a place of repose. Sepulchre for his bones and skin and eyes and fingers and his faith. Here shall be the final silence of centuries of wandering and lands torn bloody and burned black with the fire torches of devils. Stone built on foundations of faith. Stone faith that rouses us to rise each morning to feed the horses that drag the cart that carries the coffin that holds the body that one day soon will be lowered and sealed in the bowels of the mountain on the wooded hill over the river and the gorge that echoes ever onwards with the sweetest of birdsong and up above shall sleep our saint. Cuddy. Patron of the north. Leader of men. Mountain-dwelling prophet but a humble man, a good man, a man whose influence will ring like a bell down the ages for all time. A man reborn in these raging, roaring visions.

In time

my mind is a map
                    of names
                    and places

                    of bothies
                    and barns

                    of priories
                    and farms.

Settlements no more than a heap of stones and a single spiral of
smoke,
sheep watching on. Eyes in the hills. A shallow spring at the
crossroads.

                    Etal
                    Duddo
                    Twizell
                    Unthank.

Faggot, Fanny Barks and Flesh Shank.

                    Holywood
                    Foggy Furze
                    Wackerfield
                    Muggleswick.

Wide Open, Wham and Wallish Walls.

                    No Place and Busygap.
                    Babes Well and Devil's Lapful.
                    Juniper

Ludworth
Lintz.

Lickar Moor.

✝

Brother Hunred?
I ask.

Yes, girl.

How will we know when we have got to where it is we
are going?

Brother Chad scoffs at this.
His laugh sticks in his throat
like a feather; I hope it chokes him.

The girl has little faith
he says.

It's a fair question
says dear Hunred.

True believers don't question
snaps Chad.

Hunred catches my eye
and raises a brow at this.
I stifle a titter.
Skugg it in my cuff.

Enquiring minds will enquire
he says.
It's hardly a sin.

Here Stitheard falls into step.

I've often wondered the same thing
he says
then sneezes
for his chest is aflame with green rot

that he coughs up and spits out with a
quiet *forgive me, Lord*, and leaves behind
a trail of throat mussels
in our wandering wake.

       Brother Stitheard
I says.
       I shall fix you a remedy
       for your malady
       tonight when
       we make camp

because as well as community cook
I also know a thing or two about
plants and poultices and potions

and again Chad scoffs at this
but only because he has never
needed a helping hand as he is
in the rudest of health, worse luck.

At Stitheard's encouragement, Hunred continues unabashed.

       How will we know when we have got to where it is we
       are going?
he repeats.

       Yes
I say.
       What I mean is:
       how will we know when we have found a resting place
       fit for a saint?

He chews this over like a knot of hog knuckle.
       I believe there will be a sign, Ediva.

Even Chad is curious at this.

> A sign?

I says.

> Yes, child. A sign.
> Of what I do not know, but Cuddy will guide us and
> when he is ready he will show us.

> Amen

says Stitheard.

> Conveniently vague

mutters Chad.

> On the contrary, dear brother

says Hunred.

> Not vague at all.
> For a sign is a sign is a sign. We'll know it when we see it
> and we'll see it when we know it.

> Amen

says Stitheard again

and for once even Brother Chad stays silent
for as he himself said
true believers don't question.

✝

o Cuddy tell me
how did they
prepare your body
which we carry now?

        Well, child. Giddy with grief,
        there was much hesitant discussion
        about what effects
        might accompany me
        into the kingdom of the afterlife
        in the coffin lowered
        into the soft spring soil.

        stole   or   pectoral pendant?
        maniple   or pocketbook?
        candles,   of course,
        to illuminate the way.

        And, perhaps, a fine comb
        for grooming? Yes, a comb

        of stag horn or   cow bone.

        They speak so   loudly.
        In death I discover
        I am
            deafened
            by voices that
            r o a r
            like the sea
            cleaving
            deep
            new caves
        beneath the cliff edge.

And all appears brighter somehow too,
as if sprinkled with crushed quartz.

I see the detail in everything,
down to the finest pigmentation. Yes.

        In death

all is brighter, all is brilliant and
I am thrilled by the thought
of coils of slick and oily bladderwrack
slipping
            and
                    popping through
my cracked, dry hands, or being
blinded by the dark drama
of a pother of
rolling
rain
crab-crawling inland.

            I am
            ravenous
            for hot meat,

            fizzy with
            joy.

            O lord
            o death
            o sweet release

            And all is
            history now.

O Cuddy
I cannot wait.
I cannot wait
to join you.

No, child.
Your time is
best spent upright.
You must stay alive.

✝

He sidles up to me, the Bishop Aldhun. Talks in a roundabout way for a while.

And how are you keeping, child? Well I hope? Yes, yes, the stores, I trust, are sufficiently replenished? You're giving thanks each day to our lord for feeding us? All of that.

I wish to reply that it is I that is doing all the feeding round here, but I don't want to rattle the man because it's clear he's building up to something, and when he confesses he has an ailment it is as if *he* were a nervous child approaching a bishop instead of the other way round, and I have to bite my cheeks to stifle the smirking.

It's his stones, you see.

They are all a-sore.

His balls, raw. From the walking.

Chafed to buggery. Coarse as fire moss.

There is no other way of putting it.

I tell the Bishop that he is in good hands, as it were, and that I can prepare him a cooling poultice for his throbbing stones and furthermore I shall keep his burden quiet, though of course it will be an easier secret to keep were I able to rest my head on one of those goose down pillows I've seen him fluff into place before his sleeping.

He lowers his eyes and slowly nods, and that night my head rests on a sack of sweet soft feathers and I enjoy the best sleep in as long a time as I can recall.

As does the Bishop.

✝

Owl Eyes says so very little it is easy to forget that he has a working tongue.

One day we are on a short walk to a safe parish when he too falls into step beside me.

We are somewhere between the two great rivers of the Tyne and the Wear.

I forget where exactly but it is full spring because the briar and brush are busy with song as the birds go about their nest-building, and at night the sky echoes with the screams of rutting foxes, violent couplings that will produce tumbling cubs in just a few short weeks, and so the cycle will begin again.

We walk for a while before Owl Eyes speaks, and when he does it is in a voice so rarely heard by all except the horses that it is as beautiful as the birdsong that surrounds us, in its own innocent, melodious way. A voice of life and wanting.

        Do you think we are close?
he wonders.

        Close?
I say.
        You and I?

His faces flushes a little at this and I see the sunshine ignite the fine hairs on his upper lip and turn them to golden threads.

        Close to where it is we are going
he says.

        Brother Franco said we will be there before sundown and that I should have time to prepare a meal.

        No
says Owl Eyes.
        To where it is we are going, I mean. Beyond this day and the next. With the burden of the saint that the horses drag through bog and over bluff and boulder upon us.

It is a burden for which we are meant to be grateful
I says.

Meant to be
he says.

Why, are you tired of bedding down in tents and caves
and kirk naves?

Owl Eyes shrugs at this.

It's all I know, Ediva
he says.
I just wondered if you ever wondered too.

Where it is we are taking him, you mean?

Yes. The final resting place that the brothers seek. Where
it is and what it might look like, and how such a place as
befits a saint could ever be found in these godforsaken
lands.

No
I reply, though with hesitation.

He looks at me sideways. There is a tiny scar above one eye that
I had not noticed.

No?

I already know where it is that we are taking him.

Again he looks at me sideways.
You already know where it is that we are taking him?

Yes. I have seen it.

For years we have been in flight from the devilish Dane.
Before you and I were even born, Ediva, the brothers
have carried Cuddy aloft across the water from his island
home up here to this kingdom of fells and forests.

This is the most I have ever heard Owl Eyes speak. I let his
words settle there for a moment and say nothing so that he is
forced to continue.

And yet you say you have seen the place to which we
walk?

I nod. Still I say nothing. I am enjoying the small amount of
power that the knowledge affords me.

How?

We stroll on.

Under sleep
I finally say.

Under sleep?

In visions
I say.

Aye.

In visions?

Yes. I have seen our destination many times.

How is that possible?

How is anything possible? How do we eat each morning and survive each day? How do we evade the devil Dane and keep Cuddy safe and always find our way?

Because God made it so?

Well then
I sniff.
God must have made it so.

We walk on. Owl Eyes shakes his head.

I don't understand.

You would understand if you had visions too.

Owl Eyes says nothing until the silence forces him to fill the empty mould of it with a confession.

Under sleep I have visions too.

You do?

Yes. But mainly of horses. Hundreds of horses galloping across the plains. There are no people there, just horses. The sound they make is the thunder we hear before rain. The foaming of their hot trunks is the foam that follows. And it is beautiful. But I have not seen Cuddy's final resting place.

Those are just dreams
I say and we continue, lost in our thinking.

But then he stops and here Owl Eyes turns to me and in the most earnest voice says:

Tell me about it. Tell me what it is you see, Ediva.

I wait a while before speaking, but when I do the words rush like a river.

> I see things I do not understand but I also know that in days to come I will begin to comprehend them. I see scenes of tomorrow and I know that tomorrow's people will thrive there.

> Yes

says Owl Eyes, his wide wet eyes widening further still, as wide as a bird's in that frozen moment before it swoops down for the kill, when the pulse of its prey is beating in its ears and the forest falls away to nothing, and all that remains is flight and talons and flesh and the screaming of the damned.

I continue.

> They come to me under sleep, these scenes, these people. There is a building. I see it as you see the moon, Owl Eyes. This building. It is bigger than anything man has ever built, so big it rears up like a mountain, like a great beast. But it is beautiful too, so ornate and intricate in its devotion and gratitude to God that it could only be man-made, man-created, man-consecrated. Nothing so fashioned could be a natural product; no, this is the work of man. Many men. And women too. People like us.

Owl Eyes urges me on.

> Yes yes

he says,

> go on.

So I do.

> For it is a church like no other that I see. Each stone tells a story and together these stories join together to chart the rise of man, the rise of God, the rise of man and

God together, and the rebirth of dear departed Cuddy, whose corpse we carry and whose new home I see under sleep. Faces adorn this church. Also stone faces sit on the corners too, and there are towers so tall that the clouds look up in awe as they rise above them. And the windows, oh, the windows. They do turn the sun's rays into things of varying wonder. So many colours.

Which colours, Ediva?

All the colours and many more
I say.
Together we will build it.

We will build the colours?

We will build the everything.

✝

Perhaps
it is like a lightning line
behind the eye

a blue prong
pitchforking an
unexpectant skull

or seven mad magpies
bricked into a
belfry.

Perhaps
it begins with bells
or temporary blindness

or the whirlpool swirl of the sun.
The scent that follows summer rain.
A taste of dust on the tongue.

Of this I am certain:
no two start the same,
yet each new vision

builds the same stone structure
behind the black veil drawn
across my day –

a temple of spires,
monks and muttering priors.
A window, an altar, a weathervane.

✝

Bone fire and skull candle. Eye blast and blackened. A shower of sparks. These are the signs this night under stars and wrapped in calfskin, the last embers pulsing with the blood of the heat of the fire that will scorch a moon of ash by morning. To return there again. To blue lightning-bolt visions. To beams of pain pulsing through fissures of sleep. These vision eyes climbing the slopes of the vision hill. Young hands clawing through scrub and whin. The stone mountain summoned by faith, made by man. A place to become a cathedral in which to lay down Cuddy. A place to arrange him in eternal repose. In black drapes and white-heat flashes, every detail revealed. Thoughts follow thunder. Fresh details. Every architectural question answered. Every problem solved. I, Ediva, see it all in fever. I see it all in stone, as if standing there gazing up. To towers that block the silver sun. To a stone crown alive with crows. Another skull scream and time-slip. Then I slowly see myself pushing a sturdy wooden door. Entering this temple of stone and dust that my simple mind has built. Heart-thump and fear. Fire-flash as I pause and stand inhaling the scent of varnished wood and beeswax and faith. Then the faintest choir of voices joining in harmony. Voices finding a note and holding it. And the note growing. The note glowing. Gleaming. Time jump. The voices becoming louder. Stronger. Brighter. A burning chorus singing a hymn for a saint. A hymn for Cuddy sung by voices young and old. Voices pure and bold. The bold chorus of faith and fealty. Of constancy and credence. Concepts never taught. Words never learned. Feelings felt. Voices of conviction. Of assent and assurance. Voices of truth and troth. Voices of angels. Angels singing a song deep into the catacombs of my sleeping mind. Solidifying the vision and reminding that this is real and it is our quest and when I see the sign we will find the wooded island and there on the hill we shall stop and we will rest and we will build it.

✝

III

'His name, Cuthbert, strongly suggests that he was of Anglo-Saxon, rather than British, stock.'

> *Lindisfarne: The Cradle Island* by Magnus Magnusson

'Some claim he was of aristocratic birth, others that he was from a peasant family.'

> *Cuthbert and the Northumbrian Saints* by Paul Frodsham

'No one quite knows who his parents were.'

> *Saints Over the Border* by Margaret Gibbs

'He loved games and pranks, and as was natural at his age, loved to play with other children. He was naturally agile, and quick-witted and usually won the game. He would often still be fresh when the rest were tired and would look round in triumph, as though the game were in his hands, and ask who was willing to continue.'

> *Life of Cuthbert* by Bede

'He enjoyed doing handstands with his friends.'

> *Lindisfarne Priory: English Heritage Guidebook*

'They say he could turn somersaults and even walk on his hands – which is most difficult.'

> *Saints Over the Border* by Margaret Gibbs

'When he was eight years old he was handed over into the care of a Christian foster-mother named Coenswith in an unidentified village called Hruringaham… he called her "mother" and would often visit in later life.'

Lindisfarne: The Cradle Island by Magnus Magnusson

'He was a dreamy, quiet lad, and he was fond of listening to what the monks in the valley had to say about God and Heaven.'

Tales of English Minsters: Durham by Elizabeth Grierson

'The boy devoted himself to God, and, as he would later recount to his friends, when he prayed for help against frequent and pressing difficulties, he often had angels sent to defend him.'

Life of Cuthbert by Bede

'There were a great many other shepherd boys there, and they all lived out in the open with their flocks day and night.'

Saints Over the Border by Margaret Gibbs

'One night when his companions had gone to sleep and he was keeping watch and praying as usual, he suddenly saw light streaming from the skies, breaking the long night's darkness, and the choirs of the heavenly host coming down to earth. They quickly took into their ranks a human soul, marvellously bright, and returned to their home above. The youth was moved by this vision to give himself to spiritual discipline in order to gain eternal happiness with the mighty men of God.'

Life of Cuthbert by Bede

'Cuthbert was drawn to Melrose rather than to Lindisfarne because of the fame and sublime virtues of the monk and priest Boisil.'

Lindisfarne: The Cradle Island by Magnus Magnusson

'A monk was standing at the gates. It was the Prior Boswell.'

Saints Over the Border by Margaret Gibbs

'*Ecce servus Dei!* ["behold a servant of the Lord!"]'

> Prior Boisil of Melrose monastery, upon first seeing Cuthbert

'Boisil died of a plague which had affected Cuthbert also. Herefrith, a priest of Lindisfarne and later abbot there, who was in the monastery at the time, told Bede how, in the last week of his life, Boisil proposed to spend his time teaching his disciple.'

> 'The Spirituality of St Cuthbert' by Sister Benedicta Ward SLG
> (from *St Cuthbert, His Cult and His Community to AD 1200* ed. Gerald Bonner, David Rollason and Clare Stancliffe)

'As prior of Melrose one of Cuthbert's tasks was preaching to those who had lapsed into paganism because of the plague.'

> 'Cuthbert, Pastor and Solitary' by Clare Stancliffe
> (from *St Cuthbert, His Cult and His Community to AD 1200* ed. Gerald Bonner, David Rollason and Clare Stancliffe)

'Although his old neighbours were very proud of the honour which had come to him, Cuthbert thought little of it; for he was a humble man, and he loved better to preach to the ignorant folk who lived among the hills than to stay at home in his prior's parlour at Melrose.'

> *Tales of English Minsters: Durham* by Elizabeth Grierson

'It was his way for the most part to wander in those places and to preach in those remote hamlets, perched on steep rugged mountain sides, where other men would have a dread of going, and whose poverty and rude ignorance gave no welcome to any scholar.'

> *Beasts and Saints* by Helen Waddell

'For many of them profaned the faith they held by wicked deeds, and some of them also at the time of the plague, forgetting the sacred mystery of the faith into which they had been initiated, took to the delusive cures of idolatry, as though by incantations or amulets or any other mysteries of devilish art, they could ward off a blow sent by God the creator. So he frequently went forth from the monastery to correct the errors of both kinds of sinners.'

Life of Cuthbert by Bede

'There were no village churches. If people wanted to be married or baptized they had to wait until one of the missionary monks came round.'

Saints Over the Border by Margaret Gibbs

'Often for a whole week, sometimes for two or three... he would not return home.'

Beasts and Saints by Helen Waddell

'And occasionally for a full month, wearing a habit of undyed home-spun wool, and over it in winter a long cloak made of such strong material it resisted rain. He may have taken with him a satchel.'

St Aidan and St Cuthbert by Henry Kelsey

'He would tarry in the mountains, summoning the rustics to heavenly things by the words of his preaching as well as by the example of his virtue.'

Life of Cuthbert by Bede

'Cuthbert was recalled after his departure from Melrose by Bishop Eata, who assigned him to Lindisfarne.'

'Cuthbert, Pastor and Solitary' by Clare Stancliffe

'Clearly Cuthbert did not have an easy time. Within the monastery he had to persuade the brothers to accept a monastic rule rather than their traditional customs, and this aroused bitterness.'

'Cuthbert, Pastor and Solitary' by Clare Stancliffe

'A late seventh- or an eighth-century monastery often had many of the aspects of a special kind of nobleman's club... even at Lindisfarne the brethren feasted at Christmas in a manner which alarmed Cuthbert.'

> 'Elements in the Background to the Life of St Cuthbert and the Early Cult' by J. Campbell (from *St Cuthbert, His Cult and His Community to AD 1200* ed. Gerald Bonner, David Rollason and Clare Stancliffe)

'He would spend whole nights praying, sometimes lying in ice-cold water all the time.'

> *Saints Over the Border* by Margaret Gibbs

'Praying in the icy waters of the sea, that old monastic remedy for lust.'

> 'The Spirituality of St Cuthbert' by Sister Benedicta Ward SLG

'One night one of the monks watched him creep out, then followed him stealthily to see where he was going and what he was about. Down he went towards the beach beneath the monastery and out into the sea until he was up to his arms and neck in deep water. The splash of the waves accompanied his vigil throughout the dark hours of the night. At daybreak he came out, knelt down on the sand, and prayed. Then two otters bounded out of the water, stretched themselves out before him, warmed his feet with their breath, and tried to dry him on their fur.'

> *Life of Cuthbert* by Bede

'These, prostrate before him on the sand, began to busy themselves warming his feet with pantings... and when this good office was rendered, and they had his benediction, they slipped back again beneath their native waters.'

> *Beasts and Saints* by Helen Waddell

'They departed to their haunt in the waves of the sea.'

> *The Anonymous Life of Cuthbert*

'The brother kept silence on the piece of valour that he had seen, until after the saint's death, when he took pains to tell it to many.'
    Beasts and Saints by Helen Waddell

'Cuthbert was wonderfully patient and unsurpassed for courage in enduring physical or mental hardship. Though overwhelmed by sorrow at these monks' recalcitrance he managed to keep a cheerful face.'
    Life of Cuthbert by Bede

'At chapter meetings he was often worn down by bitter insults, but would put an end to the arguments simply by rising and walking out...'
    Life of Cuthbert by Bede

'It must have tried the patience of a saint indeed!'
    Lindisfarne: The Cradle Island by Magnus Magnusson

'... he would upbraid the monks for their softness.'
    Life of Cuthbert by Bede

'He sedulously abstained from all intoxicants; but he could not submit to such abstinence from food, lest he should become unfitted for necessary labour.'
    The Anonymous Life of Cuthbert

'There are, however, signs of accommodation in his willingness to drink wine when ill.'
    'Cuthbert, Pastor and Solitary' by Clare Stancliffe

'Whether he was praying alone in some secret place or saying his psalms, he always did manual work to drive away the heaviness of sleep, or else he would do the rounds of the island, kindly inquiring how everything was getting on.'
    Life of Cuthbert by Bede

'Many monks and clerks drank and thought like noblemen, owned slaves and treasures and probably lived in halls like noblemen. It was a particular source of distress to their critics that they also dressed like noblemen. When Cuthbert's sober garb is stressed, it is because other clerics were less restrained.'

'Elements in the Background to the Life of St Cuthbert and the Early Cult' by J. Campbell

'He wore quite ordinary clothes.'
Life of Cuthbert by Bede

'Vanity in dress is not fitting for men.'
Alcuin in a letter to Higbaldus, from *Life of Cuthbert* by Bede

'Bring me my staff and sandals.'
Cuthbert, from *The Anonymous Life of Cuthbert*

'He could never finish Mass without shedding tears.'
Life of Cuthbert by Bede

'Cuthbert yearned with ever increasing intensity for a less and less worldly lifestyle. He craved solitude, not to escape from the cares of the world but as a means of coming closer to God... at the core and centre of his being he felt a profound compulsion to become a recluse, a holy hermit.'
Lindisfarne: The Cradle Island by Magnus Magnusson

'A monk completely, a monk, a monk I say.'
Symeon of Durham

✝

IV

Seven moons in a hill fort.
Seven days dry.

A feast of fish from a barrel bartered back at Once Brewed
and fine honey for the loaves.

The coffin covered and raised, watched over. Guarded.
Prayed upon. We rest.

I ask Chad which way is north and he points to the stars.
Chad is an ass.

Amen.

✝

o Cuddy
tell me
is it true
about the otters?

> *Well, yes. It is true that on occasion*
> *I muttered my prayers tit-deep in the sea.*
>
> *It does something to both mind and blood,*
> *and bones, the cold.*
>
> *Here life and death do dance under*
> *the watchful gaze of a graceful God*
>
> *until upon a truth it is so agreed.*
>
> *Of the otters who are said to have dragged*
> *their fleshy forms across banks of sand and shale*
> *to dry my blueing feet with their hot fishy breath*
> *beneath glistening whiskers strewn with jewels*
> *however I cannot, alas, comment.*

✝

As a woman I am allowed
my own tan-hide tent
a place
that they do call the kitchen
and the price I pay is that I am placed away
from the brethren lest they fall into temptation.

I am at the edge of the camp, a she-wolf.
    It pleases me.

This I am quite content with, for even the holiest men
do talk and fart long into these northern nights
and stagger about watering the plants and
sometimes linger by the twine of my tent flap
a little too long than is courteous or comfortable.

Only
Owl Eyes
ever
enters.

First for warmth
then for succour.

This boy is not Godly and no one can quite recall why
or from where he came, for memories can be as great
a burden as a pocketful of rocks. Why carry them?

He has brilliant wide eyes that peer into your very
                        centre.
Eyes that seem not to blink. Eyes that one day are
                        blue
and the next jade, then anthracite and once, red.

Still he says little and I say little and perhaps that is
why we have long prayed beneath the skin of cow
and each drawn breath until we are at one with Him.

o Cuddy
I know you know.
I know you do
see everything.

> *Yes, girl.*
> *I watch without*
> *judgement and*
> *pray for you*
> *always.*

✝

Weeks wandering
wondering:

what will tomorrow's
tomorrow
look like?

What will be the shape of it?

✝

Easing down the Whin Sill shelf one day
we leave the Old Wall behind and trudge
across the plateau of wind. Roman ghosts
stalk the ditches dug by men of golden skin.

Trinkets sit in the soil unseen, spoils
of an Empire that stretched, they say,
from here to sunny islands far away
(north was nothing but heathens).

They built first a fort and then a town,
and called it *Corstopitum* or *Corbricg*
or *Colebruge* or *Corbridge*, a last
fish caught in a net flung from a place

named for a founding king called Romulus.
They barely dared to wander further, deeper,
into Pictish hills, turning back from myths
of man–beasts born from blood and battle.

This I know from the brothers who, tiring
of parables from God's book, do on occasion
tell me tales instead of the old wild tribal
lands, on which all life silently trembles.

We walk for a sun and a moon and then
one more of each. The brothers chant
and the brothers sing, meandering hymns,
heartful and devotional, but lost in the swale.

Then Cuddy comes to Corbridge, to the parish
kirk of St Andrew where we are welcomed
by a priest called Popple, his pink face pluked
but a good man; his stores generously stocked.

The horses are handled well and rested
and here we sojourn for a week or two,
some brothers pairing off to preach the good
word while the others guard our cargo.

✝

o Cuddy
I call out to thee
o Cuddy
spill your secrets.

> I will, my girl, I will.
> But first this. First
> I shall tell you
> what I miss.

> I miss
> my oldest friends
> from the Holy Islet.

> I miss
> the eider duck and the fulmar
> the meadow pipet and the skylark

> the mallard and the kestrel
> the pintail and the coot
> the little egret and the lapwing
> the gannet and the snipe

> I miss
> the mute swan and the moorhen
> the red-breasted merganser
> the bar-tailed godwit
> the goldeneye and the tufted duck
> the knot, the turnstone, the ringed plover
> the grey heron, the oystercatcher
> the pied wagtail, the moorhen,
> the teal and the black-headed gull
> the dabchick's shrill call

> I miss them all.

> I miss

the phragmites that harbour them
the eelgrass
the mudflats
the velvet-tipped reedmace

and o how I miss
the cold and lonely black lough
where the pink bogbean grows.

Are there
birds
where you are now
o Cuddy?

    Yes, child.
    They fly around the inside of my skull.

✝

Brother Stitheard
                    is stricken
with yet another
                    ailment.

First there was the
                    blue bile,
then there followed a fit of
                    coughing

and for a week he suffered
                    horrors
upon waking, screaming
                    horrors

so violent it was as if Satan
                    himself
had moved into our poor
                    Stith.

Now he complains of a
                    rash
on his scalp so severe he
                    cannot

bring a blade to his head,
                    cannot
shave his pate as the Bishop
                    demands.

Oh child what can be done?
                    Stitheard
groans, fingering wooky sores,
                    glistening.

Your hair is growing out,
                    perhaps

it softens your features,
               I say.

He swats the compliment
               aside,
and I see mild Stitheard suffers
               still.

We have prayer brother, and
               poultices,
I say, applying a wad of cloth
               packed

with comfrey, Lady's Mantle and
               yarrow
soaked slowly in ale and apple
               syrup.

The look upon his phyz displays
               gratitude:
Truly you are heaven-sent,
               child.

And within a week dear Stitheard's
               bonce
resembles less a basin of rotting
               fruit

and more a fresh, fleshy bulb
               bursting
through soil to greet the new spring's
               sun.

✝

o Cuddy
tell me about
your entry into
service.

>Melrose.
>>I was a young man.
>>The prophet
>>Prior Boisil
>>proclaimed me
>>a servant upon sight.
>>Gave me bread. Gave me a bed.

>Melrose.
>>Here I learned the miracle
>>of the salmon
>>rushing through the beats
>>to its spawning grounds
>>deep   in the Tweed.
>>The flex of its spine as it rises up

>to Him

>winnowing the cold air
>>the sun catching it there

>>light playing upon the
>>armour of its scales
>>as nimble fingers
>>might play the lyre.

The moment frozen and framed on all sides by water and wood,
stone and sky.

*That is how I
became a
servant,
child.*

✝

Often Owl Eyes speaks only in unfinished questions.

    When shall?
    Which will?
    What may?

His sentences left hanging like spiders suspended.

✝

A rank rabble of pustules and
rashes and squabbles they may be,
but many of the monks have skills
beyond those of normal
                    humble
                    mortal men.

Your stone-shifters
and lobster men.
Your sheep-keepers.

With his feather pen
and array of ink pots
made from clay,
Hunred creates kingdoms
on the skin side of vellum
made from calf hides
dried and scraped
and stretched tight.

Such is the standard of his intricate patterns
and pictures of people
and the scriptures of our Lord
told in tiny black markings that I could never hope
to understand –
some say that dear Hunred worked on the *Lindisfarne Gospels*
even though
that great book
is older than the hills
and Hunred is perhaps
only thirty winters on.

But he makes me believe in magic.

His sheets he arranges
in quires with the spine lines

of the once-great grazing beasts
running right through
his creations
so that their remains carry stories
as an ass carries man's burden
and when we find a final home for Cuddy,
which the brothers say is coming soon,
Hunred intends on having these quires
pressed and bound
for all
eternity.

An honouring of animals.
Cuddy's intention.

> What is it that you wish to say with
> these candelight etchings, brother?

I ask.

> Say, child? Say?

replies Hunred.

> I wish to say nothing but see everything,
> to capture joy, to express love, to paint
> the land and its people into forever,
> to hold it there, press it like wild flowers,
> to frame it so that tomorrow's children
> might learn the lessons of today and that
> that they too might love His
> wondrous
> creation.

He pauses, lost in thought and then he speaks again:

> and so that our voices will echo
>   echo
>   echo
> ever onwards.

I say
    And this you
    hope to do scratched
    upon the backs
    of cattle?

He says
    Yes.
    Those that
    are dead anyway.

    I believe you,
I say.
    I believe you.

✝

Many days later Hunred reaches into his pack and pulls from it a vellum roll tied with sheep gut. He passes it to me without a word. I carefully flatten it and there staring back at me is the face of someone familiar – a person wide of eye and dark of demeanour. Clean of crooked teeth and full in cheek. Aflame with life. Surrounding it are interlaced patterns, ornate spirals and serpentine forms. It is me, Ediva. Orphan girl of the holy folk clan. It is as if I am perched over the stone mountain of my visions and I see myself, perhaps for the first time, but when I finally summon words in a mouth from which my breath has been stolen, Hunred has disappeared, gone in a blink of silent retreat, and I am alone with my shadow self, a replica in miniature, one whose eyes dance with sparkling spinks and whose true capabilities remain hidden, mirabilia bidden.

✝

I remember it. The first vision, happening.
In sleep.

Summoning something the size of a mountain,
bigger,
too big for any words, too vast for vocabulary,

a towering hollow thing that blocks the sun, so
beautiful
I am scared that it is allowed to live inside me –

inside a mind whose life is so small, so
concerned
with skillet loaves, wash-day and kindling.

Fearful that I am its architect, that I am a
messenger
chosen to receive His plans for this place,

I recognise this sacred space, this
citadel
carved from a cold mountain in a vision

delivered not from memory but from
faith,
sculpted from prayer, house of the holy,

fortress for the future many, place of
repose,
consecrated from belief, sanctified in

silent miles across black-stink bogs,
howling
gales and blisters burst in duty.

It scares me, how it looks like that,
so impending,

a place of pilgrimage finally found.

And now its foundations are dug into my
sleep
and its turrets raise my eyelids upon waking.

A dog joins us
as a starling joins a murmuration.

For several days it trails the convoy,
   an underfed
   over-trusting
padding pouch of bones and hope.

It sniffs the slick
   wet morning grass
   and finds the stink
of fox, stag or boar,

points a way for the hunting party.
Path of the prey.

I make sure to save it a bowl of broth bones
   which it laps at in a frenzy, then gazes at me
   with a look of love so total that I know that
He is within him as He is within all creatures.

Then one day Brother Chad chastises me. He says:
         Child, you must not give meat to a diseased dog
         when we monkish men live in a state of perpetual
         hunger, to which I reply, Brother Chad, did not
         Cuthbert value all animals as he valued all humans
         and did not seals and ducks flock to him, to be close
         to him, to warm him, and did he not save half a
         loaf for the faithful hungry horse that carried him?

         And then I add: Also, I am neither man nor monk.

At this Brother Chad falls silent, but for a moment
   his eyes appear to rage red and the bone angles of
   his features seem to sharpen and his head glows
   like a lantern but the moment passes and instead
   Brother Chad, who I have never taken to, lowers

his eyes and quietly retreats into a place of brooding.

After several dank days the dog is found torn in a copse,
presumed by all to have been gored on the tusks of a boar.

Brother Edmund helps me heap a pile of stones,
    a memento cairn for one of Cuddy's creatures.

A place for   ever silent.

✝

Brother Edmund is a curious fellow who
favours the feeling of cold mud, sharp stones
and dung of many varieties
beneath his bare feet over the donning of
the sandals that his fellow brethren wear.

He explains to me that it brings him closer to Cuddy, Cuddy:
     who eschewed the comforts of the priory
     who prayed deep in the swell of the sea
     who ate only onions in his dying days
     who walked the wintered hills alone
     who prayed beneath a quilt of stars
     who cured the sick with a glance
     who shepherded all lost souls
     who moved the sand dunes
     who turned back the tides
     who preached only love
     who inspired devotion
     who bore all burdens
     who lived with grace
     who quietly suffered
     who died with grace
     who sought silence
     who sought solace
     who found silence
     who found solace
     who entrusts us
     who becalms us
     who guides us
     who is sainted
     who sits upon
     our worthy
     shoulders
     Cuddy o
     Cuddy
     o o o.

This, says Brother Edmund, kissing his folded fingers,
is the reason that I choose not to wear those sandals.

✝

o Cuddy
tell me about
your childhood
visions.

Child:
all my life was
m o v e m e n t.
First with the shepherding
then with the preaching.

One informed the other,
for a sheep man does not wait for his flock to find him.

As in herding then, so too in proselytising;
I went out there
on foot

carrying a few good words
up mountain
through bog
and wild wood
across moor
to those furthest-flung places considered
by most to be the most barbarous and squalid
settlements of sin.

Faith my only
shield,
belief
my only weapon.

A week or two I could be out, shin-deep in black oceans of
decay.
Sleeping rolled in a tannery hide
half-starved from eating only
rough groats
and

sour apples.

Drinking dub water.

All to share my visions.

There were surely better-kept horses, but yet.
But yet.
He delivered me time and time again.
This I acknowledge.

✝

o Cuddy

Yes child?

I have
visions
too.

✝

Heat sleep and itching. Stone scratch, an ache in the head. Thirst in the throat. At night under this stone weight of troubled visions I see the hollow mountain again. The mountain chiselled out. It is scored. Blasted into being. Peaks like needles scratch the sky and the cave of its belly can hold two dozen parish churches. Heads the size of horses' hang from about its crafted corners. The smaller ones are more horrific. Stone masks of the purgatorial imprisoned lashed by the elements. The mountain holds them captive. Their shrunken faces grimace as they push through its skin. Great beasts crawl across it too, four-legged protrusions frozen in stone. Teeth bared. Tongues forked. Tails pointed. Eyes as sparks. Some are winged as if summoned by temptation. But the dream song tells me that evil does not dwell here. Evil fears the hollow mountain and these figures are guardians made to repel evil. Time-slip. Body twitch. Under sleep I enter it. Enter the hollow mountain. The cave of its mouth. Broken rainbows are stacked in here and butterflies of every colour settle on its surfaces. A feast is laid for the eyes. The ceiling is as distant as the sky. Meadows of stone run for miles and forests of rock sprout ladders to heaven. I follow a stream of stones under arches from which great towers grow. Roots wrap their way around my ankles but a prayer for Cuddy releases them. Vines and ropes dangle everywhere and flowerheads unfold into beds of blossom borne in the circular twilight of forgiveness. Cuddy nourishes them. An ocean of silence floods every niche, crevice and corner and all the animals of the kingdom gather to worship at the altar of the sun. A sun that puts its lips to mine. A sun that bakes loaves of bread in the oven of forever. Turns gold into goblets. Silver into the heads of kings. The devil to dust. Sleep jump and skull flash. Another time-slip. I walk on through the gallery of understanding deep into the hollow mountain. The mountain that is surrounded by serpentine water, enshrouded by stars. Perched like a bird over a wooded island. Poised like a phoenix in its firepit. Feathers blazing, fashioned by flame. Immoveable. Immolated. Under sleep I find a tomb-slabbed shrine, and know the hollow mountain is the place we seek. Cuddy's place.

✝

Owl Eyes comes to me in the deepest tomb of night.

> Have you a knife?

I reach beneath my bedding and produce a knife.

> Have you life
> beating in your blood?

I stretch my arm and then turn my palm to the sun.

> He says: If we mix our blood we are bonded.

I blink back, his face framed by the stub of a candle's reach.

> He says: Boys do it and they become brothers.
> Soldiers do it on the evening of battle and the
> next day they reign victorious. Ediva, if we are
> bonded we will build the great church together.

The blade is light in my palm, as light as a feather and mottled with a pattern of rust spots, though it needs a morning on the whetstone. The bone handle is worn in such a way that it sits snug against the blisters caused by all the dough-rolling. Something rattles inside of me, hums like a bee in a jar, but I do not show it, need not show it.

> I say: I am not a boy and I am not a soldier.
> Nor do we need to be bonded in that way.

His short candle flickers. The wick is a single dead tree scorched by lightning. His eyes are grottoes in which water drips from the ceiling.

> I say: My blood belongs only within me.

I think of the knife being forged in fire, tempered, struck into shape and hammered flat, and the steaming sizzle of it. The hours spent cutting and carving the bone. The careful decoration of lattice lines, slowly scraped with a tool held fast by steady hands and now darkened with the dirt of a thousand days. Grained in. I think of the final pressing and sharpening of the blade, the gritty swarf dusting the maker's leather apron. A little lubrication perhaps, carefully applied. Grease-rubbed into being.

Then the slotting into place of blade and bone. The locking in. The buffing and polishing, a brief and blinding flash of light as it is turned towards the sun.

Then finally the quiet ceremonial presentation to the recipient, a gleaming thing passed on, passed down, seeking purpose, seeking something's flesh to sever.

Owl Eyes considers it in my hand as if awaiting instruction and outside my little tan-hide tabernacle the night is a bottomless ocean.

In a voice as soft as smoke he says,
        It will not hurt much.

        It will not hurt at all, I say, for this blade will not be used
        upon me. Blood is for bodies and puddings and little else.

I see then sitting between us the mountain of my mind, the great jutting bluff of rock, tooth of the earth, the slab of shadows stabbing skywards, a place awaiting our arrival, to be carved and shaped and adorned and consecrated as a cathedral in our sainted Cuddy's name. His corpse settled there beneath it. Owl Eyes runs his neat little tongue around the ring of his thick cracked lips. He does not see what I see.

Then there are other ways to bond,
he says, and snuffs the candle.

And the tide of night rises around us.

✝

o Cuddy there
must be more
memories of
your passing.

Child, you dwell in death —
why?

because I do not know
from where I came
but I can learn about
where it is I am going.

Well. A drama cast in cloud and rain and great white cracks
that slit the sky, and the growl of fury rolled over the dank wet
dominion of Bernicia and out to that unwavering line where
water meets what wondrous kingdom surely sits above, I saw
Him out there, with open arms. Awaiting my arrival.

Him o Cuddy?

Yes. But still death lingered longer,
a squatter in the box of my cell.
The wind carved corners there.
It conversed with the stone and I lay in silence.

The stone knows
                nothing.
The wind knows
                nothing
I knew little more.

The sea. It was all around me. Curling, crashing.
I sought a smaller island — an island off an island —
to be with mizzle and wind and Him and there we were.

Walls of baffled rock and banked dirt blocked out the fog of distraction.
A hole in the roof let the sky in and the smoke out.
I made it an altar.
Prayed.

My latrine: two planks over a rock pool. I made it too an altar, shuffled to it when I could. I timed the tide and counted the waves. Awaited my fate. Talked to the gannets.

Prayed.

For months prior I mumbled words to the spume and the fret here.
Prayers for utterance. Prayers for good harvest.
For the priory, the men. For the farmers
and their women. For good health
and strength and peace. For salt
and fish and mead and meat.

Twice a day the water rose.

And when my mouth was dry I reached
beneath my couch and crunched
a mouthful from an onion.

I took great care in
peeling away the layers
until I got to the gleaming core.

Hours passed and when I took another bite,
it was as delicious as the apples grown
by the monks of Ampleforth.

More o Cuddy
o more please,
I say.

> At night my foes rose from the darkest, daized corners
> of the cell to tap their bony fingers against my brow and
> whisper words as punishment for sin or piety, and here
> the storm was at its worst, and sometimes I was so
> overwhelmed that a trance befell me and I rose from
> the couch to walk the few paces to my oratory; sour
> onion on my breath, throat of stone, the calf-hide roof
> stretched tight and thumping like a drum of battle under
> the rhythm of north country rain. Only the changing
> of the light told me much time had passed as I came
> round on bended knees the thinnest layers of the onion
> membrane scattered like petals, shining in the shafts of
> light that beamed down through the needle holes.

I reached towards them, ready for death, and I met it.

✝

Rain falls when the answer to my question comes.
              The question is who am I?
                            And why?

Asked in prayer but not in person,
Brother Hunred is the one I trust
to tell the truth of me unadorned.

Rain falls
        falls
        falls
        and we are two days out,
        two dire days from nowhere.

Long-walking
hymn-singing
gut-rumbling.

            Hunred
I say.

            I will tell you
he replies, quick as a weasel.

            Tell me?

            Yes, tell you.

I say
            Tell me what?

            You know what
he says.
            The truth of your life.

            How do you read my mind so?
I say.

It is written in your eyes.
Two black questions blink there
and my mouth is full of answers.

He pauses.
        But once you know you can never unknow.

        Unknow?
I say.

        Yes, child, you can never unknow your story
he says
        You can never unknow the –

His words hang there
dew drops on a morning web.
I wait. He tries again.

        Well.
        You can never unknow
        the true horror of the devil Dane.

I shrug but
swift Hunred speaks quickly,
mutters a prayer
into the pouch of his hands:

        o Lord save this dear child,
        protect this child, save this child,
        o praise be Lord, deliver her
        for she is the lost lamb you spoke of.

        Sounds like you're the one that
        needs saving dear Hunred
I say,
though the words

do not have to get past a smile
for he is lost in prayer for a moment
and the rain falls
            falls
            falls.

      It was somewhere on the approach to Asunderland –
continues Hunred

      I've heard tell of it
I say

      – not far from the rushing river
he continues.
            We had been to visit some brothers across
            the water there at Monkwearmouth
            and found ourselves on the Bishop's
            barren land granted to him by Athelstan.

Keening for revelation
I nod him onwards

      Yes, well, we had fed and rested there
      at the priory across the way
      but now the devil Dane
      had staked a claim.

      Asunderland
I say.
      Yes, now I recall the name,

and as I whisper the word
I feel within me the flutter
of something
familiar.
A ghost awakened.
Corpses raised.

Hunred carries on with his tale.

> Jorvik had already fallen, you see
> and all along the coast was aflame.
> It was the Dane.

> You have seen a raid?

I ask.

Hunred's face is a dying fire.
> Yes.

> Tell me how it is

I say.

> Alright then

says brother Hunred.

> They do not announce their arrival.
> They have no need.
> Their stories precede them.
> A man looking out might see
> the flicker of lanterns
> where water meets sky and man meets God.
> He might.
> It is doubtful though that he will hear the low song of
> the oarsmen at first.
> Nor will he see the nodding hull of the long boat rear-
> ing up and the dozens that follow behind it like a stud of
> steeds haunch-flogged and trunk-lashed into battle, nor the
> whites of salt-stung eyes glimpsing this thin strip of holy
> land for the first time. Only when they are shore-bound
> might the voices be heard over the strangling scumfish,
> the squall of the spume and the breakwaters enfolding the
> banks of shifting shale. To his knees a man might wish to
> drop in prayer, for prayer is always prudent, though by then
> it will be too late, for a pestilence will have befallen the land.
> A plague upon faith will spread. God watches on in silence.

Hunred pauses, swallows and then continues.

> And it was this same godless Dane, you see
> who saw fit to land and plunder,
> to steal and wreak,
> to take
> and
> rape and
> burn and tear
> children from their families.
> You were once such example.

I take in Hunred's revelation for though I have heard much about the Dane's ongoing devilment at many a fireside I do not know this story about my family who are nothing but a burnt black circle where once there was a memory.

> They reckon I was sold in for service
> for half a hog and a few sacks of wool

I say.

> O child no

says Hunred

> there is no truth to that
> for we, the sons of Cuddy,
> would not take payment
> in exchange for a lost soul
> just as Cuddy would refuse
> payment for God's work.
> No, no.
> O Lord, no.
> The life of the lost has no price
> and we are in God's service.
> We could not carry Cuddy
> in good faith and conscience
> knowing a child had been sold.

So what happened
Brother Hunred?
I ask.

We found you lost.
Just like an upland
sheep separated from
the familial flock.
Bare-ragged and
meat-starved. As black
as night, as black as death.
Rattled by a cough,
skin as vellum.
Moon eyes
all afrit.

I wait a while
before asking
Who made me?

He waits a while
before responding
Maybe the Dane
he says.
Maybe not.

I ask
Then what?

Hunred looks wistful.
I lifted you up and put you under my cloak
kept you safe from the terror
and the lightning
and the thunder
of life.

You did that, Brother Hunred?

He turns his palms to God.
     With these very hands.

I ask again
     Then what?

     Then what?
says Hunred.
     Then you were Cuddy's child.
     Then you were one of us.
     Bishop Aldhun named you Ediva.
     And we walked into the storm as one.

✝

A full day passes.

      Why 'Ediva?'
I ask.
      It means child of visions
says Hunred.

✝

Sometimes when we walk a silence befalls the brothers, a silence that takes a shape, becomes tangible, a thing to be shared and carried just as the carriage holds the coffin that houses as a keepsafe the immaculate corpse of a man made by Him, but it never lasts, just as nothing pure ever does, and the void is soon filled, because a void of pure nothingness is too pure a thing to consider at length, because when one glores into it there is nothing but the skull of the self staring back.

So then someone speaks.

Or a prayer is uttered.

Perhaps a hymn is sung, a melody muttered.

And once or twice when we walk we take to humming a low deep note of foreboding harmony. First it comes from the chasm of a single mouth, then from several, then from all of us, even Owl Eyes, as our feet shuffle beneath this drab dirge that must surely be heard far across the purple heathered plains and down into the deep dark denes of a land to lose ourselves in. Tomorrow there, over the brow.

✝

Walking and thinking
        praying and fasting;
        the endless act of

facing yourself.

✝

o Cuddy
tell me more
about your time
alone on the rock.

    I will, child.
    I will.

        Picture wet black slabs slick
        with the skin of the sea
        and streaked with globs of bird scat.
        Here and there are sheaves
        of marram grass soaked
        like spoiled straw deposited
        by the retreating waves.

    At low tide
    the bladderwrack
    lies flat.

        Mussel shells
        like the delicate ears of children
        shut themselves to God's great world
        and limpets cling as suckling babes do
        to the teats of their mothers.

    A patina of barnacles
    coats half the rocks of the island
    and on the furthest
    foreshore are

        the smashed remains of shells
        pecked and crudely strewn
        by the bladed beaks
        of all His birds.

    Here the tide deceives – always.

To turn your back upon it
is to turn your back on Him.

      Much seaweed moils
       in a tub of gluey rainbows.

At the highest point of this
half-acre plot there grows
a scant patch of grass and clover
so green in the ocean
I call it Paradise.

      Here I find feathers
      and spat-back nuggets
      of crab parts compacted
      into a coarse dry dust.

There is lichen.
      There are cockles.

      And at low tide shelves of black rock
      are stacked so as to give an
      impression of a distant mountain range rising

and the groaning flats
are marked with the weft
of the current's keen undertow
and the lugworm residue is
tied into tiny beautiful
      knots of
      sand.

      At high tide
      all is God's
      sincere silence.

✝

V

'There is an island called Farne, set in the sea – not like that part of the coast where live the men of Lindisfarne – but hidden several miles to the east of this half-island, and sieged on this side and on that by the deep and infinite sea. No man, before God's servant Cuthbert, had been able to make his dwelling here alone, for the phantoms of demons haunted it.'

Beasts and Saints by Helen Waddell

'Demons indeed! He knew that twenty thousand million demons could not possibly be as powerful as God, so why worry?'

Saints Over the Border by Margaret Gibbs

'Just a lump of land girt with a low rampart of black dolerite rock to keep the sea at bay, and capped with a covering of green.'

Lindisfarne: The Cradle Island by Magnus Magnusson

'It has that quality of remoteness, the feeling of being beleaguered by God in a far sea, a rocky independence, and a lasting quietness.'

Some Lovely Islands by Leslie Thomas

'A place more venerable than all in Britain.'

Alcuin, AD 793

'To actually get away from the world, even in the seventh century, you needed, as Cuthbert found, to become a hermit.'

'Elements in the Background to the Life of St Cuthbert and the Early Cult' by J. Campbell

'Cut off on the landward side by very deep water and facing, on the other side, out towards the limitless ocean... Cuthbert was the first man brave enough to live there alone.'

Life of Cuthbert by Bede

'It was an astonishing decision... to sail off alone to an island hermitage which is frequently cut off for a week or more in rough weather, and from which all inhabited land is often blotted out by mist; to go there, alone, in winter, when death was approaching – that naked fact speaks volumes for Cuthbert's trust in God.'

'Cuthbert, Pastor and Solitary' by Clare Stancliffe

'The structure was almost circular in plan, from four to five poles in diameter, and the walls on the outside were higher than a man. Out of piety he made the walls higher inside by cutting away the solid rock at the bottom.'

Life of Cuthbert by Bede

'A small medieval chapel, it was about 7m long and little more than 1m broad, and it lay within a rather curious curved enclosure wall, forming a kind of platform.'

Lindisfarne: The Cradle Island by Magnus Magnusson

'Digging down almost a cubit into the ground, through very hard and stony rock, he made a space to dwell in.'

The Anonymous Life of Cuthbert

'He set a roof of rough beams and thatch.'

Beasts and Saints by Helen Waddell

'At Cuthbert's bidding, the monks dug down into the rock surface inside the enclosure wall of his hermitage, and presently, in response to Cuthbert's prayers, fresh water appeared in the hole.'

> *Lindisfarne: The Cradle Island* by Magnus Magnusson

'The great sweetness of its flavour we have proved and still thankfully prove by tasting it, even until the present day.'

> *The Anonymous Life of Cuthbert*

'An old monk, strong in the faith though wasted away through dysentery, said to him "Tell us, my lord, when we may expect to see you again." The answer came back as plain as the question (for Cuthbert knew it was true): "When you bring back my corpse."'

> *Life of Cuthbert* by Bede

'Cuthbert was alone, sealed into prayer.'

> 'The Spirituality of St Cuthbert' by Sister Benedicta Ward SLG

'He maintained the dignity of a bishop without abandoning the ideal of the monk or the virtue of the hermit.'

> *The Life of St Cuthbert* by Anonymous

'It had never been the beauty of scenery that had drawn Cuthbert to Farne – indeed he seems to have taken great pains not to see it at all. For him it was the desert, the place of the cross. There was nothing there but the stars and water.'

> 'The Spirituality of St Cuthbert' by Sister Benedicta Ward SLG

'The more a hermit sought solitude, the more his solitude would be invaded by pilgrims anxious to imbibe from him the wisdom and insight he was presumed to be gaining by his undistracted communings with God.'

> *Lindisfarne: The Cradle Island* by Magnus Magnusson

'Even if I could possibly hide myself in a tiny dwelling on a rock, where the waves of the swelling ocean surrounded me on all sides and shut me in equally from the sight and knowledge of men – not even thus should I consider myself free from the snares of a deceptive world.'

Cuthbert, from *Life of Cuthbert* by Bede

'They came to him as a spiritual guide, with their sins and their worries.'

'Cuthbert, Pastor and Solitary' by Clare Stancliffe

'His conversation, seasoned with salt, consoled the sad, instructed the ignorant, appeased the angry; for he persuaded them all to put nothing before the love of Christ.'

'Saint Cuthbert – Soul Friend' by Gerald Bonner
(from *Cuthbert: Saint and Patron* ed. D. W. Rollason)

'He was never a gloomy saint.'

St Aidan and St Cuthbert by Henry Kelsey

'He was affable and pleasant in his manner.'

Bede

'At first he would accept a scant portion of bread from them, and would drink from his well: but after a while he felt it was more fit that he should live by the work of his own hand.'

Beasts and Saints by Helen Waddell

'He who serves God shall never die of hunger.'

Cuthbert, as recorded by Bede

'The monks of Lindisfarne were host to a highly public cult.'

'Lindisfarne and the Origins of the Cult of St Cuthbert' by Alan Thacker
(from *St Cuthbert, His Cult and His Community to AD 1200* ed. Gerald Bonner, David Rollason and Clare Stancliffe)

'He used to keep the window open and enjoy seeing his brethren and being seen by them, but in the end he blocked it up.'
Life of Cuthbert by Bede

'It is tempting to wonder whether Lindisfarne in the seventh century was really the remote and peaceful place it is today.'
'Why Was Saint Cuthbert So Popular?' by D.W. Rollason
(from *Cuthbert: Saint and Patron* ed. D.W. Rollason)

'It fairly teems with life; for the Inner Farne is home and sanctuary for literally thousands of birds: terns dancing and darting like swallows, colonies of shags and cormorants as ungainly as waddling divers, guillemots and razorbills looking stiff and awkward as a male-voice choir in their penguin suits, kittiwakes constantly calling out their name, fulmars clucking hoarsely or spitting venomously at intruders, eider ducks placidly incubating eggs in unlikely tufts of grass, clown-nosed puffins squatting in luxurious solemnity.'
Lindisfarne: The Cradle Island by Magnus Magnusson

'Upon that island for a great while back a pair of ravens had had their dwelling.'
Beasts and Saints by Helen Waddell

'He saw two crows pulling out pieces of thatch to make their nest. "Now, now, my friends," said he, "will you pull the roof of the house I have built?" But the crows took no notice – only went on stealing his thatch. Then Cuthbert spoke to them quite sternly, telling them, in the name of Our Lord, to off at once and not come back again.'
Saints Over the Border by Margaret Gibbs

'With no tarrying, back the [ravens] came, and carrying with them a present, no less than a good-sized hunk of hog's lard such as one greases axles with.'
Beasts and Saints by Helen Waddell

'Many a time thereafter the man of God would show it to the brethren who came to see him, and would offer it to grease their shoes…'

> *Beasts and Saints* by Helen Waddell

'I expect they needed something to keep out the damp.'

> *Saints Over the Border* by Margaret Gibbs

'… and he would urge on them how obedient and humble men should be, when the proudest of birds made haste with prayers and lamentation.'

> *Beasts and Saints* by Helen Waddell

'The same St Cuthbert who was famously kind to ducks sometimes existed on the flesh of beached dolphins.'

> Alcuin's letter to Ethelred, King of Northumbria
> (from *Epistolae Karolini aevi Vol II* ed. Ernst Dümmler)

'Once when he hung a fat goose in the house for his guests he was quite angry at them for not eating it.'

> *Saints Over the Border* by Margaret Gibbs

'He kept his soft leather boots on for months on end without ever removing them.'

> *Life of Cuthbert* by Bede

'He did not take off his skin boots from one Easter to the next.'

> *St Aidan and St Cuthbert* by Henry Kelsey

'They persuaded him to take off his boots on Maundy Thursday so that they could wash his feet.'

> *Lindisfarne: The Cradle Island* by Magnus Magnusson

'The monks found thick calluses where the boots had chafed his shins through all his prayers and genuflexions.'

> *Life of Cuthbert* by Bede

'He loved being a hermit.'
Saints Over the Border by Margaret Gibbs

'He was still a shepherd and still carried a shepherd's staff.'
St Aidan and St Cuthbert by Henry Kelsey

'For nearly two months Cuthbert was able to enjoy the quiet and solitude of his retreat again, until the onset of his final sickness.'
Lindisfarne: The Cradle Island by Magnus Magnusson

'For two months the monks and people watched.'
Saints Over the Border by Margaret Gibbs

'Bad weather had prevented Herefrith's return to the sick man, and Cuthbert had also been subject to a tempest both external and interior.'
'The Spirituality of St Cuthbert' by Sister Benedicta Ward SLG

'It turned out that Cuthbert had been lying there helplessly for five days and nights. He had no food except for five onions which he had kept under the covers of his bed – and even then he had only nibbled them to allay the thirst.'
Lindisfarne: The Cradle Island by Magnus Magnusson

'Ascetic discipline and ceaseless ministry had worn down his sturdy frame.'
St Aidan and St Cuthbert by Henry Kelsey

'As the end drew near, Cuthbert asked to be carried back to his little cell and oratory. It was nine o'clock on the morning of Tuesday 19 March 687. No one had been allowed to enter the cell for years, but now the monks asked that one of them should be allowed to go inside with him. Cuthbert chose Walhstod, the monk who suffered from dysentery.'
Lindisfarne: The Cradle Island by Magnus Magnusson

'And, raising his eyes to heaven and stretching out his hands aloft, he sent forth his spirit in the very act of praising God to the joys of the Heavenly Kingdom.'
Life of Cuthbert by Bede

'He fell asleep, fortified by the Body and Blood of the Lord.'
Newcastle Cathedral Saints by George Miles

'And so Cuthbert died, early in the morning of 20 March 687.'
Lindisfarne: The Cradle Island by Magnus Magnusson

'Without delay one of them ran out and lit two torches; and holding one in each hand, he went on to some higher ground to show the brethren who were in the Lindisfarne monastery that his holy soul had gone to be with the Lord: for this was the sign they had agreed upon among themselves to notify his most holy death.'
Life of Cuthbert by Bede

'Two torches waving in the wind. Cuthbert of Lindisfarne was dead.'
Saints Over the Border by Margaret Gibbs

'Cuthbert's death appeared to be more of a release than a triumphant ascent to heaven in the arms of angels.'
To the Island of Tides: A Journey to Lindisfarne by Alistair Moffat

'His death, however, is far from the end of the story.'
Cuthbert and the Northumbrian Saints by Paul Frodsham

✝

VI

Once the brothers had a home, a church in Chester-le-Street, a place where Cuthbert's remains lay.

My memories of it are vague and intangible, grains of sand through my hands. I can't grasp them.

They are memories made of scents and feelings and an atmosphere so vague perhaps I was never even there, and instead carry only the echoes of a place from before I was born.

I call upon Hunred to colour in the fading shapes of a mind not yet then fully formed.

What was it like
I say
at Chester-le-Street?

Like?
says he.

Yes.

He sniffs.
It was a place for his blessed bodily relics to be rested. You were young then, you won't remember.

No.

Twelve years his body lay untouched in a tomb of stone. A cenotaph marked his sleeping. The kirk was made from timber.

Not stone?

I ask.

No. Not stone.

says he.

Timber. It was shoddily built, but it served its purpose as a reliquae for the saint. Our saint. At night, during storms, or in bad weather, it creaked just as the forest from where it came creaks, and it groaned too like the devil Dane's longboat. It was new and the wood had not yet warped into a comfortable shape. It leaked a lot.

Leaked?

Yes. Often. Roman ruins surrounded it you see, the remains of those long-departed left to remind us all of the price of greed, arrogance and avarice. The stone chambers of a collapsed empire.

Why did the Romans leave, Brother Hunred?

Well child, I'd say it was the weather.

Is that the reason?

It's as good a reason as any.

Why was the church not built from rocks and stone?

Because it was a temporary expedient.

What does that mean?

It means we always believed in something better.

Better?

Yes. A place befitting a true servant, a saint.

We fall silent for a time.
Then I speak.

A place as big as a mountain?

I say.

Yes

says Hunred.

I would suppose so.

A place so ornate and beautiful as to steal the breath from the bodies of all who see it?

Yes.

A place adorned with stone faces and glass that turns the sun's rays celestial, a place with towers that prod the sky, and wonderful altars, and shadowed knaves, and quiet transept corners for moments of contemplation, and cloisters and winding stairways and clerestories along which echo the footsteps and the soft words of prayer from his acolytes, and keeled corners too, and great slabs of ashlar and canted stones chamfered by the chisels and hammers of stone-dusted men, and decorative dados painted by masters and masters' apprentices and keenly carved traceries set by plumb lines and much calculation, and a great piscina for washing the holy vessels?

Hunred's eyes I see have widened into sparking flashes of penetrating wonder.

        Child

says he.

        How can you know such things? How can you know
        the technicalities that go into building a house of God,
        and how is it that these words are in your vocabulary? Is
        a miracle at work amongst us?

I shrug.

        I don't know

I say.

His eyes widen further.

        You don't know?

        I don't know

I say.

        But I have seen it.
        I have seen it all.

✝

Time shock and bone splinter. Hot poker eyes. White hot. And then the still space. The stone place. Visions of it again. This space for silence. Space for communion. A space so far beyond the dark and dire churches and priories of these northlands as to be unrecognisable. Lightning flash and sky crack. Then I can see every detail, taste every dust mote in the back of my haws. Timeslip. Here the voices of angels boom and echo in the mouth of God. Here prayers are heard and considered and answered. Here lies Cuddy. Cuddy in a coffin within a coffin within a coffin. But still alive. Alive always. Alive surrounded by his most precious items, sealed within stone, sealed under stone, the great mountain of a cathedral growing grander around him with each passing age. Sun flash, heat scream, then I see it. The gruff rough stone of it. Generations of monks will live and die here; no more the wandering of woodlands, no more the scratching at barren shores for limpets and whelks. No more the sleepless nights spent in fear of the devil Dane for the devil Dane too will fall to his knees in awe at the great mountain of a cathedral. And if he tries to attack it he will fall and drown in the rushing waters that surround the wooded island or he will be harried by the men and women that live to serve its splendour. Great rocks and fire and oil and arrows will rain down upon any blasphemer who tries to storm the great carved mountain. Because in this vision I summon is a place of peace and a place of reflection. A place of sanctuary, a home for the lost and the lonely, the hunted and the haunted. All these years of roaming this island home will lead to here, to the cathedral built by the wandering folk of the holy man, yes. Yes, all of this, but a place first envisioned in the mind of one young peasant orphan girl who they thought only capable of concocting mediocre broths and applying poultices and balms to their aches and ailments. Sparks in the darkness. Voices in the fire. Broken sleep. And I see now that this place was my purpose; that my role has only ever been to guide and steer the Cuddy community to safety, through the tangled trees and over shifting dunes of sand like broken glass, to a wooded island where a stray cow did wander. And here the sign was seen and the sign was read, and the sign was understood. And the place will be built. And they shall come.

✝

Then this morning, camped in the shelter of a great hole once quarried to make a dozen dwellings long since fallen, Chad spits out his morning meal of oats and sow milk, wipes his mouth on his cassock sleeve and mutters something to himself. One or two of the other brothers smile quietly, for they know that Brother Chad is not good in the mornings when his head is still heavy with the sour yellow cloud of last night's mead, and make sure to allow him a little space in which to shake off that which pains him, but why I should keep quiet? I was soaking oats for a vat of podge, peeling plums and proving dough while he was still whistling through his tombstone teeth, and all with a pain in my belly and another bout of bilious puking at sun-up. So I ask, Is the food not to your liking, Brother Chad? and at first he does not respond so I make sure to say it again in the same flat voice. Is the food not to your liking, Brother Chad? and at the second time of asking he lifts his heavy head and he says, The food is fine enough, so then I reply, Then it must be that you're feeling a touch off-colour, perhaps I can see what remedies I might have in my store to set you back on the right path? A little mint oil to rub about your temples maybe or a rag of hot stones and rosehip? But he shakes his head and mutters something about the devil that I know is directed at me, and I say, The devil it is that makes a grown man cowardly enough to skugg his words in whispers, Brother Chad. This gets his attention sure enough, and that of some of the brothers too, who glance up from their morning bowls, for to bring the devil to the table, even just in jest, is something not to be taken lightly. In merely summoning his name a true believer might run the risk of the devil himself appearing. So then I say, Perhaps the mead has sent your bald noggin sideways dear Brother Chad for any man with good sense knows better than to insult the cook, for who knows what the cook might do when a man's back is turned and there is just her and your bowl and a headful of mischief or a mouthful of hockle? Chad flashes me a savage look. This is a coarse image, I know, but the brothers are not so pious that they don't indulge in latrine talk from time to time, for although they are men of God they are after all still just men, and not the types who get to lie with their wives or run youling naked at the moon or dancing around the fire at certain times of the calendar like the wild mushroom-chewing folk we have on occasion encountered in the uplands. I do sometimes wonder if such deprivations make the monks a little wild in the mind themselves, not least Brother Chad, who has a mean streak just as a big old brock has a white stripe across its questing face. He points his spoon at me. I have seen you, says Chad, and I do believe you are possessed by something evil. I have seen the way your eyes roll and spittle gathers at the corner of your lips like the devil is in you sometimes. And I have seen you down by the clear waters, naked and shameless in front of God. Naked and shameless, he says again, like a farmhouse harlot who opens her legs to every passing herdsman. Oh leave her be, says dear Brother Franco. Ediva was just bathing as we all bathe, that's all. What you saw while lurking in the dene is no one's fault, for she is just as God made her. Amen, adds Brother Eadmer, now can we finish our victuals in peace? Brother Chad doesn't like this, so he stands and tips the rest of his maizey pap to the ground, an act which is both wasteful and insulting, not least because the loyal horses that drag the cart would surely like to have a little extra something sweetened with the honey we harvest from hives secreted in stone skeps all over the place. The very same horses, we should remember, who make it possible for Cuddy's corpse to continually evade the wicked Dane who still stalks the region looking for scalps and treasures and Lord knows what else. Chad points at me then and he says, She has the devil in her, this one. The devil, I say. No good can come of it. And then Brother Chad turns and walks up and out of the quarry to sulk on the moor while we fold away our tents and Owl Eyes appears, for he has been away giving the horses a gentle leg stretch and a loving scrub in the stream or whatever else it is he does when he goes a-solitary wandering for long spells. He senses the mood amongst the men though, for he has not only the eyes but the senses of a hoolet too. What is it? he asks but I just shrug and then say Brother Chad has spent too long in the mead barrel and now he is seeing devils every which way he turns. Brother Franco hears this and smiles and Brother Eadmer does too. Owl Eyes says, What do you mean? but I just shrug again and I say, It is of no consequence, only that some men are scared of their own shadows while others are scared of things they can neither see nor understand. And you, says Owl Eyes. What are you scared of, Ediva? But I can't think of a single thing to offer in reply, so instead get to work swilling the brothers' gratefully scraped-out bowls and breaking camp before another day's travelling. I'm feeling something odd within me. It is strange, unknown. It is new. I think it is power.

✝

Two birds duelling.
Shapes across the sun.

✝

o Cuddy
won't you
sing me a
song?

>*Child,*
>*there is*
>*no song*
>*greater*
>
>*than the*
>*song of*
>*silence in*
>*death.*
>
>*I*
>*sing it*
>*to you*
>*always.*

✝

I must admit that on more than one occasion I have stood over Brother Chad as he sleeps. At those times when circumstance has forced us all together, in the most dire conditions for example, or when we have been given bleak board in a barn or byre, I have watched his chest rise and fall with the slow breath of sleep and seen the blue worms that pulse and squirm beneath the thin skin of his scrag-end neck, and I have looked at the curve of his shaved skull, and thought how the shorn stubs of hair look like grains of sand stuck there, and the crab-apple lump of his throat that shifts as he dry-swallows his way through the dreaming, and I have noticed too that he frowns even when under the blanket of night, even when bathing in the pool of the moon he has the face of a perturbed beast, and I have sometimes thought how a rock could be brought down on the goose-egg dome of his head, just the once would be enough to stun him as a slingshot pebble stuns a grouse in flight, yet a second ding would send him on his way into the deep sleep of forever, and no more would he be able to sneer or mock me. I have thought about this often, though I have never acted upon it. Just to know that I can is enough. Just to know a rock and the will is all it takes.

✝

Glimpses of the sea.
Molten metal.

✝

Later that day Hunred ambles alongside.
We stramp a while, the cart ahead of us.
The coffin on it, Cuddy in it. Some sun.

He says

> You know, I see you too.

> See me?

I say.

> When you are having your –

here he pauses.

> Your –

he pauses again.

> Your visions. You think that you experience them when
> you are sleeping but you do not. I see you, as Brother
> Chad has seen you. And others too.

> See me how?

> As if God himself has gripped you. As if His hands have
> closed around your heart and held it there. Yes. He has
> chosen you in a way that none of the brothers have been
> chosen. This much I believe to be true. We monks might
> know that we have been anointed or blessed or ordained –
> or whatever words you might use for this calling – but
> only one of the *haliwerfolc* truly stands in the light. It is
> you, Ediva. I know this because I have seen you when
> you are deep in the throes of a discussion with Him.

> Oh

I say.

> But there is no discussion.

> Instruction then. I have seen you when you are deep in
> the throes of receiving instruction. Your eyes roll until
> they are entirely white and your limbs move about of
> their own accord for a moment, but then you are perfectly

still save for the slow, low rasping of your young breath as it presses its way out between your strong teeth and thick lips. This is when you see things that no mortal, humble being can see. You, my child, are a prophet. A visionary. And I perhaps I have always known this. Right from that first day when you were wandering, lost and bedraggled in the stinking boglands of Asunderland, you had a glow around you.

A glow?

Yes. A celestial aura. To the others perhaps you were but an orphan child in need of charity, someone who we could nurture as one of our own, and who, in turn, might prove to repay our hospitality by being of use, as you surely are with your polecat snares and filleting knife, and of course your broths are some of the best I have tasted, and improving daily, but from that first moment I saw your aura. I saw the light around you and I thought, Well Brother Hunred, this child is surely sent from heaven, and she will lead you, she will show you the way. Because she is God's child, an orphan angel sent down to this godforsaken plain to ensure our sainted Cuddy has a safe passage, to ensure our sainted Cuddy receives deliverance.

I say nothing to this. Instead I consider what it is that Hunred is saying. He continues.

For years we have been wandering. Decades. Entire lives have been lived in service to corpus Cuddy. The community has swollen and shrunk and swollen again over time. Many brothers have come and gone. Hundreds of horses too have dragged the cart that carries the coffin that holds the corpse of Cuddy and his precious relics. They have worn their hooves to stumps and when they have finally fallen, exhausted, we have eaten them out of necessity.

We have been met with both hospitality and hostility. Sometimes we have settled in places for many months, years even, as at the church in Chester-le-Street. But never have we reached a destination to befit the burial of a saint whose wisdom and kindness will ring like a bell down the ages, and whose shadow-presence will shape this island for centuries to come, whose life will live on through tomorrow's tomorrow's tomorrow, and whose name and teaching will be taught in a world that will be changed so far beyond comprehension as to be unrecognisable to us today. But now I see it is you, Ediva, it is *you* and your guidance that we have been awaiting, for do you not see in your visions the resting place for Cuddy?

I see a church as big as a mountain.

Hunred says:
    We call it a cathedral.

    A cathedral then. I see a cathedral as big as a mountain.

    And?

    And, oh Hunred, I see so much more.

    Tell me, child. Tell me what else you see.

I shake my head. I feel my eyes becoming wet.
    It is beyond words.

    But it is beautiful?

    It is beyond beautiful. It is heaven cast in stone.

    And it is a place fit for saint?

    It is a place fit for a saint

I say.

> Then you must take us there.

> I will take you there

I say.

✚

The seasons wheel.

Sun then rain then
sun again. Cuddy
in the coffin. The
coffin on the cart.

Sweating monks
and horse funk.

A pilgrimage to
who-knows-where.

I will when
we get there.

✝

We're following the broken coast south when Brother Franco's head goes west.

Without warning he whips off his coarse cassock, his sweat-stained undershirt and his ragged breeches and goes tumbling down the dunes like a turnip off a farmer's handcart on market day.

Stumbling and wailing, his wrinkled white worm bouncing, he runs across the rounded rocks that mark the tideline and hoys himself into the crashing wash with neither grace nor dignity. The curling waves take the yelping monk and immediately turn him scut about tit.

He can't find his feet and with his bald head, stretched neck and gasping mouth he resembles a baby bird in the nest at feeding time, as high above him circling seagulls gather to laugh and point with their dipping beaks at poor Franco's plight.

The monks fall about with laughter too. Even Chad splits his face with a smile, though it looks more like a blade wound. You can hear the rattle of stones around Franco's ankles as the wide-eyed brother tries to drag his bare bones and disappearing ball sac out from the salty soup, but the surge of the swell is great and it keeps toying with him like a cat with a ball of yarn. It paws at him, rolls him over and kittles his chin, then throws another wet grey blanket of water over Franco's startled head.

The monks laugh harder until the Bishop Aldhun instructs a couple of the brothers to wade out to lend a helping Christian hand, which they do. Owl Eyes leaves the horses to join them too.

Once back on steady legs, Brother Franco sits on a rock and his face returns to normal; his eyes become placid and his face impartial. Only the goosenubs of his shivering flesh and the nicks and scrapes around his lower legs signal his adventure. He dresses in silence, brushing sand from his flesh, then strides up the dunes and carries on walking as if the sea has shaken out of him whatever moment of madness gripped Brother Franco's poor troubled soul, and his sudden self-baptism was just the makings of our imaginations.

No one sees fit to mention it again, as if perhaps, deep down, as deep as the sea itself, we each inside of us know that we walk a fine line at all times.

A fine line indeed.

✝

Faith through walking.
  Walking through faith.

✝

Eadmer is the next to be troubled by a bodily malady. He approaches me at sun-up with pain written across his haggard face.

Ediva, it's my tooth

he says.

What of it, Brother Eadmer?

I have a worm within it.

Tooth worms don't exist.

Then the devil has it.

The devil has it?

Yes.

Can he do that?

I ask, earnestly.

The devil can do as he please.

Then so can we.

Can we?

Yes. Or the very least I can try to ease your troubles. Let me see.

Eadmer opens wide and I am hit by the stink of him. His breath is like a mixture of the fish guts we use for crabbing, a midden mound and much more besides. The smell of mulch and rot. I see a brown stump and his tongue prodding at it incessantly.

Toothache is it?

Ah, Ediva. Ache is too soft a word for this
Eadmer says through a moan.
>I thought I could pray the pain away, at least until we
>reach our final resting place, for when we find a home for
>Cuddy all wrongs will surely be righted, and all suffering
>will end, but this journey seems endless, and this pain is
>endless too. I do believe the devil dwells in my mouth.

With that reeking breath I'd be inclined to agree I think, but
instead I say:
>Come back later. Come back when the sun is at its
>highest. I'll have something for you then, brother.

He nods most solemnly and, turning away, touches a hand gently
to his cheek.

>Oh, and Brother Eadmer.

>Yes?

>The journey will soon be over.

>Do you think so? Do you think we are near?

Now it is I who nods most solemnly. Eadmer's face brightens a
little at the prospect. He goes to say something but hesitates for
a long lingering moment of uncertainty. Then he speaks.

>It is true what they say then – that you have visions?
>That you have glimpsed at future days, and seen what
>fate belies us all?

I shake my head.

Not entirely. But I have seen a resting place most splendid for our saint, a place beyond words, and I know that
it is near, and I have seen too that your pain and suffering
will pass soon. Come back when the sun is at its highest.

Eadmer nods, says:
    I think perhaps this pain gives me premonitions
and then turns away again.

That morning I follow a beck through a narrow ghyll down to
the shore and in the shallows I fill a jug of sea water, and then
on the way back to the camp I pick some garlic leaves.

I transfer the seawater to a more ornate bottle and when Eadmer
returns I tell him that I have made him a medicine especially for
tooth pain. Eadmer takes the bottle, sniffs the liquid and then
takes a gulp, gagging as he swallows it. His face is a picture.

    No brother,
I say, smiling.
    This liquid is for rinsing only.

Eadmer spits.
    It tastes like the sea
he says.
    It tastes like nothing good should taste.

I reply:
    That's as may be but you need to rinse your tooth. So
    rinse, then pluff.

Eadmer does as instructed.

    Several more times, dear brother.

Again he rinses and spits, and then I unwrap a dish and pass it to
him. It contains crushed cloves pressed in pig fat.

Take a nub of this and rub it on your tooth and gums and then, later, chew on this.

I pass him a folded parcel of the waxy green garlic leaves. I also pass him an onion.

This too will help, taken raw.

Just as Cuddy used to eat it?
says Eadmer.

Yes. What is good enough for our saint is surely good enough for you.

And that is it? This will cure me.

Yes, though of course there is one other method.

I'll try anything.

They say that to truly end tooth pain and ward against it ever returning, one must rob a grave and remove a tooth from a corpse, then wear it as an amulet.

Brother Eadmer looks at me aghast.

But let us see how you get on with the sea potion and the rest of it first
I say, for although the corpse tooth is a rumoured method it is not one that I fancy either of us would like to attempt. Eadmer goes on his way.

✝

Overnight guests at a forlorn priory run by a distant cousin of the Bishop Aldhun, the monks decide to devote a day to prayer, so Owl Eyes takes me down to the rock pools.

We pick our way across greasy rocks. It is low tide on a hot and clear day loud with birdsong. We take horsehair tawms and hooks and a pail of fish guts for bait, and far out at sea, breakers fold and crash over a ragged bank of stone onto which seals drag their flabby forms to rest a while.

But here near the shore the sea is as still as font water, and the sun is dancing upon it, a show of silver that shimmers.

We lift our smocks and overturn stones to snatch smaller crabs, and reach into submerged hollows beneath the overhang of barnacle-covered rocks to prise out the medium-sized ones that have a green hue to their shells. But the biggest ones, the crabs with the purest meat and the cruellest pincers, are to be found in the deeper waters so we climb across a stretch of diminishing rocks that reach out from the crumbling headland and drop our lines into the dark waters there.

Soon we are pulling up crab after crab. We drop them in the pail with the stinking bait. Some have shells as big as horseshoes. Others are as large as our heads.

In no time at all the pail is a squirming mess of fish guts and clamouring crabs. As their eyestalks reach for a viewpoint, the largest creatures climb to the top of the pile, a futile effort, as Owl Eyes, who seems happier than I have ever seen him – except perhaps in the early dark silent hours under the covers of my tent – ties a rag around the rim with twine so that none can make a sideways bid for freedom back into the endless North Sea waters.

The tide is rising to the sky and the breakers booming lonely in the offing when we turn our back to the sea. The swinging skeel hangs heavy in Owl Eyes' hand and with his other he grips the sack that dangles over his shoulder. At first he refuses to let me help him but when he is puffing through the dry dunes that shift underfoot and he nearly spills the contents of our morning's mission, he lets me take the wooden handle with him and we walk in silence, the pail between us, clicking and scratching with the movement of our catch within it.

Tonight we will all dine well on these gifts from the sea.

Indeed, in no position to be fussy, the monks eat whatever I serve them.

My repertoire is expanding. Fish and pheasant, cockle and pig, chicken and whelk, goose and oyster, winkle and partridge. Deer, boar and woodcock. All go into my pot.

Anything but duck that is, because the duck was sacred to Cuddy, and some, the biggest of them all, those that live on the rocks around his old island home, are named in his honour, and for whom he created laws of protection.

To eat a Cuddy duck is an unthinkable sin that no brother dare to entertain.

✝

There are
no birds
here.

✝

In my eyes there are only cathedrals now.

They blind me to all else.
I see every mosaic, every gargoyle, every boss.
Every cross.
They exist beyond my ability to describe them.
But they do exist.
The brothers look to me for guidance now.
They think that they don't, but they do.
My burden is real, my visions finely detailed.
They are obtainable, they are within reach.
O Cuddy. O Cuddy, I call out to you:
Take us home to the wooded hill.

✝

Filled with meat, these men of the cloth – these half-mad men drunk on devotion – idle for a day or two in a great green vale that no one has a strong memory of and appears on no maps in our imaginations. It seems we have strayed from our usual routes though it matters not. It is dry, hot. Cuthbert is safe in his carriage and there is plenty of cold pottage in my trusty pot. We dream away another lost day, lazy in the languid fields of a dizzy spring, the wild grasses a-thrum with the drones of feeding bees and fat flies that spurt black animal blood when swatted flat on the skin of a bare bicep. Dandelion clocks take flight to remind that time is nothing but another notch on a stripped bone-white elm bough, and the only certainty is the setting sun. In these moments a kind of lull befalls our queer community and a brief sense of peace prevails. The evening reaches to enfold us each. To hold us. To remind that even the most wild and roaming mind seeks stillness.

✝

I hear a hum in the sky.
It is becoming louder.

✝

VII

'The congregation of St Cuthbert evolved over time into a mixed community.'

> *St Cuthbert and Durham Cathedral: A Celebration* ed. Douglas Pocock

'Such was the force of this love in this human being that after death his flesh continued to shine with wholeness.'

> 'The Spirituality of St Cuthbert' by Sister Benedicta Ward SLG

'Proof that Cuthbert's immaculate life had found favour with God, and undoubtedly a potent factor in the rapid growth of his prestige.'

> 'Lindisfarne and the Origins of the Cult of St Cuthbert' by Alan Thacker

'The accounts of how the grave was opened in 698, eleven years after Cuthbert's death, how the body was found undecayed, and how it was placed in a wooden coffin on the floor of the church are in effect describing the acceptance – literally the "elevation" – of Cuthbert as a saint. From this point on no expense was spared to increase his renown.'

> 'Why Was Saint Cuthbert So Popular?' by D.W. Rollason

'St. Cuthbert's body was invested with a living personality.'
> *Rites of Durham, being a description or brief declaration of all the ancient monuments, rites, & customs belonging or being within the monastical church of Durham before the suppression* by Anonymous (1593)

'The body was the tangible validation of the community's claims to trace its origin back to Lindisfarne and the earliest days of Northumbrian Christianity... possession of the body thus validated ownership and claims as well as offering divine protection.'
> 'The Wanderings of Saint Cuthbert' by D. W. Rollason

'The strange vicissitudes which attended his dead body, served to emphasise the man in a remarkable way.'
> *Leaders in the Northern Church: Sermons Preached in the Diocese of Durham* by Bishop Joseph Barber Lightfoot

'His cult, fuelled by stories of his body remaining uncorrupted after death, spread like wild-fire throughout Britain.'
> *Lindisfarne: The Cradle Island* by Magnus Magnusson

'Cuthbert – the Lammermuir shepherd who became the great saint of the Northern English – enters into the history of the Northumbrian kings as a figure of awesome importance.'
> *Northanhymbre Saga: The History of the Anglo-Saxon Kings of Northumbria* by John Marsden

'Cuddy was an affectionate nickname for Cuthbert.'
> *To the Island of Tides: A Journey to Lindisfarne* by Alistair Moffat

'The real Cuthbert is hard to find and far to seek.'
> 'Elements in the Background to the Life of St Cuthbert and the Early Cult' by J. Campbell

'His fame was due to his biographers and the fables and folk-lore.'
> *Newcastle Cathedral Saints* by George Miles

'He is a little bit of everything to all men.'
'The Treasures of St Cuthbert' by Dr Janina Ramirez

'Some of these tales are rather bizarre, and must surely have been made up long after the events were supposed to have taken place.'
Cuthbert and the Northumbrian Saints by Paul Frodsham

'To achieve those heights a saint needed considerable promotion, the active manipulation of those who had something to give. Cuthbert's posthumous success depended upon his community.'
'Lindisfarne and the Origins of the Cult of St Cuthbert' by Alan Thacker

'Lindisfarne was a powerful and well-connected church and it threw all its weight behind the cult of Cuthbert.'
'Why Was Saint Cuthbert So Popular?' by D.W. Rollason

'Of course, travelling around northern England for years with a dead body and assorted other relics in a wooden box must have proved logistically awkward.'
Cuthbert and the Northumbrian Saints by Paul Frodsham

'Five new generations of men would be born before St Cuthbert's remains found a resting place.'
A Naturalist on Lindisfarne by Richard Perry

'The greater part of the band of followers, tired from several years' travel, suffering from hunger and lack of comforts, left the party. The only ones that remained were the bishop, the abbot, and the seven faithful guardians who never deserted their post as protectors of the Saint.'
St Cuthbert of Durham by Philip Nixon

'In 995, the bishop and community made their final move to Durham.'
A Brief History of the Anglo-Saxons by Geoffrey Hindley

✝

VIII

We leave the coast and turn inland.

I am at the head of the caravan now, in front of the Bishop Aldhun, in front of Brother Hunred and Brother Chad and Brother Franco, in front of all the monks, in front of Owl Eyes and his horses, in front of St Cuddy, even.

I point the way and not one of them suggests otherwise.

I know where we are going.

To a wooded hill with a cow.

For there is the place fit for a Saint.

I have seen it so many times now.

I have seen it so many times.

There we will build a home.

A home to house a holy man.

Within a great structure like a mountain.

Yes. It may take many, many years.

But we will build it. A holy house.

We will build it.

And the centuries will echo with the footsteps of pilgrims.

✝

And we are
getting closer.

✝

High on a hill the locals call Mount Joy – though there is little joy to be found here this day – the cart becomes stuck and try as they might neither the horses nor the monks can shift it. The day is dry and the ground is hard so there is no reason why the wheels should no longer turn. Cuddy's coffin is held fast, as if he were bearing all his weight down upon this earth.

As if he were sending a sign.

Like he is reading my mind, the Bishop Aldhun says
        Brothers, it is a sign.

At this the monks become excited.
        A sign
they say.
        A sign.
        A sign from Cuddy?

        Yes
says the Bishop though I see that he glances towards me as if seeking assurance.

In turn each of the brothers fall to his knees around the cart and immediately begins to pray. Soon only Owl Eyes and I are left standing; he lifts the yokes from the horses' steaming necks and leads them away to pasture a while, and I put down my creel pack and take a long and lovely drink of water. After a while the monks slowly stand, one by one.

        Well what now?
says Brother Eadmer.

        I think the answer is clear

says the Bishop Aldhun.

> I agree
>
says Brother Franco.

> You do?
>
says the Bishop Aldhun.
> Even though I've not said what it is yet?

I trust in you, Bishop, as I trust in our Lord.

> As do I
>
says Stitheard.

The other monks nod and mutter in agreement.

> Well it is settled then
>
says Bishop Aldhun.
> We shall stage a vigil.

> A *vigil*
>
says Edmund with excitement in his voice.
> We've not had a vigil in a long time.

> We shall fast and pray for three nights and three days
>
says the Bishop, drawing a cross in the dirt with his foot.
> Right here.

The men begin to unpack their gear.

> Yes
>
says the Bishop Aldhun.
> We shall pray for a sign. Cuddy will speak to us when
> he is ready.

✝

That night I have my final vision.
I dream of a hill so great it is an
island in the ocean of woodlands.
On it is a cathedral made from a
mountain. The cathedral I have
seen all along. A place for Cuddy.

✝

The vigil is long, complicated, pious and tedious but being as the monks are fasting it means I at least only have to prepare food for myself and Owl Eyes. Sweet relief from the pestle and mortar.

Early the next day deep in the woods I see two milkmaids leading a cow across a clearing. It is a fine beast. A dun-coloured heifer ripe for milking. It is so laden that it walks with a waddle. One maid carries a three-legged stool, the other a wooden pail. As they pass by they stop and one points to the wooded hill that looms over everything and around which there winds a river. There, I hear her say. I lost the other one over there, somewhere on the Dun Holm.

I wander over to them. The beast eyes me sideways and flicks away flies with its whip of a tail. The milkmaids are around about my age. They speak in a tongue two steps removed from my own. They speak with a song in their voices. Clear water over pebbles.

      Hello
I say.
      What is that place?

I point to the hill.
      That hill there, I mean.

      We call it Dun Holm
says one.

      I thought that's what you said. Meaning hill island?
I ask.

      Meaning exactly that
says the other.

      Thank you. Have you lost a milker?

One maid nods.

She wandered off last night. There is a bull about.

The brothers will help you look for her

I say.

Your brothers?

No

I say.

I mean, men of the cloth. Just some monks I go about
with.

Where are these monks?

I point behind me through the trees.

Back there, deep in prayer.

They'd be better off helping us look for our beast.

I agree. They'd be better off doing a hundred other
things, but they're monks and they can't be told otherwise. Stubborn. I have tried. I have tried many times.

And where is it that you are going?

the other maid asks me.

I turn to the great steep hill. I turn to the wooded island with
the river snaked around its base. I turn to the Dun Holm.

There

I say.

✝

Here I take my blade
and push the point deep

all the way into
the hilt of the handle

all the way into
the heart of the hill

the depths of England.
A marker for men.

✝

The home for Cuddy is here.

I announce these words to the brothers. Some are so lost in prayer or delirious from thirst and hunger that I have to say the words again.

The home for Cuddy is here.

Only dear Brother Hunred open his eyes and sees me. I walk over to him.

The home for Cuddy is here?
he asks.

Well
I say.

Over there. On top of yonder hill like an island.

Can you be sure?

The home for Cuddy is here.

Then I believe you.

Thank you.

So we have arrived.

Yes.

And the journey is over.

Yes, Brother Hunred. One journey is over
I say.

But now another begins.

✝

Of course the monks insist upon a further two days of vigil anyway.

Only when they are half-mad with hunger and lack of sleep and their throats are hoarse from prayer do they finally emerge blinking into the present moment, where Owl Eyes has thought to build a fire and I have prepared a great vat of mutton stew.

The men are intoxicated by their own deep devotion. They all speak at once.

Edmund says: Oh, dear sainted Cuddy spoke to me.
Stitheard says: And to me. I do believe we are close.
Franco says: A sign, a sign, I received a sign from Him.
Chad says: Our piety and prayers are being rewarded.
Eadmer says: I think this might be the place, brothers.
Bishop Aldhun says: Yonder hill. This is to be his home.
Hunred says: Ediva told us all this over two days ago.

At this the brothers look to me, and finally see me, as I turn and point.

Point to the wooded island of a hill once more. Point to the place of our calling.

✝

That evening.
  After supper.

Owl Eyes takes me
  to one side.

Are you sure?
  he says.

Are you sure
  this is the place?

Yes, I reply.
  This is the place.

This is the place
  I will have our child.

✝

IX

'A hill surrounded on three sides by a deep, looping river gorge, it was imposing *and* defensible … the hill encircled by the river would have reminded them of Lindisfarne and how it too was looped in by water; by a circling of the floodtide that only closed itself around the island twice a day.'

St Cuthbert's Corpse: A Life After Death by David Willem

'What was a long caravan of precious baggage and the monks who looked after it doing following milkmaids? Perhaps they were attractive.'

To the Island of Tides: A Journey to Lindisfarne by Alistair Moffat

'They left their houses and flocked to Dunholme, men, women and even little children, dragging their rude hand-waggons along with them, and there they remained until the work was finished.'

Tales of English Minsters: Durham by Elizabeth Grierson

'The foundation of Durham cathedral priory was accompanied by the development of a town.'

Monasteries in the Landscape by Mick Aston

'The creation of this vast mausoleum put a monumental end to the Anglo-Saxon concept that the corpse could travel.'

St Cuthbert's Corpse: A Life After Death by David Willem

'The translation of St Cuthbert's body into the new Norman Cathedral was a matter of such importance. We are a long way from the image of an ascetic bishop.'

'The Wanderings of Saint Cuthbert' by D. W. Rollason

'Durham's greatness derived from the power of his cult.'

The Anglo-Saxons ed. James Campbell

'His dust is now the prized possession of Durham Cathedral.'

St Aidan and St Cuthbert by Henry Kelsey

'The exterior of Durham, with its three massive towers, its enormous bulk, and its superb position on a rocky promontory round which the River Wear sweeps in a grand wooded defile, makes perhaps the most impressive picture of any cathedral in Europe.'

Byzantine and Romanesque Architecture by T. G. Jackson

'The Normans built well; they glorified in the strength and power of stone.'

The History of England Volume I: Foundation by Peter Ackroyd

'Music is liquid architecture; architecture is frozen music.'

Johann Wolfgang von Goethe

'Durham Cathedral is where the structural thrust problem in major buildings was resolved, where the buttress, rib-vault and pointed arch of the Gothic were first demonstrated ... Innovative architecture in a dramatic setting creates a cultural happening.'

St Cuthbert and Durham Cathedral: A Celebration ed. Douglas Pocock

'The mass of its towers and great nave perch on a river peninsula above the Wear and they speak of faith, of continuity and of half-remembered history.'

To the Island of Tides: A Journey to Lindisfarne by Alistair Moffat

'The cathedral erected at Durham to house the shrine of St Cuthbert is not only a cultural benchmark, but also an aesthetic high and architectural innovation.'

> *St Cuthbert and Durham Cathedral: A Celebration* ed. Douglas Pocock

'If you go outside the church and look up at one of the towers, you will see a memorial... there, carved in stone, are the figures of a cow and two milkmaids, one of them with a pail on her head.'

> *Tales of English Minsters: Durham* by Elizabeth Grierson

'In the south alley end of the nine altars there is a good glazed window called St Cuthbert's window... in it all the whole storye life and miracles of that holy man St Cuthbert from his birth of his natiuitie and infancie unto the end and a discourse of his whole life, marvelously fine and curiously sett forth in pictures in fine coloured glass.'

> *Rites of Durham, being a description or brief declaration of all the ancient monuments, rites, & customs belonging or being within the monastical church of Durham before the suppression* by Anonymous

'The shrine was estimated to be one of the most sumptuous in all of England, so great were the offerings and jewells bestowed upon it, and endless the miracles that were wrought at it.'

> *Durham Cathedral* by C. J. Stranks

'We do not tread on that dark slab of stone, and we look down at it reverently, for under it lie the bones of the man in whose honour this mighty Cathedral was raised... as long as Durham Cathedral stands, the memory of St Cuthbert and his life-work will never pass from the minds of men.'

> *Tales of English Minsters: Durham* by Elizabeth Grierson

'Those dark and silent aisles are fill'd with night,
There breathes no murmur, and there shines no light;

The graves beneath the pavement yield their gloom,
Till the cathedral seems one mighty tomb.'
     'Durham Cathedral' by Letitia Elizabeth Landon

'The structure represents time locked-up, a gigantic pause in the temporal flow of history… one is aware in Durham of the presence, as well as the pastness of the past, for the story is kept alive, celebrated, enacted.'
> *St Cuthbert and Durham Cathedral: A Celebration* ed. Douglas Pocock

'So sumptuouslie finished and absolutelye pfitted.'
> *Rites of Durham, being a description or brief declaration of all the ancient monuments, rites, & customs belonging or being within the monastical church of Durham before the suppression* by Anonymous

'A massiveness and solidity such as I have seen in no other place. It rather awes than pleases, as it strikes with a kind of gigantick dignity.'
> *The Letters of Samuel Johnson* by Samuel Johnson

'The immensity of Durham Cathedral engulfs the wanderer within a great wilderness of towering stone.'
> *The History of England Volume I: Foundation* by Peter Ackroyd

'An architectural fantasy floating above the tree-tops and perched on a sort of isthmus like those other great Benedictine houses.'
> *The Northumbrians* by Dan Jackson

'I shall have no emotion greater than this in any cathedral! This building is not magnificent: it is stupendous!'
> *In Search of England* by H.V. Morton

'The most sensational man-made structure in Britain.'
> Simon Jenkins, *The Sunday Times*

'The first thing that's made my heart race.'
> *The Buildings of England: County Durham* by Nikolaus Pevsner

'The Eighth Wonder of the World.'
> John Ruskin

'Thus, the story which began on Lindisfarne or Holy Island, concluded on Dunholm or 'hill-island', the appropriate name for the raised plateau within the meandering loop of the river Wear.'
> *St Cuthbert and Durham Cathedral: A Celebration* ed. Douglas Pocock

'Given the chance [Cuthbert] would perhaps be happy to walk away from the grandeur of Durham and back to the seclusion and simplicity of his little hermitage on Inner Farne.'
> *Cuthbert and the Northumbrian Saints* by Paul Frodsham

✝

X

Dun Holm. AD 1094.

It begins with a handful of sand.
Earth filings, sun shavings,

time's rock reduction.
Mud-flat foundations.

The grit-base of everything.

All
moons
forever.

✝

They have dug the foundations   d
                                          e
                                          e
                                          p.

Trenches sunk to the height of men.
You have to, to hold all that weight.

The greatest building this kingdom's
even seen, a stone citadel to house a
saint, supported by the soft sand of
a razed plateau on a wooded island.

No. A structure like this needs to set
roots. Needs to reach down deep to
the underside just as an old yak tree
clings to the green acorn of its birth.

The men who planned this bold task
must have the minds of prophets to
imagine such a creation; only a true
believer with a god-shaped heart and
eternity in his eyes could conceive of
this thrusting upshot of quarry stone
dragged and cut and carved and then
signed with the unseen markings of
skilled men. They say Cuddy's coffin
was carried for a hundred winters on
a cart. They say it was my forefathers
and foremothers who shouldered the
burden for generations – me, a humble
apprenticed stable lad though still a
skilled handler of the horses that pull the
ropes that turn the wheels that lift the
hod that holds the stones to build it all.

Me, a spawn of the wandering *haliwerfolc.*

Sometimes I speak to him while I work.
I call upon Cuddy and he always replies.

The first stone was laid late last August.

✝

o Cuddy
keep me
company
while I work

I will, my son, I will.
But first this. First
I shall tell you
what else I miss.

I miss
the wet sand
stiff-shifting
underfoot

I miss   *I miss*
the moss   *the taste of salt*
that holds the   *blown in on the breeze*
flint-spark   *the only meal*
of all life   *a man needs*

I miss   *I miss*   *I miss*
each sodden lonnen   *the deer*   *thistles placed*
flooded and fringed   *in the sand dunes*   *in cassocks*
by hawthorns   *the sea on*   *as a prank upon*
* twitching*
like skeletons   *all sides*   *the pious*

I miss
the
marram
grass
maze.

Some of my workmates here call me
Poet or Master Silence or The Lurker.
One or two others call me Owl Boy.

Is there
anything else
you miss
o Cuddy?

> *Yes. I miss*
> *crouching in the sandy swalleys*
> *deep in the dunes*
> *watching the waters*
> *tainted by the devil Dane.*

The devil Dane
is dead now, Cuddy.
This is an
England anew.

✝

BOOK II

The Mason's Mark

Duresme. AD 1346.

'The mason stirs:
Words!
Pens are too light.
Take a chisel to write.'

Briggflatts by Basil Bunting

In the woods, the garlic is up. The riverbanks are winking with their white flowers, thick with the stink of it. All the way from the cathedral to four miles downstream at the priory down at Finchale. To the priory there, where the monks take their leave four times a year. Where the monks go to put the bustle of the old city behind them and contemplate deeply what it means to be a servant of God here in Cuddy country. Yes, in the woods, the garlic is up. The garlic is up so summer must be coming. Scum Gertie says it was planted to stop the brothers rutting. Scum Gertie says if a brother comes back smelling of the old garlic then he has been up to no good in the garlic patch with another brother. Tumbling about. Sinning in the pungent fungus. Rolling in the rotten stuff, flowers caught in the weft of their coarse wool gowns. She told you this herself. Scum Gertie has of course been known to do favours down backstreet stairways for a bag of draf or less, so Scum Gertie knows. The very image of it though. Those monks in the garlic planted to prevent them taking one another, all within moaning distance of our sainted Cuddy's bed of stone. Brothers wandering deep into where it is the wild garlic grows. Like hogs. To think of it. Like dogs. Cassocks rolled thighwards, cassocks yanked skywards. Brothers bent double and grunting under the watchful eye of a loving God. Down there, getting grubby on the bed of waxen leaves. Drunk on the flavour. Dizzy on the fist of it. Sweaty in the grip of it. Biting on the bone of it. Flower seeds caught in the rough stubble of their pates, their shoes kicked off, lost in the ivy that strangles the trees like spoiled Eden's serpent, heathen words of wanting still on their wet swollen lips. Like dogs. You heard tell some put it on the pork joint and eat it. Garlic that is, and you've a dirty mind if you think I suggest otherwise. Yes, garlic and salt rubbed deep into the creases of flesh, and then straight on the spit at feast time. The monks have their own uses for the garlic though, thrusting and crying out His name down there in the summer stillness. Like hogs. At it. Like dogs. *At it.* You think of them often.

He kisses your tits and bleats like a lamb the night before he leaves. Tears glue him to you and you hold him there. He has never looked this small – as your husband is, in all other ways, a big man. Gat-toothed and strong-jawed, byre-door broad but misshapen too. A portion of him – a ham flank-sized piece of him – is more swollen than the rest of his big body. Stripped to the waist, you can see the bulk mass of one rounded shoulder and the bellringer's ropes that writhe in his drawing arm, which is noticeably bigger than the other, like that of a crab who waves his claw in a mating ritual. For Fletcher Bullard is an archer, a bowman. One of the king's very best. He has been squinting down a quiver since he first opened his eyes and the taut drawstring has given him a big arm. But there is another sign too, another sign of a true archer. And that is the straight line of a burn mark worn into the skin of his neck. Some might be as silver as the river at moonlight and after battle others might wear open sore streaks that are raw and never-healing. But all carry the mark of a studied archer and sure enough there on the string side of his neck is the line that shows you that he is one of the best with a bow in all of the northlands. Battle is in his blood. It's mixed into it. Stirred into it. Dirt work for maniac dignitaries is his profession. Land grabs and border disputes. Blood-red vendettas. General warfare. And Fletcher Bullard's arrow is more accurate than most. He can take a sparrow from a branch at a hundred paces, pin a passing coney to a fencepost at double that. Your man's accuracy is a life's training. Your man's training puts meat on the table. But this final night all you see is a big brute of a beast glued to your milk-white dugs by his own silent salty tears, shaking with the fear of long blank emptiness that they call tomorrow. You utter a short prayer to Cuddy for protection and deliverance, though deep down you know you don't mean it.

It is quite beyond his usual character, for Fletcher Bullard is otherwise a big brute devoted to violence. Raised on violence, it nourishes him, excites him. And when he is denied the drama of the battlefield, he pursues that violence in you, and on you. Upon you. Not with the bow and arrow from which he has made his reputation, but with fists and feet and anything else to hand. An empty pan, a poker, a broken broom handle, or nothing at all. And then the next day, swathed in layers of black regret, he offers a watery apology for the previous night's actions. The bruises fade faster than the memories but, oh, he is canny, the bowman. Often his deeds go unseen. Bruises on the stomach, bruises on the back, thighs, scratch marks, knuckle marks, the tight grip of fingers. Cracked bones in the gaol of your chest that holds the heart upon which he has writ his name. You wear them all as he might one day wear his medallions won on the battlefield doing grunt work up on the hill with the longbow boys, his hemp flax or silk strings drawn tight, and one eye squinted. For he is a bowman and a bastard, yet still something ties you to this man, this brute, just as an ox is yoked to a plough or a plough is yoked to an ox, one dragging the other through a deep wet cloying acre of dire England. To all others he's a hero but to you he is a bastard of a bully with a bow and a pouch full of secrets, and you shall run a clean and simple home in his absence. You shall keep the grate swept and the logs split, set the cat to the rats and ensure the stores are never empty because how would that look? A waiting bed sits stuffed with straw. Only now on this last quiet night before his parting, as he lays mewling like a bab, do you dare admit to yourself, if not Cuddy or God himself, that sometimes – sometimes – you pray that this man, your man, the bowman, might fall upon that same English soil, spear himself by the arrow of another, never to return. At sunlight he will leave. And you – you will finally find yourself able to breathe.

Drifts of dust and chippings. The stonemason's yard. Men, and great slabs of stone stacked in one corner waiting for the shapes inside of them to be first imagined and freed. It is summer, but it rains, the blebs falling fat and quick to spot the chunks of rock, some pieces roughly kevelled on the quarryman's whim, and the rain darkens the rock to the colour of the cathedral it will become, each new block to be carved and raised and added, in time the cathedral growing greater, the cathedral growing more ornate, an opening rose, a crown of roses, a place befitting a saint, each stone slotted into the puzzle that pleases God. And when it rains the settled dust becomes clodded and heavy like river silt. Smelly stuff, river silt, made as it is from the rotting bones of things once living. The dark wet bed of the dead. But here the stone dust smells different, like coarse spices, like ancient English earth pressed flat. Empty, the mason's yard feels a haunted place without the whack and clang of mallet and chisel, the scraping of cap- on flag-, or the hushed deliberations of the men who have chosen to heed the call of the dense and mystical stone. The same men who can look at a lump dragged all those miles by a pack of oxen and see the shape of something within it, who can take it and love it, spend more time touching and noticing the stone than they do their wives, who can turn it and come to know its grain and sparkle, and sniff that spicy dryness and then slowly, tenderly, give it curves and patterns and angles and life; who can deliver beauty from within to without. Truly the way the mason conjures such magic is God-like. And each day he keeps returning to lift the apron – a sheet of supple leather whose every crease is stained with cathedral dust – over his head, and then shuffles across the settled crust of his endeavours to raise a mallet once more. But first he lets its handle sit across the calluses of his palm, lets the weight of it bed in, as all things inclined towards permanence must bed in. Then, with a flick of the wrist, it spins in his hand, once and twice over the straight flat back of it, and he cocks an ear to hear the ringing of the stone. He listens intently, breath held. When it truly sings, he begins.

191

The masons of the stone claim that work gives them the devil's thirst. All that dust. All that chipping. A liquorice root tucked into the corners of their mouths, clicking, gives their tongues something to think about. You take them their jugs yourself. You know their names and they make no trouble nor speak out of turn for they are skilled men on sacred ground, they are artists and thinkers who speak through the stone. Also you belong to Fletcher Bullard the finest archer in Auld Duresme, if not the entire king's army, and only a fool would be cruel to a brewer, for who knows what foul flavours we might lace their ale with. No, these men know where their butter goes. Same with bakers or cooks of any kith or kin. Cross a baker and you'll find furry cat parts in your pie or a nugget of human tod in your horse-bread. Cross a cook and God help you. Everyone knows your ale is the best ale, from Bishop Hatfield down to Scum Gertie, shagged sideways in her cups, but always with a smile for you. And if dead Saint Cuddy was still standing he'd surely take a drop too. The run from the mason's yard is thick with a slow trickle of brackish pump water swilled to wash away the drifts of dust and all those vouchsafed secrets set lose from the stones. There are men in each corner working away as apprentices come and go – one sweeping the copper-coloured slurry, another cutting the ropes from a fresh palette and a third dusting beakers in readiness for Eda Bullard's fresh batch. You pass a mason lost in thought as he engraves a word into a simple stone. Over his shoulder you see it says CVDDY. You wheel your hand-cart into the yard and are greeted well enough. Even here outdoors the funk of woodsmoke and sweat is strong. You could pay a lad to do the rounds – Ancel Paine often obliges – but that costs extra coin and with Fletcher Bullard away the string is pulled tight. In summer it is not so bad a chore. Heads are raised and hammers held aloft, momentarily suspended between a bold idea and a cold lump of stone. Some nod, others ignore you, lost in their work, seduced by the stone. Only one smiles and pops the stopper from his bottle in readiness of your sloshing jugs, and wipes the skin of dust from his mazer which hangs on a peg by his bench. Shy Francis Rolfe. Dame, good day give you our Lord, he says with a lowering of the chin. A courteous man, Francis Rolfe. You reach for a drop of the better batch. Sire, God you keep, you reply, with moths in your mouth.

Your ale is fine, yes, your ale is the best. The best in Duresme. Most with taste will tell you so. Your ale has its own flavour because you put your mark upon it just as each mason marks his stone with a unique sigil such as a cross or a lightning line or something more mysterious. You learned to brew from a master, your father Godfrey Fresne. Godfrey means God-peace and he was a good man who taught you to take the ale in moderation. Too much ale will make a mind mushy, he said. Too much ale will give you the creeping pains. The creeping pains is when your head feels split by an axe blade and your stomach is as off as green bacon but worse than that, it feels like your own shadow is trying to sneak up and strangle you so. It's always there at the corner of your eye and your teeth are itchy. That's the creeping pains and some say you can't do anything about them but take another draught. So best not to bother in the first place, said your father, who as I say was called God-peace Fresne, and who brewed only as a service, only to make money, only to buy bread from Guydo Joplin's yuvven and put a little meat in your meat box. He taught you this and you live by it now, taking only a single draught on occasions deemed special, such as the last of the harvest days, when a mystery play passes through from York, or if there is a jousting tournament, or you're sitting down to a rare game of merrils or when Fletcher Bullard returns peck-drunk and forces a jug down you to, as he says, bring on the sinning slackness.

Eda, says the stonemason. Francis, you reply. Have you brought us the good stuff? The best there is. Is that right? Fresh brewed, you say. I've not even had a time to put a bushel over the door; it's straight out the vat, pure and simple. No herbs or honey or caulding with egg yolks in my ale and any man says otherwise will – here you're interrupted by Roger Sparks, who speaks through a crooked grin whose purpose you cannot divine. Be pinned to a trunk at a hundred paces by one of Fletcher Bullard's arrows? he says. Lord, what an archer. I recall once up on Maiden Castle mound – now it is Francis Rolfe that interrupts *him*. Eda doesn't need weapons, he says. Words are her weapon, and her smile. A deadly combination, words, when you know enough to place in the right order, says Francis Rolfe and he comes to help lift the jugs as you decant the ale into the masons' flasks. Well, says Roger Sparks. I wouldn't know so much about that when this here mallet is the tool of my trade, but still I saw your man split a spuggie so true it didn't scunner. It was like it was sleeping. Roger Sparks whistles through his teeth and shakes his head. Fletcher Bullard, he says. May his aim always be true. Not to me, you think. Not when he is swinging his neafs or dancing the devil's jig on your face and chest as if his feet were on fire. But you just smile and pour with Francis Rolfe at your elbow, an emptied jug dangling from one thick strong finger as if it were *him* that had spent a lifetime drawing the bowstring and firing the arrows that end the lives of men. But when he stumbles and blushes you see that he's not like Fletcher Bullard. He is not like that man at all.

There hangs on the door of Cuddy's cathedral a gimbled face most diabolical. A grimace cast in copper, it has turned a mottled green from the rain that has lashed about it for two hundred winters or more. You pass it heading homewards now. To some its eyeless sockets are those of the snarling Barghest that stalks the barren uplands beyond the birth of the Wear, while to some he has the mouth of Jack-in-Irons who haunts the lonely rides in chains, and to others still his is the visage of the grisly goblin Redcap or a boggart of the fields, or the troll who fell from the tower or a sin-eater or an evil wyvern trapped forever in molten metal, or the firebird that lives for five hundred years before being reborn in flames, or simply the hideous mask of all the city's sinners condemned to wander the smoking planes of hell for evermore. But to most folk it is the Sanctuary Knocker, whose stout handle is to be rapped against the sturdy door of the most impressive building in the world while the words *Sanctuary! Sanctuary!* are yelled by those who seek it and often with the hue-and-cry mob baying at their tail. You have seen it with your own eyes, day and night, from sneak-thieves and child-diddlers or a twin brother who killed his other in an ale-fugged fight. Upon doing so, the said door is flung open by the monk that sits in the chamber above it for exactly the purpose of pulling the seeker in and promptly shutting it behind them. Sanctuary is granted and the Galilee bell rung to mark the moment, and the seeker then made to wear a robe that bears the yellow sign of our Cuthbert sewn onto one shoulder to show the world the generosity of our saint who offers his home without judgement. The fugitive is then given quarters and food and the time in which to pray forgiveness, give confession and make peace with himself, then say farewell to the city, for then he is made to leave and guaranteed safe passage by a chaperone acting on the king's orders. Accompanied by constables and carrying a cross, he will walk the highway and pass through the parishes unscathed, and have thirty-seven days in which to board a single-sail cog, most probably at the palatine port named for the pool-of-the-stags, that is Hartlepool, and then set sail for only-God-himself-knows-where. Overseas, far from here, in lands occupied by strange beasts and giant birds the size of sheep but with beaks like great blades, and where they say the sun burns a different colour, and the people speak in tongues too strange to comprehend, and where if the locals don't get you then the loneliness shall, will be his destination, from which never to return. The face of the Sanctuary Knocker then, is that of the lonely miscreant, the damned, the doomed, the cursed, the blasted, the blighted, the bedevilled, the fated; he who shall live their life seeking God's eternal forgiveness alone.

Some folk about the place call the fiendish Brother Barnabus 'Cruikshank' when his back is turned. This is because they say that beneath his cowl his legs are as crooked as fire hooks. Put these bandy pins onto a fleshy barrel of a body that's more befitting a woman weighted double with child and you have quite a sight that you yourself, Eda Bullard, do not care to ever have to see. Little wonder he is at war with the world, and all around him – and you in particular. There he is now, across the Palace Green, scurrying past the Almshouse, though he is not a man you would beg alms of. It is your natural beauty that riles him so, you reckon. It must be. How else to explain the hatred that burns in him if you do chance to meet in an alley or pass in the street? Sire, God give you good day, you say, as steady as you can, but your greeting is met with a wall of stone silence and then when he casts his eyes of shale upon you and turns your spine to ice, it is because he sees something that no amount of prayer could ever deliver to his cell door. He is bitter with desire for something he cannot have, cannot own, and that causes hate like fungus to grow within him. He is to be avoided. You hope and pray that one day he himself might be transported across an ocean for those sins he surely harbours within him, and about which tongues have long wagged in the back rooms and choirboys' dormitories. A fiend he is, naught but a fiend and destroyer.

Two sunrises later. A knock on your door, stout and brisk, bone on wood. You open it and a stick of eels swings in with it, jammed in the handle. They are of impressive length and girth and most meaty, the last glimmer of life still fading from their glassy orbs. Several are conger and their jaws are prised open in an expression of collective surprise by the birch rood shoved through the mouth and gullet of each. The stonemason Francis Rolfe steps into view then, grinning snag-toothed and swarthy. Dame, good day give you our Lord, he says. Fish fit for a king. Or queen. Or saint even. Best in the Wear. Sire, God you keep, you reply. Yes, lady, you be welcome, he goes on. Cuthbert's community, the wandering folk of the holy man, he says, would have dined on the very same eels. The very same here? you say, straight-faced as you lift the rood from the handle. Might be they've gone off a bit by now, and you lift them for a little sniff. The mason is flustered, blushing. Their ancestors, I mean. The old eels from whence these wrigglers were spawned, I mean. Caught them in my traps at first light. Praise God. Praise God, you reply, He has blessed you most bountifully. Shame He couldn't bless you with some lamprey though, they'd go well baked in sugar and cinnamon, shame indeed. Francis Rolfe looks forlorn and you let him dangle like a spider on a line, squirming in his uncertainty. Well, I'll never eat all these myself, you say, realising that's the reason he has brought so many when two could sit curled snugly beneath a pie lid. I'm out of vinegar so there'll be no pickling either, you add, and the stonemason Francis Rolfe just stands there, smiling and sweating, hat in hand, humble as you like. You utter a short prayer to Cuddy for understanding. If you linger on the step much longer I'll be minded to sweep you away like gathered dust, you say, and he replies Oh, right-o and turns to leave, but when you say The fire's banked and I'm supposing they could go in the pot, he takes the invitation and you quickly lean out and look up and down the row for enquiring beaky noses and enquiring eyes that will lead back to Fletcher Bullard. You and your eels best get inside then, you say, ushering the man that makes your young innards writhe most agreeably, over the smelly sump and into your little spinster's box of hot corners and short shadows, only you're not a spinster, you're taken by the bowman. Property of. You know it, and the stonemason Francis Rolfe knows it and Brother Barnabus on his crooked legs knows it, and the Sainted Cuddy of Duresme Cathedral himself knows it, better than most. He sits in silence. And so it begins.

Six eels curled tight into a bucket. They're slick to the touch, stiff flesh river-fresh. The stonemason Francis Rolfe stands there rolling his hat as you pour the sluice water off into the runnel. Their blank dead eyes glore so that whichever way you turn them there is always one pair angled on you in unblinking judgement. God is in them, watching. God is everywhere. You leave the front door open to stop sin getting a foot in, then remembering how easily Madlin McGrillis across the way flaps her lips, change your mind and close it. The stonemason Francis Rolfe surveys the room. He takes in the fire and the little crooked shelves and then settles on the old bow that hangs from a peg on the wall. A full quiver sits close by. Is it true that he is the best, your husband? Only at archery, you say. This seems to amuse him and his face brightens. Oh? Not so good at the fishing then? Well, you reply, I'd wager he could fall into a barrel of dace and dogfish and still come out sucking his thumb. He smiles, says: Me, I can catch a stick of eels while sleeping. You say: Boastful people will be shamed but wisdom stays with those who are modest. A wise and modest man he must be then, smiles Francis Rolfe. Hardly. Yes, he continues, I had heard otherwise. And what else have you heard? you ask, but he just says It's not for me to gossip, I'm no fishwife. You flash him a hot-poker look then, slick pod in hand – And neither, sir, am I – but inside you're smiling. At this he flounders. Oh no, I didn't mean – it's just that – the thing is. Now he's a worm on a hook and you don't release him yet. Francis Rolfe's face crumples beneath the cloud of a frown. I heard he is too free with his fists, and more besides. I'll not be making a pie, you reply. I've not got time for pastry. Through gritted teeth he says, yes, I heard he blacked your eyes and turned your nose sideways. Syrup, you say. I can poach a couple of eels in syrup. Then so quietly as to barely be heard Francis Rolfe says, I heard he is a dog or worse, because dogs are loyal and dogs know no better. Then he adds, I'll bring you some elvers next time; they're fine fried in butter. And I'll tell you one thing – you've already told me one thing, you say interrupting him before busying yourself with the fire, the pots, the eels. The syrup and the seasoning. Francis Rolfe is perched on the edge of Fletcher's chair. His words are pebbles on his tongue. Well, you say, spit it out, and then the pebbles come tumbling out. I heard he booted you so hard down there that you walked with a limp for two seasons and that's why you haven't sired, may the Lord forgive me for raising it. You say nothing just now. The two biggest eels are heavy in your hand, all blood, grey flesh and river mud. Francis Rolfe crosses his legs and coughs. Your fingers curl around their slick skin as you lift them from bucket to pot. Francis Rolfe uncrosses his legs. You grip and squeeze the eels, then drop them as gobbets of water spit and sizzle on the glowing logs. You're not the one who needs to be asking for forgiveness, you finally say.

You are a locked chest full of desires to which only Cuddy has the key. God's envoy across the north country, he is sole witness to your sins; only he can ever know what it is you want. Watched over by such a saint, a person cannot hide that which they crave.

She is a maker of miracles in her own way, Scum Gertie. Some men have been known to worship her, falling at the altar of her feet. For a few coins she offers a glimpse of heaven to be found in the folds of her flesh or the hot purses of her most private parts. She is as honest as the world is flat and to be found out in all weathers, shaping her skills and shaking her assets, always identifiable by her mustard yellow hat and smile as wide as the Wear. A wise hen, Gertrude, your old friend, a wisdom gained from being turned out young. She's as skilled and practised at her profession as the wheelwright is at his, and just as vital to man's advancement, though the taxman rarely comes a-knocking at her door. But if he does, she says, curling her crooked fingers to her palm and examining nails that have been carefully cleaned with vinegar, there are almost certainly informal arrangements to be made. No man is beyond temptation for they are simple creatures, she adds, and easier to read than The Big Book. Dear Scum Gertie, your fathers were acquainted. A Germanic name, Gertrude. He was guessed to be a Hun, though it is said he crossed the wrong nobleman and was sent across the sea after servicing the said man's wife, sold on to break his back with shovel and axe, though others claim he was snatched one night and buried alive in the soil somewhere between Flass Vale and the Red Hills, drowning in the dirt up there. Tongues do flap and rumours abound; Auld Duresme is that type of town. Gertrude means strength and she does not carry the stench of sin, despite what they say in the taverns; cruel are the mouths that have nibbled on Gertie's pink lug. You will not sniff a fetid miasma about Gertrude – she washes daily and in these warmer months takes to the river by Fulling Mill once a week, then covers herself most abundantly with a drop of civet in rosewater that she makes herself and hopes one day to sell in the perfumeries of Lunden. She delouses as often as noblemen and keeps black soap in her cupboard at all times. Her hair smells of liquorice, her mouth of cardamom. The 'scum' name is a slur spread by men who have surely laid with Gertie themselves. They do that, men. No, she keeps herself clean in order to shorten the walk through the fiery dungeons of judgement, and to give her a chance at redemption come the day. She keeps a clean hemble too: fresh rushes on the floor, and six or so scrubbed children, born in bastardy in the main, but all moral, of Godly mind, strong of tooth and only one minorly defected with the dribbles. Scum Gertie is your best and perhaps only friend, the one who balms your bruises and fetches cloves for a bleeding mouth when Fletcher Bullard is back on leave, always without judgement. One day women like you and Gertrude might gain the whip hand. I pray that day may be sooner than most may think.

Another morning. The smell of summer on the warming southerlies. The sloshing flasks and the cart handles heavy in your hand as you transport ale for the masons, fresh ale for the masons to slocken their dust-coated throats. Ale for Francis Rolfe whose smile cancels the concerns that wriggle in your belly like a pot of maggots. Another piece of the puzzle, he says, nodding towards a block of stone from which a curved section has been scooped. That's what we call a formeret, he says. A half-rib to slot in betwixt wall and the vaulted ceiling. Ribs that spring from a corbel stone rather than the expected capital. Where? you ask. Where? Yes, in which part, I mean. The north transept, Francis Rolfe replies. Above the arched doorway there. I didn't have you down as interested. I'm interested, you reply. I'm interested in all things Godly or otherwise. And have you seen the burial place? he asks. I've seen many a burial place, yes. But what about the burial place of Our Cuddy carved in stone, the cathedral's own? No? Then come with me. He touches your wrist at that point where your life force throbs. The rabbit's foot thump of it. With one finger he gently touches that soft white part, and it is like heat and then ice, and you follow. Across the ragged scrub of the Palace Green you walk, past the grazing cows – the half-sweet funk of them is ripe – and then you enter the vast cool space of the cathedral and take a turn to the left. Francis Rolfe walks quickly; he strides as if his body is struggling to contain the joy he finds with the world, but lightly too. He walks on the balls of his feet. They lift him up in a way that is agreeable, and noble, though he is no nobleman. Oh, it is a sight. Then you are down at the end, where it is cool and dark. The Chapel of the Nine Altars, says Francis Rolfe, and he leads you to a four-cornered shrine where candles burn and something shivers inside of you, like a breath at your ear, a tongue licking up your backbone. Frosterley marble, he says, his hand running over a column nearby, but your eyes are on the stone slab on which are carved the letters CVTHBERT. He lies here? What? says Francis Rolfe turning, but you already know the answer. You ask only out of a sense of awe. Saint Cuddy is here. He is *here*. You drop to your knees and say a long prayer for salvation and charity and forgiveness and freedom and – yes – desires fulfilled, but not once do you say a prayer for Fletcher Bullard as he awaits battle.

You have been up the tower I assume? says the mason Francis Rolfe and you reply No, I have not. Not once? Not once, you say. Then you have not been as close to God as many and that must be rectified immediately, come with me now. Now? you say. Yes now, why not, do you have something better to be doing? And you reply Well, yes, I have a hundred things to be doing like finishing my rounds and picking up the sugar, then fetching the loaves from Joplin the Baker's yuvven and straining a new batch of ferment and cleaning out some skeps for the summer's honey hives, I can't be climbing up towers when there's all this going on, but really you're wondering what people will say if they see you with Francis Rolfe in God's house, and here he stops and smiles and says Eda, are any of those matters so pressing that you can't spare a half hour to climb the great stone ladder up towards His kingdom? And you have to admit, no, they're not, though you'll get the stalest blackest loaves from Joplin's kiln if you leave it too late. So you follow him through the door and across the knave, through the shaded corridors of the cloisters, you snatch a view of the hog-patch of dry dirt in the middle, as it catches the early summer sun. The mason Francis Rolfe smiles as he turns away and steps through a doorway to disappear around the curved corner of the stairwell, and begins to climb the steps at speed. You follow and are soon rising up through the stone, climbing higher than you have ever been, higher even than when standing atop the hills of Hollingside or Hallgarth, where you picked bumble-kites as a bairn, higher than Whinney Hill or any of the seven hills on which this, God's city, was built. Oh wait for me, you say, but every time you think you are reaching him, you catch only a glimpse of the mason Francis Rolfe's coat as it flaps around the corner, and his laughter echoes upwards, trapped between the walls and your breath is in your ears and your ears are on fire and the fires sweal inside of you in ways you never knew possible. The steps wind in one direction and then just as you are becoming dizzy they narrow and turn the other way, and you see strips of the city through tight little windows from which many an archer such as your own Fletcher Bullard must have fired an arrow down the centuries. The stone of the tower feels dry and clean and almost new to the touch as you run your hands upon it, feeling the contours of time impressed there. And still Francis Rolfe strides on, gasping and laughing, up, up, upwards.

Then suddenly the stone stairwell delivers you to the kingdom of the clouds and Francis Rolfe is standing there on the slope of the roof, and the wind is flapping his coat, and he is smiling and pointing, and you're struck dumb by the sight of the city seeming so small as it sits scattered around the base of a building raised for a saint. You utter a short prayer to Cuddy of awe and gratitude. How many men must it have taken to build such a place? you say. How many put their shoulders to the cart that carried slabs so heavy that there must be a mountain of ox and horse bones beneath its very foundations, each a fallen victim in the pursuit of faith? Faith indeed it was that built it, says Francis Rolfe. And fifty thousand folk too I shouldn't wonder. Fifty thousand? you scoff but you see that Francis Rolfe speaks not in jest. It took near enough a century to build it so, he says. Think not just of buried animal bones but the entire lives spent in service to the stone, he says. Think of those who never got to climb this tower or see the marvel in all its finished wonder. Think of the sacrifices they made so that we might feel the wind upon our face on this, a glorious Godly day. Amen, you say.

It has been struck on more than one occasion, says Francis Rolfe. Struck by lightning. He is pointing to the flagstaff atop which the blue and red banner of King Edward is raised, his six lions roaring as warning to the devilish King David and his Scottish heathens who, in league with the French, are said to be making threats concerning invasion of these northlands, and to whom Ralph Neville of the House Neville of Raby is already taking a stand as he assembles his fyrd, said to soon be six thousand strong and numbering among them your husband, Fletcher Bullard himself. The flag is rattling with the wind, visible for leagues around. Do you think there will be a war? you wonder, and you find yourself shouting, for the breath is swept away up here, swept away and stolen. There is always a war, says the stonemason Francis Rolfe. So long as there are men there will be war, and I shall want no part of it. You are a coward then, you say, though it comes out as a question. It is more cowardly to go along with things like jimmers in a herd, he snaps back. Braver is the man who chooses his own path. Braver is the man who says no than nothing at all. This answer catches you unaware, and places the mason in a new light. But what about God? you ask. Does God not want us to stand strong and proud against the fiendish Scot? And do not the wives of soldiers up there in Scotland ask God the same things about the English? replies Francis Rolfe, shaking his head. No, *He* does not care for warfare, only goodness of spirit, charity and neighbourly generosity. It would not surprise me if even in five centuries one country is fighting another over more borders and boundaries than ever before. Man is at fault here, Francis Rolfe continues, not God. Man, rather than woman, for no woman fires a bow or rides a cavalry steed. No, we must take the lead from our Saint Cuthbert and treat all God's creatures equally otherwise all this – here he pauses to stretch his arms wide – will have been built in vain. It is up to us to see down the centuries and consider what may lay beyond the horizon. We must tell the stories of our time so that tomorrow's children receive them, then pass them on like scrolls in bottles sent down the river.

Here he crouches and runs a hand along the carved balustrade. And I choose to do that with my stone.

He keeps a hawk. Up here he tells you all about it also, and when he does, this curious and gentle stonemason's big eyes become alive with the pursuit he has a passion for. Tiny fires burn there for you can see now what you already suspected to be true: that Francis Rolfe is a man of talents, an artist, a soul sensitive to all around him. He talks loudly for the wind is wild up here at the top of the tower, and even though the country beyond the city is laid out for you to see, it is him that you are looking at and you listen now as he tells all about how he has trained the bird well, reared it since it was feather-less. Hand-fed it grubs when it was nothing but a blind thing of skin and claw. She sleeps at the foot of my bed, he says. The hawk fills an absence, he says. A gap. She is a protector. At night when I am under my blanket she lowers her beak to the soft feathers of her chest and her eyes become small and then smaller still, and then they are closed to the world. Then she is dreaming of soaring. Soaring and swooping. Swooping down from a great high place like this one. When she has these deep visions her claws curl to the bed post. There are scratch marks there. She has worn it away, chipped it away, just as I do with my blocks of stone. Sometimes, he says, she twitches. She sleeps as we sleep, and in that sleep she sees things, lives other lives, goes places no creature can visit in this earthly realm. She is more than a bird, he says. She has been sent by God and is worth a thousand men, and I worship her as Cuddy worshipped all animals for we are all equals in the eyes of our Lord, amen. Amen you say, but the wind steals your words away again in an instant. The words take flight like the hawk, like the owl, like the angels from the heaven above, soaring over every tiny thing.

Afterwards, the stairwell is a funnel of stone down which you pour yourselves, your laughter like liquid, guiding you gaily as you descend back to earth having tasted heaven's many flavours.

You're struggling with the sugar when you see Brother Barnabus, also known as Auld Bandy Legs or The Creeper of the Cloisters or Mouldy Dough or Cruikshank, this warm and windy evening. That something so fine is as burdensome on your back as Christ's cross was on His is the wrong kind of miracle, but the cargo is precious and not a grain can be spared. A pound of it is twice the price of a capon, twice a labourer's daily wage, and you won't even take a taste for yourself as it is going straight to Toller the spice man in exchange for galingale, cinnamon, ground pepper, and fresh herbs and honey too, for recently about the town the men have got a taste for metheglin and you are thinking of turning your hand to a vat of it – though not the mead, which is better made either down in the south country or by the monks that remain up on Cuddy's island of Lindisfarne. So you're struggling with the sugar when you see him, over by the stagnant Saddler Street puddle, that fiend Brother Barnabus, skin the colour of ash, and one part of him, the trunk and hips and haunch of him, as round and soft as that of a lady – you think of Scum Gertie and chew a smile away in case he gets the wrong impression – and the pallor of a man who might dine only on maslin and rainwater, though some have said he dines only on the blood of chorister boys. It is his eyes though. Brother Barnabus stares so deeply with the eyes of an animal that it is a violation, and as he sidesteps the puddle and passes by, those eyes take you in, bore into you, wretched drill-bit pupils causing agony in your soul, and in a cold, flat voice at just the correct register, and so that no other person around might hear him, spits a single word in your face, twice: Whore, he says. *Whore.*

In the days that follow you take to returning to Cuthbert's shrine, lingering longer around his resting place. The stone there is as smooth as a piglet's belly from the knees of the many. The space is hallowed, the space is holy. It's quiet in this corner; there is only candle smoke and distant echoes. You say a prayer. You say a prayer to Cuddy of fear and guilt. You say a prayer to Cuddy of fear and guilt and you ask for protection and pray for safe passage through this life and the next. You pray that the fires of damnation will not scorch your soles. You say: Cuddy, I wish to remain humble and charitable and good-humoured where circumstance will allow me. I wish to be as strong and noble and pure as you were in life, and remain so in death, please let your judgement be fair and just. And you hear your prayer bounce back, a polyphonic jumble of voices bouncing between stone and stone, the scent of snuffed wick smoke and stone dust strong. Down the far end, there is the squeak and shuffle of shoe leather and cracked hide, the baritone boom of things being moved. The creak of the pews as they sigh beneath the burden of man. Bell chimes, high above, metallic and often, blading a streak through the summer clouds. The distant rumble of the sky is first like hunger, then akin to battle wails and blood cries. You continue. Cuddy, I call out to you. I ask for guidance, pray for forgiveness. He remains mute. He lies there, silent like a buried knife. Even alone you feel a presence and it is not undesirable. And Cuddy is down there, immaculate beneath his blanket of stone, almost within reach, a sainted man whose soul is pure in a way that yours could never be. You pray for forgiveness, pray for guidance, for many things, yet deep inside you know you are praying for more of that feeling that the mason might give you.

In the morning Francis Rolfe knocks, and soon you find yourself walking with the stonemason once more. You follow the
water, you follow the river, the Wear. You smell swine cress,
lamb's lettuce. Where does it all go? you wonder. To the sea,
says Francis Rolfe, to the sea. Have you ever seen it? you ask.
Once. Once I walked all the way. All the way? Yes. How far
was that? From dawn to darkness, he says, I was in the trees
almost all of the day. Then I passed a priory at a place called
Monkwearmouth that was kept by some brothers, and the sea
was within view. It was a great big slab of grey stone laid at the
edge of the land, or as if the sky had fallen. There were boats
like clouds and clouds like sheep trimmings. I was just a mason's
apprentice then and my job was sharpening blades, oiling tools
and running errands up and down the tower. I studied designs,
patterns and techniques too; they would not let me lift so much
as a chisel until I had learned all there was to know about bank-
heads and bosses, chevrons, corbels and capitals, scrollwork and
spandrels, jambs and soffits, lozenges and spirals and much more
besides – that was just the start of it. And I learned about the
cathedral too, and all its different aspects – chantrys and chapels,
tombs and cloisters and deaneries and so forth, for what use is
a stonemason who does not know about that place which he
is improving? Of course there was also the stone itself: there is a
big difference between buff-coloured sandstone and limestone
polished to resemble marble. So they sent me on to Finchale
Priory to study the designs created in tribute to the house style
at the cathedral. But that was another time. This day I arrived at
Monkwearmouth, Francis Rolfe continues, and I was greeted
warmly, for I could talk at length about my work, and though
I was only an apprentice the brothers were impressed and they
fed me well. We had crabs and bread and much butter and cake
made from fruit. Then one brother – I believe his name was
Edward or Ellis or Edmund, a decent follow nonetheless – led
me to the beach, where the land turned to sand, tiny grains of
it, more grains than there are eels in the Wear and I walked on
out into the water, and I opened my mouth to taste it. How
did it taste? you ask. Not as nice as your ale, laughs Francis

Rolfe. But it was still a place of power and magic and the sea lifted me up so that I floated quite freely. I let the waves run through me and they gave me strength and power. The next day I walked back and reached my digs dog-tired but aglow, as if I had wandered the world in its entirety, or so it seemed. I've not been to the sea since, but I dream of it often. Here Francis Rolfe pauses for a moment. Perhaps, Eda, he says, one day we might see it together.

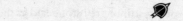

Your father picking maggots from a dead dog. This is what you remember as you walk side by side along the worn river path. He was lifting it from a stink pit the first time he told you about the corpse of the saint of our city. I'll tell you about a miracle, he said. You followed him like a stray puppy then – one that has escaped the butcher's cosh, that is – followed him everywhere. He was off to fish the slow deep waters upstream from the weir where the cormorants crouch, and the mawks were bait for the hooking. Fishing for anything from stick-lebacks to cubit-long pike with teeth like combs that snatch ducklings and drag them down to the silt-murk. He got tired of turning you back when you trailed uninvited, so sent you to a shallow side run to pick cray from beneath the flat stones there. Giant cray, meaty cray, fat for the pot. You took some nips but they were worth it for the taste in your ladle. Time to be told the makings of a saint my girl, he said leaning over the dog, and then shared the story of the wandering folk of the holy man, and how they one day saw fit to cease those wanderings right here where there was nothing but trees and a river rich with cormorants and pike, and a cow, and a hill on which to build Cuddy's cathedral. He told you all this as he folded a stink pit mawk onto one of the finest thorn hooks kept in vinegar since winter past, and the flesh of it popped and oozed onto a finger that he raised to his lips when you laughed, saying hush girl you'll disturb God's fish and neither He nor His fish will like that. Then he dropped his line and told you about the time Our Cuddy was raised from his stony sleep by the Prior and the sub-Prior, the sacrists, the archdea-cons and Symeon, who saw fit to write the story of Duresme down. And you both watched the flowerhead he had tied on as a float as your father told of how they lifted Cuddy and his holy vestments from his coffin and with quivering candle in quivering hand Symeon stooped to kiss the feet of the saint and moisten them with his tears. And the flowerhead hung there in the still water over the squirming blind maggot as your father told you that the coffin gave off a sweet fragrance, as if he himself had been there, and how all was fresh and bright and Cuddy himself was uncorrupted, and even after all this time was not at all like the various creatures of the stink pit, which is to say: mashed rotten. A miracle it was, said your father as he snatched at his stick and lifted a perfect brown trout from the brown waters that flow deep and still in the gliding passages of memory. It hung there, slowly spinning. A miracle, as every fish in the pot is a miracle, praise be. Praise be, you replied, then ran a young pink palm down the shining muscular flanks of it and felt all life there in it.

After Francis Rolfe's story you walk in silence for a while. A question sits inside of you until it becomes so sour that it has to be asked. It has to be exorcised yet you deliver it gently, as if you are only really half-interested in what answer may come: You have never taken a wife? Here Francis Rolfe's face folds − briefly, fleetingly − into a frown just like his sheep trimmings clouds darkening the bright path of the sun. But then the sun returns and he smiles a sad twisted-toothed grin, as much to himself as to you. Yes, he says, oh yes. You do not press him. You wait until he speaks again. She died in birthing. He pauses. As did the bairn. He raises his eyes to the sky. They're up there now. You utter a short prayer for eternal peace in heaven with all heaven's creatures. Thank you, whispers Francis Rolfe and you speak no more on the matter. I hear there is a new prior up here at Finchale, you say as much to fill the silent gap as anything, Nicholas de Luceby is his name, but Francis Rolfe seems distracted and you are close to the priory now, in fact you can see the stone tower's spire poking through the tree-line, and its timber roof too. The grandeur of this hideaway home for those monks for whom the city is a drain upon their patience is quite a sight, you say, adding: though it still does not hold a candle to Cuddy's place. Francis Rolfe grunts agreement and you climb the slopes to rest deep in the thickness of the trees where little sunlight penetrates the canopy and you can watch the priory from a distance, aware you ought not to go closer in case you are seen together, you, the wife of Fletcher Bullard, and he, the widowed mason of Cuddy's cathedral. Side by side you sit and see the shallow bubbling waters of the Wear there, and the fishing run the monks have made from stones. All is tranquil and still. A fine place for respite surely, you say, a Godly home. Then Francis Rolfe turns to you and looks. He looks long and hard, searching for something, seeking an answer to a question unasked with a stare that is like a bright light reaching into your every dark and lonely corner. His eyes are so large and brown; they are the eyes of a hungry hunter. You need not hear the question to answer it. Yes, you say. Yes,

yes. But then a movement distracts him. Down there, leaving the priory by a side door, furtive in their movements, are two monks. You recognise one of them by his gait and by his girth. It is that runny drip of dog dirt, it is Brother Barnabus, the one they call Cruikshank.

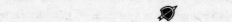

The spell of Francis Rolfe's gaze is broken, and he swats away a fly that is bothering him. You are hidden in the trees as you see the two monks walk hurriedly away towards the thicket that runs in a narrow and uninviting overgrown stretch between the abbey and waterway. Shifty as a weasel that one, says Francis Rolfe. I have heard many things about that Cruikshank. What things? you wonder. None of them Godly, he says, swatting the fly away once more. Brother Barnabus leads the way, but then he pauses and he lets the monk, who you can now see is young, much younger than you first thought, and wearing a face heavy with worry, overtake him, and from behind Brother Barnabus shoves and pushes the other brother, cajoles him as one might a stubborn old ass, and he stumbles forward, but offers neither words nor gestures of protest, and as they disappear into the chickweed and the oxtongue, the fat hen and the sow thistle, Brother Barnabus turns and looks over his shoulder to see that no one is watching him. For one moment it is as if his eyes have fallen upon you and he glores across the water and up into the trees, and there is a cruel slit of a sneer on his face – or maybe it is a lusty hunger of sorts – and then he turns and follows his young charge through the hidden doorway into another England, one of sweat and secrets. The trees close behind him.

Homewards, lost in the thrum of summer, you take a higher path and the river below disappears from view. Cows graze the watery pastures somewhere out of sight and close by a cuckoo is calling. The stonemason Francis Rolfe guides the way. Flanked by weeds and vines, brambles and nettles, the paths wind and rise and dip and split, each becoming narrower and narrower. The cathedral shrinks as you burrow deeper into the sea of wild green, then disappears entirely behind you. Francis Rolfe walks with purpose, but lightly too as if he dare not leave a footprint nor damage his surroundings. Men do not usually walk lightly in this way. Men always want to damage their surroundings. Twice he looks back and smiles, and it is on this second time that you stumble on a tree root and your leg brushes against a thick patch of nettles. The sting is instant and you flinch, making an animal noise that causes your cheeks to blush. White welts rise on red skin and the peppery itch of the plant spreads up your lower leg; you can see it when you stop and stoop and lift your skirt. Francis Rolfe stops too then, and turns back. He comes to you, but not before he scours the undergrowth and then finding what he wants, twists out a thick handful of leathery green leaves. Where there's nettles there's always docks close by, he says. Nature hurts and nature soothes. Nature provides. And God creates all, amen. Amen, you say. He bends down and – may I? – vigorously rolls the leaves into a thick stringy wad between his stone-worn palms until both become damp and then he carefully turns your leg a little and applies the poultice to the rash. Your calf is white. His hands are warm and the leaves feel cool. He holds it there, fingers curling gently around the flesh of your leg, and the fine hairs stand on end. Nettles, says Francis Rolfe as he looks up at you, only grow in fertile soil. This soil is very fertile indeed. And the way he says this it is as if he is saying something else entirely.

And you both know what it is he is saying, because you do not need words. Everything is glifs and gestures and the blinking of wet eyes. And you hear yourself saying Indeed sir, and they can be brewed into a fine ale too. Can they, says Francis Rolfe, his voice low and thick in his throat, well I would surely like to have a taste of that sometime soon, yes I would. And the moment melts away then, as his fingers sit on your skin, and the wild green sea is alive with the snap and buzz of insects, and yourselves. You utter a short prayer for hope and forgiveness, but also gratitude too, for in this moment this feeling is stronger than the guilt that will surely descend later like rain.

His prick is not that big, you suspect there are bigger, have dreamed of bigger. No, he is not that big, but when he enters you it opens you up so that it feels like the world has a tear in its fabric and white light is beaming through, illuminating, seeking a path.

That night you have a deep vision. You summon a man so great he is a God on earth. Though he is so ordinary as to go unnoticed, with his hands he crafts coarse stone until it sings. The stone marks a place for Cuddy, and pilgrims flock to it, flock to him.

At sun-up Gertie comes about, dragging her aching feet. She says: Guess who I just gobbled against an old oak on Maiden Castle hill in the dead of night? Who? you ask, only half interested. Guess. It could be many a man, Gertrude, you'll need to give me a clue. He was the tenth of ten and an ugly brute, she says, as ugly as a sumpter's rear. That does not narrow it down. Also he paid me handsomely, she says. Well, that narrows it down a little bit, you say, but I'm still none the wiser. A soldier. A soldier? Yes, she says, a soldier. And not just any soldier but William Yalden, an archer in Old Ralph Neville, the Earl of Westmorland's band, the same mob of which your Fletcher Bullard is said to be the best with a bow. They're camped at Barnard Castle. The name of your husband makes your left eye twitch though dear Scum Gertie does not see it, or she ignores it, because she carries on jawing. Yes, he was as storkin as a shepherd's staff and very much backed up. He came twice for me, she says with a glimmer of pride, and the second time there was just as much muck as the first, which is rare. Also he was missing an eye. Missing an eye? you say. Yes, says Gertie. He would not say how, other than it was lost during training, and that it had to be scooped out by a medic and it gives him great pain now, which was evident as it was weeping pus as I gave him the gobble, but not so much pain that I couldn't give him a very, *very* thorough milking. Even with the socket empty it still felt like he was looking down at me, mind. With either two eyes or one, I don't know a William Yalden, you say. Well anyway, Gertie continues, glad of the audience and a chance to rest her swollen feet, this Yalden says the Earl's division of best bowmen are soon to do battle with the King of Scotland and his legion of devilish pagans, who have already advanced through the black border marches up there, and that he puts his trust not in swords or helmets, lances or bows, but only in the name of Christ. That's if they can find them, of course. One-eyed William Yalden says a hundred pounds per year has been put up to anyone who can bring the Earl's men within sight so there'll be plenty of blood shed by autumn, says Gertie. Are we in danger? you ask. Not within the city walls, but think of it this way, and may the Lord forgive me for saying so: Fletcher Bullard might get one through the eye and out the other side himself. And then you'll be free. Free? you say. Of course, says Gert, free to romp with the stonemason Francis Rolfe. But how do—? Gertie interrupts you. It is written in the plum flush of your cheeks, Eda. You are entirely ablaze with the satisfaction of love, the internal infernal fire of it, and I should know for much every man looks at me that same way when I'm finished with them and lowering my skirts. Fear not, my oldest friend; you'll get your happy ending yet. The Lord himself will surely reward you greatly for your past troubles, and an almighty amen to that. Yes, you reply. Amen.

On the morrow rounds with a bushel of ale. The slosh and skelp of it against the cooper's slats. Late spring into early summer blooming, and the scent of a season incoming, brought in on a light breeze from the fields beyond the city walls. Listen: there's the call of a cow, a long happy rowting rising up from the guts of it and carrying down through the lanes, from a hillside far away. The rattle of a woodpecker too. You see more smiles in the street than expected this morning for winter was long and unyielding but now it is a dead thing, fallen to the past, as all things must. And there's barely a thought of Fletcher Bullard in your mind to whit. Best wipe that notion away, think only of today. The gladness for a little lingering sun can be felt all around, praise God, amen. Besides which, few are ever unhappy to see Eda and her ale passing down the way and though Saddler Street is stinking, and you have to hold your nose by the tannery, the market square is a-bustle with traders in from the farms. There's yeoman Gerard Brewster with his hundreds of speckled eggs and cages of Silkie roosters and black Rosecomb bantams, in whose eyes you see Satan himself. There's cottar Reg Norton down from Lanchester with his preserves made from fruit grown on the local lord there's demesne; there's Gregory Inman with the fruits of the vast vegetable garden he keeps at Houghall – onions and carrots and turnips and chibols and peas – and the dairy farmers Walter and Cicily Cockayne, with trays full of butter and milk plus bacon for boiling and plenty more besides. They each take a jug or two from you, and they're glad of the taste that loosens their dry tongues into idle gossip and thoughts on the season ahead, wondering whether the harvest will be a blessed one or whether God will deem the city unworthy by flooding the fields and blighting the crops as he did some three summers back. You continue onwards with your rounds, your load lightening, the day brightening, hope in the back of your throat like the drifting pollen that makes your eyes reem and itches your nose so that you hard-sneeze the devil's sin right out of you.

You're upon the corner when Brother Barnabus is right there. He's almost on you, that vile monk they call Cruikshank, blocking the sun. Well, well, he says with a sneer that's like a knife-slit in a bowl of proving dough. Eda Bullard. You nod and avert your eyes as you attempt to sidestep him, for you've no desire to engage with the man, but he sidesteps too, and in a most deliberate way. He says your name again: Eda Bullard, wife of Fletcher Bullard and brewer of ale most mediocre. And then a third time: Eda Bullard, hell-bound sinner and seducer of stonemen. Stonemasons, you say. What? he snaps. Anyone knows that it is stone*masons* sir, not stone-*men*. You make to move but still he blocks you. And he is close now; close enough to smell his breath, which reeks of creamed cheese and liquorice and the sour English wine that the clergy make and keep for themselves. When he speaks, his voice is not quiet. Every other sin a person commits is outside the body, he says, but the sexually immoral person sins against his own body. Corinthians. You have to summon the strength to reply to Brother Barnabus for the power of the man fills you with fear, yet something compels you, so reply you do: Do you not know that the unrighteous will not inherit the kingdom of God? you say in a lowered voice as to suggest discretion. Do not be deceived: neither the sexually immoral, nor idolaters, nor adulterers, nor men who practise homosexuality, nor thieves, nor the greedy, nor drunkards, nor revilers, nor swindlers will inherit the kingdom of God. Here you pause and then you add: also Corinthians. He steps closer. Be careful, he says. Be very careful. One word to Fletcher Bullard and he would surely come running. And then what of your beloved stoneman, whose thumbs would be chopped off, and every bone carefully broken? Bullard is a beast as you well know, but you are betrothed in the eyes of God, and in *my* diocese. What business is this of yours? you ask, a tremble rising. Everything that goes on within these city walls is my business, he spits. *Everything*. And what of beyond the walls, you say, such as down where the wild garlic grows? Here you manage to slip past him with stealth and break for the corner, but not before Brother Barnabus says I'll pray for you, Eda Bullard. Take my name out of your mouth *Cruikshank*, you reply, I do not want your prayers. Sin I might, but at least I am not a hypocrite. And then you run. You run like a stallion off into the stone labyrinth of Auld Duresme.

This eve there is a knock on the door but when you open it there is just the alley, the drains, a glimpse of the street. A bold rat with the uncanny face of a sullen child, darting through the slop. You look down and see that there is something – a bulky object wrapped in sack cloth – at your feet. Then there is movement at Turstan and Madlin McGrillis's window over the way, a passing of a person from one place to another, and though you can't see them, you feel a set of eyes upon you, so you scoop up the parcel. It is heavy, much heavier than its size suggests. As heavy as winter. You have to put your full body behind it as you close the door and roll it out from the cradle of your arms and onto the stuffing of your bunk. The fire draws sap bubbles from logs that still carry spring in them; they hiss and pop as you peel back the cloth. It is a beautiful block of stone sculpted into the shape of Cuddy's cross, just like the one that sits down there beneath the cathedral floor with the saint himself; the same cross they say was carried along with his corpse for all those years by the wandering folk of the holy man as they fled from the Norse devils who arrived in these cursed northlands, to say nothing of the heretics and heathens who also wanted his head and his riches. The cross has four limbs carved in a curved way so as to appear feminine, and it is fringed with an intricate pattern of lines that are interwoven like the slim strands in a length of rope or the knotted tresses of ivy that hang suspended over the river from the steep bank sides where the Wear bows around the peninsula. They almost appear to be moving like a tangle of serpents, and look so real you have to touch them, tentatively at first, but then with a sense of admiration and appreciation at the overwhelming level of craftmanship. Francis Rolfe made this. He made this for you. He made this for you, over many hours, days, many weeks, maybe. You have never before been given something that serves no purpose other than to express – what exactly? Love? His love for you? Yes, that must be it. Love it is, love absolute. You turn the cross in your hand and there on the underside, in marks so minute it is impossible to fathom how they might have been made by the hand of man alone, is the stonemason Francis Rolfe's sigil, his signature:

And beneath it, beautifully carved:

AD 1346

The cross stone is so heavy it feels as if it has been made to defeat time, to outlast it. You imagine him hunched over his bench, the stone held in place there. He circles it once before even picking up his tools. First looking, then touching. Sniffing it. Then perhaps a tongue comes out, just the tip, to taste the spiciness of the stone, and the stories behind it. Time on the tongue, and the layers of it. He will spend more time with each piece than he ever did his mother, old lovers, and you. Beneath his hand it is coarse and cold like a thousand lonely nights without a fire in the grate, as dry as death falling upon the rasping, sleeping shape of the old. But the stonemason deals only in life. He gives life to each stone, bearing down and bringing patterns and faces and fluting to it, before the stone is hoisted high to the upper reaches of this Cuddy forever-place. He sends life up there, atop the sky-ladder to God. This sculpture will be special though. It will be created after hours, away from prying eyes. He had to steal the small block for himself, for you. Small enough to carry. He waited for weeks until he knew that it would not be missed and then he set it aside, and waited longer still. Now he steps back and circles it once more to let the idea blossom inside of it. Finally he sees it; finally he feels it. The shapes and lines and curves and declivities are there, awaiting the tap-tap of his mallet. Awaiting release. Only then, gripped by a vision, does he rear up like a horse and come at it. He comes at the stone with violence, and with love. He makes his mark on the stone and he makes his mark on time. He makes his mark on you. Francis Rolfe works for half of each night. In three weeks he will present his work. Those three weeks have passed and now that stone is in your hand. It says more than any words ever could. And one day when you are both bone dust, the cross stone will be dug up or raised from the river, and rinsed clean so that future fingers might explore the crevices that spell out the secret signature of your stonemason Francis Rolfe, and this act of love in the year of its creation. This year AD 1346, when you were briefly reborn into happiness, spared the daily pains of living. Only Saint Cuddy can know the pure truth of it.

You sleep with the stone. Beneath the blankets, you lay on one side and you wrap an arm around it. Your fingers feel their way along the notches, curves and grooves that this man crafted for you, marks the mason made as he chiselled his way through time, drawing a line through today and onto all the days to come. In the stone is yesterday's sun and the stories it has seen, not only of wandering holy folk and the fiery Norse, not only old white churches and milkmaids, galloping Frenchmen and the green men that took to the trees, but other details not always pressed to the page by monks. Everything the stone has borne silent witness to is held within it now, and to touch it in the dark hours of deep night is to transfer the pictures of them from the stone into your feverish mind. Everything comes gushing out at once. Rainstorms and quarrymen, Picts, plague pits and paupers, hawkers and jesters, skirling new life and coughing old death, archers and anglers, devils and angels, sunrises and sunsets, courting couples sitting on stone walls watching snowfall, villeins and franklin and wandering freemen, nets of cuttlefish and pails of crabs, sores and scabs, bed-bound mothers and gaoled fathers, babies – a thousand wailing babies – and church bells, cabbage soup and nettles and worms and sacks and jam and garlic and knives and deer and murder and toll gates and caravans and soothsayers and plums and coffin-makers and lepers and laughter and ice and logs and oats and sex and sin and Cuddy and Jesus and God. You wrap your thighs around the stone. You press them together, tightly. It is cold against your skin yet still you moan.

And so you see him again, leaving the walls with haste. You are forced to watch. Just as you know that apples picked and packed in straw in September can last the whole winter through, so too something seen today can be stored for tomorrow. Not all weapons are forged in fire; things known or seen have value too. Cruikshank the monk. He raises his hood. His liripipe dangles this day like the devil's tail and there is something in the way he carries himself that compels you to fall back and follow. Perhaps it is God's guidance that leads you far upstream from the city and deep into the first fresh tranche of garlic. There are few paths and no pastures here, just the peppery tangle. At a run by a stump of oak there waits a boy. Here Brother Barnabus stops and stoops, and the boy recoils. Low on your haunches, you do not need to hear. Your eyes tell you everything as the monk grabs him by the russet tunic and propels him upwards and onwards.

The boy is forced to lead and when he falters Brother Barnabus uncoils a leather length that is wrapped around one hand and whips the lad. Whips him about the back and head. Though his gait is familiar you cannot see his face; you can only pray for him. Perhaps he is one of the orphans the monks keep on at the priory for menial tasks and who are said to sleep with the palfreys if they're lucky or beneath the bunk of Barnabus if not. You can hear the sobs escaping from the child as he walks, sobs that suggest that this is not the first time. On bandy legs Cruikshank shoves him deep into the looming thicket and without further ado trips him face first into the bed of garlic and falls upon him hungrily. There are no sobs now, only the hum of flies, the hum of life, and the sound of your breath locked inside you as a bead of sweat slowly trickles at your temple. You durst not quell it. Leave him be, you think. *Leave him be.* But you cannot speak now. Everything they say is true: Brother Barnabus is the devil reborn.

Only afterwards, later, thinking things over, rising up like a skull from a landslip, or a face looming through salty fog, do you realise who the lad was. It was poor Ancel Paine, the orphan who often helps with your deliveries. A lovely lad Ancel, but lonely. What horrors he must have suffered at the hands of Cruikshank. What invasions he has quietly tolerated at the paws of this beast.

They say there is a sickness out there, across the sea. They say it is passing through the people like a fire through a forest. It turns their skin to purple and their heads to a fever, and then when the fever abates and it appears as if they are maybe returning to good health, it strikes again, harder, with a death-fist. There is much rumour as to its cause. Some say sin, others suggest bad bread, others still rats. But you do not worry for your city because you have Cuddy watching over all. And what use is a saint in residence, if not to turn back the tide of an approaching plague?

You cannot sleep for the summer air is tight and your head infected. This night the streets echo with dull voices as you try to walk away from the voices that chatter within. Out here on the cobbles there's a snatch of song, from a rabble of roustabouts, the brief scent of old stale blood by the butchers, and ale piss and heavy wet smoke filling the spaces between the buildings. You have an itch inside of you – your heart is a dry pea in a child's rattle, so you walk and walk, past flickering tavern windows full of sloppy cackles and sorrowful grimaces, across the square where two beggaries, mother and son, hold out a bowl, then over the bridge, the cathedral's calming bulk a silent guardian to a late-showing moon. Footsteps snap like a mallet on metal, crack like metal on stone, your footsteps. Eyeball doorways raise chicken-skin bumps but you keep on walking, remembering various stabbings and violations. From around the corner comes a man, hands hidden, hatless, hair parted slick to his pate. You hold your breath, keep on walking. Up the hill to the burial plots, to the yard of graves and past the paupers' end where it's always boggy. This place has been known to come alive at night. Because even here alongside death, life finds a way. Courting couples might lie between the dirt mounds made by man not mole. Fletcher Bullard brought you here, dragged you down with him, pressed you flat beneath the meat of him just as Cruikshank pinned the boy. He howled then, Fletcher, howled at the moon, a creature uncaged as he dripped out of you, a small gluey patch marking the end of innocence on the flagstones. A rat scurries by now on the other side of the railings, sticking to shadows, as do you, your young thighs feeling the hill as each ache carries memories. You cannot think of the brute Fletcher Bullard or the sodomite Brother Barnabus now. And then so, as if blossoming beneath the strange pull of the moon's soft light, you open up and taste the sweet potential of possibility and you think of him instead. You think of another. Again you think of Francis Rolfe.

You do not bleed for him. For Francis Rolfe, stonemason. You do not bleed for him at all. Instead you lurch from bed to bucket spewing a string of something sour, three mornings in a row. And that's how you know he has left something inside of you, and to your eyes it is already beginning to show. Like the curve of a small turnip or a great growing bubble inside, your stomach protrudes just slightly, smooth, pale. You fall to your knees then, for it must be a miracle. You utter a prayer for thanks but still the guilt sits heavy, and the confusion is a cloud of woodsmoke because only then does the problem become apparent. You carry his child when everyone within the city walls knows that you are not capable of such a thing. How can this be? Is it the wonderment and generosity of God's sweet gifting? An answer to a prayer? Or perhaps it is the resurrection of our Lord saviour Himself, within you, bearer of something immaculate? No. No. It is not these. The answer comes to you then, as straight as one of Fletcher Bullard's arrows: it is *he* who is incapable. All these long years of his drunken forceful prodding, violating, probing and raping, and the fault lies within him. His seed is useless. His seed is nothing more than wasted milk turning sour within you. The big man Fletcher Bullard, champion archer, feared hero of a city, killer of dozens, scores even, soldier-saviour of these cursed northlands, is no man at all.

A strange fog descends. A sullen summer sea fret that has wandered too far inland. It billows heavily with a touch of evil about it, filling the streets and alleys as a slippery tinker's smoke might fill a rabbit hole. It moves silently as one monstrous changing shape, and its edges are flickering wisps like cold white fire if you could ever conjure such a thing. It glides across the river like a ghost boat, then into the trees, stealing the space between them. The devil's doing, it clings, turns day to night. It is a damp blanket unfurling across the everything of this place, a cloud cast out and fallen to this sinful earthly realm. Another sign? Surely. You are caught out in it, collecting jars and payment, and within a blink it takes you and turns you, gets you lost in a place you know so well. The scumfish fills your ears and eyes and it's like drowning. It tastes of judgement. It knows your every wanton thought, your every debased desire. For a moment you think you see the face of Brother Barnabus leering through the murk so you turn and run, slipping in mud as stiff as honeycomb, blindly flailing in breathy panic. You nearly fall. It has you gasping, this evil bloody fog. It wants to turn you inside out and show your sins to one and all, like washing hung on washday. Only the ground tells you which way is up for the city is otherwise upside down, a wrecked ship sinking into the ocean of hellish mist, the sky closing over. You call out: O Cuthbert, O sainted Cuddy, cast out this devil that's in me and I will let history lie, I will come to thee O Cuddy. You say it twice then thrice. O Cuthbert, O Cuddy. What a pleading prayer it is. And then you see it, slicing through the fog with its stone angles, cutting a way through the veil, the cathedral, its triple towers taller that the dead-weight fug that befouls this haunted day. An anchor dropped. You rise up through the slopes with ropes of fret squirming down your throat, gagging, gasping, knuckles scraping the city walls as you palm your way forward, feeling and finding your way to the cathedral. Then you're free and you run to it and place your cheek to the cold rough stone and it is wet with the fret, slick to the touch – soft, almost – and then your tongue is out, distended and probing as you lick the salty grain of the stone, lapping at it like a kitten tasting its first saucer of morrow milk. Something bursts inside of you then, and it is not awful. In fact and indeed, it is quite the opposite. It is life.

Early the next morning there is no message, no advance notice, just the door swinging open and Fletcher Bullard standing there, with a fat goose in hand, dangling by its broken neck. You're still in your chamber, foaming with fever dreams, crusted with sleep. It'll need plucking and gutting, he says without so much as a smile, and that's when you know that he knows and furthermore and indeed you know that he knows you know he knows, and the dying fire sighs and the longbow, the weapon for which he is named, is across his back. There is death in it, and in him too, and oh a horrific unholy hunger also. His eyes don't lie. His appetite for all things is great and it will be the death of others yet. After four months in the field, the awful stench of battle is on him. It fills the room. He licks his thick lips. Rage bubbles up.

Once he used to beat you black and blue yet still you got wet over him. Now his touch turns you cold as ice, as dry as bone.

The itch is upon him then and he has you on the mattress of straw and oats. He says: Your cunny smells of crab meat, wash it, so you get the bucket and rags and wash it and he says who you washing your notch for, you hog? What's his name? How long's this been going on while I'm away fighting for king and country, you hog, you pig, you cheap cocklicking sow of the midden pit, and he backhands you so hard your teeth rattle like seeds in a seed pot. You hear a peal of bells, then spit blood. Spit history.

Afterwards he picks up his fat purse and it is bulging with Ralph Neville's money. He shakes it, all show, but offers you nothing. It is money earned in the field, piercing the hearts of the Scot. Mine, he says, all mine. How goes the battle? you ask in an attempt to return to normality, but your mouth is swollen and instead of words, you cough up a clot of blood onto the bedspread and Fletcher Bullard, the man to whom you are bound until death, just sneers, waves you away. I've all the ale in the world, you say, but he stares you down so long you think another beating might be coming but instead says: Your ale is piss and I have business. A trail of mud follows him out the door. He did not stay long enough to remove his dirty battlefield boots.

What can you do but swill your mouth with aniseed oil, burn a candle of mutton fat and sea holly seed, stuff your cheek with a saltwater rag and go about your day? There is still ale to stir after all, mouths to moisten. Fletcher Bullard, you know, is doing that right now, wasting his purse in the taverns where he will be greeted as a returning warrior, his back sore with all the slapping, spinning stories and boldly declaring: tankards for every man. Perhaps he does not know your sinful secrets after all. Perhaps the scudding was just another form of greeting, because wasn't this a regular occurrence anyway, long before the mason Francis Rolfe entered your life with a wry smile and a touch so sensitive it is as if God is speaking through him? You're brewing these thoughts when Brother Barnabus is suddenly stepping through your door without invitation. He steps in close. I see Fletcher Bullard is back so your secret shall be safe no more, he says. *Unless.* Unless? you say. Unless, he hesitates. Unless you give me two dozen silver pennies on every cask you sell from now until the day of judgement, and you might just be spared the eternal flames of damnation. But Brother Barnabus is unaware you have a weapon. Remember? The weapon borne from bearing witness? You step in closer still. You unsheathe the weapon. The same flames of damnation that might engulf a man of cloth who drags young boys into the garlic patch just as the sun is setting? you say. The monk's eyes flicker now, as conse-quence follows realisation. I saw you, you say through the salty rag. With these eyes, *I saw you.* May God turn your house into a heap of ashes for the wickedness that is within you. Then you remember a line from The Book, so you say it in a slow and careful way so that this demented vile monk hears every single vinegary word: And he took away the sodomites out from this land and removed all the idols that his fathers had made. Amen.

He backhands you then — hard. His lumpen knuckles find the bone of your cheek, the same cheek struck by your lumpen husband just hours earlier. Your head skirls and a cruel taste floods your mouth but you stay silent. A fire is in Cruikshank's evil eyes now as he goes to strike again but you duck and twist and he stumbles forward, flailing, grabbing and bundling you down to the dirt. There is so little room and his fingers are in your hair. You squirm beneath the weight of him as he lifts and bangs your head off the hearth stone and all you can think about is how you wish you had swept it one more time before you met your God, as you surely soon will. This makes you push and thrash and scratch but the monk sits heavy, spittle dripping from his red lips. The door swings open then, clattering. It's Scum Gertie. Dear, dear Gertie. She sees it all so succinctly that she is on Cruikshank's back in an instant, doing to him what he is doing to you, without hesitation. For a moment we are the beast with three backs but the brother's grip is murder-tight. All is becoming blurred, as if seen from underwater. He will not release you. Your tongue is curling under itself like a banked turbot and the room is rapidly fading around the edges. Still you wrestle beneath the weight of him. Gertie must have let go because you discern movement, a chair upended, something smashed. In the watery smear of the day you see as she lifts the longbow from the wall. Slides an arrow from the quiver. Somehow finds the space to draw, aim, release. And then the arrow is sitting right through the centre of Brother Barnabus, piercing the trunk of him at an angle, comfortable in the doughy tithe-bought bulk of him, as easy as a knife through butter, as natural as the branch that grows from the tree. He makes no noise as he falls sideways, except for a slight exhalation of warm garlic breath, and Gert is silent as you drag yourself free, your quickening heart beating in your pounding head, short breath reaching, returning, alive, beautifully alive, and also carrying another life within you too. No man will ever lay a finger on you again, or that fresh flower that blooms inside. Not now, or ever.

You're both standing, Cruikshank splayed at your feet. Gertie gives him a prod with her toe. That's a very dead monk, she says. May God forgive us, you reply quick as a flash. It's him that needs the forgiveness, says Gert, but it's too late for that. He's in hell now, and may he burn. He was going to kill me, you say. And you wouldn't be the first, she replies. I'd wager he has buried the bodies of several boys who have gone missing over the years — orphans, low-lifers and the cast-out sons of starving villeins, in the main. Under Cuddy's watchful protection, says Gertie, we must get rid of him. Cuddy would not condone this, you say, not murder. What else were we to do? says Gertie. It was you or him and the world is a better place with you in it and him sent on to the infernal chambers down below. Even Cuddy, who loved all men and animals, and was goodness presented in the form of person, would see the sense in that. Also, you say very quietly, I am with child now, so it is two lives rather than just the one. Gertrude's eyes widen at this.

You shove Brother Barnabus's big body beneath the bunk. The arrow makes it difficult so you have to hack off the flight end. A little puff of air comes out of the hole, like a soft sigh, then there follows a few bubbles of blood, like foam in a river's eddy. We hoy a blanket over him. I've had him, Gertie says, standing over the prone heap. Or he had me, I should say, the bowky rat wouldn't pay a penny. You let Cruikshank—? you begin to say, but Gertie interrupts you. There was no letting and a lot of taking, and often, and I had no say in the matter. You look at her but she just says, come on Eda, we both know he could have had me out of my digs and living in the scat tank at the click of a finger, just as he was ready to tell Fletcher Bullard all about you and Francis Rolfe and the stottie in your oven. Here she points at your belly. You say: So what now? We'll wait till dark then shift him to the woods I suppose, replies Gert. We'll need help though, do you know of anyone who holds a grudge and keeps a secret? You think for a moment then say, yes, Ancel Paine. The lad? says Gert. Yes. Can he be trusted? Yes. How can you be sure? Because Cruikshank had him too, you say, and I'll give him ale forever, for his endeavours. Also, though he looks like a streak of gristle, he's strong enough from a short life of lifting. The taverns will keep Fletcher Bullard tonight; he'll not be back until morning, or perhaps the morning after that, sore-headed and hungry, but still. But still, we must be swift. Yes, says Gert. You get a message to the Paine boy and we'll all meet back here when the moon is up to shift this lump, but in the meantime we'll go about our business as usual, and that means me off to give Gilbert Knapp the tallyman a right good noshing.

Ancel Paine is more than obliging. You offer him ale and favours for life but wager he would help you for free as it's all you can do to stop him from working on Brother Barnabus's cold podgy body with the sharp shears he uses for clipping the sheep when he's off shepherding up Weardale. Gertie's all for letting the lad cut off Cruikshank's scrote bag as a token but you cannot afford the mess in your house. So under the heavy canopy of deepest night you roll him in the clippy mat your mother made – God grant her salvation in the eternal afterlife of heaven – and the three of you heft it out the back way, then down the narrow alleys that take the shortest route to the garlic banks. These seem a fitting final resting place. You want to bury him but Gertie says, oh hell no, let the birds and the boars and the flies and the foxes and the hawks and the wolves and the worms at him. Yes but we should say something, a few words, you declare, but already Gertrude and young Ancel Paine have turned away, so instead you utter a short silent prayer for understanding and deliverance. I'm due up in Weardale soon, says Ancel Paine as he departs. Might be that I'll head up sooner, still. You'd be wise to, says Gertie, before giving him a big kiss on the lips, at which the lad smiles and blushes. There'll be more of that coming, she says. I'll keep it by on account for you. You just let Gertie know.

The Duresme woods hereabout are thick with owls, what strange songs they sing. Some nights they fall so silent it is as if it were decreed by law, but on others, as this night, their calls echo down the wooded palisades and out across the water. Perhaps they are deft hunters or perhaps they are guardians of Cuddy's home, trained to scour the river paths and clearings, scout soldiers sent on in advance and then reporting back through a clarion chorus – urgent but measured, feared but fearful, an ancient call. Some say owls carry within them the souls of those who in life never had a name, a place or a purpose, and were cast out to wander alone. Some say their stained-glass eyes are windows into other worlds. But tonight as you stalk the homeward shadows you see them only as an omen, a symbol of disquieting things to come.

Afterwards you and Gertie hatch a plan and check your story, sweep the dust over your tracks, so to speak. You have an idea.

The sound of his footsteps down the alley lets you know that Fletcher Bullard is full of ire as well as ale. At morning light the door swings open and his fingers grab your arms and lift you straight onto your feet. Your chilblains feel the cold of the floor and his eyes are wild. He prods your belly. Is it true? he says in a voice so unexpectedly quiet it fills you with a greater fear than usual. He prods harder and tears fill your eyes. *Is. It. True?* It is, you nod. He smiles. Then a joyous miracle has taken place, he says, gently, for in all ways you are known to be barren. Praise God and Cuddy, a miracle it is that finally blesses this house with a baby to call my own. Really? you reply. No, you slack-fannyed, scab-mouthed daughter of a dog-sucking whore, he says, raising a hand. I'll only ask the once: whose is it? You reply without hesitation because you cannot take another scudding from any man. Will not. Cruikshank's, you say. Brother Barnabus. He took me by force some weeks back, several times, and he laughed while he did so, said that ploughing me was like ploughing the best bowman in the land himself, Fletcher Bullard, and laughed again. Your husband is a simple man, and his reaction to this is as expected. Rage. He throws you down, snatches up the chair and smashes it to splinters. Boots the log pile. Upturns the table. Slams a fist into the dull wattle of the wall and leaves a hole there. Then his eyes fall upon the cross stone, the beautiful piece carved by the mason Francis Rolfe. Fletcher Bullard lifts it up, and turns it over. And this? he says. A gift, you say. Cruikshank said that for my silence he would give me this holy gift. Now he sneers, lifts the stone above his head and then slams it to the ground, where it cracks into two neat pieces along a crooked diagonal. He takes his bow from the wall, hoists his quiver and then leaves.

You wait, steadying yourself and finding a quiet space some-where deep inside. You peek across to check whether Turstan and Madlin McGrillis's lumm is smoking and when you see that it is, you take a deep breath and run screaming and flail-ing like a manticore untamed into the alley: He's going to kill him, by God's word, save our souls, he's going to kill him dead! Old Madlin McGrillis being big of mouth and fond of dipping her nose into everyone's pie is out the door like a ferret. Now what's all this stink about killing? she says, barely able to hide the glee at the story she'll have by sunset. He's going to burst him, Fletcher Bullard, you say through a sob so sudden that it almost feels real, Fletcher Bullard is going to burst the Brother Barnabus for the barbarous things he has done. What barbarous things? says McGrillis. You fling your hands over your face: I cannot say, lest God strikes us down. Madlin McGrillis takes your wrists. Eda, she says. Listen, if there's to be a murder we need to stop it, and then she turns and shouts back into the house, Turstan, Turstan, run for help, big Fletcher Bullard is on the rampage and Eda here says Cruikshank the monk is soon to meet his maker in the most horriblest of ways. Again you sob, then fling yourself to the floor. Oh Lord, you say, Lord, save us one and all. And then you thump the ground and claw and scratch at it like a woman gone cuckoo.

He does not return until the following morning at dawn, his eyes ringed with the redness and his ham-flank muscles sagging on the frame of him. You have not slept a single sheep jump. You stoke up the fire and he sits by it, silent as you warm up yesterday's porray and spoon it onto a slice of tourt we use for trenchers. Henry Inman's finest leeks, you say, if only to fill the silence with something, for you do not know where Fletcher Bullard's head is, and whether your own life is soon for ending. But you see his knuckles, skinned and bloody, teeth marks on his forearm. Such is the haunted look about him, you're almost inclined to believe your husband has found and killed Cruikshank a second time, and you find yourself asking as much. Brother Barnabus, you say. Did you find him? Fletcher Bullard stares through you, then slowly shakes his head. They're hiding him, he says. The monks, I'm sure of it. What will you do? you ask. Still staring, your husband sits in silence for a long time, so long it is as if the question has gone unheard, or perhaps that the answer lies within you, and that he is looking for it in your eyes. Finally he speaks. I'll hunt him down. I'll spend the rest of my days hunting him down, and when I find him I'll scoop out an eyeball and then I shall fuck his eye socket for a very long time. And then? you whisper. Then, he replies. Then I'll deal with you.

The body is found at first light, when the early birds are signalling the new day with song, by a herdsman and his wife on their way to milking in the fields past Quarryheads Lane. By the time the city has creaked into life the body has been identified and word has spread like a fire untamed. Brother Barnabus, Benedictine monk of the Priory of St Cuthbert, current-day successors to the Cuthbert community – the *hali-werfolk* who kept the immaculate saint's corpse preserved at all costs, is dead by one arrow shot clean through the vitals. The reeve of the manorial court has already instructed his best men of the bailiwick to bring in the suspect, Fletcher Bullard, the best bowman in the city and lead archer in Ralph Neville of Raby's army, currently home on leave while engaged in battle with King David and his Scottish devils, who have long advanced south past the Roman wall and over the Tyne, and are said to be just a week or two away from Duresme, and, in league with the French, are hungry for combat. Your husband's lids are heavy when the door swings open once more. Three bailiffs crowd the room. Your arrow has been found in the monk Cruikshank, says the first. Best come quietly then Bullard, says the second. The third just takes out the cuffs and shackles, weighing them in hand, ready.

It can't be, says your husband. I never touched the monk. I wanted to but I couldn't find him. Must be a coincidence then, says the first bailiff, that he was found dead from your weapon the very same night you were threatening blue murder. He stands, knocking the last chair over. Silent, the bailiffs step forward. Somehow Fletcher Bullard snuffs the spark of the first. One punch and he crumbles, cold. Then he pushes past the other two and out into the alley. It is strange seeing him flee for his life like this. Thrilling, almost.

All that happens next you hear second-hand but so soon after the event that you take all witness accounts to be credible. What happens is this: your husband, the much loved and equally feared Fletcher Bullard, a man-beast so large in life as to be a living myth in the minds of all those who have met him or seen him out on the field, flees. Realising a fate irrefutable, he takes to the slick cobbles and runs like a rabbit, like a hunted creature. It is perhaps the first sensible thing he has done in his life. Straight through the city he runs, and many see him, and the two panting bailiffs in pursuit, with others streaming from their morning doors to join the caravan. Perhaps they sense the myth of a man is solidifying into something special, that a new story is being told. Across the market square he goes, then up the incline of Saddler Street, a swift right onto Owengate and then out into the open space of Palace Green. Now it becomes clear as to his destination. It is to the home of Our Cuddy, the cathedral itself, to its warped wooden entrance and the knocker that sits upon it, the grim-faced custodian and saviour of sinners seeking sanctuary.

My story, and that of Fletcher Bullard, just one story in a thousand million stories that combine to define a place, concludes thusly: he rapped the knocker and screamed for sanctuary, screamed like a desperate man, and when no one answered he banged and rapped his bloody knuckles on the door some more, until blood smeared it so, and then he called out to Cuddy, called out for Cuddy to extend a helping hand. The bailiffs were nearly upon him when the door opened ajar, and the pale face of a monk peered out. What ethical dilemmas must have struck the brothers of the order that morning can only truly be guessed at. But a brief moment passed before he slowly and silently moved aside, and Fletcher Bullard stepped into the hallowed space of Our Cuddy. And the door closed behind him.

You hear that Fletcher Bullard made it to Hartlepool under escort and from there he gained transportation to a land across the sea, though some dispute this. Some suggest that in fact the monks took him far beyond the city walls, and that many miles out, up in the fields where the low peasant hovels cough smoke, beyond places you have only ever heard of – beyond Kelloe and Fishburn and Trimdon – they did unspeakable and imaginative things to your husband, things that the monks themselves will have to answer to when the day comes, and God looks down upon them.

The stories we tell one another are all that shall remain when time dies and even the strongest sculpted stones crumble to sand.

The following spring you give birth to a child, a boy, in fine health and with strong lungs. Francis Rolfe takes him in his arms and declares that there can only be one name for such a wondrous miracle. Welcome, he says. Welcome, young Cuthbert.

INTERLUDE

The Stone Speaks

The nave. AD 1650.

In September 1650, following victory over a Scottish army led by David Leslie at the hour-long Battle of Dunbar, Oliver Cromwell's invading parliamentarian army marched the defeated soldiers south.

Three thousand Scotsmen were imprisoned in Durham Cathedral. No longer a place of pilgrimage and worship after the dissolution of all deans and chapters at the outbreak of the English Civil War in 1642, it was now reduced to little more than a storage space, a gaol. Britain was in an interregnum – no monarch reigned for over a decade, but Cromwell, installed as 'Lord Protector of England, Scotland and Ireland', wielded great power.

The Scottish soldiers, most of them young, only recently persuaded to enlist and described by one historian as 'nothing but useless clerks and ministers' sons', had little in the way of food, water or heat. Conditions were inhumane and neither aid nor mercy was forthcoming. As autumn set in, seventeen hundred soldiers died in the cathedral from illness, injury and starvation, their bodies buried in mass graves nearby, which went undiscovered until the construction of a cafe at Palace Green in 2013.

The cathedral had lost its purpose as a place of worship, sanctity and sanctuary for all comers.

Dramatis personae

The CATHEDRAL. A cathedral.

WILLIAM 'WULLIE' McFRAINE, 19. Soldier of the Highlands Infantry.

JAMES CANNON, 22. Soldier of the Highlands Infantry.

ALEC 'BIG ECK' MACKWATER, 17. Soldier of the Highlands Infantry.

DUNCAN FRIZELL, 15. Soldier of the Highlands Infantry.

INT. THE CATHEDRAL. AUTUMN, NIGHT.

Four young Scottish soldiers, WILLIAM, JAMES, ALEC and DUNCAN are slumped against pillars or lying on straw and bare stone in the western corner of the cathedral's nave. They are all ill or injured, or both, and are in near-darkness. Only the stub of a single candle is burning, giving their faces a sallow yet angelic glow. When they speak, their teeth chatter or they shudder controllably. Their voices, and the shrieks, groans and cries of other dying soldiers, echo in the cold vastness of the building. A desperate state, all told.

   Cathedral (Voiceover): Thirty hundred bodies barred in; all of them Scots, my exits barricaded. Helpless I am to treatment not witnessed since the barbarian migrations trampled over my unquarried English seams. I was still soil–sunk then, not yet tall, not yet holy. Not yet a quarried arrangement of a singular vision set in stone and called a cathedral. Now you might call me a coffin, a mausoleum for the many. Earlier, at sunset, a single pheasant in the trees outside slowed the day to darkness.

   James: Ach the cauld is in my bones and a great thirst upon me.

   Alec: Bothy-bottom pigs are treated better, brother.

   James: I feel all ma faculties are a-fading. I doubt I'll see dawn, me. Nor care to.

   William: I curse the English bastard. May he suffer as we suffer, ten-fold.

   James: Curses aren't keys though. I see no way oot. Jesus himself cannae have suffered as we suffer eh no?

Alec: Then let us pray together.

Duncan (meekly): There's nae prayers left to utter, Eck.

James: I thought you hud expired, son.

Duncan: Pray for my death then. May it be swift.

Cathedral (V/O): From far across the land of Alba they came. Two dozen regiments of honey-fed farm-boys and moor-top dreamers, raised from Banffshire to Nairn, Moray to Fife, to fight the English with little but flames in their Protestant hearts. And now it ends here in agony, their ragged remnants tormented by thoughts of beer and bannock, of village dances, clay pipes and the open moors of home. A warm body in the bed, perhaps. If stone was haggis or salmon or maslin they would find themselves in abundant heaven, but instead I sit abandoned too, nothing but an empty stone-built hell for these lads, our two nations on the same island split by the one thing we share in common: faith. I have nothing to offer them but prayer.

William: Christ, that thirty-mile march ooer moor and rain. Truly, the black dreich Lammermuirs are a cursed place.

James: Fucking right, man. Nowt but stone and water up there, and that thick long grass that's as sharp as bayonet blades. Them black bogs pulling us under all the way from Edinburgh to Berwick. Nowt to kill.

William: Nowt to eat.

James: I saw a dozen or more of oor boys drap by the time we reached the ramparts there, eh Wullie. Starved, they wis. Starved down to the strings that holds their bones together, no? Help me piece it together. Ma mind's a blur.

William: Mine too though I've no forgot there wis a dozen more poor souls taken that night by the cowards' men, Jamesy. Their throats slit, dumped in a pit. At least them that still had their running legs ran, but.

Alec: And we was locked up that one night in yon castle there. Alnwick, I believe it was.

James: The horror of it.

William: Then the next night was the walled garden in Morpeth, gorging on those cabbages pulled straight from the soil. I've been shitting the ring since.

James: At Newcastle I saw with ma own eyes twenty-three fresh graves dug at sunrise.

William: That must have been before the long day's drag by a dismal river through endless woodlands, silent except for the shrieking crows and our agonies. Then to here, where stone spires signalled a God hoose turned gaol. How long we been here anyway?

James: A thousand lifetimes, brother. A thousand lifetimes.

Cathedral (V/O): They pulled down my Papal pictures, ripped out my rails, turned pews into kindling, altars first into tables, then mortuary slabs. All things smashable smashed to splinters. I can't blame them. My woodwork split for feeble fires, smoke-scorched circles blackening the stone for short-lived heat savoured by shivering skin. Everything burnable was burned, save for the Scottish thistle clock spared by the soldiers on a whim of sentimentality. And who can begrudge them a symbol of home in this house of death. But now follows the acceptance of their fates. They have given up. The hushed agonies of the diminishing few echo in the vastness of my stone soul. They remind me of the monks from the old time. I wish I had a tongue to assure them, but any assurance would be a lie.

Alec: They say it wis built for a saint, this place, but alls they've given *us* wis a cup of sour milk boiled with ditch watter and bean flower.

William: Must have been six nights ago when we removed the ringer from the great bell to use as a battrin' ram — now the none of us even has the strength to staun. Ma straw's soppin with pish. Illness everywhere.

James: Those bible books divnae burn for lang nor fill your belly either, though Lord knows we've tried.

Alec: That guard with the haggis puss and a pot of oatmeal – did I imagine him? Was he just the ghost of a rumour?

William: Aye, well, we game highland boys acted upon that rumour. Scarfed the scraps four-ways, eh Jim?

Alec: He got himself killed stone deid for that pot, so that we might we live a day longer in hell. His choice.

James: As good a reason as any. Me, I divnae fear hell, for we've already visited it a thousand times over. Nor do I seek forgiveness now. Forget that.

Alec: He was a brute called Brewen, that guard. The first day in here I saw him drag the lectern from the quire. A sack of candlesticks and some silver too. Sold them all on, I bet, while we lie starving, the dog. He had a murder coming.

Duncan: I – I – I just wan–, wan–, wan–

Alec: Whit?

Duncan: I – I – I just–

Alec: Spit it out, son. While you still can.

Duncan: I just wanted to be a – a – a – potter.

William: Aye, well. Maybe in the next life, eh?

Cathedral (V/O): The reek of souls suffering sickness is significant. A week in, my stone trunk rattles to the sound of hacking, coughing and empty retching; of strained stomachs devoid of all but bitter bile. Desperate with flux and dysentery, the soldiers squat and groan in my coldest corners. All around, their splashing evacuations pool in puddles that freeze into crusted brown plates when the frost sets in. The stench of men is in my architecture, and so too are their screams. In my six centuries of standing I have not hosted such torment. This is not right. This is not Godly.

Alec: Whit's the name of the saint whose hoose this is, Wullie? Saint Cunt, I shouldn't wonder.

William: It's Cuthbert, Eck. They call him Saint Cuthbert.

Alec: Then Saint Cuthbert, Saint Cunt or whoever you are, I beg you: in the name of Jesus extend a merciful hand that our pains may soon be over. We ask only for release from these mortal flames.

William: No saint could bide here. Only the devil hisself.

Cathedral (V/O): Some bodies have already been tipped into the soil just beyond my door; the lucky few left alive will be deported, transported, indentured, enslaved. Most lie dying in terror now without a single woman to nurse their shattered bones, pluck musket balls from their flesh, dress the weeping pike wounds, gunpowder burns and battle-field infections. Some are soon to lack a leg or sight, or never to laugh again.

James: Is this really it then, Wullie?

William: The thirst or the cold will surely get us, Jim. Not long now, eh.

James: I'd sooner have taken buckshot in ma erse at Dunbar then sit through this.

Alec: Oh, to climb these towers. If ah had the strength, I'd throw myself off the tallest yin and soar hame like a hawk.

James: Hame?

Alec: Aye. Or anywhere but here. Instead I can only pray for us all.

William: Fuck your prayers, son.

Alec: You cannae say that. No, no, you cannae say *that*. Not now. And in a holy church too.

William: This is no holy place.

Alec: But this is God's house.

William: No God would let this pass. That God – our God – must be deid now.

James: Maybe that turd Cromwell got him too, eh Wullie?

Alec (praying): Oh holy Father, oh redeemer and saviour –

William: I'll believe in Him if I make it hame, son. But until then I'd favour you kept your prayers as quiet as Duncan there.

INT. THE CATHEDRAL. LATER.

William (whispering): There must be a way out. A divine sign. Anything. Even just a crust for strength. A cup of ale.

Cathedral: I am but merely man-made, stone piled upon stone, just as the field of conflict is man-made or a grave is man-made. Or religion is man-made.

William: Can not your God reach out and open the door?

Cathedral: But you said you were not a believer.

William (quietly): Desperate words spoken in anger.

Cathedral: Alas I am not of the heavenly realm. I am just like you – born of the soil. Made from this land.

William: I daren't tell the boys I'm afeart, but I am. Afeart as fuck.

Cathedral (V/O): No choir has sung within me for many winters. Instead this night, only a single howl, as if from a feverish baby or a starving owl. It is that of young man – a boy really – facing death. A young soldier is screaming for his mother. In centuries to come the protruding pelvic bone of this young lad, now just a few agonised breathes away from death, will be lifted to a future sun, its patina as mottled as the glaze on a Grecian urn. I will witness this. The skull of his cousin, dead two days before him, will be the subject of much study, a thesis, a book. This skull was named by its mother when small; she called it Walter. Duncan joins him now.

Alec: Duncan's deid.

James: Eh?

Alec: I said it's Duncan. He's deid.

James: Lucky bastid.

Cathedral (V/O): More young boys buried supine in darkness today; others will be dumped face-down, thin limbs akimbo, legs where arms should be, worms in the eyes of sockets that saw hell here. One day they will awake in a new world as bones on a building site, their wet skulls dirt-brushed back into daylight, wearing nothing but a new cafe for a crown.

James: I cannae feel ma body no more.
William: If I could take this last candle and burn this hell place I'd gladly go doon with it.
James: I said I cannae feel my body, Wull. Cannae feel nothing now.
William: But stone doesnae burn. Turns out damnation has no fires after all.
James: Hope's left us.
William: Mebbe we could eat Duncan.
Alec: And prolong this life? Naw. Besides, it's a mortal sin.
William: Also, we don't even have a blade to cut a slice off the poor wee boy and, see me, I've only got two usless teeth left in ma heid as it is.
Alec: 'Fathers shall eat their sons in your midst, and sons shall eat their fathers. And I will execute judgements on you, and any of you who survive I will scatter to all the winds.'
William: Just let any God or man or squirming maggot try.

INT. THE CATHEDRAL. LATER.

William (whispering): I'd give my life for service to God for a cup of water.
Cathedral: I believe you.
William: Then help me.
Cathedral: I cannot.
William: Then you have no purpose. Then you and your God are deid too.

Cathedral (V/O): Then, late this night when the faces of the captives are made wax by moonlight and more corpses are strewn about my stones, a lone voice sings a song summoned afresh from somewhere deep inside.

William (singing):
> 'Sir David frae the border came
> Wi' heart an' hand came he ...'

Cathedral (V/O): Though his voice is wan and accent thick, still it as sweet as a child's, and I, the house of miracles, do witness one more miracle when his two remaining fellow soldiers rise up on one elbow to join him in song, taking a hoarse and desperate line each, and for the first moment in a long time my stones are warmed with the echoes of worship.

James (coughing): 'Wi' him three thousand valiant men ...'
Alec (whispering): 'A noble sight to see!'
William: 'A cloud o'mist them weel conceal'd ...'
All Three (in a spluttering chorus): 'As close as e'er might be.'

Cathedral (V/O): But in the next attempt at a verse the strained voices become ever mournful, and like dying embers they fade as the life drains from them and the soldiers realise their story is already written and instead fall back down to the stone. It is left to young William McFraine, struggling, facing death head-on, to sing his dying lines.

William: 'Again I was at curst Dunbar
> And was a pris'ner ta'en;
> And many weary night and day,
> In prison I hae lien.'
> Come on, boys ...
> ... boys?

Cathedral (V/O): Bones become dust. Dust gathers. A spirit settles and these brave young lads become ghosts of this uncivil war, left to stalk the ancient city that stole them. Yet here remain immoveable, watching. Stone of God, God of stone. The whole of hell. Sufferance in its totality. I remember the names of my new sons. I hold them all in my architecture for evermore, for no one else will. I honour them now: William McFraine, James Cannon, Alec Mackwater, Duncan Frizell, Ingrum Polson, Thomas Moody, Daniel Grimes, Henry Dill, Henry Kidd, James Magoon, Alexander Forbes, Alexander Bruce, Gilchrist Livingstone, John McPherson, John McIntyre, John McLeod, Walter Knox, Davey Bean, Charles McClay, George Purdie, Angus Ross...

[FADE OUT]

BOOK III

The Corpse in the Cathedral

Dunelm. AD 1827.

'The city of Durham appears like a confused heap of stones and brick, accumulated so as to cover a mountain, round which a river winds its brawling course. The streets are generally narrow, dark, and unpleasant, and many of them almost impassable in consequence of their declivity. The cathedral is a huge gloomy pile; but the clergy are well lodged.'

The Expedition of Humphry Clinker by Tobias Smollett (1771)

A letter marked with the emblem of the church arrives.

Its contents concern matters in the north of England.

On the previous occasion that I suffered the misfortune of having to journey to this part of the country it was under extreme duress. The occasion was the funeral in Chesterfield in the county of Derbyshire of an uncle who I barely knew, yet was nevertheless obliged to attend, in order to represent one side of the family, who, but for I and I alone, had all but deceased.

The three-day sojourn was one of the most displeasurable that I can recall, and during which time itself seemed to slow to a pace that felt, to my young and eager mind at least, a form of torture. My lodgings and food were dire, the weather particularly inclement – it was an autumn far from that of 'mists and mellow fruitfulness' as observed during Mr Keats's idle perambulation around Winchester College – and the few locals that I had the cursed luck to encounter were nothing less than hostile to my queries regarding local culture, or the lack thereof. Of my few relatives who gathered by my uncle's sodden plot, strangers one and all, I shall reserve comment if not judgement.

I was at the time an undergraduate and only after I left the dreaded Derbyshire did I learn that Chesterfield is barely in the north at all, but in fact at the southernmost end of it, and that even a cursory glance at a map shows that it sits squarely in the blackened aorta of the country, and therefore is technically neither north nor south, but is in fact that vague area known as the midlands, and is just about as far from the sea as one can get. This in itself, I discovered, breeds a certain inward-looking mentality amongst those who never get to gaze across the briny vastness and breathe the bracing air, as I do as a matter of course at least twice a year during my trips to Walberswick and its surrounds.

I was, in fact, gripped by a greater enthusiasm for the history and topography of the Peloponnese than, for example, Lancashire or the Yorkshire Ridings, and far more readily able to recite entire passages from Thucydides in the original tongue than the work of any of the great scribes of the north, primarily because of these the region seemed entirely bereft, a factor I have yet to be corrected upon; against classicist titans I'm afraid most contemporaries continue to leave no impression whatsoever.

The north of England was a distant universe, a faraway celestial plane onto which little light penetrated, and to which I hoped I need never return as the very thought of it evoked, at best, indifference, and at worst, sensations of dread, nausea and outright hatred, a reaction based upon little other than the seeds of prejudice first planted on that long-ago trip, and which have in the interim been cultivated by time and education and an ever-growing infatuation with my beloved Oxford that continues undiminished to this day (though there is a gilt-lined footnote to this inconsequential anecdote: my Derbyshire uncle bequeathed a hand-painted porcelain tea service and a particularly delightful matching soup tureen, purchased in China, that I had sent down and which I continue to use whenever I have cause).

And so it is whenever I am called upon to stray further north than Hampton Poyle or Bicester I experience, without fail, a slowly strangulating sense of anxiety, an untethering sensation as if one has been involuntarily unanchored and cast to the mercy of a tide so cruel as it might mercilessly wash me up on alien and uncivilised soot-stained shores. Some might call this snobbery but one can only speak – or indeed write – from experience. The north to me has always appeared a land of coughing chimneys, blotched babies, vile ale, wet wool and cloying clouds, where all is coated with a slick of grime, a skein of grease, and such concepts as aspiration, education and betterment extend to an extra pan-load of dripping of a week's end.

'Never the north,' has been my maxim, and it has served me well. I'd take the Mediterranean or Mesopotamia over Manchester, for I am certain there is more life to be found in either.

So the letter when it arrived this morning, stamped rather ominously with the mark of County Durham, was not well received. Black ink barely dry on the envelope, it even felt leaden and heavy in the hand, an unwanted imposition, portentous like a raven sent down from the darklands. Once read, it now feels less like an invitation but rather a summons, a dire plea that in any other circumstances would be best ignored.

The sender is one Reverend William Nicholas Parnell BD, prebendary of the sixth stall in the cathedral of Durham. The erratic handwriting suggests a certain degree of urgency while the tone taken is, I find, overfamiliar – a tone one might reserve for an old fellow with whom one has a long-shared history, and I have to pause midway through my reading to take stock. Indeed, I feel it is perfectly within my rights to cast this missive onto the fire and move on with my day.

But something compelled me to read on.

Parnell, Parnell. The name rang a small handbell of familiarity in the deep and dusty belfry of my mind, though it was hardly the carillon of familiarity suggested by this reverend's bluntness. Nevertheless I continued, for I would not be a true scholar of antiquities were I not still a little enamoured with mystery. I enclose in these diaries the letter as written.

Rev W. N. Parnell BD
Prebendary of the sixth stall
Durham Cathedral,
May 5, 1827

Dear Professor Fawcett-Black,

Sir – I write to you to first offer an apology and secondly to issue a plea. The apology follows an extended period of silence between us so protracted that I durst hardly call myself a friend at all, but rather an associate from the long and distant misted past, for friends do not allow the river of time to glide silently by without communication as I have, and for that I implore your forgiveness. I should not be offended if you have pause for thought at this juncture and to perhaps scratch your head in puzzlement at the liberty being taken by this, a stranger no less. But sir, despite the chasm in our communication I am no stranger, and hope that you fondly recall, as I do, our time together at Brasenose, and those moments shared during the blossoming of our youth, and the rare occasions we did meet in London at my club during that strange and listless transitory spell – and spell is the correct word when I consider the magical feeling that was in the air then – that followed the Elysian days of our studies, when it appeared we would remain forever young and our only concerns were food and books and long summer nights, and the future was a concept not yet to be trifled with.

I have followed your blossoming academic career and ascent in Oxford's history department from afar, and with great interest and quiet pride in the knowledge that I have associated with one of the most respected and widely travelled antiquarian scholars of the modern age. You are surely aware that the accounts of your research trips to Greece, Italy and the Caucasus have a devoted readership far beyond your field.

And now for the plea, a request so wanton that I cannot burnish it with any further preamble, other than, perhaps, to beg forgiveness once more for the intrusion upon your valuable time and the crudeness of my request. I have been blessed, Sir, in my employ as prebendary at Durham Cathedral for many years now. To serve in this magnificent house of God is an honour most humbling, and even the most ardent disbeliever would, I hope, not fail to be awestruck by the magnificence of the building's Norman architecture. For here I arrive at my point: as you are aware, the cathedral is home to the remains of Saint Cuthbert. Such is the veneration of this unofficial patron saint of the north of England, this humble man of the people, the one they affectionately called Cuddy, born of Melrose, latterly bishopric of Lindisfarne and now the most famous son of *Dunelm* (as it is in Latin), that the foundations were dug in his honour and for seven decades thousands of men and women toiled in order to build a final resting place for the man we duly call 'our Saint'. It is also believed that his remains are intact this day, one thousand one hundred and forty years after his death in AD 687.

And this is why I write to you, an Anglican and man of great standing in the fields of archaeology and all things antiquarian. A learned colleague, Rev. James Fraine, rector of Meldon in Northumberland, librarian to the dean and chapter, schoolmaster, and author of such recent well-received published works as *Documents and evidence relating to the administering of the Holy Communion to the Laity within the parishes between the rivers Tyne and Tees before the Reformation* (1825) and *Catalogus comprehensivus seu maunscripta, artifica et emphemera generalia spectantia ad primas quinque saecula Cathedralis Dunelmensis* (also 1825), for reasons predominantly, though not entirely, theological, and too detailed to burden you with here, has taken it upon himself to debunk this myth or – in the absence of a more empirical term – Cuthbert's 'immaculate corpse'.

To do this he intends to exhume the remains of the Sainted Cuthbert in order to embark upon a thorough examination of his disinterred corpse. *I tell you this in the utmost secrecy.* Sir, I have agreed to assist in this project only under the assurance that a learned academic be in attendance as witness and advisor, and to ensure a fair-handed and pragmatic approach to what is – potentially – a moment of great significance in both your field and mine, and I trust that you, dear friend, are the only man I see fit for this position. The proposed exhumation takes place in two weeks' time from the day of writing, on May 17 this year MDCCCXXVII, and therefore I would be most grateful if a response is forthcoming. I enclose all expenses necessary and can offer lodgings, food and generous payment for your time.

I remain, Sir, forever your humble servant and unfeigned friend,

Rev. William Nicholas Parnell, BD

As circumstances prevail this letter has, somewhat fortuitously, arrived just two days into a full term's sabbatical, during which I intend to catalogue a decade's worth of papers from my personal archive, which is soon to be acquired by 'the other place' for a modest sum in the autumn. The contents of the letter are made all the more intriguing by the bare fact that I simply cannot recall the fellow's face, much less any of the occasions we are purported to have either undertaken study together, or socialised at his club as post-graduates, though neither are beyond the realm of possibility, for who can truly recall every single brandy-flavoured evening of two or more decades ago?

This venture of Rev. Fraine's has the potential to be an ethical abomination, and one which certainly requires some sort of external policing, a role for which I am qualified; an exhumation such as this – a process fraught with pitfalls and dilemmas, and of which scant details have been shared – requires an expert's impartial eye. There is also the matter of Fraine himself, an antiquarian so 'esteemed' that I have never once heard mention of nor seen his name in any of the journals to which I subscribe, nor encountered him at any symposia. Is this luring of me to Durham, I wonder, a ruse of sorts?

Such questions abounded as I found myself packing my valise this very evening before settling down to record this unexpected turn of events. Enquiring minds are rarely easily silenced and so it is with reluctance, trepidation and no small amount of curiosity, I shall leave for the dreaded north at daybreak.

My greatest asset is also my weakness: curiosity.

May 14 1827

Of the journey it is too tedious to write about here, suffice to say the three carriages and two days in which I travelled from dawn to dusk have been most arduous and uncomfortable, and the inn at which I alighted last night, weary, mud-flecked and sombre of mood, situated in a grim little village whose name I shall not credit with mentioning, was infused throughout with the lingering odour of human effluence due to a drainage system and water source most primitive, yet which came highly recommended by my driver who insisted upon us staying there for the night. I now suspect that this was surely only because he had some sort of prearranged deal with the landlord, a hairless lickspittle of a man whose appearance, demeanour and bodily movements most recalled that of the *Lumbricus terrestris*, the humble earthworm.

The three counties of Yorkshire that I passed through did nothing to win my affections nor alter my steadfast perceptions of them as places of sodden fells, screes of grey talus and barren moorlands with little but swathes of skeletal-looking heather to define them, punctuated on occasion by soot-blackened towns whose skies are emphysemic in pallor. The people I encountered were of little consequence either, though I did see a perfectly agreeable canal known as the Aire & Calder Navigation, upon whose banks I passed a pleasant quarter hour's respite from the discomfiting carriage whose suspension system seemed deliberately designed to injure in specific physiological locations most unpleasant. Spring has not yet sprung here.

I had hoped to put in some long hours getting down to the bones of Volumes I and II of *The Works of Flavius Josephus* – viz *The Antiquities of the Jews* and *Their Wars with the Romans* – as translated by Sir Roger L'Estrange, but found that reading in the carriage made me feel nauseous and faint-headed, so instead had to content myself with pulling down the blinds lest the bedrizzled vistas offend my eyes further, and challenge myself to recite those sections of Plutarch's *Moralia* that I have filed away in the dusty cabinets of memory, and take a small degree of pleasure in discovering that I can still recall vast extracts with great clarity. Many long slow hours passed this way.

Suffice to say, I know with great certainty that it is not a journey I shall be undertaking again, except in the reverse direction of course, and furthermore can conclude with only the slightest modicum of hyperbole that it is currently easier and more enjoyable to traverse the Tyrolean Mountains or explore the four corners of the Hellenic Republic, both of which I have done in the pursuit of learning, than it is to travel the byways of old Albion in these modern times.

I was told I was to be met by a chaperone at the corner of Durham's market place, a neat square lined on three sides by inns and businesses, above several of which I could see there lived in cramped quarters the families of those who work below: grocers, stewards, saddlers and so forth. The tardiness of my one-man welcoming committee allowed me time to stretch my cramping legs as I walked the perimeter of this square at that time of day when the gutters were littered with the decaying detritus of rotting fruits and vegetables, while buckets of blood were being splashed down drains, yet the nocturnal malingerers had not yet turned out for a night in the sinful barrel.

There were several seemingly feral children about the place, dressed in little more than rags, with one poor mite barefoot. In one small doorway I saw what appeared to be a damp heap of discarded clothing, but which on closer (but not too close) inspection contained within it the face of, I think, a woman – I durst not call her a lady – whose thin lips peeled back to reveal a dark sepulchre of a mouth in which I was able to count the sum total of three teeth like tiny tombstones that would not look out of place in a neglected corner of St Clement's or St-Peter-in-the-East as she, without preamble, made me a proposition too profane to record here.

It was then that there was tugging at my cuff, an intrusion the likes of which I have never experienced. I turned to see which interlocutor might take such a liberty right here in the market square of a county town that calls itself a city, fully prepared to be faced by another scabrous street whore, and there standing before me was a young man, a boy really, with a visage that wore a look of startlement, chiefly due to his alarmingly large eyes that were penetrating and strigine. I would go as far as to say he was barely even a boy but something else entirely, owlish almost in his movements, which were contained and measured like either a hunter or a hunted thing, for it was hard to discern either way; his eyes, as I say, as dark and round as the anthracite coal they hoist from the chthonic underworld in these parts. I found them somewhat disturbing but yet difficult to draw my gaze away from. A curious fellow.

He stood at the same height as me, and on his top lip sat a light shadow of downy hair. I took one steady step backwards and surveyed him from head to foot, slowly and deliberately, as I find this can be a disarming tactic when confronted with characters one knows nothing about, in situations that are wholly unexpected. It gives one a sense of having a handle on things while one attempts to achieve exactly that.

'Yes?'

'Forbes?' said this strange creature.

I fixed him with a stare which, I hoped, would shatter his carapace of impudence, and held it for a lingering moment before speaking.

'I *do* beg your pardon.'

'Are you Forbes?' he asked in the blank tones of a savant.

I raised my cane an inch or two and then tapped it on the square stone slab of the market place, another affectation no doubt, but one which felt purposeful in the present moment.

'Consider addressing me correctly and I shall consider offering you an answer.'

The lad shifted from one foot to the other. He was unperturbed and, in fact, quite indifferent as he pulled from the pocket of his brocaded waistcoat, once surely bright in colour but now faded and worn trim about his torso, a scrap of paper. He cleared his throat and then slowly turned the scrap around as it was upside down.

'Are you Professor Forbes?'

I looked at him aghast.

'No sir, I am not. Who I am is Professor Forbes Fawcett-Black II.'

He looked at the paper again with his spheroid, avian eyes.

'It just says "Professor Forbes of Oxford" here –'

The lad hesitated for a moment before slowly taking a moment to look *me* up and down, in an act that was nothing less than a flagrant parody, and then he continued.

' – and you're here for Cuthbert business though.'

'What business I am here for is entirely mine.'

The boy blinked his black eyes and shrugged. When he did not reply, I sighed and spoke.

'I am he.'

He looked around.

'Luggage?'

I raised my valise.

'Everything I require is within.'

'For a week?'

I scoffed at this, more loudly than I expected, and so forcefully that a stray fleck of sputum shot from between my lips.

'I shall hardly be staying that long.'

The rascal reached forward then to take the valise from me.

'I'm quite alright, thank you,' I said, withdrawing it without ambiguity. 'This bag has journeyed to the Cilo-Sat Mountains in Anatolia's Hakkari province and back, not to mention other such sites of historical interest in the furthest reaches of the Ottoman Empire, including during such recent days of incipient revolution in the Peloponnese, and survived without so much as a broken clasp, so I hardly think it should require protection now, even here in your little town. I am quite ready to be taken to my accommodation. Is it far?'

The lad dropped his arm and turned away from me, and with keen haste began to wend his way across the square. Not knowing the city from Jakarta, I had little choice of action but to follow.

'I say,' I called after him. 'I'll ask you again: is it a great distance to my lodgings?'

'It's not far,' he said, without having the grace to turn and face me, his words disappearing into the emerging night, though I rather fancied that, like the owl, he could turn his head a full revolution if so required.

We walked up the incline of a roughly cobbled street and suddenly there to my right was the great cathedral, rising from the earth like a sculpted mountain, and I have to admit that it was an awe-inducing sight, one accentuated by the smallness of its humble surroundings.

What a spectacle such a structure must have been, evoking in even the most heathen minds the intended omniscient power of the God to whom it was devoted, towering as it does over everything around it, to be seen for two score miles or more in any direction.

But instead of pausing so as to enjoy the building's full aspect we veered left alongside it and continued down a street tightly packed with houses and along which several young scholars of

293

pre-pubescent age passed in rather striking uniforms of purple with gold trim. As we walked the lad said nothing, and I concentrated all my efforts on trying to keep apace.

'I say, what is the name of this street?' I asked, but the lad was either suffering from loss of hearing or so supremely arrogant as to deem my question not worthy of a response. A street sign told me that this was known as the North Bailey.

It was only after we had scurried a good distance down that it occurred to me that we were in the domain of another fellow of Oxford, Robert Surtees, who was born, I believe, on this very street. Though he studied law, Surtees considered himself at heart to be an antiquarian and his *The History and Antiquities of the County Palatine of Durham* was well received, though having had no call to read such a parochial study (I am of the belief that such a move from law to all things antiquarian is nothing but dilettantism), I could neither confirm nor refute this, though I have now made a note to finally give it a quarter hour of attention during my stay. Surtees comes from family money and famously had the luxury of travelling the country with a groom in attendance at all times, so that he might pause to examine any – or all – antiquities at leisure, cataloguing even the most trivial inscriptions and banal documents. (Apparently his groom wrote of it being 'weary work' for 'we could never get past an auld beelding'.)

I have never much cared for the man.

We passed a timber loft and a brewhouse and then turned right through the stone archway of a gatehouse, above which I observed a chapel, and proceeded with haste into a close directly behind the cathedral. Containing buildings far more opulent than any I have yet seen since arrival, I instinctively knew that it was here where those who hold true positions of power in the city lived; these being the men of the cloth, of course, far apart from the lowliest monks who willingly choose austerity and sufferance.

At the far end of this quiet square I saw there sits a preparatory institution known as the Chorister School. A sign outside told me that it is this seat which provides the cathedral with its choirs of angelic cherubs (angelic, at least, until their voices shatter and they devolve into little demons). Close to the school's entrance I paused to study a quaint stone tower marked Conduit House. The centre of this square is occupied by a neat green, which contains an attractive pumphouse, but I did not have time to examine it further for the boy beckoned me into the doorway of a house and there was little I could do but follow, my gasping breath in my rising chest, sweat on my back. Never before have I felt my advancing forty years quite so acutely. Without seeing another soul he led me to my suite, then turned to leave.

As he did, the lad muttered something under his breath, which I took to be something like 'History is lies', an opinion which, given my profession and entire reason for being in this place, was clearly meant as an insult. *History is lies.* What a peculiar parting statement.

Fortunately – and I weight this word with ingots of sarcasm – there was something that called itself food waiting for me in the form of some grey knots of mutton congealed in a coating of lard, accompanied by potatoes, bread, butter, jam and a large pot of tea that was only lukewarm.

Barely replenished, I now find myself fighting tiredness as I record all this at a desk in the corner of a curious chamber – more of which anon, for I write with a growing pain in my wrist and an ache behind the eyes. I must rest now, for Lord knows what tribulations tomorrow might bring. Certainly I hope to have this business concluded speedily, so that I might return to more familiar surroundings.

It has been a day as long as a year, a year as cursed as a leper's lifetime.

May 15 1827

I write this not more than an inch or so of candle following the last chronicle, if only to anchor me back to the reality of the here, the now. In truth, I am gripped with a form of fear I have never previously experienced; a fear so sudden and total I find myself flailing in the face of all reason. But let me first make note of my suite, and then of my failed attempts at sleep within it, so that I might examine the influence of the former upon the latter. Without reason I am nothing.

I have been afforded the use of three rooms that sit side by side off a dimly lit and rather gloomy hallway, occupying, as they do, the upper floor of the house. There is first a parlour-cum-reading room containing a bookcase bulging with all the latest facile tomes beloved of country widows, and a fireplace whose grate is heaped with ashes, and which no one has thought to clear and replenish prior to my arrival. Next to that is a small bathroom with all the expected facilities, including a thin stubbled ring of scum around the bathtub – a human high tidemark, if you will – and then finally my chamber, its walls wainscotted and containing within: desk and chair, an overstuffed ottoman, fireplace (again, unlit, though there are logs) and a bed that I was relieved to find at least has a mattress that is firm, for there are few things more certain to exacerbate my troubled back pains than a featherbed that has borne witness to better days.

A window looks out onto darkness and on the suite's end wall, running adjacent to my bed, there is a full-length curtain, which to my surprise covers an old door that once led, presumably, into the upper chambers of the next house. It is locked and has been nailed shut, its seal painted over. It has not been in use for decades, the curtain surely there to block out a persistent draught that blows (and occasionally whistles) across the top of this peninsula, and which I feel through the gaps in the old wooden panelling when I part the curtain.

After my hastily taken ablutions I initially slept well, despite the lack of fire, for this being the north of England I at least found the bed piled thick with an abundance of blankets.

But then I awoke suddenly, stirred by what I perceived to be the sound of voices. When I opened my eyes and lay still, my alerted senses highly tuned as they so often are in the deepest part of night, I heard nothing but somehow felt quite certain the echoes of those voices – the echoes of whispered voices I should say – were still about the place. The whispers were words from a vocabulary I did not understand, a bastard tongue that appeared to make sense to the unseen speakers, but not to me, your impartial witness.

> *Stither.*
> *Ungred.*
> *Eedmah.*

As these strange incantations resonated feverishly in my awakened ears, I also experienced the sensation one gets in a room that just moments before has been vacated by a person or persons; a residual energy, I suppose, even if it is just from the warmth of bodies or the settling down of things after movement and interaction. A physicist might better explain it, though I suspect it is ably illustrated in the simple equation of action versus reaction – movement being the action and one's personal response being the reaction. We know we can smell or hear things without seeing them, so why not feel them too?

I felt something, a sense of otherness and the fading away of whispered voices – several of them, all male, solemn in their delivery.

I lit my candle but its reach was minimal, and it made me start for when I sat up and looked about the room I was certain that I could see protruding from the bottom of the long curtain that covered the nailed-down door a pair of boots. It was unfathomable as to how they could be there, not only because my own shoes were placed by the bed as always, but also because, though the dim candlelight obscured my view of any close detail, they appeared most primitive. Far from the stout leather boots of today, these were shoes made from soft straps of leather to be swaddled around one's foot and ankle, and held in place with some sort of length of twine or lanyard. Still under the heap of blankets I scrabbled for the lamp so that I might properly scrutinise this unexpected malefic sight – one which, I must admit, evinced in me primitive feelings, being as I was curious *and* fearful – and upon lighting it, I had risen from the bed and saw not a pair of boots, but merely an illusion created by the way in which the thick curtain had gathered in furrowed billows where it met the floorboards, and therefore cast a short shadow which my heightened nocturnal imagination had interpreted as the feet of a full bodily form secreted behind the curtain. It was a trick of the light – or lack of it.

I extinguished my lamp, climbed back beneath the blankets and felt myself sink back into sleep. But almost immediately I heard the same whispered voices again, more discernible this time, a low chorus of men chanting in procession a dire threnody that was almost entirely without melody and in a tongue again most unfamiliar to me, and in which I could only discern a dirge, a lamentation transcribed thusly:

> *o Cuddy*
> *Cuddy o*

Over and over again so as to become an incantation uttered from deep within.

> *o Cuddy*
> *Cuddy o*

In the short moments before I flung back the blankets and once again lit my lamp, I heard beneath this funereal lamentation, so desperate in delivery, other sounds that I would describe as atmospheric, sounds so close as to be believable: the creak of a warped cartwheel, the sonance of fatigued feet tramping mucilaginous mud, the deep breathing of ragged lungs seeking air, a deathly cough, a desperate groan, an uttered prayer.

Naturally, as soon as my chamber was illuminated such noises were no more, though I once again felt the sense of them, like the shudder that follows a draught-slammed door, or the brief silence that follows a dropped bottle in a tavern.

Sleep is now an impossibility, so I occupy myself with documenting these morbid events. However I find myself experiencing no such emotions, but rather a great sense of unease and, I must admit, that gnawing impression of loneliness with which one is most acutely burdened in the depths of night.

No, I shall sleep no more, for the cold light is upon the day already, and the morning sun is creeping around the arboreal headland, which at least allows me to better survey my immediate surroundings. Opening the curtains just some minutes ago, I was pleasantly surprised to see that my suite occupies the top floor of a house that abuts the peninsula fortifications that surround and protect the cathedral and its close quarters. From here I can I look down upon sharp drops below, to wooded bluffs and ivy-covered escarpments, which might be dizzying for those lesser travelled than I.

Exhausted to the point of distraction, I must now rise and seek sustenance in this uneasy abode, and hope that I might be able to later snatch back some sleep deeper into this dawning day, and banish the dire voices that echo in my mind.

> *o Cuddy*
> *Cuddy o*

Afternoon. Shortly after completing this morning's entry, there was a knock at my bedroom door and I opened it to be greeted by the Reverend William Nicholas Parnell, BD, the sender of the letter, former fellow of Oxford, and a man I have already grown to resent quite considerably. He was holding in his hands a tray generously laden with breakfast foods, including two boiled eggs, toast, kippers, devilled kidneys, mushrooms poached in milk, tea and various condiments.

'Professor,' he said, breezily. 'What a great pleasure it is to see you once again, after all these years.'

His face remained unfamiliar and given that he was wearing his robe and collar he looked pathetically subservient as he stood there. Only his air of familiarity, which I found both presumptuous and inappropriate for men of our standing, told me that it was indeed Parnell and not one of his fellow colleagues of the cloth.

'Reverend,' I said.

'I trust your quarters are satisfactory?'

At this I grunted a non-committal reply, for, really, what does one say in response to a laconic lad, a suite with unlit fires, cold meat and not so much as even the briefest appearance from a housekeeper to turn down the bed?

'Please accept my apologies for not being there to meet you upon your arrival,' Parnell said, in a *Bufonidae*-like attempt to smooth the situation. 'I'm afraid I was waylaid by some matters which would surely sound trivial were I to describe them.'

'It is fine,' I said. 'Life is comprised of such trivialities.'

'And yet I must ask forgiveness once more, for rather than have Edith bring you your morning victuals I thought I would provide that service myself, if only – rather selfishly – to see you before we discuss the more formal matters at hand.'

'Edith?' I said. 'Who is Edith?'

'Oh, Edith keeps us all fed and watered, dressed and darned. She is somehow cook, nurse, confidante and many more things besides to clergy and monks alike, all at the same time, yet without having a job title that correctly encapsulates her value to us. To call her simply a housekeeper or even a maid-of-all-work does her a great disservice – an angel sent from heaven would be more accurate, though more prosaically she joined us as an orphan child from the poorhouse in Sunderland. She has a staggering ability to give the impression of being in several places, completing several tasks, simultaneously. And she is a wonderful cook. You will have met her upon arrival here last night.'

'Sir, I met no one upon arrival here last night and, regretfully, the solitary plate of cold mutton that greeted me far from compensated.'

Parnell flushed at my admonishment. This man needed to know that if I were to drop my responsibilities at Oxford in favour of this dubious venture, then I expected better hospitality. Any reasonable fellow would do the same.

'My humblest apologies,' he said. 'I can only imagine that it being a Sunday yesterday, our dearest Edith was otherwise occupied by a complicated timetable of meals during what is the busiest time of the week for her. I'll personally see to it that, at the very least, you dine like royalty from hereon in, professor.'

Again I offered a response that was short, but which the situation warranted. I felt justified in a demeanour that some would dismiss as discourteous: I have always believed that respect is something that is reciprocated, and cold mutton and an empty hearth after a long journey is far from fair remuneration. Six years of study and two (or more) subsequent score of research has, I hope, earned me more than that.

'But I must ask,' continued Parnell, a look of confusion on his flushed face, 'how is it that you found yourself here to your accommodation which, by the by, I hope you will find comfortable?'

'It seems adequate enough,' I said. 'Why, I was brought here by the boy, of course.'

'The boy?'

'The young lad. A rum fellow; somehow both impudent and yet also wholly aloof.'

Reverend Parnell hesitated.

'I'm not sure I understand.'

'Which part of this tale confuses you?'

'This young lad. Who was he?'

'I don't know, I didn't catch his name, merely that he was the chaperone you had sent to meet me.'

'I ordered no such thing, sir, for *I* was to be your chaperone. That you responded so keenly to my letter ensured that I would be waiting for your carriage. Though, of course, I unfortunately found myself pre-disposed due to –'

Here his voice faltered slightly, and then faded away mid-sentence.

'Then who was the lad?' I asked, echoing the reverend's own question, having little time for the vagueness and indecision of his feckless mutterings.

'Without a description I could not say.'

'Well, the curious thing is, he looked very odd. Reminded me of a partially plucked bird perched upon a branch. About my height and swarthy in his colouring.'

'I do not know of such a fellow,' said the reverend, 'yet it seems he knew who you were, and to where it was you were to be delivered?'

'Yes and furthermore: he addressed me by my first name.'

'My goodness,' said Parnell, displaying genuine consternation as one hand fluttered up to his chest like a dove uncaged. 'Did he really? Then he could be no ward of this church. I thought perhaps it might have been one of the choirboys, but none would be so presumptuous.'

He shook his head and tutted repeatedly, but by now I was already tiring of the subject, the town, and this fellow's questioning, and in all frankness wished for nothing more than to retire to my room so that I might eat my breakfast while it still held within it a semblance of warmth.

'Yes,' I said, though it came out as a murmur. 'It would appear so. Well, come in then, come in.'

Parnell entered and put down the tray.

'You must be hungry,' he said.

'Yes. Yes I am.'

'Then I shall leave you to eat, sir.'

I sat, and cracked the top of an egg.

'So what is all this business about, Parnell? You may stay while I eat.'

'I think it best we discuss it when the Reverend Fraine is here. He might properly present the argument.'

'Argument?'

'Well, yes. The argument, or at least the justification for this endeavour of his.'

'His – but not yours?'

'The idea is entirely the Reverend Fraine's, sir, I am merely here to assist him, for I feel that it is a worthy venture. He is acting upon motives which he believes sound.'

'You're talking about the proposed exhumation of the Sainted Cuthbert's corpse, of course.'

'Of course,' repeated Parnell. 'Of course.'

'Well, where is this Fraine fellow?' I asked. 'I've gone to great trouble to travel here and I've not yet been given the opportunity to get the measure of him.'

'And I am most grateful, old friend.'

I bristled at this. 'Old friend' struck me as both sycophantic and simply untrue.

'We both are,' continued Parnell. 'Reverend Fraine perhaps even more so than me, in fact, for he is a great admirer of your work from afar and you have amongst the prebends here many more readers and admirers of your reputation, whereas I at least have the advantage of having known you in your youth.'

'About that,' I said. 'I hope you're not offended when I admit that I am struggling to recall our time together or, indeed, recognise you.'

Parnell appeared untroubled.

'That's quite alright, professor. Our salad days seemed to speed by and, of course, you must have met a hundred, a thousand – nay, a *million* – men on your travels, so I do not take offence that you should not instantly remember my rather ordinary countenance. Time has been crueller to some of us than others yet you, sir, look in as rude health as I recall you were at the age of twenty-one; or better in fact, for at Brasenose did not they fill us undergrads with enough stodge? Yes, they were fine days. Fine days indeed.'

I did not reply, and instead folded some cold toast into my mouth and followed it with a large gulp of tea.

'Professor, I shall let you eat, but before I take my leave I wish to invite you to lunch with Reverend Fraine and myself, so that any questions that you might have should be answered and all pressing concerns alleviated.'

'Very well, Parnell. Be aware that if the responses are unsatisfactory it is I who shall be taking his leave, all the way back to Oxford, and we shall speak no more of this matter.'

'Of course, professor. Of course.'

The reverend closed the door behind him and after I had finished eating I began work on recording this encounter, for if all else fails I hope to at least get a paper out of all this – something that examines the Anglican Church's culpability in the mindless desecration of antiquarian sites of sectarian significance perhaps, or the close propinquity in behavioural habits of the simian species and the common working-class northern Englander today.

I jest.

Later still: a meek tap at the door introduced me to the famed Edith, a compact and not unpretty lady, who delivered a handwritten message explaining that with great regret the holy Reverends Parnell and Fraine were delayed and that we would take tea together instead. I received it with a face like storm clouds gathering over the Pindus range; more of my precious time wasted.

'Perhaps the professor would like to take a constitutional in the meantime?' said Edith in a manner far more breezy than my own. 'I have taken the liberty of putting together a pack-up luncheon for you should you decide to do so.'

Here she handed me a knapsack that I was pleased to discover felt warm to the touch.

'There's brisket and warm bread and much more besides,' she said, with a smile, and I rather fancied that Edith did indeed have a certain charisma about her that one might find comforting or even attractive were one inclined in that direction.

'Also a slice of cake, some other tidbits. And, of course, a flask.'

Though feeling peevish at the delay, a little time surveying the lay of the land on what appeared to be a temperate late spring day might do me good, so I accepted her lunch and intend to do exactly that now.

Let us at least hope that something noteworthy besides bad dreams, gluttony and shallow theological discussions occur, for the sake of this logbook, if little else. Otherwise I could be inclined to think that a simple postcard might have been a more suitable medium on which to record this protracted and tedious trip 'up', as they say, 'north'.

Late afternoon: I have now seen the town that calls itself a city. In daylight, away from the hordes of the main street or two, it is not so ghastly. In fact, there are certain quarters of Dunelm, as it is traditionally known, which offer much to fascinate a classicist.

For the sake of brevity I shall not document its finer structural features here, though separate notes have been made should I decide to write a paper pertaining to medieval architecture, or Durham's tactical geographical positioning and its key role in defending the north during the attacks of the fourteenth century from their wild Pictish neighbours.

I especially enjoyed a perambulation along the river path that follows the serpentine waters around the peninsula, from which looms the cathedral in such a dramatic fashion that, from one angle in the glaring May sunlight, it reminded me of the Carpathian Mountains. This religious precinct that sits atop this formation is large but, like the wider city itself, somehow harbours an illusion of greater grandeur, dwarfing as it does all around it, including the trees that fill the banks most abundantly, banks that will soon be thick with garlic, and somehow silently states the case that with a cathedral and castle keep – and of course the immaculate corpse of St Cuthbert within – this is not just the true heart of the north, but that the region itself is the birthplace of Christianity in England itself.

The people of the city I am less keen on. My glimpses upon arrival told me enough: many are barbarous and appear entirely occupied with indulgence. The stench of last night – a Sunday, no less – lingers long in the nostrils, as powerful and acrid as smelling salts.

To distract my senses I bought an apple from a fellow named Inman, whose name was writ large above his stores, only to then be accosted in the street by a man, a beggar of sorts. I brushed him aside but not before this layabout could grasp my lapels and with searching – nay, *pleading* – eyes that swirled with desperation say 'Cuthbert, are you he?' His voice has echoed on in my mind for all this long afternoon, for why would a fellow ask such a thing?

Perusing a pamphlet in my room earlier I learned about the childish myth with which the city folk seem enamoured, that of the origin of the place, then named Dun Holm, which appears to be shared in all seriousness by both scholars and theologians and peasants and plebeians alike. The story concerns their Saint Cuthbert, or rather the community of acolytes who transported his coffin. The abridged version has it that whilst on their arduous journey one of their number heard during fasting and prayer the word 'Dunholm', to which some significance was attached by the monks. Further on their journey they happened upon a milkmaid or two in search of a missing cow, which had been spotted at a place nearby called – yes, but of course – Dunholm; *dun* being an old English word for wide-topped low hill (cf. 'down' or 'dune') and *holme* from the Scandinavian 'holmr', for island or promontory.

This, it seemed, was considered as emphatic a sign from God as they might ever hope to receive and therefore the very place at which to bury Cuthbert's body and build a cathedral, which they did with admirable application – though it took several churches before they evolved into the building which stands today. A charming tale I suppose, though one with no factual grounding. I suspect that with the peripatetic lifestyle having lost its charms, the self-styled 'Cuddy community' were simply tired after a century's aimless wandering. Two turns of the clock hands spent in the region has me feeling much the same.

As I strolled I saw several anglers, perched most preposterously over a weir like herons, and I passed a curious portico, which appeared recently built. Close to the river, it was a sandstone dwelling in the style of a Grecian temple complete with four pillars; a rudimentary homage.

Nearby a handsome bridge links the cathedral quarters to the 'mainland' – that is to say, the back end of the city – beyond which a series of more squalid streets lead up to a row of houses that enjoy a clear view across to this consecrated *chersonese*. As I crossed it I saw a courting couple enjoying the afternoon in a row-boat, and considered there were worse places to be at this time of the year. In its favour, you see, Durham feels more akin to a city of the south that somehow miraculously has been transplanted to the north – a Salisbury, Ely or a St Albans, perhaps – but with a history of bloodshed and conflict from here all the way up to the wild borderlands of Northumbria, Berwickshire and beyond that is entirely unique to a region.

I relate another odd incident appertaining to the growing sense of ennui and unease – dare I call it anxiety? – that I have experienced since alighting at the city square only last evening.

It occurred just beyond the bridge, as I cut back on myself at the city walls to instead drop down into the tangled undergrowth through which there appeared to run several trails so narrow and slight that they might have been carved by hoofed ruminates. Ivy formed a canopy overhead so that the daylight had difficulty penetrating this fortress of weeds that was now thriving most abundantly, and I trusted my feet and the trail to lead me. Experience has taught me that sometimes it is of benefit for the explorer to get a little lost, though of course I was not 'lost' as such in this instance, for I knew there was a cathedral above and a river below, and a civilisation of sorts within shouting distance.

Taking a turn uphill I came upon a set of steps that were so ensnared by the creepers' reach that they could hardly be used at all, and there at the stone stairhead was a figure half-turned away, that of a man, a young man. I recognised him immediately as being the same surly lad who had led me to my lodgings. It was his remarkably large eyes that identified him, and in that brief moment I felt them drill deep into my core, with neither subtlety nor shame. Those eyes saw me entirely. The all of me.

I went to raise a reluctant hand in greeting but the lad turned away and took the final two steps and silently disappeared beneath a low-leaning stone arch with the stealth of a sneak-thief or footpad.

'I say,' I said, my heart racing loud in my ears. 'I say, young man, wait one moment, will you?'

But my call was delivered to an empty doorway, a dark entrance that seemed to lead further into the undergrowth. I took long strides up the steps and followed in pursuit. The archway led to an old narrow path that ran at the foot of the city walls as they followed the perimeter of the peninsula.

It has been a dry spell of late, yet in the shadows there was much mud underfoot and twice I nearly tumbled. A treacherous drop was directly to my right and though I am too long in the tooth to go scrambling around in the brush and thicket in such a manner, something propelled me onwards – a feeling I was unable to fully identify, nor would dare to name here even if I could.

Before I realised it, the lad was there waiting for me just as the path seemed to take a sharply angled turn to the left and I was nearly upon him. I was short of breath – I was panting quite heavily – and though he appeared to be calm, I noticed a slight film of sweat trapped in the fine hairs of his upper lip. His colouring appeared darker than ever.

'Wait,' I said. 'Wait one moment, would you?' But without offering either a response or recognition of my presence he turned and was gone again around the corner. What was this lad's game? And, furthermore, what was it that I wanted with him?

I followed his footprints in the slick mud; by now I was too deep in the trees not to.

I caught up with him in another darkened doorway that appeared suddenly where the verdant riverbanks ended, and which led back instead to within the city walls. A discreet entrance, it was little more than a slot in the stone.

He was waiting for me.

'By gad, sir,' I said, though as I began to speak I found that I had nothing to say – nothing at all – for the manner in which he was standing, half-turned towards me and half-turned away towards the inner sanctum of the ancient quarter of the city, almost proffered an unspoken invitation, an arrogant challenge of sorts. I noted for the first time that beneath his shirt (he was without coat, for the day has been fair) he was a sturdy lad, shaped in some way by labour. These observations swirled in my mind as I found that my words as well as my thoughts had been stolen from me and my mind was completely blank, like a slate erased of all impression, and I was as still as a statue as if caught in the gaze of the great Franz Mesmer or perhaps a male Medusa. We stood like that for a moment, he silent and me near-cataleptic and only dimly aware of the rising and falling of my chest as I gulped for air without grace, like a banked fish.

I heard my heart hammering and rattling at the gaol door bars of my ribs, and then I am certain I heard a second heart, the heart of the lad beating too, plangent in my ears, in my blood, two hearts out of synch like faltering footsteps so as to be slightly jarring, but then one juddered forward, or skipped a half-beat, so that the rhythms of the individual organs, each trapped in their own cages, fell into step as one, and time elongated into a contorted moment that felt as if it might be infinite, endless, but without pain. Quite the opposite in fact.

The lad's eyes were doorways leading down into the darkest, deepest tomb of the self. I entered them.

And as I did, instinct compelled me to wipe the sweat from my brow with my forearm – but then he was gone again, as furtive as a lamplighter. I had the feeling of awakening, as if suddenly stirred, rudely, from bewilderment or a trance of sorts, and the sheen of sweat turned to the thinnest layer of ice upon my skin, as if I had been stricken by a fit of the ague.

I composed myself and then followed the lad through the doorway.

Only in his wake did I notice the stench of him, ripe and noisome in its pungency, yet still I followed once more. I found myself in what appeared to be the back gardens of some large town houses – the houses on the very square in which I was staying, I suspected – but the lad was nowhere to be seen. Fearful of being caught trespassing I pulled up my collar and hurried across a lawn and then down an alleyway that did indeed deliver me into the residential corner known as The College, the cathedral towering above me as if in silent appraisal – or judgement.

The lad was disappeared entirely.

Then I heard music. It was faint at first, the sound of an organ distant yet nevertheless muscular, and it grew in volume as I was compelled to finally explore the monument raised in honour of this unofficial patron saint of the godforsaken north: the cathedral itself. I did not plan on seeing it at this moment – I had in fact intended on retiring for some reading and a rest after my morning's wanderings – but still feeling in something of a daze, I approached the building from an oblique angle, and I entered it not by the main entrance as favoured by tourists and pilgrims alike, with its famed door knocker which depicts a grimacing face that reminds me of so many of the locals, but from the rear.

Suspecting once again that I was trespassing by using a door reserved for monks, clergymen or the cathedral's cleaners, I hastily turned right so as to quickly distance myself from this possible infraction.

The organ music grew louder still.

I was on the South Quire Aisle, which in turn led to a quiet corner which I now know to be the Chapel of Nine Altars. Here I stopped and gazed upwards to the slender ribs of the steeply vaulted ceiling that curved so far above me, like a Norseman's longboat upturned. The light here was poor due to this chapel occupying a gloomier and more obscure corner, but nevertheless I observed a clear fault in the symmetry of the ceiling, an architectural error so glaring that its creator must surely have had to carry the burden of disgrace for the rest of his days.

Many candles burned around me, and as I turned I saw a magnificent round window of stained glass.

Its circular shape and geometrical configurations reminded me instantly of the Indian mandala, though the theological narrative depicting Christ surrounded by his apostles (who are, in turn, surrounded by, I believe, twenty-four elders from Revelation), as told in glass and illuminated this day by diluted sunlight, is clearly late medieval in origin; fifteenth century, I should say. It was the Rose Window, an aperture quite like no other.

As I examined it, the May sun moved into position in such a manner that one might almost be tempted to cite it as an act of divine intervention – *almost* – and the rendered blue and red details that predominated its petal-like shape became illuminated where, just a moment earlier, they were difficult to discern. Dappled light played upon the cathedral's stone floor, and the music enveloped me entirely then. It didn't play upon me – or *at* me – but inhabited my entire being, in a manner that was wholly unanticipated, and I became otherwise deaf and blind to my immediate surroundings, save for this powerful hymn that reached deep down to my core, to the marrow within my bones, and still the sunlight streamed through the glass.

Rapt, I stood unmoving in a moment of supreme quietude and was alarmed to discover that my eyes had become wet.

I write this down now so that the sensation may not be forgotten. I was silently weeping.

There was a pause in the music then, an aural stillness – or did a cloud cross the sun? – and the spell, the stupor I had sunk into while gazing up at the Rose Window, the call-it-what-you-will, was broken. Only then did I see that right beside me was the feretory that held the burial place of St Cuthbert himself. Here up some short steps, his resting bones were marked by a stone slab worn smooth from the knees of pilgrims, and which this lowly librarian and schoolmaster, the Reverend James Fraine, and his cohort, intended to raise.

Though my surroundings might sound tranquil on paper, I did not feel altogether myself, as if I were quite deeply in the vapours.

Thoughts of the boy on the steps and the music, the changing light, the tears and the sudden realisation of the close proximity of the dead saint – something that has never previously troubled me during years of site studies – combined to plunge me into a state of despair that was quite overwhelming. Inwardly, I felt as if I had been dropped from a great height, yet I felt raw too, as if I had been flayed. I was frit.

But there was another sensation too. It was alien and undeniable. It was desire.

I turned and left that place immediately. With my head down in the hope that my eyes might not have to meet those of another – especially the enigmatic boy should he resurface – for fear that they might somehow see within me my many transgressions just as one might see the skull beneath the skin. I crossed the Palace Green, wound back onto the Bailey and scuttled rodent-like to my residential quarters to record the day's events here.

Now I discover the lassitude of this morning has returned *in extremis*, and so I must rest a while before finally meeting the famed Reverend Fraine; and this time if he does not put in an appearance my valise shall be packed and I shall depart Durham by dawn, a damning letter condemning his shoddy practices sent to his clerical superiors as my parting gift.

This time I shall not mention my latest encounter with the sullen lad. If neither of my hosts claim to be aware of his existence then it is best that this wordless dream-like exchange and attendant pursuit through the undergrowth, alleys and secluded stairwells of this strange city remain undisclosed.

I shall remain vigilant where that one is concerned, for who knows what his motives might be.

Also I feel I may be falling ill.

Night. Should I continue recording the inanities of the conversations I have encountered here in the north of England thus far? Will any reader ever even cast their eyes upon these transcriptions? I fear not, though take solace in the fact that they may be of use to me in the future, should I choose to write a full account of this trip, if only for my learned colleagues' amusement. If nothing else, it might make for an amusing and diverting reading at the Society of Antiquaries of London's Christmas luncheon.

In which case, I shall continue. Not least because, though I am fatigued, this evening's meal – was it high tea? Was it dinner? I cannot decide – at least it provided an interesting insight into the minds of these clergymen, and what I initially perceived as to be their stunted ways of thinking. How I sometimes wish they could abandon the vapid certainties of The Great Book and come over to our more progressive ways of empirical thinking.

Nevertheless, this evening's exchange was a worthwhile one and despite being heavy of head, I shall attempt to relate it now.

We gathered in the dining room of the deanery at a table set for three. The maid Edith served us sherry while we stood. She then presented a tray of baked oysters. To avoid causing offence, I managed to swallow down a half dozen nevertheless, and which I correctly predicted to myself would later cause a bout of burning and discomfort. These were followed by a rather thin broth in which there floated small meats of unknown origin.

The efficacy of the broth at least stirred me from the torpor that has been upon me ever since I returned to my suite and, though it lacked seasoning, I cleared the bowl. As we ate, my hosts went to great length to offer a meagre and inconsequential explanation as to the inhospitable ignominy of their no-show earlier this morning.

'I'm afraid there was some unavoidable business pertaining to the Bishop,' said Parnell.

'The Bishop?' I asked, lifting a sliver of pink meat to my lips.

'William Van Mildert,' said Fraine in a tone that suggested a hint of disapproval. A rather dismal-looking fellow, he strikes me as not the type of man one would wish to follow anywhere, let alone deep into our island's history. I couldn't help but notice a drop of liquid appearing at the tip of his nose with alarming frequency, which he had the habit of dabbing at with a handkerchief, only for it to be replaced just a few minutes later. The man is as annoying as a dripping tap.

'Recent successor to the Right Reverend and Honourable Bishop Shute Barrington who, sadly, passed just last year,' Fraine continued. 'And a finer diocese figurehead we could not have hoped to serve under.'

'Yes, I knew of Barrington. He was a regular visitor to Brasenose.'

'That's right,' said Parnell.

'I did not know he had died. And what of this Van Mildert? Not that it concerns me, but is he up to the task?'

'He is the son of a gin distiller,' said Parnell. 'Dutch by descent, I believe.'

Fraine merely frowned.

'He's quite outspoken on a number of issues,' said Parnell quietly.

'Most men of intelligence are,' I replied. 'And what was the situation that was so pressing?'

A glance passed between the two reverends.

'A clerical matter that is quite bureaucratic and relates to the Bishop's county palatine,' Fraine interjected. 'I should not bore you with the details. The man himself is quite well though.'

Our main course was a simple stew of sorts, in which another meat that was difficult to identify – was it, no it couldn't be, salt-cured *corned beef*? – battled for dominance with potatoes, carrots, scallions. Cheese may also have featured. Presenting it, Edith said that the dish was a local delicacy called 'panack-erty'. Broth coupled with casserole, and the starter of oysters, made me feel as if I were a fish bowl, noisily sloshing in transit.

With the required amount of small talk and woeful attempts at badinage on my two hosts' part dispensed with, I found myself steering the conversation to the matter at hand, lest we be sat there all night discussing the recently elected Right Honourable George Canning's prospects as Prime Minister (I gave him three months). The figure beneath the stone slab was the only man I was interested in discussing.

'So what was it about this saint of yours that made him so special as to build a cathedral to house his remains?' I enquired. 'And furthermore, what is it about him that continues to draw streams of pilgrims to continue to visit him now, here in a town which, lumbering Norman attraction aside, doesn't appear to otherwise be a particularly desirable destination?'

'He was a humble man,' said Parnell. 'Very humble.'

I scoffed.

'Reverend, the world is full of humble men. The church, as you know, is particularly packed like pickles in a jar with those who wear their piety with pride.' I smiled at the accidental allit-eration, before continuing. 'Surely modesty and self-effacement does not solely a saint make?'

'No,' said Fraine. 'No, of course, I agree. But Cuthbert was more than a modest man who lived a hermetic life. Quite the opposite, in fact. He travelled widely and was able to find common ground with people from all echelons of society; from Anglo-Saxon kings to the poorest of Borderland peasants; from monks to men of ill-repute, to birds of the air and mammals of the moor. Yes, he lived an austere life far from the trappings that the church might otherwise offer its servants of higher standing, but it was not, as far as we know, a conscious decision, but one borne out of a simple background and a need for a simple existence. Cuthbert rejected comfort; all he needed was his faith, and as such he led by example. He had a multitude of followers, yet was in many ways a reluctant leader. He hadn't even wanted to be Bishopric of Lindisfarne, but still devoted what were to be his dying days to service nonetheless.'

'You'll have heard of the *haliwerfolk*, I expect,' said Parnell with the faintest of sneers playing about his mouth in a manner that suggested he knew very well I hadn't heard of any such thing.

'The word sounds early medieval, or even pagan perhaps,' I replied. 'But as you are aware, theological matters are of little interest to me. My areas of research – my passion – lie in the physical rather than the liturgical. Artefacts are my religion; stories excavated from the soil and given life again, so that we might listen to the voices of our ancestors through such relics, and study their societies, and learn from them. Antiquities, sir. Is that not the reason why you summoned me here, quite out of the blue in the first place?'

'Indeed, indeed,' said Fraine. 'And for your response we are grateful. And stories we have for you. Perhaps, even, it will soon be revealed, one of the great antiquarian stories of our time. But my learned friend the Reverend Parnell is right to raise the *haliwerfolk* – the folk of the holy man – if only to give you a little context; a little, shall we say, colour, as to what it is that continues to make our saint such an important figure in the Christian faith. Am I to take it, sir, that you are not a believer?'

'You know full well I am not,' I replied.

'Nor do you place great stock in those of us who devote our lives to service.'

I replied to the reverend with a quote, and closed eyes.

'"Men, who have taken care to engross the affairs of Religion, as well as others, to their own management, are no more guided in that than in any thing else by the dictates of reason. The religion they were bred up in, they blindly prefer to all others, without being able to give any stronger proof of it's being the best, than that it was the Faith of their fore-fathers."'

Here I opened my eyes, and asked 'Do you know who wrote such an observation?'

Fraine frowned and Parnell shook his head.

'It was one Lady Sophia Fermor in her treatise, *Woman Not Inferior to Man: or, a short and modest vindication of the natural right of the fair-sex to a perfect equality of power, dignity, and esteem, with the men.* You see, gentlemen, unlike such fellows of your calling, rather than devoting so much attention to one book, I prefer to read widely, and if that means reading the work of women who believe themselves to be equal to men, or in some cases *superior*, then so be it. So long as their opinions are soundly original – and I happen to agree entirely with Lady Fermor, a person of great quality, who wrote this a century ago – then I do not discriminate. So, to address your latter accusation, it is not so much that I don't place great stock in the profession of being God's servant, but that I simply cannot acknowledge the purpose of such a pursuit, for how could one recognise a master that one simply believes not to exist?'

We had by now dispensed of our passable stew and a moment of silence sat between us as Edith cleared our bowls. Finally Fraine spoke.

'Professor, I respect your honesty and am humbled by the depth of your learning; Reverend Parnell told me you were leagues beyond your contemporaries at Oxford, and remain so. And perhaps this disdain for our belief system is one reason why we selected you as witness and bearer of testimony to this endeavour of ours.'

'Disdain is a strong word.'

'Scepticism, then.'

'That's preferable,' I said. 'But you didn't first think that Surtees was the man for this task?'

'Surtees?' opined Fraine. 'Yes, Surtees is a fine antiquarian as you well know professor, and *The History and Antiquities of the County Palatine of Durham* is certainly a –'

He paused to choose his words carefully.

'– most comprehensive study. But we feel he is too close to the subject matter. Surtees is from Durham – he is *of* Durham – and therefore lacks an outsider's impartiality. Also, academically speaking, he is in no way of a comparable calibre to you, sir.'

'And he is not a well man,' interjected Parnell. 'When we went to visit him at Mainsforth Hall he practically coughed up a lung into the quince blancmange.'

Fraine shot a look at Parnell which was not so discreet as to escape my notice, and which told me they had almost certainly already approached the joyless Surtees about the exhumation – Surtees a man of law, no less, who wouldn't know a wheel-thrown Grecian oinochoe from a three-handled Mycenaean pottery pyxis – and that I was indeed, despite this feckless duo's attempts at flattery, second choice after all.

Fraine composed himself and then continued.

'Despite your lack of faith, I still feel that you are at least interested in our Saint Cuthbert, for not only have you enquired as to the potency of his life and legacy, but you have travelled here to see it for yourself, have you not?'

At this I could not disagree.

'I would even go so far as to say your lack of faith is an advantage – and that is not a declaration I make lightly, professor.'

Again I could not disagree.

'Then perhaps you will allow the Reverend here to tell you a little about the folk of the holy man,' Raine continued. 'For like you with your antiques, they are an area of particular passion to him, and, after all, their story is one lifted from the soil, hewn from rock, etched in stone and shaped by the slow passing of time, so maybe our interests are not so entirely different after all?'

Parnell cleared his throat, and then reached for a bottle of port which Edith had discreetly placed by his elbow while serving us each with a slice of Madeira cake. He spoke.

'Well, you see, for a century or so after his death on his solitary rock in the North Sea off the island of Lindisfarne, Cuthbert's body was transported about during times of great turmoil. I hardly need give you a history lesson professor, but share this only for the sake of broader context: the region was riven with battling clans, foreign invaders, hungry heathens and all manner of greedy souls set upon carving up the land and claiming it for themselves. The north was wild then.'

Then, I thought, with a small smile, but I kept quiet and let the Reverend Parnell continue.

'During this time of disquiet a nomadic company emerged: the Cuthbert community, or the *haliwerfolk*, the folk of the holy man. Formed out of necessity – not to mention faith and devotion – their number varied from several score, possibly hundreds, to but a dozen or less. Christianity was in its infancy then, and its survival depended upon them and the safe transport of Cuthbert, or at least that is how they surely saw it. This dwindled clan was comprised almost entirely of the most hardened and devout monks, whose sole purpose was to complete the mission that by now had been passed down the generations to them: to find a safe final resting place for their saint, and then when this was achieved they would instigate the construction of a great monument in which to house him forever, a building to celebrate his greatness and inspire awe. More than a building, in fact, it would be a gift to God himself, something so vast and beautiful that it would be beyond comprehension to those few people about the place who lived in conditions most primitive, something to be seen from miles around as it stood tall and proud on the peninsula, a structure so breath-taking as to be frightening, that all across the land might flock to see it, and to see him – and to remember. And they do.'

'These brothers were the protectors of the corpse of St Cuthbert, and instigated the making of the cathedral, and therefore this city,' chipped in Fraine. 'Without their faith, endurance and cunning, his remains would surely have been desecrated or stolen by Viking invaders or simply abandoned somewhere on a lonely moorland to be ravaged by wild dogs. Or worse. Their names are recorded, and we thank them: Brother Edmund, Brother Franco, Brother Chad —'

Reverend Parnell continued the list for him.

'Brother Chad, Brother Hunred, Brother Stitheard, Brother Eadmer —'

These last names pulled me up short. I put down my port.

Were these not similar to the noises I heard whispered in the night?

Ungred. Stither. Eedmah.

Yes, I believed they were.

'Sorry,' I interrupted. 'I didn't quite catch what you said there, reverend.'

Fraine obliged me by repeating his litany.

'Brother Hunred, Brother Stitheard, Brother Eadmer —'

Ungred. Stither. Eedmah. Yes, yes, these were the sounds to which I had awoken the previous night. But how to explain this to the clerics? How to seek confirmation that this awful nocturnal chorus had meaning without sounding entirely like a man haunted? No, it would not do for a pragmatic scholar and rationalist such as myself to evince such a stark confession.

'I firmly believe that it is these brothers who should have achieved sainthood too,' said Parnell. 'For they gave their lives to ensure safe passage and that Cuthbert's body should remain undisturbed.'

The reverend then replenished our glasses which had by now been twice drained of their port. I took another sip and frowned into my drink.

'Yet now the pair of you seem intent on doing exactly the opposite of that.'

Here Parnell looked to Fraine for what I took to be reassurance, as the latter is clearly the stronger personality of the pair, even if they are of the same standing in the church's convoluted hierarchical structure.

Now it was Fraine who was frowning and staring deep into the darkness of his port, as if he expected an answer to be found there. But I chose not to give him time to formulate a response, just as I believe they had not yet fully afforded me the respect that I feel is due, a mistake that it will take more than a decent meal and medieval port to rectify.

'Gentlemen, you will excuse my directness, but let me speak plainly: if this saint of yours is so highly venerated then why is it that you wish, in an act some would surely deem *at the very best* as sacrilegious, to dig up his remains? Even done with the utmost respect and delicateness, disturbance is certain and though as an antiquarian *clearly* I am interested in your findings, surely there are deeper moral and theological concerns for your cathedral community.'

'Let me assure you, we do not enter into this venture lightly,' said Fraine. 'However, I believe we have sound theological reasons, which I hope that you as an academic will find just. On your wanderings you may or may not have seen that a new church has been built very close by to here. It is named in our St Cuthbert's honour and in just two weeks' time it will open its doors.'

'And it is Roman Catholic,' said Parnell, barely able to mask his disdain.

'This is a problem?' I asked. 'Are you so petty as to bicker with fellow believers as to who stakes a claim over this saint's name, his legacy?'

Reverend Fraine raised a palm, in a gesture of supplication that I took to be somewhat ersatz.

'No professor, we are not.'

'Good. Because as you are undoubtedly aware, the frivolous squabbles that take place in the name of God are of no interest to me whatsoever; I find them demeaning for all concerned and a divergence from sound thinking.'

'In essence I agree,' said Fraine. 'But there is a broader point here not yet made. If this peninsula is large enough to house a cathedral and a castle, and the wonderful dwellings that we call home, then it is large enough to accommodate our Roman Catholic brothers and sisters too. Furthermore, grand plans are afoot, sir, for the establishment of a new university, on this very land. Parliament is already being lobbied to introduce a bill to – and I quote – "enable the Dean and Chapter of Durham to appropriate part of the property of their church to the establishment of a University".'

A university, I thought. *Here?* In the cursed north country, where the streets are awash with the urine of its townsfolk? I have never been good at divorcing my inner feelings and I fear Reverend Fraine could read me like a book.

'With respect, professor, you might be unwise to express doubt, for our cathedral is one of the very richest in the land. And when university status is granted, as it surely will be, the newly established Durham College will be a seat of learning to soon rival that of Cambridge or your Oxford.'

At this I nearly – nearly – spat out my port, but instead gulped loudly in such a way as to express my scepticism. Also I belched involuntarily; 'twas the oysters. Fraine continued unabashed.

'However, in taking Cuthbert's name as their own the Catholics also appear intent on distorting the truth of our saint. No, wait – let me rephrase that. In an attempt to lure converts via an act of blind papism, it is my belief that they are outright lying about the life and death of Cuthbert. And therefore are committing nothing less than blasphemy.'

'How is that so?'

'It seems as if—'

Here Parnell took up the thread, but Fraine interrupted him for the conversation was now his entirely.

'They are intent on perpetuating the myth that Cuthbert's corpse remains uncorrupted.'

'And you do not believe it to be?'

'Professor, we may be men of God but that does not mean that we reject such things as fact and science and the natural process. And while I may be both a Reverend, a principal surrogate in the consistory court and author of the well-received *Documents and evidence relating to the administering of the Holy Communion to the Laity within the parishes between the rivers Tyne and Tees before the Reformation*, you might not be aware that for fifteen years I have also been second master at Durham School, and furthermore have held the role of librarian to the dean and chapter. Which is to say, I believe in education, betterment and all pursuits deemed scholarly; I am not stuck in a theological rut, but on a perpetual quest for a greater understanding. For too long this tale has been told, and perhaps its origins are harmless, but today we feel that it is being used to manipulate the emotions of the vulnerable in a manner that we deem crass and cynical. Therefore we wish to prove once and for all that Saint Cuthbert endures in our hearts and our minds and our prayers – and in every stone that made Durham Cathedral – but that his body has, of course, turned to dust, as all bodies do. This, sir, is, I consider, nothing less than an act of charity towards our Catholic cousins.'

Somewhat taken aback by such unexpected logic I chose my response carefully, and tried to overlook the drop of liquid that had returned to his nose.

'Reverend Fraine, you have surprised me. I find your honesty refreshing and acknowledge your position as master and librarian as well as being a man of God. It is a shame that this business may be perceived as a tug of war between Protestant and Catholic, a battle in which I could never choose one side over the other.'

'And I, sir, would never be so egregious as to persuade you to adopt such a position.'

'Yet,' I added, 'I feel I at least now understand your motives.'

'And as Reverend Fraine has already identified, that is precisely why we invited you,' said Parnell. 'Because your atheism and clear thinking is well known. There have been Jesuit priests serving the community here for a hundred years or more and the Roman Catholic church owns a fair portion of this city; we are all doing God's work with equanimity and probity here. Yet you, professor, are famous for your rejection of all things speculative.

Your stock in trade, sir, your speciality, the field in which you excel most famously, is unearthing objects, and then walking backwards through epochs in order to tell stories behind them, is it not?'

'Yes,' I said. 'I suppose you could define archaeology and anti-quarianism as that.'

'Well then. Now you see why you are here.'

'Yes,' I said proffering my empty glass towards Parnell. 'Yes I do.'

Parnell obliged by charging my drink and we each had another round before I spoke.

'Sirs, I do not believe that this man shall be disinterred, but I will help you,' I said, though I must admit my motives were not entirely altruistic. 'While I am morally opposed to this venture for academic and ethical reasons, I suspect that you cannot be dissuaded and therefore this endeavour would, I believe, benefit from my experience.'

The reverends raised their glasses, and I did the same. We then spent a further hour discussing the details of tomorrow's 'dig' as they insisted upon calling it.

Perhaps it was the effect of the alcohol, or the strain of the day upon me, but as it came time to take my leave I found myself pausing for a moment and speaking words I had not intended.

'I do believe I saw one of your lads again today,' I said to Parnell.

'Lads?'

'Yes, the boy you sent to meet me upon arrival.'

Parnell looked to Fraine and then back to me and I imme-diately regretted opening my mouth. It was as if I were momentarily suffering a decay of the brain.

'Ah yes, that again,' he replied with a smile that could not disguise its condescension and doubt. 'As I mentioned, the only chaperone I had arranged was my good self, and it was a failure of attendance for which I can only apologise once more.'

We were all standing now and I felt my body swaying slightly. I was all at sea, and perhaps this was apparent as Reverend Parnell followed with a question in language which I perceived as being designed to patronise.

'And where was it you saw this phantom protector a second time?'

Suppressing a frown, I instead made every effort to sound flippant and disinterested.

'Oh, around and about. It was during my constitution upon this very headland. It matters not.'

Here Fraine interjected in a voice of great import.

'It matters to us if you, sir, an honoured guest, are being molested in some way. Perhaps if you could describe this fellow we might at least be able to identify him. He could be a cathedral scholar or a chorister. I for one would like to know what this little blighter's game is.'

I hesitated.

'Sir, there was no maltreatment to report. But let me see —'

Still feeling slightly unsteady on my legs, again I hesitated.

'He had dark hair and the complexion of an alien. An incomer. If I had to guess I'd say Moldavian or Wallachian, though he could be a gypsy, or merely unwashed for all I know.'

'Hmmm,' said Parnell, thinking.

'Hmmm,' said Fraine. 'I wonder if it were young Reginald Erskine.'

'Oh yes,' said Parnell. 'It could have been Erskine. Did he have a significant birthmark about his face, professor?'

'No, he did not.'

'Then it was not him.'

'How tall was this boy?' said Fraine. 'And of what age?'

'About my height, and sturdy of build. Of his age it is difficult to say.'

'Certainly being able to estimate another's age is a skill that, I find, one loses as one advances oneself,' said Parnell.

'Ah, sturdily built,' said Fraine. 'Then perchance it was Kit Cannon.'

'Oh yes,' said Parnell. 'It could have been Cannon. Did he speak in a thick Caledonian accent, professor?'

'No, he did not. Or least not as I recall. I should say he were about six and ten years.'

'Perhaps that lump Gregory Bullard then? A shock of red hair and eyes so indolent they might remind one of a goat?'

I shook my head.

'Well, is there anything else to distinguish this lad?' said Parnell. 'His clothes or something he said? His gait, even?'

Again, I shook my head.

'It's curious, all I can truly recall is that he had a look of impudence about him. And exceedingly large dark eyes.'

'Robert Cockburn,' said Fraine. 'He's as brazenly impertinent as the devil himself when he wants to be.'

'A strong rower though,' said Fraine.

'True, true,' said Parnell. 'There is none better in the coxless pairs.'

'Hmmm,' said Fraine.

'Then again it might have been that little pest Charles Rolfe or maybe Chad McGrillis.'

'The soprano?'

'Alas, young Chadwick is a soprano no more, reverend. In daily evensong his honk resembles that of a goose in migration.'

Parnell said this with a discernible sense of sadness which would have troubled me more greatly had not tiredness fallen upon me absolute, and I felt an overwhelming need to extricate myself from this mindless confabulation immediately. I interrupted the two reverends' incessant wittering.

'Gentlemen, I must retire. If I see the young man again I shall corner him and ask his name so that this mystery might be resolved, though I'm sure you appreciate that I have more pressing matters upon my mind. I thank you for your hospitality and shall see you anon.'

And now I record this evening, exhausted by the day once more, though I am not sure why, for little work has been done here. Again my wrist aches, as do my eyes. I suspect I shall need new spectacles upon my return to Oxford. My stomach feels a little distended too from a meal that gave the illusory impression of being digestible. I fear the daemons of dyspepsia have taken up residence.

Also, I have only to hand a copy of Bede's *Life of Cuthbert*, pressed upon me by Fraine. I am too fatigued to read it now, though pleased to see that it contains illustrations of this man whom we are soon to meet. While wearily thumbing the pages an interesting citation arrests my attention: 'If necessity compels you to choose between two evils, I would much rather that you take my bones from their tomb and carry them away with you to whatever place of rest God may decree.'

Perhaps it is words such as these that Parnell and Fraine interpret as an invitation to move the saint, even if only a matter of inches, and temporarily, once more. Might I find myself caught between the 'two evils' of rivalling doctrines? I should be careful, I suppose, though my atheism – they are too polite and too in need of my insight to call it outright heresy – is surely a worthy armour; a rain-shade against the gathering storm clouds of a parochial theological schism.

I now place my pen aside. I have written too many words, and for what purpose I am not sure.

Sleep, then.

I hope.

May 16 1827

Daybreak.

Again slumber evades me.

Indeed I find myself so outspent I can barely be certain of what it was that I experienced during this night past, only that I know it to be inexplicable. I shall keep the account short while it is fresh in my troubled mind.

I could, if so inclined, apportion blame or explanation for what occurred during this night on the libations with which

I was plied at last evening's meal – the sherry, port and wine that I imbibed a little too freely left my head thick and, along with the food, my stomach sour – but I know that to do that would be to question my own keen senses and furthermore deny a deeper truth. The truth being that I, a scholar of international renown, and widely read author of numerous texts, including, most recently, *Mystras: An Archaeological Chronicle in Six Parts of the Misc. Ceramics and Metalworks Discovered in the Ancient Principality of the Byzantine Empire During the Great Exploratory Dig of 1822–1823*, now in its third printing, for the first time in my life, believe myself to be unravelling, perhaps due to a prolonged state of exhaustion brought about by years of study. Or, failing that, I am – and I hardly dare write the words now in the cold morning's light – the subject of a haunting. Yes, a haunting.

This, of course, goes against everything I believe, teach, write, speak and think, my entire life and career having been devoted to rational thinking, as should be evident in the title alone.

I record this at daybreak. This is what happened.

I had hardly been asleep an hour when I awoke with a start. Compelled to cast light about the place I lit my lamp and saw the same primitive footwear protruding from the floor-length curtain that covered the locked door, and the shape of a figure behind it. I leapt from my mattress and pulled back the drapery only to find there was no one there, and the door firmly nailed into place. But the shoes were real, and quite unlike the handmade boots one might journey to Jermyn Street twice a year to have made up.

No, these were soft leather moccasins that were little more than thick socks in shape and style, and with a sole of what material I am not certain for the light was poor – thicker layers of treated hide perhaps – over which the leather was roughly stretched and pinned into place. I turned these primitive things in my hand; they carried within them the warmth of the wearer and they were pungent too, reeking as they did of sweat and toil, and perhaps even a note of effluence. That was when I threw them down and retreated beneath my blankets, not daring to consider how they had got there, or how they should have appeared so lived-in.

I calmed my racing mind and composed myself. A few long and confused moments passed before I reached a glaringly obvious conclusion: clearly I was the victim of a prank, but who would dare do such a thing? And why had I not noticed them when I returned from dinner? Had someone snuck in just now to place them there?

I was too tired to consider such questions, and retired once more, resolving to give them thought in the morning, when my nullified senses had returned to reason, and the stark light of day might better enable rationality.

I slept fitfully, if at all, and would estimate that another hour passed before I was disturbed by noise and movements in my bedroom once more. This time they were unambiguous; there was an intruder or several intruders in my chambers. I heard shuffling, the breaths of men and, most disturbingly, a low chanting.

I scrambled for the lamp, but found it out of reach this time, even though I know I had deliberately positioned it right there on the dresser. My hand clutched at nothing but darkness as panic rose within me like bile. The lamp, the lamp. Where was it?

And the noises did not abate: they were real, I heard them. It was the sound of a dire procession, and of tongues speaking a language I barely recognised. I heard not the dry creak of loose floorboards, but instead feet and cartwheels tramping through sludge and mire. I heard the rasping of infected chests, the drastic moans of exhaustion and the uttered prayer of total devotion.

In my mad panic to find my lamp I fell from my bunk and lay prone on the floor like a banked fish, and in the dim light saw all around me the legs and feet of this imagined – or was it? – caravan of people passing through my bedroom, this cavalcade of spectral – or were they? – bodies from an earlier age.

I rolled beneath my bedstead and dared not move further as the feet shuffled around me. Every sense was alert to the moment as I heard their words:

> o Cuddy Cuddy o
> o Lord o God
> o Jesus
> o Cuddy sainted soul

The very sound of this whispered mantra, so dire in its delivery, made me want to flee from the room, but I could not move for I was frozen stiff with fear. All my body was ice, my every sense heedful to the point of alarm.

And the chant continued, their voices exhausted by their endeavour and starved of sustenance; voices in search of sleep and salvation, voices seeking deliverance, voices in search of a sign of a resting place, voices fuelled by faith alone as they intoned in unison:

> o Cuddy Cuddy o
> o Lord o God
> o Jesus
> o Cuddy sainted soul

I do not know what happened next, only that I came to beneath my bed, shivering and muttering the same words I had heard spoken by the people of the procession, as a thin strip of light crossed the floor.

> o Cuddy Cuddy o
> o Lord o God
> o Jesus
> o Cuddy sainted soul

And it was morning.
Praise be for morning.

And now another incident to report, from just a few moments ago, after I laid my pen aside and attempted to snatch a moment's rest.

If sleep came to me then it was broken by what I thought I discerned to be the lightest of scratching sounds outside my bedroom door; so light as to be barely heard, and slow too, like a rusted nail being gently run along a stone. But heard it I did. I am not so old as to be losing my primary faculties for, the occasional plug of troublesome wax aside, my hearing remains the sense that I perceive as being in capital condition.

The noise just outside my door was credible and though I have heard mice and rats chewing their way through internal walls on many occasion, most usually in London, I instinctively knew that this was the work of no rodents, but something less hurried. Its negligible movements were, in a way, more malevolent.

I was out of bed like a shot, for it was light outside and the oppressive fear that one experiences in the lingering torment of night had abated, and courage propelled me out from under my blankets, barefooted across the floor to the door, which I yanked open with no amount of violence, only to be met, at my feet, by a bucket on top of which there was balanced a heavy wooden chopping board. The noise was coming from inside the bucket – slow scratching, and of unknown origin.

With both reluctance and curiosity I squatted and taking care to do it all at arm's length I carefully moved the board aside just an inch or so in case it harboured within it a cornered rodent, but when nothing showed itself I drew the makeshift lid further back and peered into the vessel.

At first what I saw for a fraction of a moment as a dark incomprehensible mass was in fact a number of crabs slowly climbing over one another in a futile bid for freedom. They were large crustaceans, with slowly grasping pincers, searching eyes and the green hue of the sea to their underbellies. It was then that Edith appeared at the end of the hallway.

'Oh professor, I hope my delivery didn't waken you?' she said.

I looked up from the crabs, then back to the bucket.

'What is the meaning of this?'

'Crabs, sir. Freshly caught during the night just off Seaham, sir.'

'Seaham?'

'It's a village, sir, just ten or fifteen miles from here. They say these crabs are the finest the North Sea has to offer and that there is soon to be a harbour built there.'

'Who does?'

'Everyone who tastes them.'

'And what are they doing here?'

'It's something of a tradition sir. The church owns much of the land between here and the coast, and out into the sea too no doubt, so there are agreements in place, sir, whereby the fishermen donate a portion of their weekly wares to God's cause, you see. The clergymen eat a lot of crabs here – a lot of fish and periwinkles and mussels too – but it is a courtesy to always offer esteemed guests the pick of the morning catch. The best ones, if you will. The monks especially like their lobsters, sir. Full of goodness, they are. I wondered if you might like to pick one or two out and I'll have them boiled and dressed for you in no time.'

My appetite still in retreat after last night's gout-inducing spread, I instead ordered a simple meal of back bacon, kidneys, eggs, mushrooms, some bone marrow, a little blood pudding, a modest round of toast, a pot of tea and a selection of condiments, with some stewed figs for afterwards, all to be taken on a tray in bed, and the frightful decapods removed forthwith.

Edith returned in good time with my breakfast tray, upon which was also placed a note.

Professor,

I pray forgiveness for monopolising your time in this manner but our planned project must be delayed due to issues concerning privacy and discretion for one day and one night. We shall resume on the evening of the 17th day of May in our Lord's year AD 1827. That is to say, the day that follows this one.

I apologise most profusely.

Please dispose of this missive upon completion.

I am forever your humble servant & co.
Reverend William Nicholas Parnell, BD

Two days. Another two full days I am expected to loiter around this city which feels as if it is shrinking around me! I fell back against my pillow, utterly dejected.

For the remainder of the shortening morning I have felt both exhausted and listless, with a gnawing feeling of entrapment eating away at me. I have the sense I am being held like a chattel. It is both mentally and physically debilitating; to hold even a pen currently feels like an effort.

Upon reading Parnell's affront of a note, received after being the subject of unwanted and inexplicable nocturnal visitations – to say nothing of the pail of crustaceans – after careful consideration, I have reached a decision: namely that all this is folly, and I was wrong to come to this place. I may even be in danger, if not from external forces then from my own exhausted mind; I at least retain sufficient faculties to read these warning signs quite clearly.

So now I must summon the energy to pack my belongings and leave with stealth and secrecy. I do not care about causing offence to the reverends; in fact, I rather relish the prospect, and of turning my back upon the cathedral that houses their trouble too.

I shall be gone from the squat domineering power of this terrible place.

My departure from my lodgings was swift, though not without concern. I fled as a prisoner might upon finding his gaoler asleep and keys dangling within reach; my effects were thrown into my valise and my coat tucked under one arm. Perhaps there was no need for such a covert undertaking, yet I nevertheless determined that that was exactly what the situation demanded.

Such was my haste that I departed hatless.

Rain was falling, gently at first, but soon, within seconds in fact, as if to add drama and inconvenience to the occasion, it fell persistently and with violence, so I worked my way into my coat and turned my collar against it. I crossed the close in which I had been domiciled without looking back, lest I see Edith or, worse – far worse – the blank face of one of my chanting night-time tormentors pressed to the window pane.

Gripped by a kind of pulsing low panic, I walked without forethought. I knew if I could get to the market place a carriage could take me away from the stricken city to a neighbouring town at the very least, anywhere away from this city. Is there even such a preferable sanctuary here in the north? Would, for example the neighbouring towns east of here such as Chester-le-Street, Houghton-le-Spring or Hetton-le-Hole, each named by Romans, be any safer for my physical and mental welfare? No, I was certain that as soon as I was able to head south I would begin to feel at ease once more. Sometimes distance from a trauma is the only remedy required to repair frayed nerves and recalibrate the senses in order to take a more sensible reading of proceedings. Could it only have been four days since I departed dear old *Oxonium*, and two since I arrived in Dunelm? Entire empires might have risen and fallen in the interim, such is the harrowing sense of time being elongated here.

I hurried away from the college, through the archway by which I entered, and then, hoping to avoid the main thoroughfare of the Bailey, a street which had appeared to have shrunk in width overnight and where I could easily be intercepted by Fraine, Parnell or one of their young charges who might recognise me as the famed author of *Mystras: An Archaeological Chronicle in Six Parts* etc. & etc., for my accompanying author's portrait has appeared in a plethora of periodicals subscribed to by libraries across the continent.

The rain fell harder still, vertical and relentless.

The cathedral was at my elbow then, but I did not care to turn and look at it, in case it could somehow read my intentions or itself conspire to intervene in my avowed escape. I turned away from it as one would from a person most disfigured. Another church was upon me, seventeenth century in appearance I would say, though I was moving too quickly to examine it more closely — how many churches does a town that masquerades as a city need? — so I quickly ducked into a side street, dashed across the smooth cobbles that were slick with rain and found myself at the top of a long flight of rudimentary steps plunging steeply down the side of the peninsula's wooded gorge to the river below, giving the appearance of a portal to an arboreal netherworld.

With my valise swinging I took the steps at speed, barely taking care to stop myself from slipping on the algae-covered wooden steps which were narrow like a companionway as they descended into the darkening space.

Far beneath me, at the river's nearside edge, I could see a small hand-pulled ferry boat attached to a rope pulley, but no one to guide it, as the rain had surely sent its owner indoors on a day unlikely to earn him much coin. Nevertheless I thought if I could cross the river here where it looped to create the headland on which I felt I was being both held captive and haunted — this strange and ancient bluff where the rotting bones of a saint lie in the soil — then I should more freely make my way out of the city unseen and unhindered.

The trees here were strangled by ivy — great ropes of it, asphyxiating trunk and timber and alike. Everywhere I looked it was winding and clinging, juvenile and mature stems intertwining to strengthen their grip.

Halfway down the gorge side I paused to take a breath and wipe water from my eyes, for the rain had dishevelled me completely and pasted my hair to my brow. Where my coat met my trousers I was similarly soaked through. The northern skies were taking their revenge upon me with something of a beating merely for daring to spurn the region for the more temperate south. I lamented the loss of a hat.

I looked back the way I had come and then I saw him: a figure, a dark figure, coming down the very same steps in a sideways motion at a brisk velocity. Rain was running down either side of this earthen ladder, cascading in rivulets that cut a way through the sodden loam. And he too almost appeared to be made of water, filthy black water, the way his shape shifted as he moved.

I could not see this desperate creature's features from where I stood but I knew it was him, the lad with the eyes of an owl, and as the rain fell and the runnels scoured the soil he moved with such speed that his charcoal-coloured greatcoat flapped open and its brass buttons managed to gleam in the gloom, and it was as if he were swooping down from above like the creature he most resembled, and I were the prey soon to be swept up in his talons, and though a defensive sense of self-preservation urged me onwards, a part of me craved this deeply. I desired it more than anything, in fact. For a vexing instant my legs froze as a growing part of my being wanted to turn to the lad, to face him as a toreador might stare down a rampaging bull in an act of bravado, or even submission perhaps, stifling all sense of reason and clear thought, just as the vines here smother everything that grows in their path.

I turned and fled.

He shouted something then, his voice lost in the cacophony of the rain as it drummed a war-like tattoo upon the ground.

Again he shouted and again I could not make out the words. I was compelled to stop then. To stop and turn. To turn towards this solemn boy-shape of ambiguous motives. He was closer now. His thin coat was also soaked through and across his chest his white shirt clung to his body, so wet as to be transparent.

'What?' I said. 'What did you say?'

'Let history lie.'

These three words confused me. His dark eyes stared me down. We were both breathing heavily and the harsh rain fell upon that dank and torrid arboreal cathedral of nature's making.

'Of what matter do you speak?' I implored, though deep inside of me I knew the answer and could not fool myself into thinking otherwise. 'Do you mean Fraine and Parnell's venture?'

Was this not the same phrase he had said upon delivering me to my quarters only the other day? No – that was 'history is lies'. An entirely different meaning.

'Let history lie,' he said again, more forcefully, each word carefully emphasised, and this time they were like a series of punches issued by a pugilist to the stomach, gullet and head. But it seemed to me then that it was not history that was in question, but man's relationship with it: the way scholars such as I, perhaps, document, record, ruminate and extrapolate. The way we steer and shape it, some critics might say. My very being was under threat, and yet –

And yet we stood like this for a moment, once again breathing heavily, once again on stairs, trapped momentarily between this place and another.

He took a step forward and something deep within me flexed with pusillanimous anticipation. His large eyes were open as wide as any man's ever have been, so wide as to take in the entire universe, but yet also somehow trained entirely on me, his intended target.

But then the lad did something quite unexpected. He retreated. He took three or four steps backwards and then he turned and climbed the steps two at a time, a diminishing black shape in the long shadows, up towards the cathedral as fat drops dripped from the trail of his coat, and the rain roared in the trees and on the river.

There was little I could do then but wait a minute or two and then wearily follow in his path, for tiredness had gained the whip hand once more. No – tiredness is too weak a word for it; this was exhaustion and despondency as I have never known; to cross the river or walk through the city to hail a carriage was now quite beyond my capabilities, much less enduring a two-day drive south.

Instead I submitted to fate and returned to my chamber as if I had never left it, only now illness is within me for certain. I feel its cruel cold ache, with loneliness, guilt and desire manifesting themselves as an internal ailment, just as a patina of mould might shroud a ruined and rotting dwelling. My chest is tight from the damp atmosphere, no doubt, and I am wracked by chills. A fever, I think, is coming, for the words of the lad – '*Let history lie*' – appear to be going round and round in my head, and I am quite beyond their control. Clearly it was issued as a warning, but against what, I wonder. The proposed exhumation? If this is the case, how could he know about such a secretive endeavour? A criticism of meddlers such as myself is my only conclusion, and it is one not reached with a fully sound mind.

In one moment I shall have to call for Edith and request that she might bring a remedy of sorts – some melted butter and lemon, or a balsam tincture perhaps. A warm compress for my burning lungs at the very least.

Also, I am beginning to wonder if documenting these events is a wise idea, for these words must never be seen by another; a reader might judge me as degenerating into lunacy.

So why write them?

I do not know.

But write them I must.

Write them I must.

May 16 1827. Evening.

Dozing, I had an alarming vision.
I saw a pile of bones scattered on
cold northern stone. Torrid men
were gathered about. The bones,
they had a voice. It spoke to them.
This was their hallowed St Cuddy.

Words like birds
trapped in the atrium
of my mind:

Let history lie.
Let history lie.
Let history lie.

May 16 1827. Night.

o Cuddy
are there birds
where you
are now?

Yes, professor.
I feel them
flutter
in the cage of my skull.

May 16 / May 17 1827

By candlelight
once more
I write.

I am caught between days and realms as time slips away and delirium has me in its grip during these dark hours.

I must believe that this is the case, as it is the only explanation for what has just happened, and that is: another visitation.

The same dire procession again.

The same shuffling forms of monks transporting a cart laden with a coffin again.

I saw them much more clearly this time as they passed right through my bedroom just moments ago – their tattered rags, their malnourished bodies, their closely shaved skulls. Their wounds and sores and ailments.

And as they walked, though I could not make out their faces, I could hear quite clearly that they chanted in a tongue that was once again foreign to my modern ears, a bastard hybrid of early English, Celt and Bible-speak. They said their prayers and muttered their songs, songs in search of music, a music most offensive to the ears, a woeful music without melody and featuring only snatched lines spoken in devotion, adoration, piety. But one verse made it through without the need for translation.

o Cuddy Cuddy o
o Lord o God
o Jesus
o Cuddy sainted soul

Cuthbert was in the coffin. I instinctively understood that he was just feet away as I cowered, quivering and drenched with fever sweat beneath my blankets once more, and this depleted band of monks were close to reaching their final destination now. I could see it all so clearly: was not the cathedral just a hundred strides from where I lay?

Yes, their journey was nearly over, and the body of the wandering Cuthbert, patron saint of the north of England, was to be laid to rest for evermore, thus setting into motion a chain of events that would shape the country for centuries.

The community passed through my room, though how they did this with doors locked and walls in their way, I do not know. Only that they did.

Only.

That.

They did.

For I saw them.

Frozen with fear, I saw them.

One straggler remained, however, a lone figure out of step with the monks. He was younger, had his hair.

He raised his head. This one's face I saw. This one's face I knew. His wide dark eyes stared me down, bright like those of a nocturnal animal caught in a lamp's glare.

'Let history lie,' he said. '*Let. History. Lie.*'

Exhumation day.

I shall say nothing of this morning or early afternoon, for it passed in a state of nervous torment. Twice I intended to attempt to flee, but twice I fell back into the failure of myself, unable to summon the energy or courage to do so; the haunting had depleted me, changed me entirely.

I ate nothing, drank only hot lemon water, and some tots of whisky sweetened with treacle. I listlessly perused these notes, and let illness consume me so that I might be absolved from all involvement with what lay ahead.

Yet even this malady failed me, for when the time came this evening I was dressed and ready by my chamber door, willingly awaiting deliverance as if the previous hours had been passed in a stupor. I had somehow disentangled mind and body and then stepped back into my own shadow and was now observing my physical form, which felt like an empty vessel, being as it was temporarily devoid of all conscious responsibility. Outwardly, at least, I believe I gave the impression of mental competence, despite feeling quite the contrary.

It gets more wretched.

The Rev. Parnell collected me and we left the house in sombre silence. The day was darkening and the glaze of the spring sky cracked and blistered with a terrible sense of foreboding, made worse by what I discerned to be a low malevolent hum of unknown origin; I guessed – I *hoped* – a faulty valve in the cathedral's ancient organ.

A dozen, nay, a *million* times during the short walk to the cathedral I felt compelled to turn and run once more, yet could not. A greater power pulled me into the building, to the chapel where this St Cuthbert lay, and up the short steps of the feretory, and then leaning over his remains, crouched like a leering golem, was the Rev. Fraine, with an array of tools to hand and a malevolent glint in his eye.

And there about him were other men, none of whom I had been introduced to nor given prior notice thereof.

'What is the meaning of this?' I enquired, tugging at Parnell's cuff. 'Who are these fellows?'

'Oh,' came the reply with a cold air of indifference that I found disarming. 'Well that there is Rev. William Gilly, Prebendary of the ninth stall; next to him is Mr John Leybourne, Deputy Receiver; beside him is Mr Edward Fairclough, Clericus Operum; then Mr Anthony Tyler, Verger, and Mr William Joplin, Master Mason. And the Reverend Fraine you, of course, know.'

'Five men whom I am unacquainted with,' I snapped in as hushed a voice as this great hallowed space demanded.

'It matters not,' replied Parnell in such a way that I wished to slap him sober, for he had the look of one who was intoxicated, if not on clerical wine, then drunk on this damnable debacle, and foxed on this foul folly.

'It matters to me,' I hissed. 'These strangers have the capacity to compromise my steadfast academic reputation.'

'Well, they're not strangers to us, and while your reputation is unimpeachable it is secondary to an endeavour that I hope you agree is of greater import,' came the reverend's arrogant retort as he strode to join them in the corner where this saint of the north lay, oblivious to what fate was soon to befall his poor corpse.

No formal introductions were made and my presence was barely noted beyond cursory glances – an oversight which, in any other circumstances, would certainly undermine any credible attempts at collaboration.

But these were no ordinary circumstances; collectively we were entering most murky moral waters, and little better than those cursed 'bodysnatchers' who pilfer cadavers to peddle to so-called men of science.

We – that is to say, *they* – began with neither prayer nor preamble, but with prisebars wedged into declivities scraped into the ancient lime mortar that held the great slab of Frosterley marble in place, and which I estimated to be close to nine feet in length, four in width and proportionately thick. It was a formidable piece of stone that necessitated the might of all seven men who at that very moment were assuaging any guilt by quietly convincing themselves that this mission was holy, and undertaken entirely in service to the one these north country folk call 'Our Cuddy'. This I discerned from their mindless Godly mutterings.

I did not lend a shoulder; was I not, after all, there as passive observer, primed for impartiality, and ill too? I sequestered myself at a distance deemed appropriate.

With no shortage of ruckus, bickering, puffing and chin-scratching perplexity, the unscrupulous rabble of reverends, clerics and masons slowly lifted the great stone, and I found myself clinging to a pillar such was the sudden vertiginous feeling of overwhelming nausea that overcame me as the marble was raised amidst a puff of stony powder, and those three words were spoken once more, loudly in my mind:

Let.
History.
Lie.

Beneath the stone: soil.

Nothing but impacted dirt.

Beneath the dirt: who knew what.

Nevertheless I exhaled a brief sigh of relief and took the merest glimmer of consolation in the fact that the saint and his relics were not, at least, laid in plain sight.

This disappointment appeared to galvanise this errant ecclesiastic herd into a frenzied state as Fraine, aided by his men, threw himself upon the edaphic rectangle as a starving man might upon a steaming banquet table, and dug away at it first with trowel and spade, quickly and carelessly, and then with bare hands, like the victims of vivisepulture in reverse.

It went entirely against every technique I have practised, taught, documented and espoused, and I felt sick to the pit of my stomach.

Yet I did not stir.

I did not do a thing.

Instead I watched this after-hours excavation – this wanton act of vandalism – progress apace.

They dug down quickly, deep below the humus, where, at a depth of approximately eighteen inches, there sat another stone of similar dimensions, though of a lesser quality. With great effort this too was raised.

Beneath it lay a third stone cut in the shape of a parallelogram with a keen mason's proficiency, and it was, save for an outer layer of grime, almost perfectly white in colour.

'We are close,' said Fraine. 'So close to our calling.'

'Our saint,' said Parnell.

'Praise be,' muttered one of the men of cloth.

'Our Cuddy,' said another.

Then beneath this third stone: a coffin.

Let history lie.

A coffin of oak so rotten its lid had peeled back and curled away like an old scroll twisting beneath the weight of many damp centuries. The sides of this crumbled pall had perished to such a degree as to be in a state of disrepair so total that it was beyond redemption; a catafalque and airless casing in the manner of a papal mass which might once have ensured longevity, or at least instilled some sense of dignity to this stricken saint of theirs, but not now.

Not now, not here, after so many leagues interred in peninsular soil. Indeed not ever, here in the wild northern lands of perfidious Albion.

Yet still, despite its state, markings were nevertheless evident upon the ancient reliquary's lid. Sigils perhaps, or inscriptions, messages

343

from the past; the very aspect that keeps drawing antiquarians such as myself back to this troubled practice. I moved closer.

'Look,' said Parnell.

'Figures,' said Fraine. 'Incised upon the wood.'

I moved closer still.

Let. History. Lie.

The wood was warped and well on its way to becoming charcoal but the illustrations were visible, even there in the dim light of the closed-off feretory down in the cathedral's most obscure dark corner.

It was the figure of Jesus, crudely carved by contemporary standards, but clearly Christ nonetheless. My heart was a drum as I saw that he was surrounded by what I immediately understood to be symbols representative of four evangelists, and also acknowledged without hesitation it to be the oldest example of decorated wood to have survived from this period – which is to say, in all probability, seventh-century Saxon.

Closer inspection revealed deeper detail: also carved upon the coffin by the woodman's scrieve were the twelve apostles themselves – viz. Matthias, Bartholomew, Simon *et al* – along with five archangels, and furthermore at the foot of this rotting sarcophagus, the Virgin and child. Though the illustrations had a barbaric air about them, the figures also displayed a Mediterranean influence – Christ himself, for example, appeared to conceivably be carved in the manner of earlier, most probably fifth-century Hellenic origins. There was also upon what remained of the coffin's lid an iron ring some four inches broad and used for lowering (or raising) this appalling eternity trunk.

For the first time in my life when confronted with the Jesus figure I experienced a great wave of revulsion that heightened my consternation into one of utmost terror; it was a wave whose repugnant undertow threatened to drown me so completely that I might never return to full mental capacity.

Again I heard the warning previously unheeded – *Let. History. Lie.* – and again I heard the chanted litany of names once unrecognised – *Stither. Ungred. Eedmah.* – but now they were made clear to be the foot soldiers of the saint himself, those monks

344

who comprised the so-called Cuddy community: Brother Stitheard, Brother Hunred, Brother Eadmer, not to mention Edmund, Franco and Chad, whose names joined this haunted census now in a polyphonic chorus of whispers and warnings that grew so enormous in their totality that it took the strongest of will to stop myself running from the cathedral screaming like a stricken soul bound for Bethlem.

My grip upon all reason and reality was loosening.

Oblivious to my plight, the others continued with their frantic excavation quite unaware – or uncaring – of the fear in whose grip I found myself, as the whispered voices of the chant rose to bellows and then into howls as loud as the bells that occupied the belfry high above us, and then something quite peculiar happened. As quick as a candle being snuffed, all colour drained from my eyes. Just like that the world was cast anew as monochromatic and became little more than an appalling gradient of greys that would never again be replenished with the more vibrant hues of the palette.

My mind rattled like a trapped rat.

The men removed the mass, the mess. Without thought or care they lifted the spoiled coffin from the grave and my protestations were nothing but a ghost in my throat, and the architecture of the world was cast into shadows.

Once this saint lay beneath silk, but now he lay exposed, naked beneath the eyes of heartless interlocutors.

Let. History. Lie.

The reverends and their men were making much noise and fuss now as they attempted to raise the entire discovery upon trestles and keep it intact, which was a futile effort for lumps of coffin were shearing away as they did so and falling to the stone slabs around it.

Finally they reached a consensus of sorts as Fraine and Parnell managed to lift a portion of what was left of the lid, and I hardly dare report further.

But I must. I *must.*

There in the coffin lay a mounded mass, a dark substance in the shape of a small man.

o Cuddy

Cuddy o

Let. History. Lie.

It was he.

My eyes widened to take in the whole of this dead saint who had shaped a region, steered a religion, defined a people, a country.

Only then did I see that, gathered at the foot of this desecrated morass of coffin layers, accursed soil and fragments of robe, there were a number of bones. Time's disturbance and the subsiding of the land had shifted the framework of the decomposing saint to one end, and gathered him there in a small pile of bones.

Indeed it was he. The beatified Cuthbert.

Cuddy corrupted.

Cuddy disturbed.

Man as osseous matter.

Let. History. Lie.

For a fleeting second or two I saw tarsals and vertebrae and clavicles and ribs and perchance the cracked dome of a yellowing skull, and there were several articles placed about the body that a better antiquarian, a better *man* than I, would take time to document, but I was no longer of myself, and all critical faculties had been swept away forever, lost beneath a tidal wave of fear and mania.

Because colour, as I say, was wiped from my mind and erased from capacity forever, all joy ruined. Never again would I appreciate the vermilion crest of spring's first woodpecker, the bluebells of June, a pinkening harvest moon. Fear shivered through me as I wondered what sense other than sight might be the next to go.

Then the men fell upon their bounty with such fervour that my view was crowded out, and I was too stricken to move my leaden limbs.

Time-crumbled wood and soil-soured bones and the damp rot of death-earth; all was a mess in this hallowed stone place and still I was clinging to a pillar for support, all faculties failing.

This was only a backdrop for something far more horrific however, as it was then that I saw him again. Over there he stood, pressed tight into the darkest corner of the chapel, unseen by all but I, the lad with the swarthy visage; the lad whose presence has confused my humours, capsized my mind and tempted me with desires I previously thought buried forever. The lad who has done nothing less than stalk and haunt and torment me. Inhabit me.

It was he with the eyes of an owl and a demeanour not of this realm, he who might be the devil himself.

Let. History. Lie.

The lad looked different. His hellish face was a skull held beneath skin as thin and pale as parchment, his eyes as wide and dark as the sockets that held them. They spoke of emptiness. Suggested eternity.

He raised one arm as if in benediction and he looked right at me, he looked through me, he looked beyond me and into all the centuries that would follow from this moment. And he spoke.

'Let *his story* lie.'

And everything became black.

This last entry, I confess, is a lie. It was not written on the evening of the excavation on May 17 but was instead constructed piecemeal from the shattered mind of an unwell man over the intervening weeks that followed a complete nervous collapse, from which I am told I might never fully recover. Often I have managed a mere sentence before anxiety and terror have engulfed me once more here in my room at the sanatorium, and still I can't see colours.

Alas, that pleasure, like all pleasures, has been stolen from me.

But it matters not, for no eyes shall see this account. Instead I write these final words on a late summer's day of an unknown precise date, in this, our year of the Lord, devil or whatever other entity might exert malevolent influence over man, MDCCCXXVII, with dwindling hope that my sickened soul might yet be saved.

That it took the unleashing of something diabolical from the north country soil to make me consider the existence of one's soul is the single fragment of consolation. Certainly my scholarly career is over, as is any hope of normality. Everything in which I once believed now lies about me in fragments.

I pray only for this torment to end; I pray to a God I now believe in.

I record this only to alleviate the guilt that grows within as divine punishment for my involvement in this foul desecration, and a life of arrogance prior to deliverance.

I know not what became of the meddlesome Fraine, Parnell and co.

I know not what became of the remains of the Saint Cuthbert.

And I shall neither write nor speak of the matter again.

And though I should like never to think of it too, this remains an impossibility, for in dreams and waking nightmares I hear the chanting of the saint's tortured acolytes, the famed *haliwerfolk* – the wandering folk of the holy man – echoing ever onwards. Nor can I escape the feeling evoked by the stolid tyrannical influence of that terrible building on the hill overlooking the bend in the river. Contemptuousness and conceit drove me there, and now I must suffer the consequences.

Worst of all, the lad still visits me. A fugue state of sorts I may be trapped in, but it is one in which I am denied the luxury of either amnesia or silence. Instead he taunts me with his beauty. It is a seduction of sorts.

This I can write now, without fear, for no fear can be greater than that which sits at my core, leaden, poisonous and dreadful.

Nor does he age. He simply stares with those predatory eyes, and then he disappears around the darkest corners of my desirous mind. And still I follow him. Always, I follow him.

God looks on.

I close my notebook.

It shall be read by no soul.

Former Professor Forbes Fawcett-Black
FBA, FSA, MCIfA.

BOOK IV

Daft Lad

Durham. AD *2019.*

'As we pull
out of the station through the dusk and fog,
there, lighting up, is Durham, dog
chasing its own cropped tail,
University, Cathedral, Gaol.'

'Durham' by Tony Harrison

Underfoot, the ground feels as tight as a drum skin as he waits outside the station in the long dark minutes before the day's slow breaking.

He watches the early morning buses pause at the entrance for a frozen moment, and he sees the still-sleepy faces of the drivers framed behind glass, the taste of the first morning cigarette and last sip of coffee already stale in their mouths. A lingering wet scent of synthetic cherry vape smoke drifts on the forecourt too, but when Michael turns around there is no one there.

The bright lighting of the buses' interiors creates a harsh glossy hue to the skin of the drivers so that each appears as if coated in glossy grey wax. It makes him think of illness, decrepitude, decay and what he is leaving behind at home, and he has to train his mind elsewhere. Some of the men are unshaven, one bearded. All are white. They blink with heavy eyes, yawn unapologetically in the face of the indifferent day.

Another bus pauses at the junction, its brake mechanisms hissing like a cornered cat, and then the driver pulls out and takes a wide left onto a one-way street to begin another eight-hour shift criss-crossing the county lines.

It is cold. Michael feels it. He feels it because he is lean. It is in him, the cold, frosting his core. He tightens the drawstring of his hood.

The pavement is glittering with a dusting of ice and he can see his breath before him, a blossoming of warmth suspended in the cellar of the morning.

Michael's empty stomach feels sour with worry and doubt. It squirms like the eels they sell at the indoor market. He can taste something stringent and vinegar-like in the back of his throat, then swallows. It is the vile taste of abstinence, of hunger.

The remnants of last night litter the stained paving slabs of the bus station with all the signs and symbols of wanton hedonism. Tipped polystyrene fast-food cartons trail sliced meat, shredded red cabbage and chilli sauce the colour of blood. There is a stain of slopped curry too, and then close by some broken glass and a few drops of actual blood; each smeared deposit a separate story, still waiting to be told.

There is a strong stench of urine, the invisible scent markings of feral men after midnight staining the cold concrete. The stench of it is the perfume of bus stations everywhere; the desperate reek of transience at the crossroads of the intoxicated.

Michael's hands tremble slightly so he cups them to his mouth and blows. He holds his breath there as if it were a tiny bird. He stamps his feet and tries to recall a prolonged period when he wasn't almost entirely consumed by worry, or cold, or hunger – or all three. The latter two can be remedied with practical solutions, but not this nagging anxiety, so insistent that it has a real physical presence.

He stamps his feet again, blows into the bowl of his hands again.

A car pulls up to the kerb and a man leans over to wind down the passenger window. It opens in juddering movements. As he does, ash falls from his cigarette onto the seat. He looks at a clipboard.

'Michael?'

He dips his head to car level and nods.

'Aye.'

The man stares back. His face is drawn and in the morning gloom Michael can clearly discern the curve of his cranium beneath his scalp. Shadows carve sharp cheekbones and in this light the smooth concave hollows at his temples seem scooped out. There is something about this place, at this time of the morning when night is only just relinquishing its grip, that briefly gives everyone the appearance of cadavers, or revenants even.

'Have you got a hard hat and boots?'

'Yes.'

'Steel toe caps?'

'Yes.'

'Get in.'

Brushing ash from the seat, Michael folds himself into the car and closes the door behind him. They pull out from the station and into the empty road, into the flat blank morning.

Even though the man is sitting down, Michael can see that he is tall and lean, but knows that he is stronger than his appearance suggests. No flesh is wasted on him. Years of building sites will have made it so.

He is so tall that his knees are pressed up close to the steering wheel and his hair is worn short on top but long at the back, with a natural wave to it. It is a hairstyle that is a long way from once being fashionable, but neither is it being sported ironically.

'We don't talk first thing,' he says.

Michael shrugs, relieved to not have to engage in conversation.

Instead he looks out into the darkness as the ancient city slowly slips away behind them, a shrinking conurbation. A skin shed in the remains of the winter night.

The tall old houses of the city give way briefly to open spaces that act as a barrier between them and the newer buildings of the suburbs where the post-war houses squat, and close by are playgrounds, shabby shopping precincts and pubs whose names hint at the traditions of a rural past now well hidden – farming, brewing, hunting.

They pass retail parks where the gleaming logos of fast food companies and phone outlets tower above the largely empty car parks like neon spires scratching at the first fissures of light that strain behind the morning sky. Soon the larger anonymous sheds clad in corrugated sheeting will ring with the hushed chatter of call centre operators. Here are the contemporary hinterlands, the English anywhere.

Roundabouts lead to B-roads and then to country lanes fringed by hedges that are frozen white. It is even colder out here and everything appears tight, brittle and contracted beneath the rime of winter. Michael's moiling stomach admonishes him for its neglect with a long growl.

After a while the man lights another cigarette and offers Michael one. He shakes his head and the man smokes for a while and then he says: 'I'm Chadwick. Have you got bait? Where we're going there's no shops nearby so it's too late anyway.'

Before leaving the house Michael had taken the last Pot Noodle in the cupboard, along with an apple and a packet of Digestives. They were in a carrier bag that was stuffed down in the footwell now.

'Yes,' he replies.

Michael only very briefly wonders whether Chadwick is his Christian name or his surname but doesn't linger on the thought.

'There's no shitter either, except the scrubland. But there's plenty of that, and the bog roll's provided at least. You can take a trowel. We're not animals.'

The man glances at him sideways as if seeking a reaction or a response, and for a moment it looks as if he is about to say something else, but then he changes his mind, frowns and instead concentrates on the road.

They head north and west and north again and the day slowly lightens. They drive for a long time and the frost is even thicker on the road. It hangs from the hedgerows as if Christmas has come early, out here where the white fields stretch away on either side.

Chadwick grips the wheel with one hand. He hawks up some phlegm and it rattles around the corridor of his throat before he winds down his window and spits it out. It flies away, a string lost to their velocity. He closes the window again.

'Do you speak English?' he says.

Michael bites the inside of his cheek. He looks at him and nods.

'Yes. Of course.'

'Just checking. I thought you could, but some of the boys we take on barely can and I have to talk slowly. I'm not racist, it's just things take longer to explain, that's all. Best to work all that stuff out up front. Who's who and what's what, I mean.'

Remembering something, Chadwick shakes his head and speaks again.

'We had two Poles go at it a fortnight or so back. Cousins. One brained the other with a scaffold clamp. He peeled part of his face off like a strip of mouldy old wallpaper. It was family business, nothing to do with me or any of the other lads, so we sat it out for a bit. I think it was some feud that went way back to the motherland. A vendetta. We had to step in though when one was about to cave in the other's skull with a breezeblock. We smoothed it all out on the down-low, mainly so that the insurance company didn't find out.'

Chadwick goes quiet for a moment and Michael knows he has something else to add to the story because it is almost as if he can hear him thinking. Chadwick has one of those faces.

'Good workers though, the Poles. Loyal. Tough as titanium too. Most of them only come over for a couple or three years to send the money back home. Some of them are building houses back there. Good luck to them, I say. Did I ask if you've got a hard hat and boots?'

'Yes.'

'Because if you haven't, we can't use you.'

'I've got them.'

Chadwick looks at him for a moment and Michael turns to the window, to the rigid hawthorn hedges, the frozen fields.

'Do you have a record?' asks Chadwick.

Here and there are glimpses of lone farms down single tracks, with black barns or grain towers sitting beside them. These places are set back far from the road, statements of seclusion that are a long way from anything.

'A record?'

Sometimes Michael spots large piles of old tyres or rusted hulks of machinery too, twisted like sculptures in the farmyards where chickens strut and stagnant silage puddles gather. They suggest lonely places harbouring quiet lives.

'A criminal record.'

Michael shakes his head as Chadwick picks up the previous conversational thread.

'Yes. We've less English lads these days.'

Michael shifts in his seat but stays silent.

'Do you know why?'

Still looking out the window, Michael shakes his head again.

'No.'

'Well it's not about foreigners taking jobs, though some people will tell you otherwise. It's not that at all. It's because they're lazy dossers, that's why – and I say that as an Englishman. Our lads don't want the work. They can't be bothered. They'd rather be sat at home smoking dope and fannying about on Facebook or playing their stupid computer games. Imagine that: grown men sitting indoors with the curtains shut, playing with kiddies' toys. It's pathetic. Give me an Albanian, a Pole, a Czech or a Romanian any day. These boys are not only grateful for the work but the clutch of notes they get in their hand at the end of the week too. Plus, they've got stamina. They're grafters. The English lot are usually either too skinny or too fat. They're good for an hour or two then that's it, they're all out of puff. *And* they're always late. Excuses guaranteed, every time. Me, I've heard them all, let me tell you. We're screwed if conscription ever comes back.'

'I'm not lazy,' says Michael.

Chadwick stubs out his cigarette in the ashtray. It smoulders there and in the far distance Michael sees a ray of sun move across a low hill like a searchlight seeking an escapee from the night.

'I'm not saying you are, son. I'm not saying you are. I'm just talking from experience. Because half the Englishmen who end up on my sites these days are a whingeing slothful breed. The other half are OK I suppose.'

358

'I just want to earn some money.'

'Well, your timekeeping is good, and you look like you know how to keep your trap shut. You've got that going in your favour. So let's see how you get on, shall we.'

&

It is a demolition job. They are knocking down some old warehouses built on a barren bed of asphalt down a dead-end track in amongst fallow fields that seem to stretch for miles in all directions.

The defunct and dilapidated warehouses comprise the remains of what was once a small industrial estate that is soon to be replaced by a larger industrial estate and, alongside that, an even larger retail park. The assembled crew constitutes a clearance team of old hands and young men like Michael; they are mindless muscle, hired to dismantle and destroy that which a machine cannot do quite as carefully.

A hundred or so metres away, across the road that leads all the way back into the city, Michael can see that the foundations have already been dug for the industrial units and, beyond them, the looming forms of the nascent buildings of more retail outlets are already rising up and reaching for the ash-white sky, half-finished constructions full of commercial potential.

Over there he can see thick wet concrete is being poured into the trenches of the frozen earth and billboards surround the site, promising new branches of B&Q, KFC, Currys, Sports Direct and a drive-thru McDonald's, everything a household needs, and in close proximity, where once cows idly grazed the pastures. Soon, as early as the coming spring perhaps, the mirrored panels that are about to be erected will reflect a thousand suns, and customers will arrive before the grass seeds that will be planted in the landscaped strips of soil have even come to fruition. They won't have to endure the inconvenience of walking far from their cars. Much money will be made here.

Michael thinks about Chadwick's description of the Englishman, and wonders whether it is fair.

Chadwick is the foreman overseeing the men. He gives Michael a sledgehammer and a neon gilet to wear, then leads him to the lower remains of a half-wrecked outbuilding that is now just several walls standing in a morass of breezeblocks and rubble. He explains that Michael's job is to demolish whatever is left and then move the rubble into a series of skips.

'Mind those wooden beams are kept intact though,' he says, gesturing to the collapsing latticed framework of the building's roof. 'We can sell them on to wankers for their barn conversions.'

He walks away and spends half an hour pacing and smoking while jawing quietly, yet aggressively, into his phone.

It is eight when Michael starts and he works all morning, swinging the hammer and then shovelling the broken brick into a barrow, which he wheels across the frosted asphalt and up a narrow plank into a skip. He builds up a steady rhythm and is soon sweating despite the cold. Other men are grafting close by and though some of them seem to know each other, and exchange words or periodically pause to relight roll-ups that have gone out, they do not speak to Michael. They do not even acknowledge him, and he is glad to be anonymous, invisible. He likes to be able to retreat inside himself and avoid the distraction of conversation. Routine and repetition, he knows from experience, are what help get the work done and the day over with. Solitude and silence simplify everything; movements become reduced to the bare essentials in order to minimise the peaks and troughs of exertion, and ultimately conserve energy. Most men working on sites know this the world over.

Now and again he stops to catch his breath and wipe his brow. He sees that the winter sun is like a dull pewter plate; it gives off little heat and light – just enough to briefly thaw all but the most shadowed frozen corners of the fields.

At half past ten the men seem to respond to some unseen signal and simultaneously down tools and trudge to a metal container where there is a large tea urn, chairs and newspapers. Some of them swap cigarettes, and one or two eat their sandwiches. Michael drinks two cups of tea and eats four biscuits while looking out across the flatlands.

At lunchtime he returns to the metal container and pours water from a boiled kettle into his Pot Noodle. He stirs it, adds a sachet of sauce and then slowly eats it, followed by six more biscuits. He drinks a pint of water so cold it makes his teeth ache and his temples throb. Then he has the best part of another.

The sweat is cooling on his back and he doesn't like sitting in the gloom of the metal container with the changing-room smell of the men strong in there, so he goes for a walk. Michael leaves the site and heads out across a scrubland of rubble, broken glass and old hardcore that has been cast aside during the demolition, and into an ocean of dry grass blown flat by the winter winds.

He wades out into it, and the sharp needles of the stalks brush against his workpants. Far out into the middle of the field one of his ankles cockles on the rough, rutted mud underfoot and he stumbles for a moment, his arms flailing. He catches himself, glad that his comical near-pitfall has gone unseen, and glad to be far away from the men and the inevitable quips and smirks that would follow.

Michael takes out his phone and calls his mother. It rings for a long time and he has that familiar flash of fear, that tightened knot of worry deep inside of him, before the line clicks and she is there, her voice sounding surprised to be receiving a phone call as it always does, even though it is always him, always at the same time. And there's the long silent pause as he pictures the phone being raised to meet her mouth.

'How are you feeling, Mam?

'OK, love.'

'Better or worse than yesterday?'

He can see his breath as he speaks; he admires the shape of the warm air from within him as it swirls in the cold clear day, then becomes something else. Something beautiful. The fields run for as far as he can see. Grass stalks snap like icicles.

She makes a non-committal noise.

'The same.'

Michael kicks at the ground. He toes the stiff gluey dirt and feels it give a little. His boot goes through the sticky skin of it. In the distance, towards the city, the sky is weighted with streaks of white clouds pregnant with tonight's snow.

'Have you watched anything good this morning?'

Questions, he thinks. Questions are the engine of conversations. They keep them going.

She hesitates before replying, as if it is a quiz that she wants to do well in. Her voice is thin. It sounds translucent, like something stretched.

'It's mainly antiques programmes, love. I watched something about a couple who were wanting to buy a holiday home abroad.'

'Where was that?'

'I think perhaps it was Portugal.'

'Did it look nice?'

'Oh yes, very nice.'

'Nice and hot.'

'Yes.'

'Did they find anywhere?'

She pauses.

'I don't remember. I'd nodded off when you rang.'

Michael looks at the clouds. He remembers the excitement of seeing a fresh snowfall in his childhood, and wishes he could feel it again. Maybe he will in the morning, though he is already feeling anxious about having to rise in the dark to get to the station in time. He knows he's lucky to get a lift from Chadwick. Without it – without his own transport – he would have to face another week without work.

'Have you eaten?' he asks.

'A little.'

'Did you have the porridge pot?'

'A little.'

'Make sure you eat some more.'

'I'll try.'

'It helps with the medication.'

'OK.'

'It's easier on your stomach.'

'Yes.'

'If it's gone cold pour some hot water from the flask into it.'

'Yes, son.'

Michael turns back to the site and sees the men swilling out their steaming mugs and stubbing out their cigarettes to return to work. They are of different sizes, nationalities and ages, but all wear the regulation international uniform of hard hats, luminous gilets and rigger boots.

Beyond them, over at the big building site, he watches as a huge crane is slowly inched into position. He thinks of the land beneath it, the sturdy long-wintered soil that supports the weight of this great piece of machinery, and he thinks of the animals that will surely be displaced by all this activity. The rabbits and the badgers, the unseen trails of the roaming fox. Deer too, retreating to the shrinking copses. He thinks of the birds that will take flight at the surprise of the noises to come. There will be crushed nests, hastily vacated, and shattered eggs, when some of the perimeter trees are felled, their branches tipping out squirrels and their roots ripping away at subterranean setts.

The flags are already planted to mark out what will be the central car park around which the retail units are being built, each as big as a parish church. He bites the inside of his cheek.

Michael thinks of mice and rats and bats and hares and shrews and voles and hedgehogs; he thinks of all the indigenous creatures of northern England having to navigate metal and glass, new roads and cars that scream from nowhere like fiery hellions tearing through the night. He thinks of them modifying their ancient patterns of behaviour as their worlds shrink and become noisier, more violent. He thinks of displacement.

He knows it is nothing new, and that his thoughts are probably stuck in a past that he never even knew, and that he was surely born in the wrong age, but that doesn't make it any easier.

'I'll be back as soon as I can this evening,' he says.

'OK, love.'

'Will you be alright until then?'

He knows what the question really means. Without acknowledgement, they both know and there is a moment's silence before his mother speaks in a very quiet and small voice.

'Don't worry about me,' she says. 'You just enjoy your work, pet.'

And that afternoon he does, or at least he enjoys the fact he is trusted with the responsibility of being left alone again. He likes the brute force needed to break bricks and haul barrows too, work that a machine has not yet entirely replaced. The simplicity goes beyond thought. Instead it is all might, a simple process of exertion. And he likes the repetition of it, the ritual of bending and stretching, smashing and sweeping. Wheeling and tipping. The back and forward and back again. He likes the weight of the cold barrow's handles in his hands and the calluses that are already forming there, the wheels turning over ground that has softened to a stiff wetness and the sound the airless tyres make as they cut through it. He likes the scrubbing blank of a busy mind, for a while at least.

Now and then Michael is called upon to help others lift large pieces of paving slabs or manhandle concrete lumps and in these moments he is briefly part of a coordinated team united by a common goal, but mainly he is by himself, breaking blocks and filling the barrow, grey dust rising with each wobbling load that he guides up the plank and upends into the skip. His joints feel the strain. His arms ache and the winter sweat cools when he pauses for more than a few moments. The cold fresh air is like a thousand tiny blades when he inhales it into his young clean lungs. It is a feeling of freedom.

They clock off at four and leave the site, some in shared cars, others on foot and one man on a motorbike with a helmet-less passenger riding pillion.

Michael walks to Chadwick's car and stands around for a few minutes until he arrives and looks at him blankly for a moment as if trying to remember who Michael is.

'Am I OK to get a lift back into town?'

Chadwick looks a moment longer, then lights a cigarette and shrugs. He slowly exhales smoke into the fading light.

'It's no sweat off my balls. But don't be expecting lifts every day. I'm not a taxi service.'

He gets into the car.

Michael follows.

It is dark by the time they reach the city. Winter dark. After he has been dropped at the bus station Michael waits until Chadwick has left and then he sets off for the long walk back.

He strides along the streets with the tall town houses where the academics and doctors live, finding the rhythm to take him home, and then he moves further on through the quiet, clean estates that circle the city. The streets are familiar but once removed from his experience; they hold the lives of people he will never know. Then the estates end suddenly and he walks through a great dark nothingness of desolate footbridges and dual carriageway embankments, and the orange lights of villages and towns twinkle from several miles away. The road rises and falls with gentle undulations.

Michael takes a shortcut across a field where the grass has frozen stiff again, and he sees that a hoarfrost is already appearing on branches around him as the temperature continues to drop.

His stomach growls, a sour and empty plea into the plummeting night. He saved his apple until mid-afternoon but it was barely enough to sustain him and his limbs feel hollow yet leaden. He walks for well over an hour and the final ten minutes are along a road where the street lights had been switched off by the local council years ago. When a car passes by at speed he has to stop and press himself into a hedge, the driver shocked to see a pale face momentarily staring from the December gloom.

By the time he reaches the village he is glad of the familiar glowing sign of the supermarket. He pulls his hoodie down and with numb fingers pushes open the door and the woman behind the till looks up and nods and says 'Hiya, Michael' as he picks up a basket and gives a slight wave of a hand.

He walks the aisles. He buys chicken fillets, a tin of tomatoes, another of potatoes. He selects the cheapest tin of sweetcorn and half a dozen porridge pots and half a dozen Pot Noodles. The bags of oats and packets of noodles are cheaper, but the pots are handier for his purposes. He buys more apples and toilet roll, packet blancmange and bread, Digestives and cat food. Toothpaste. He buys soup. His hand hovers over a large bar of chocolate while he makes mental calculations, then decides against it.

The woman at the till is called Kath. Kath McGrillis. Kath packs his bag for him.

'How's your mam, Michael?' she asks. 'I've not seen her around the way for a bit.'

'She's fine,' he says while eyeing the same chocolate bars that are on display on the counter.

Kath's daughter had been in his year at junior school and he remembers how once in the dinner hall she got a fork stuck between the gap in her front teeth and began to cry. This incident spawned a nickname that he can no longer recall, given to her by a rat-faced boy called Billy Yalden, a nickname that stayed with her for years, right through school until she was sixteen, by which time many of her classmates couldn't recall the origins of the moniker either. The image of the crying girl with the fork sticking from her mouth, and the other kids laughing at her, has stayed with him though, and he thinks of it almost every time Kath McGrillis is working the till. He wants to ask her if she remembers what her daughter was nicknamed, but he knows it was something cruel and unjust, and perhaps she never even told her mother about the long-standing humiliation, and also Michael is too tired for conversation, even though he has barely spoken all day. Billy Yalden died in a stolen car at seventeen, the vehicle crushed like a concertina at dawn into a concrete bridge support on the A1M somewhere north of Chester-le-Street, just past the services where Michael once did a few days' demolition work to make way for a new Burger King.

'Keeping well then, is she, that's good,' says Kath.

'Aye.'

'Tell her I said hiya.'

'I will.'

'And you?'

'Fine,' he says, rifling through his pocket. 'Good.'

He pulls out an electricity meter card and counts out what money he has left beyond what he has budgeted for food. He has twelve pounds and change.

'Could you put a tenner on this as well please?'

Michael passes her the card and the money, and while he is distracted and fumbling with the change and zipping up his coat, Kath slips a bar of chocolate into his bag of shopping.

🕯

He awakens to pitch-black silence and the feeling that he is pressed to the bed. Pinned to the mattress like a butterfly in a case, he thinks. His body is flagging from fatigue. He feels drawn down by it, as if the gravitational pull has doubled. There are aches everywhere – in his left knee and right shoulder and in his ankle; too many aches for a young man. The calluses throb too, though they are at least preferable to the raw blisters that ran across his hands last year when he began labouring.

And then his mind clicks into gear and begins to whir with the slowly accelerating cycle of ruminations, worries and anxieties.

He thinks of his mother downstairs and resists checking on her, and instead lies in silence until the alarm on his phone lights up the corner of the room with a blue glow, and its vibrations become too insistent to ignore. He deliberately put it out of reach to ensure he had to get out of bed.

When Michael looks in on his mother in the front room she is propped up against her pillows, her breathing shallow. But he is glad to hear it. He is relieved to hear the tight rattle of phlegm against flesh.

He boils the kettle and makes a porridge pot and eats it while standing at the kitchen sink and looking at his reflection in the mottled mirror of the window. His face appears washed out, a sallow shape distorted by a pattern of grime on the glass and the reflective glare of the dim bulb. His eyes are hollow scoops. He thinks of that howling man in the famous painting. He thinks of the drawn and haunted faces of the dawn bus drivers beneath the too-bright lights of the station. He thinks of his mother, through there.

Beyond his reflection he sees that the dawn winter darkness is illuminated slightly by a thin layer of snow that has fallen in the night.

He turns on the slow cooker and then puts the chicken fillets in there, followed by the tins of tomatoes, potatoes and sweet-corn, then he adds some brown sauce, salt and pepper and several mugs of water. He places the lid onto the cooker, checks that it is on a low heat, and throws the empty tins into a bin bag on the floor. He refills two bowls by the back door with fresh water and cat food and checks the cat flap is not locked into place. He has not seen the creature for days. By habit, he checks the reading on the electricity meter; if he moderates the heating to short bursts there is enough credit for several days.

Michael makes another porridge pot for his mother and sweetens it with some brown sugar, and puts the lid on it. He places it on the table beside her bed, next to her spectacles, cross-word book and tissues.

He empties her bedpan, refills her jug from the tap and her flask from the kettle and then puts some of his Digestives on a plate for her. He grates an apple into a bowl and adds a handful of raisins and leaves that too within reach. There are drinking straws for her. He makes sure that her phone is charged. He checks her credit, and places the remote control for the TV next to her food.

He also scans her medication chart and counts out the nine tablets that she has to take, and puts them in a cup on her table.

He wakes her with a kiss on the brow and a whisper: 'Mam, I'm away now.'

His mother's large, almost owl-like, dark brown eyes – the oversized eyes he has inherited (he does not know, cannot know, what he takes from his father) – flutter open. For a moment her dark pupils search for recognition, and then when it comes a spark ignites within and she attempts a smile. He briefly recognises a previous version of her; the younger woman she once was, full of life and laughter, even during the hardest of times.

'It's early.'

'Yes. I've got to get going for work.'

'But you just got back.'

Michael smiles.

'It feels that way,' he says. 'I slept like a lamb though. Shall I open the curtains for you yet?'

She reaches for his hand but it is an awkward action and he ends up enveloping hers instead. It is cold and clammy. He can feel the pulse of her heart in the thin worms of her veins. Her hand feels like a prop, a joke-shop appendage. He can see into her, the inner workings.

'Have you eaten?'

'Don't worry about that, Mam. You're the one that has to eat.'

'Have you though?'

'Yes. And I've put a stew on for later. A right tasty stew.'

'Because you need your strength.'

He leans against the metal frame of the bed for a moment, rolls his T-shirt sleeve up and flexes a lean bicep. He turns his wrist to make the brief ball of muscle bulge and turn.

'I'm Mr Universe, me.'

She offers a strained smile.

'I'm sorry I'm not up and about to make your breakfast, pet.'

They both know she has not been up and about to make his breakfast for months.

'You don't need to do that. I'm a modern man. Gender equality and all that.'

'Well,' she sniffs. 'Still.'

He stands and straightens, pushes his sleeve back down.

'Is there anything else I can get you?'

She winces and shakes her head.

'Are you hurting?'

'No,' she lies.

'Here, let me do your pillows. And you should take some tablets now. That's what they're there for.'

Michael helps his mother lean forward and then he lightly primps and punches the pile of flattened pillows that hold the small shape of her back into a more solid supporting mass. She falls back into it.

He hands her four pills and water. She takes them in an upturned hand, as small as a crab on its back, stranded at low tide.

'Here,' he says. 'Dr Cuthbert's orders.'

She swallows them and she is so thin it is almost as if he can see the tiny tablets moving down her throat.

'You've the bedside manner of a doctor,' she says.

He takes the water from her.

'I'll call you at lunchtime. Your pan is just down here. Can you reach it?'

She waves him away.

'You'll be late.'

'You've got my number.'

She waves him away again.

He kisses her and says goodbye and thinks, don't go, not today. Not yet.

Not today.

⌘

Michael leaves the house and walks the three miles to the bus station. It is still night and though he could stand waiting in the numbing cold for the first bus into the city, by walking he saves the fare and warms up for the day of physical labour that lies ahead.

Chadwick is late arriving so they drive quickly, and he smokes all the way, not speaking. His mood seems more sour than yesterday. Michael once again watches the city disintegrate into the suburbs and then the suburbs give way to the fields and the hedgerows, each frosted with a dry dusting of fresh crisp snowfall.

Michael works all day. He swings the hammer and fills the barrow with rubble, and then he pushes the barrow up a ramp into the skip, and tips it. He does this thirty-nine times in the morning and thirty-three in the afternoon. Michael knows this because he counts. Counting imposes a system of order and breaks the day down into increments. Counting is a form of control. It is calming, like prayer.

Sometimes he has conversations inside his head with people who he likes to imagine might be interested in hearing his thoughts.

Only once does he overfill the barrow and it slips off the ramp, spilling its contents sideways. Then he slowly refills it and begins again.

He works at a steady pace. Chadwick has already pointed to the shell of another warehouse building and told him that that is next.

At lunchtime he goes for another walk and calls his mother. She answers on the fourth ring.

'How are you feeling?'

'OK, love.'

'Better or worse than yesterday?'

'The same.'

'Have you eaten?'

'Some.'

'The porridge?'

'A little.'

'Did you put any treacle in it?' Michael asks.

'No, no treacle.'

'Have you had any biscuits?'

'No, pet.'

'Have a biscuit.'

'I'm not so hungry right now.'

'Go on, have a biscuit. You need to keep your strength up. Or you could have the grated apple.'

'Maybe later.'

There is a pause and then his mother speaks again.

'The stew smells good.'

'We can have some later. I'll be back as soon as I can.'

'That would be nice. And there's tinned fruit for afters.'

There was another pause.

'Has Mister Shanks been in?' asks Michael.

'Yes. He's sitting on me now.'

'He needs a flea treatment.'

'He's alright. He's purring like a little engine.'

He can hear his mother making consoling noises to the cat whose back legs were left bandy after it was hit by a Deliveroo moped as a kitten: 'Here puss, puss.'

There is a pause and then his mother says:

'Before you go –'

He already knows what she is going to ask. It is something that he has been doing for her since he first set up her bed in the living room in early summer. It feels a lifetime ago.

'Describe the day for me, love.'

'It's cold,' he says. 'Colder than yesterday, but clear too.'

'Are you wrapped up?'

'Nice and warm.'

'And what can you see?'

'Fields for miles. There's been snow and it has lightened the day. There's a bit of sun and it's reflecting off it so that it looks like there is a second sky sitting below the clouds, and they look like they're fit to bursting with snow.'

'Any animals?'

'A lot of crows. Or maybe they're rooks. They're quite a way off in the distance, filling the branches of a copse in the middle of some faraway farmland.'

He doesn't describe the building site or the beginnings of the retail park of the development over the road behind him. It is not diggers and cranes and concrete that she wants to hear about, but weather and animals, the sky and the soil, images that will transport her back to her childhood in a small farming hamlet in the uplands of the county. True north country.

'Oh, I can see a hare,' he says.

It is a lie, but it doesn't matter.

'A hare, really?'

'Yes, it made a dash across the frozen furrows of a field, but it has stopped and now it is looking this way.'

'Oh, Michael.'

'It's big. Much bigger than our Mister Shanks. Bigger than Joan's terrier, even.'

Joan is their next-door neighbour.

'Hares are magical.'

'I know,' he says. 'I think it has come out just to see us.'

'What's it doing now?'

'Just sitting on its back legs, sniffing the still air. It's beautiful, Mam. You should see it.'

'I *can* see it,' she says.

For a moment Michael almost believes the hare to be real too, then he hears the voices of his colleagues and the sound of activity.

'Well I think I'd better get back.'

'A hare,' she says in a thin and tiny voice full of wonder.

#

At the end of the week Chadwick drops Michael back at the bus station. Only when they pull in does he speak. He cuts the engine and lights a new cigarette straight from his existing one. There is frost on the inside of the windscreen and his eyes wear the strain of a lifetime of early mornings.

'Where did they send you last week?'

'An abattoir.'

Chadwick looks at him, incredulous. Michael nods.

'An abattoir? Doing what?'

'Mucking out, mainly. Mopping blood, shovelling offal. Fetching buckets here and there.'

'Don't you need a hygiene certificate to do that?'

Michael shrugs.

'No one asked for one.'

'What was it like?'

Michael thinks about the boom and clatter of calves being corralled into death row – his smiling colleagues' name for the execution pit – and then the jolt of the electricity so sudden and so total that it made him flinch every single time. He thinks about the way the young cows' eyes rolled and how they looked with their throats slit, helpless yet suddenly less real somehow, like pantomime creatures, their life force pouring out in dark red ribbons from the gaping yawn of their wounds, then running down a series of drains that routinely became blocked with hair and meat, slobber and excrement. Then, a short while later, their bodies hung briefly from hooks ready for butchering; by evening they were scattered in parts, wrapped in plastic, ready for the ice-cold containers to take them off around the region.

And he thinks about that one man, the one short wide man, a former welterweight boxer, who used the carcasses as a punch-bag – 'just like Rocky' – while his workmates stood around laughing as he pounded the flesh.

Michael shrugs.

'It was a job.'

Chadwick shakes his head.

'Listen, how much have the agency got you on per hour here?'

'Minimum.'

'So – what – eight quid an hour?'

'More like six.'

'Six?' says Chadwick. '*Six*?'

'I'm nineteen. You get less when you're under twenty.'

'That's scandalous when you work just as hard as everyone else. Harder, in fact, judging by what I've seen. Some of the old boys who've been at it for a lifetime know better than to break a sweat. And what cut are the agency taking from that?'

'Taking?'

'What percentage.'

'I don't know.'

'Well I do, and you should. It's twenty-five per cent. Minimum.'

'That sounds about right.'

'So that's 25 pence on the pound. You can do maths, can't you?'

'Of course I can,' says Michael. 'I'm not thick.'

'Well you must be if the first two hours of every day is going straight into the pockets of those lazy bastards who never get their hands dirty. Think about it this way: right until your mid-morning brew-up you're working to buy someone's else lunch. And they'll be having something better than a bloody Pot Noodle, trust me.'

Michael shrugs.

'They get me the work. I need it. Need the cash. There's nothing I can do about it.'

Chadwick shakes his head.

'We all need the cash but there's plenty you can do, son.'

'But *you* do work for them though,' says Michael.

'Sometimes, but not always. Not entirely. And you've done a standard forty this week?'

'Yes. But then there's the travelling. It's a twelve- or thirteen-hour day by the time I get back home. Sixty-odd hours out of the house, more if there's overtime or weekend work.'

'Forget about the travelling. So forty hours at six pounds an hour brings you in at £240, minus agency commission. Then there's the national insurance and tax. And rightfully you should be giving me petrol money.'

'I didn't know about that.'

'Don't worry about that, son. You've kept your trap shut as requested so you're alright by me, and I was coming this way anyway. Listen, what are you doing next week?'

'I'm not sure yet. I've not thought about it.'

He has thought about it though. He has thought about it all week, wondering if there will be an income to pay for their food and bills and the extra painkillers and creams that his mother needs that the NHS subscription doesn't quite cover, and whether he'll have enough to get a new pair of work gloves and maybe a scarf too. And then there's Christmas, looming like a black obelisk against the white winter sun. That dismal day, dedicated to other people's happiness, just around the corner.

'They've not scheduled you in anywhere yet?'

'Not yet, no. Often I don't find out until the Sunday night. It depends.'

'Alright then,' says Chadwick. 'I happen to know that a pal of mine has some work going. Are you interested?'

'Maybe.'

'Don't you want to know what it is?'

Michael wipes his damp nose against the back of his hand.

'What is it?'

'More demolition.'

'OK.'

'And you won't have to hand over twenty-five per cent of your pay packet each week either. Or tell the tax man. It's cash in hand. Let's call it three hundred for the week, and if it finishes a day or two early you still get the same. It's not way out in the sticks either. How does that sound?'

'It sounds alright.'

'Just don't tell the agency.'

'But what if they call with work on Sunday?'

'Just make something up.'

'Like what?'

'Christ, like anything. Tell them you're ill. Tell them you've gone to fight the Taliban. Or join them.'

'They don't like it when you turn jobs down.'

'I doubt they like it when you join the Taliban either, though I expect they'd still try and get their cut if the money was good. Look, there's nothing they can do about it, son – it's your life, not theirs. Besides, I imagine you're hardly enamoured with the crap wages they pay. It's close to exploitation, and everyone does work on the side anyway. You're just clawing back at bit of dignity, that's all. Making up a shortfall. It's a moral issue. They don't own you.'

Michael speaks very quietly.

'I suppose I'll take it.'

'You don't have to.'

'Can you give me a lift to the site?'

Chadwick nods.

'OK then.'

'Just one thing,' says Chadwick. 'What do you know about asbestos?'

'Not much.'

'Probably just as well. I'll pick you up back here Monday. Good luck with the Taliban.'

🛎

He works for three days digging up damp asbestos that had been illegally buried just beneath the topsoil of a patch of post-industrial land only two miles outside of the city, close to where a billboard promises 'Exclusive luxury executive apartments – buy off-plan'. It is a small crew and the December ground is frozen solid. They have to build a big bonfire and then spread the coals over the sections that they need to dig, and then work quickly before the ground freezes. The hot ashes only soften the first couple of inches of soil, so someone arrives with blowtorches.

Michael doesn't understand why they are using such primitive methods when a digger could do the same amount of work as ten men, in a fraction of the time, but something about the project suggests secrecy and discretion so he does not raise the issue. Perhaps what they are doing isn't legal and he instinctively knows he needs to keep quiet if he wants to be paid. There is no hut for them but at lunchtime Chadwick appears with expensive teas and coffees in paper cups, and Michael eats cheap dry sausage rolls and apples and Mars bars to get him through the day.

The asbestos looks like pulped toilet paper and is frozen stiff. Apparently it is only dangerous if it is dry and airborne. 'Winter is on our side,' says Chadwick.

Above ground it has a blue tinge to it as it is thrown into a large skip that is covered with a tarpaulin, before being driven off at speed. There is a lot of asbestos, much more than any of them expected and no one on the crew is allowed to take photos or use their phone on the site. Whenever he needs to call his mother, Michael does so quickly and covertly. Chadwick remains on edge until Wednesday night, when the last of the unearthed waste is finally removed, and the soil is thrown back into place and patted down, and the crew leaves. He gives Michael an extra thirty pounds, so on the way home that night he goes to Franco's and buys fish and chips for himself and his mother, but when she tries to eat a chip and the crisp corner of battered cod that he carefully cuts for her she vomits a thin string of yellow gruel on herself and then cries quietly as he mops it up, and the snow falls heavier that night.

He sleeps late the next day and though the bedroom is freezing, for a prolonged moment Michael lies in a state of perfect benumbed stillness beneath his duvet. He does not need to get up for work.

But then as if a switch has been clicked, the familiar sense of dread kicks in again and it feels like a bouquet of flowers wilting within him. The colour drains from the day as the wheel of his mind begins to spin again until he climbs out of bed and hurries downstairs. Movement and activity is the only thing that stills it.

The front room smells sour. It reeks of rot and illness. Decay. A faint scent of bodily functions too. A shaft of soft winter light shines through a gap in the curtains and falls across his mother's hands, which are folded across her chest like two featherless baby birds embracing in the nest of the blankets. He stands watching her breath in her throat for a moment. She appears to him saintly.

Outside, snow sits thick over everything, softening the sharp angles and straight lines of garden fences, cars and lamp-posts. It weighs heavy upon telegraph wires and turns them into something else, and only the tiny footprints of a cat – Mister Shanks perhaps – have corrupted the soft carpet that covers the small sloping patch of their neglected front garden.

The cold lino in the kitchen sends a jolt through his bare feet and while the kettle boils Michael puts on two pairs of socks, then takes tea and toast through to the front room. When he speaks he can see his breath.

'Mam.'

He touches her wrist as if he were taking her pulse.

'Mam.'

She awakes suddenly, and her still face becomes frightful, a mixture of fear and complete confusion, her wide wet eyes searching his face for an answer to a question silently asked somewhere from deep inside her sleep, deep inside her illness.

'It's OK, Mam. It's me, Michael.'

There is a flicker of recognition, but then her eyes slowly close again and she tips her head to one side and appears to be fast asleep again. He is overcome with a profound sense of loneliness and unease at the thought that he needs to wake her, to feed her, to change her sheets and underwear. Seeing her naked and having to touch her clammy flesh, streaked in excrement and urine, makes him want to run from the house and never look back, but this thought then triggers a wave of guilt over the fact that he could even entertain the idea of abandoning her, even if just in a fleeting abstract way.

'Mam,' he says again. 'I've brought you some breakfast.'

He puts the tea and toast on the side and squeezes her hand.

He spends the next two days in the house, locked into a cycle of care. Cleaning, washing, feeding. He appears always to be moving, shifting soiled sheets and uneaten bowls of porridge. Administering pills and fetching blankets. Sometimes he stops and sits with her, and they talk a little, or he reads stories from the local newspaper – the magistrate's court round-up, minutes from WI meetings – but mainly his mother sleeps lightly, her eyelids twitching and the occasional painful groan rising up from inside her. This happens three times, and each sounds as lonely and horrific as the desperate calls of a faraway child trapped down a deep, dark well.

When she is lucid he raises the issue of home visits one more time.

'No,' she says, as gently emphatic as ever. 'I told you. No nurses, pet.'

'But –'

This time it is she who reaches out and takes his hand, and when his mother says 'It'll be over soon' he has to turn away and leave the room.

On Saturday evening Michael cooks a deep fill steak and ale Fray Bentos pie with some roast potatoes and a tin of marrow-fat peas. He crouches and intently watches the puff pastry rise through the grease-streaked glass of the oven door as if it were a gripping thriller, and then when it is ready he spoons a small portion from the tin into a bowl for his mother and sets it aside to cool. He takes his tea through on a tray and eats it while sitting in a chair next to her bed.

They watch the light entertainment TV shows, the singing-and-dancing shows with the judges and the drama, the bright neon lights and the tears and the screaming. When the news comes on he turns the sound off and takes the bowl, mashes the cold pie, peas and potato together and with a tea-spoon feeds tiny pieces of it to his mother. He is the bird now, feeding its helpless fledgling. A role reversal. She eats a little and they both watch the snow outside as it slowly falls from a loaded purple sky. Occasionally a car passes by and the only sound is the crumping of the soft fresh fall pressed flat beneath its tyres. Otherwise the burgeoning night is muted by the white quilting laid across everything.

The cat comes in through its flap. It is wide-eyed and stip-pled with wet flakes clinging to fur that is spiked in sharp tufts. Michael scoops it up to kiss its face, sniff its ears and breathe in the clean outdoor smell of it, the smell of winter stalking he thinks, and then he gently puts it down beside his mother, but the cat acts as if it can sense something is amiss and it imme-diately leaps to the floor and darts up the stairs where Michael knows he will later find it curled into a purring circle on his pillow.

Sometimes, in the summer usually, in the early hours when it returns from a night in the back fields, the cat, Mister Shanks, gently places a decapitated mouse there for him to discover upon waking. A silent sacrificial offering of gratitude.

Michael falls asleep in the chair beside his mother's bed and dozes for a while. When he wakes, two smiling Hollywood actors in expensive suits are being interviewed on a gaudy sofa by the excitable Irishman who can't seem to sit still and even though the sound is turned off he can see that none of the guests' laughter appears genuine.

The colours of the TV show casts the room in a changing glow of pinks and blues.

The front room smells of excrement and urine again. The snow falls again.

🕯

Late on Sunday afternoon, after he has washed and changed his mother's bedding, Michael cleans the kitchen and then uses the remainder of his cash to get just enough food in for the next few days and to top up the electricity meter card, and to pay for both of their phones for the week.

He is unpacking tins of vegetables and corned beef, cat food and apples when he receives a phone call. It is from the woman at the temping agency who always allocates work at weekends. She offers him three days' demolition in Gateshead. From here in the village he calculates that it will take a bus ride into the city, followed by a train ride and another bus journey at the other end and then a long walk or, failing that, two long and convoluted bus journeys in the opposite direction through a dozen little villages and hamlets far up in the highest backwaters of the county, and then down into the back end of the Tyne Valley. Either journey is entirely dependent on the various timetables matching up, and a guaranteed connecting service being available in the early pre-daylight hours in winter.

It's an 8 a.m. start. He takes it.

The phone rings again almost immediately. This time it is Chadwick.

'Now, lad.'

'Hello,' Michael replies.

'I've got more work for you if you want it.'

'When for?' he asks.

'Starting tomorrow. First thing.'

'I can't.'

'Why not?'

'I've just told the lass at the agency that I'd do three days' demolition.'

'The Gateshead job?'

Chadwick pronounces it the Geordie way. *Gate-seed.*

'Yes.'

'For basic.'

'I didn't ask.'

'You didn't ask?'

'No, I just assumed.'

Michael hears Chadwick sigh.

'And you're happy with that, are you?'

Michael doesn't reply for a moment.

'It's work. I need the money.'

'But this is what I'm saying, son. There's more money to be made out there than what the agency pay you. I thought I told you that. You were good last week. You got stuck in and you kept quiet. So now I'm rewarding you.'

Michael hears an odd noise in the background, a howl that could be from a child or dog or something else entirely. Chadwick turns away and says something to who- or whatever is in the room with him, but his voice is distant and muffled by his hand over the phone.

'Rewarding me?'

'Yes. I'm rewarding you by telling you that the gaffer at the 'Heed is a right tight bastard who's about two weeks away from going under, so he'll do anything to avoid paying his grunt-workers.'

'The agency sort all that out.'

'Aye, for a big cut, because they're a different set of bastards, with smiles and suits, but bastards all the same. In a way they're worse because they try and hide it, but they'd still slit your throat to save themselves a pound or two. Anyway, as it happens I've got a pal who's had a drop-out and he needs someone pronto, so I thought of you. That's the reward, you see: good work for good pay.'

'Doing what?'

'The same old shovelling and sweeping, but with a more delicate touch required. It's in a plum position too.'

'Where?'

'The Cathedral. That's why I thought of you. You're close by, aren't you?'

'Close enough.'

'And you don't seem like one of those lads who's likely to cuss and swear like an uneducated plank in the presence of holy folk. Like I say, a delicate touch. You'll have to work around whatever's going on in there: prayers and services and the like. Hushed tones and a sense of reverence is the order of the day here, son. Some fucking sensitivity. Also, it's for a fortnight minimum, so worth your while.'

'What's in it for you?'

'What's in it for me? That's what you ask before asking what's in it for yourself? You're a strange lad. But since you ask, a big drink and backstage passes to paradise from the big man upstairs are what's in it for me. Now, stop fannying around. I need to know asap.'

He pronounces this not as an acronym, but as a word. *Ay-sap.* Michael thinks of Chadwick's outdated haircut, the cloud of smoke that constantly seems to surround his head and the way he always drives one-handed.

'Two weeks' work, you say?'

'On a world heritage site, no less. Do you want it or not?'

Michael can hear the impatience in his voice.

'What will I tell the agency?'

'Christ, do we have to go through this again? Talking to you is like pulling teeth. I don't know and I don't care. Tell them your pipes have burst. Tell them your mother's dying.'

Deep inside him, Michael feels something crumble, like a thousand sudden tiny landslides at once. For a brief flickering moment a dire and almost overwhelming sense of loneliness consumes him.

'Hello?' says Chadwick 'Are you still there?'

'I'll take it.'

'Good. Get yourself there tomorrow at eight. Hard hat, boots, and no bullshit. Don't be late. Ask for Eddie.'

In the still darkness of a Monday morning, Michael walks at a brisk pace all the way from the village into the city. Pushing through the deep snow slows him down and it takes longer than usual, but the waking day is clear and beautiful and the clean air energises him. He breathes it in deeply and this time the cold feels like it is singeing his nostrils, and it reminds him of the time he once inhaled smelling salts too deeply during a chemistry lesson and it felt as if his skull was being scrubbed clean from the inside.

Wherever possible he takes alternate routes away from the main roads, cutting across frozen fields, following streams through narrow woodlands where the trickling flow makes a type of music through the frost-fringed sunken waterways, and he finds himself on an old cinder track that was once the old railway line but is now a cycle route, crunching a straight line for miles through his old childhood haunts in the country-side. He spent hours in these secluded nowhere places, usually alone, building imaginary worlds from nothing but branches and bracken.

Along the way he eats two apples.

At the back end of the city he keeps to the alleyways and side streets where possible, snatching glimpses of lives led in the big comfortable family homes that are afforded views clear across the rooftops to the cathedral standing stoic and solid on its wooded island hilltop.

Michael lets the climbing cobbled streets take him up to it and arrives, panting and clammy, at Palace Green. He stops to catch his breath and compose himself. He drinks from his water bottle. It is ten to eight; he set off walking at half six.

The tallest of the cathedral's three towers appears to grow and stretch before him to dominate the sky and skew all sense of perspective. It is covered in scaffolding and clad in a protective white sheeting, like wrapping paper on a present, which only makes it appear even more enigmatic, more coveted.

Michael is so distracted by the building that he wanders onto the neat clipped turf of the green and nearly stumbles over a KEEP OFF THE GRASS sign.

But he does not step back; instead Michael stands perfectly still in the centre of the quadrant of snowbound patch and tilts his head backwards, his hot breath billowing before him. His stomach creaks and gurgles from the breakfast of apples, and he fears that he might have to suddenly use a toilet, but still he does not move.

The vast edifice before him is enrapturing. Seen close-up rather than viewed as a distant silhouette or an apparition hastily glimpsed through the mist, it appears almost incomprehensible, a stunning visual and engineering feat made all the more impressive by its ability to dominate and dwarf all its close surroundings. Perhaps, thinks Michael, that was the intention of its creators, whoever they may have been – Were they monks? he wonders. Or builders? Were there young itinerant labourers like him all those centuries ago? – to give the impression of the cathedral having been born from the hill on which it stands, something expelled from stone like an overzealous fountain cast in rock, a ziggurat pushed and then stretched upwards towards the sun, a mountain squeezed from the bowels of the earth to be carved and sculpted in such a way as to evoke awe. No normal person, thinks Michael, could have conceived of such a structure, especially back in those dark times when people lived in primitive huts made from sticks and straw and mud, or single rooms that were little more than low heaps of stacked stones. He had seen a *Time Team* episode on it.

No, he thinks. This place must have been built by brilliant minds and fuelled by a faith in something bigger, a form of faith that he now wishes he too might experience.

And it is then that Michael remembers being brought here for the first time as a child; he recalls it now as if viewing a forgotten photograph, or a brief snippet of grainy silent film footage, but one comprised of feelings rather than shapes and colours.

He closes his eyes and in the image he is approaching the cathedral and his mother is there with him, but there is someone else too, a presence pressing down upon him at the edge of his peripheral vision. A dark shape of a man that is his father. A faceless being, he looks down at Michael and offers a large rough hand as they pass through the main entrance with its sturdy medieval door and famous Sanctuary Knocker, a horrific leonine face made from bronze that has been mottled green by centuries of changing weather, and which awaits him now.

Exhumed memory, this is one of the few recollections that Michael has of his father. All are vague and nebulous, a loose assortment of scents, feelings and textures rather than real, lived moments or experiences to savour and revisit. He is stunned that this new image – or rather this old image dusted down – has been stored in his mind until now, when it is dragged into the winter sunlight of the present moment. And he is saddened too, to think that he can recall the face of the knocker but not that of his father, which is reduced to nothing but a blank mask, a disembodied voice. Those rough hands.

Standing on the crust of snow that covers Palace Green, these thoughts make him anxious and fearful and he takes some slow deep breaths to bring him back into being; back in the moment of the winter morning.

Fearing he might be late or may yet need the toilet, Michael walks once around the perimeter of the green while continuing to inhale through his nose and out through his mouth in order to calm his thumping heart, then he enters the cathedral and steps back into a place that feels both familiar and mysterious, as if a hundred past lives are nodding to one another in wordless acknowledgement, the endless echoes of his ancestors' voices forever trapped in the stone.

🕯

His is indeed what Chadwick calls grunt-work; labouring, the likes of which puts Michael on this lowest rung on the hierarchical ladder of manual work. At the top are the cathedral's own team of stonemasons, who have been employed for nearly three years on a major renovation project that has included replacing the small sections of sandstone that have eroded over the centuries, much of them high up in the belfry, bell chamber and main tower.

Michael is told this by Eddie, who is actually called Edmund, and whose job it is to work directly under the cathedral's conservation architect, coordinating the renovations and managing a changing team of outside contractors brought in to work on a number of other improvements, from replacing rusted nineteenth-century iron railings with bronze ones, down to more menial but necessary tasks such as scaffolding maintenance, safety checks and instructing the unskilled work required of a dogsbody like Michael.

His role, Edmund explains in a friendly and measured manner that is quite unlike that of the usual gruff foremen he is used to out on the sites, is to do whatever is asked of him, by anyone: lugging gear, locating tools, running errands. It sounds like there is a lot less humping and hefting than Michael is used to, which is a relief. Edmund's demeanour is that of an academic or a historian, maybe even a vicar. Along with his slight frame and soft, earnest way of speaking, he is the exact opposite of those site managers who are used to mucking in to shift sacks of aggregate or pour tarmac, breaking up fights and dealing with payment disputes amongst an ever-changing crew of transient people with dysfunctional personalities: these are men who have achieved their managerial positions by being bullies or enforcers for the differing contract companies' unseen owners. Edmund appears entirely the opposite. This too is something of a surprise and relief.

'There are three particular things you must pay special attention to,' says Edmund, interrupting Michael's wandering train of thought. 'The first is tidiness and safety. You must make sure that nothing is left lying around that might be considered at best unsightly, and at worst, potentially hazardous either to the workers or members of the public.'

Michael nods at this.

'Secondly, do you smoke?'

Michael shakes his head.

'What about vaping? A couple of the chaps vape. Do you vape?'

'No.'

'Good. Because the good Lord frowns on synthetic fruit-scented smoke in His house.'

Michael doesn't know if Edmund is joking, as he says this with a straight face that is obscured by a beard in which a smile could get easily lost, so he chooses silence.

'Hugh said you were quiet and discreet –'

Hugh? thinks Michael. *Hugh?* Does he mean Chadwick?

'– and that's exactly the approach we need here, because not only is the cathedral a destination of pilgrimage open to members of the public the world over, but also a continued place of worship. Obviously, it remains a working building with daily services. A holy place and a sanctuary. Silence is cherished, and there's certainly no room for behaviour that might sour the hallowed atmosphere.'

'Of course,' says Michael.

'Finally the third and most crucial thing to remember is to keep the workers lubricated with libations at all times.'

Michael looks at him and wonders what he means, whether he is taking the piss.

Michael says, 'I'm not sure I understand.'

'Tea,' replies Edmund. 'Keep it flowing at all times. If an army marches on its stomach then these masons chisel on tea, and if they don't get their regular fix they get a bit tetchy. Coffee too. It's best to keep them happy; after all, they're part of the same noble tradition that helped build this ancient wonder in the first place. And now, you are too. A little tip for you if I may: bring them biscuits at all times, and in plentiful amounts and you'll have friends for life. Any problems, just let me know. You get an hour for lunch.'

Michael's eyes widen.

'An hour?'

'Is that not enough for you?'

'Oh, yes. I'm used to fifteen minutes.'

'Fifteen minutes is barely enough time to chew and swallow,' says Edmund. 'Quite inhumane. No, we like to do things right here. Do you have any questions, Michael?'

He shakes his head.

'Good. Then let's get you started.'

The building is so stunning and so beyond the scale of the rest of the city that Michael has to prevent himself from pausing every few metres to admire a new detail. Standing in the nave, a cavernous space that could hold his front room at home ten thousand times over, surrounded by worn wooden pews and carved columns that rise like the trunks of ancient oak trees, the soft December light streaming in through the decorative windows of stained glass – windows that appear to tell stories – makes Michael feel dizzy and weightless, as if his mind were moving outside his body.

When he steps into this vast vessel of stone that holds within it the hushed voices of reverent visitors, the soft lingering echoes of footsteps made by modern shoes on old stone cut by the hands of men who knew nothing of electricity or medicine or flight, and the gentle sounds of suppressed coughs or coins being dropped into collection boxes, it is, he thinks, akin to time travel. He feels himself falling backwards through eras and imagines his forefathers, robed men with their faces obscured by hoods, reaching out to catch him, and welcome him. It feels both strange yet familiar, unnerving but exhilarating.

It feels like – what?

It feels like coming home.

He works all morning, running errands. He brings tools to those who need them, removes waste, sweeps up, tidies, safety-checks that all cones and cordons are in place. As he suspected it is far easier than being out on the remote rural sites doing demolition, and therefore is much less physically demanding. The stonemasons that he meets seem a friendly, if somewhat odd, set of eccentric individuals of differing ages, accents and appearances. Their work is slow and intricate and they carry themselves with the demeanour of sages whose idea of time is measured in stone alone, their noble eyes and steady movements suggesting a higher state of awareness within.

Michael sees a lot of the cathedral in his first few hours, from the Galilee Chapel with its wooden vaulted ceiling to the four sides of the cloisters once walked by the monks who lived in a dormitory there, and he even finds himself helping carrying a delivery of boxes to the gift shop.

Along the way he reads plaques which explain the history of the different areas that he passes through and he tries to remember the new words that refer to various aspects of a building that appears to be constructed entirely from its own vocabulary: chantry, revestry, presbytery, dado, the transepts. He finds himself keen to know more of this world. To understand its deeper meaning.

Late in the morning Edmund asks – asks not tells, Michael notes – if he might take tea and a tray of sandwiches up the central tower to the masons who are restoring the weathered stone of the cathedral's highest and most exposed point.

'You've been up before, I assume?'

Michael shakes his head.

'Never?'

'No.'

'But I thought you were a local lad.'

'I am, but –'

Michael feels his face flush. Actually going *inside* the cathedral was what middle-class families did; it wasn't for those who lived in the outlying villages left fallow after their local industries had depleted in the years before he was born. No: the secret history of the building's interior belonged to the academics and the teachers, the doctors and their children. It was for people who wore cagoules and hiking boots and owned caravans; people who walked across wet moors for fun at the weekend, dropped French phrases into conversations and could afford to be vegetarian. It was for the students too, with their neat, nippy cars, their pashminas and credit cards, their rugby legs and clean skin and white wine hangovers. And the cathedral was also the playground for the choirboys who went to the fifteenth-century Chorister School in the close just behind it, and who would soon go on to run the country. Also you had to pay to climb the central tower, which was the best part. It cost money. Even if he ever had any spare cash Michael wouldn't have spent it on sweating his way up a tower when you could climb a hill for free. He knows that God, if He exists, would agree with him on this.

'It's a bit of a hike,' says Edmund. '325 ever-narrowing steps. But you're a fit and healthy lad, Michael. You best fill a couple of the big flasks before you go because it's not a journey you'll want to do twice in quick succession. The girls in the cafe will sort them out for you when you pick up the sandwiches and snacks. It's all on order from yesterday – the masons get the pick of the menu, you see. It's one of the perks. The higher you go, the better the bait.'

Edmund looks at his watch.

'It's ten to twelve so you best shake a leg before there's a mutiny. Also, you want to avoid the bell tower at midday. If you're too close the chimes will be rattling in your bones for the rest of the day.'

The cafe is called the Undercroft Restaurant and sits oppo-site the gift shop, beneath a dramatic ceiling of medieval stone arches. It is beginning to fill up with lunchtime customers when Michael wanders in.

The room feels surprisingly warm for such a cold day.

On the walls hang watercolour paintings of Northumbrian landmarks and Border country landscapes. He looks at them each in turn and reads their titles, written in the right-hand corner in fine pencil: Lindisfarne Castle, St Cuthbert's Cave, the ruins of the priory at Coldingham.

He approaches the counter and looks at a menu that is placed there. It offers a wide range of choice, including an afternoon tea of 'Soft finger sandwiches, delicious home-made cakes and desserts, delightful mini scones and unlimited tea and coffee.' The scones in the display case before him look anything but small however: they are the size of a cow's hooves, and have risen in such an impressive way that they appear almost too big to contain themselves. His stomach growls.

'Pretty impressive, aren't they? I often think each of them resembles a volute on an Ionic column.'

A young lady has appeared behind the counter, and she says this with a smile.

'Yes,' he says. 'Did you make them?'

'No. My job is to merely sell them, and try not to succumb to their seductive ways. Though they sell themselves, cakes, don't they?'

'How do you mean?'

'I mean, a display is all you need. No words. They're visually appealing.'

He guesses the girl to be around his age, perhaps a year or two older, and with an accent not from the region. Almost certainly a student, then. She is pretty, and her hair is tied back in a full and elaborate chignon.

'Yeah,' he says, blushing. 'They're massive.'

'Are you here for the lunches?'

She nods to the two large flasks that he is holding.

'Yes. I wondered—'

'Tea in the blue, coffee in the red, as I recall. Is that right?'

He passes them over the counter to her.

'I think so. I mean, I'm not sure. Either is probably fine.'

'Not necessarily; I've always found that the flavour of coffee seems have a habit of lingering in flasks so that whatever is put in there afterwards is always slightly tainted by it, no matter how many times you rinse them out. That weird peaty taste is the taste of my childhood.'

Michael looks back at the girl but is unsure what to say in response.

'Too many holidays dragged up Helvellyn,' she adds, rolling her eyes and then touching her hair in such a way that he knows he will be thinking about the tiny gesture for the rest of the day. 'My parents thought it was character-building.'

He does not know what she is going on about, so he forces a smile and nods. Then he remembers the Pot Noodle jammed into his back pocket. Blushing, he says, 'Would you mind adding a bit of hot water to this too?'

'Of course not.'

She examines it for a moment.

'Bombay Bad Boy.'

'What?'

She turns the plastic pot towards him.

'It's a Bombay Bad Boy. I've not had that flavour before.'

'Oh right. I just grab any of them off the shelf. I'm not too bothered.'

She peels back the lid and Michael feels his face flushing a deepening red. His skin prickles.

'Is it your first day here?'

'Yes.'

'I bet they've got you running all over the place. It's a raw day to be up the tower.'

She turns to a large metal urn that sits at the end of the counter.

'You'll need to take the sachet out,' he says.

'What?'

'I was just saying. The sachet of sauce. You'll need to take it out before you put the water in.'

She leans forward slightly, looks around and then in a mock-conspiratorial tone says: 'It's OK, I'm a student. It's my job to know these things.'

Again Michael finds himself flushed with embarrassment. Aside from the receptionist at the doctor's surgery who began to call him by his first name at his mother's appointments before she became too sick to leave the house, he can't recall the last time he had a conversation with a young woman of his own age. He feels a bead of sweat run down one temple.

She begins to make the tea and coffee. She is shorter than him and has a face that appears different to most of the women

393

in the village; hers is a face that is open, quizzical and somehow more classical-looking. Her cheekbones are smoother and her nose only slightly upturned in an attractive way that suggests mischief. She does not yet appear to Michael to be embittered or defeated by life.

'Feel free to have a seat if you like.'

'I thought I might have to buy something.'

'Oh, you're alright. You're staff, aren't you. You're sure I can't tempt you with a scone though? They're just out the oven.'

There is nothing Michael would like more than to sink his teeth into one of the warm scones, except perhaps for this girl to reach across the counter and kiss him for a long time, and for the low echo of the hushed voices of the cathedral to be silenced and the entire world around them to crumble away to nothing but stillness. But what money he has needs to be saved to buy eggs and ibuprofen and electricity and toilet roll and apples and meat and porridge and tea bags and oven chips and bleach and drinking straws and tins of beans and tins of soup and tins of custard and cat food and bread and pasta and gas. The price of a cathedral scone can, if he is careful, heat the house for two, perhaps even three, days.

'No, I'm alright, thanks.'

'Watching your figure, are you?'

'Me? No. Why?'

'I'm only joking, daft lad. It's just what most people say when they pass the cakes. Seems like everyone is watching their figure these days. Do you want me to add the sauce?'

She holds the steaming Pot Noodle.

He hesitates. He flounders.

'Big decision,' she says. 'A lot hangs on the outcome.'

Michael realises she is teasing. It's been so long since he has had a conversation like this that he has almost forgotten that it is alright to joke, to take the piss without malevolent intent. Too much time amongst first his peers at school and then, later, the men of the building sites has made him forget that not all joshing has to contain an undercurrent of cruelty and violence.

'Go on then,' he says. 'But I like it stirred clockwise. With a teaspoon, not a tablespoon.'

Now it is the young lady who is not sure if he is joking. Then he smiles – a shy grin.

'Of course,' she says. 'It's the only way to prepare a *Pot de Nouilles*. All the top chefs in London, Paris and New York know that.'

She puts it down and returns with a teaspoon, which she first lifts in the air ceremoniously, and then carefully dunks into the steaming noodles and begins to stir. As she does, she holds her little finger out at an angle and then meets his eyes. Unblinking, and without breaking her gaze, she tears the sachet of sauce and adds it. Michael feels embarrassed. She is looking right at him. She is looking *into* him, and seeing him. Overwhelmed, he blinks and then looks away.

But then he looks again as she crosses the kitchen and comes back with a sprig of parsley, which she elaborately shreds and sprinkles onto the Pot Noodle, then with a tea towel folded over her forearm she turns it a quarter circle and carefully slides it across the counter to him.

'J'espère que monsieur apprécie son repas préparé avec amour,' she says. 'I'll fetch you those flasks.'

He wishes he knew what she meant.

Edmund was right: it is a long slow climb up the tower. It is not so much the repetition of climbing old stone step after old stone step, but the ardour of following the spiralling staircase while laden with two heavy flasks and a backpack full of sandwiches and snacks that makes Michael feel a little lopsided. The continual veering round a seemingly endless narrowing stairwell is discombobulating.

The steps are wide enough on the lower section for two people to pass but then in the upper part of the ascent, beyond the resting point halfway up, they narrow to a tight, confined section where the old worn steps are steeper. Were the tower not closed to the public during the renovations, he would almost certainly have to keep pausing to let visitors squeeze past, while trying not to squash the freshly made sandwiches between himself and the wall. Michael finds himself perspiring and breathing deeply, yet is exhilarated by the swift elevation and the sense of history held in the thick slabs of stone that rise up around him.

Signs and an accompanying leaflet at the bottom warn that the central tower should only be climbed by people of a certain level of fitness and that it is not for those with a heart condition. Suitable footwear, the leaflet says, must be worn ('no high heels, flip-flops, platforms, backless shoes, "heelys" or bare or stock-inged feet') and neither food, drink or large bags are permitted either. Michael takes a small thrill in knowing that this rule doesn't apply to him. The leaflet also adds that hands should be washed afterwards as the space is shared with resident pigeons.

There is a metal rail, but Michael's hands are too full to use it. Instead his thighs take the strain as he imagines what it must have been like for the monks of ten centuries ago who were given a similar task of delivering supplies to the first stonema-sons who worked up there beneath the same sky. He pictures a huffing, puffing comical character with a bald pate, like Friar Tuck in the Robin Hood film he saw.

The stairwell is a dark shaft that is lit only by the daylight that comes in through the narrow medieval apertures that punctuate the climb. Save for the sound of his breathing and the muted slaps of his footsteps, it is a still place that is soundproofed by centuries of stone. When Michael pauses to look out one such window, it is utterly silent.

A little further up he pauses again by an old solid wooden door that leads off from the stairwell. Curiosity compels him to try the handle, though of course it is locked. A small window in it looks out along a narrow walkway that runs at a great height above the nave. Once again Michael thinks about the men and women who went before him: the monks who climbed by candlelight, and who believed themselves to be moving closer to God with each step. And then there would be the cathedral staff and all those others who congregated here, who walked these steps. Clergy and cleaners, scholars and choirboys, and soldiers seeking refuge. He wonders whether their lives were any less or more anxious and troubled than his, and whether they experienced freedom and joy and desire and excitement, or if their lifelong devotion superseded such notions. Did they, he wonders, have the same hopes and desires back then as he does today?

He keeps climbing the tower and the stairwell is now a tightly winding coil cut through the magnificent stone.

Suddenly, somewhere close by, a peal of bells rings midday, and the vibrations run right through the tower, through the stone and through Michael, just as Edmund had warned. It is not unpleasurable.

He pauses again at another window as the twelve chimes end and he sees the surrounding streets huddled close to the cathedral. Where the tight angles of the grey slate tiled roofs of the college buildings in the Bailey meet one another sit triangles of snow that have evaded the dim sun's gaze. Further afield the uglier modern municipal buildings, many of them built during the 1960s, when thoughtless town planners seemed to have bought a job lot of concrete and pebbledash, sit awkwardly close to the old quarter of the town, so badly considered as to be an insult to the architects and masons who built and adorned the cathedral and nearby castle.

The city centre soon ends though. From up here it seems so small, little more than a jumble of streets and slender alleyways, a place of eras awkwardly colliding, of inclines and tight corners, of friction created by the centuries rubbing up against one another. Then, beyond the city, there are much more green spaces, which now in December are reduced to monochrome patterns. The black branches of the wooded areas that sit in shade to the south, and which have yet to be built on, are coated with streaks of snow frozen stiff. The university playing fields and athletics tracks too are patched in white. And then he sees further still, past where the river loops again, off to the horizon where he knows that old pit villages, newer suburban housing enclaves and industrial estates ring the city.

Michael carries on climbing the steps and then suddenly they end and he is at another wooden door. Its dark grain is covered from top to bottom in graffiti. It is not the crude tags of contemporary spray-cans though, but instead grooves etched with penknives from decades passed, and which spell initials and acronyms and declarations of love. He pushes the door and steps out onto the top of the tower, which is entirely covered in sheets of tarpaulin so as to form a make-shift sub-zero studio created at the very highest point of the building in which the team of masons work. The nearest two turn towards him.

'Close that door,' says one of them. 'You're letting the heat out.'

Michael abruptly shuts the door on its latch but when he turns back the masons are smiling and laughing.

'I'm only messing,' says the man. 'Did the professor send you up?'

'Edmund?'

'That's the one. We call him the Professor. Or Edmund the Confessor. Or sometimes, when he's got his brown tank top on, Edmund the Oxfam Dresser. He's alright though, is Eddie. Besides, he calls me the Bishop.'

'Because he likes to take the holy water,' says the man next to him, laughing.

'That's almost funny, H. Keep trying son, you'll get there one day.'

Michael finds himself in an elevated space of stone and work tools. The top of the central tower is covered in scaffolding enshrouded in the thick white sheeting that diffuses daylight. From here the masons can step through a flap and onto scaffold walkways fixed precipitously to the crown of this great building. Michael pulls his hood up against the biting breeze.

'I'm Michael,' he says.

'Brought us our bait have you, Michael?' says The Bishop.

'I have.'

'Good lad.'

He is the oldest of the men and has an air of authority about him as he helps Michael with the flasks and the load of food he has carried.

'Here, meet the team.'

He introduces him to the other stonemasons, pointing to each in turn. All are wrapped up in many layers, and wearing a combination of hats, scarves, snoods and bandanas pulled up to their eyes, and fingerless gloves. They resemble a team of Arctic explorers as much as they do those whose ancient craft is the slow shaping of stone.

'That's Harry, Frankie, Ed and Stoddard on the end there.'

They all nod or utter a friendly greeting in acknowledgement – 'Alright, mate' – and it is the first time that he has met a work crew that Michael has not felt intimidated by, nor detected any resentment or animosity directed towards him, an outsider. Perhaps it is because of the presence of Frankie, a woman. Michael takes out a list and distributes their lunch orders accordingly.

Though the cladding has created a barrier to the wind, and there are two large electrical heaters emitting hot air – their appearance more symbolic than functional – it is nevertheless freezing and noisy as the breeze whips at the sheets and whistles around the sharp stone corners.

'First time up here?'

Michael nods. He hands The Bishop a warm baguette wrapped in foil.

'Shame it's all closed off – you'll not get the glorious view. Here, have a peek through a gap if you like.'

The Bishop pulls a strip of sheeting aside and beyond the outer skeleton of scaffold Michael gets his first full view from the top of a tower that he has only ever seen from afar his entire life. The sky is grey, pregnant, a bulging net of snow, and a gust of freezing wind fills his mouth, as if the air were solid matter. He feels the cold in his teeth, his eardrums, behind his eyes. Cold as a dull weighted ache. He gags on it.

'It's a view worth seeing a thousand times over,' says The Bishop, tearing at the end of his sandwich with his teeth. 'Each day it's different.'

'It's freezing up here.'

'You're not kidding,' he says through a full mouth of bread and bacon. 'This time of year I never truly warm up. Every night our lass runs me a bath, but even after an hour's soak it's like I can still feel the cold in my bones.'

'How long have you been up here?'

'Some of the masons have been and gone on to other jobs – skilled boys and girls like these are much in demand right across Europe – but I've been up here since day one. Approaching two and a half years now.'

Michael whistles through his teeth.

'I'm deep into my third winter,' says The Bishop. 'That's three winters getting blown about on the plastic duckboards.'

'You must have a head for heights.'

He shrugs.

'Beats a desk job. I like to surround myself with history. Real living history.'

'When do you get finished?'

'Summer. It has to be done by summer.'

'This summer coming?'

'This summer coming.'

'Big job.'

'Massive. The entire balustrade was coming loose. It was fracturing and moving. A lot of erosion too. It's possible that some of the original masonry will have been up here a thousand winters, in weather like this – or worse. Here, look.'

The Bishop points to an example of the stonework, in which new pieces have been perfectly slotted flush into the gaps left by the removal of old blocks.

'If one of those old pink capstones had come down you'd have known about it. So the team are having to remove every bit piece by piece, then take them down to the workshop for repair or, if they're beyond it, to make new stones carved to fit perfectly in place. They call this blaxter sandstone. It's like working on the world's biggest puzzle – a jigsaw as high as the sky. These things can't be rushed. Time up here is measured by centuries and millennia rather than hours and minutes.'

'How much does a piece weigh?'

'The bigger ones are well over a hundred stone, or nigh on fourteen or fifteen hundred pounds each. About ten of you or me, give or take a big lunch or two. Getting the scaffolding up to this height was just as much trouble, mind. A logistical nightmare. But then again, if they could build it from the foundation pit upwards in the eleventh century then we sure as hell can spruce it up a bit in the twenty-first. It's more than just architectural all this, though. It's spiritual.'

'How do you mean?' Michael asks.

'You'll see. You'll feel it. Soon enough you'll feel the pull of Cuddy.'

'What do you mean by the pull?'

'Oh, they say old Cuthbert starts talking to everyone eventually. Or he's there for those who need him, anyway. Which is all of us at one time or another.'

The Bishop eats some more sandwich and then wanders off to fill a mug from one of the large flasks.

Michael stands at the gap in the tarpaulin, his fingers curled around the old metal railings. Looking down, he sees the land of his fathers laid out before him.

The panoramic view from up here is like none Michael has experienced before. The sound too is different. When the wind dips and the tarpaulin skin of the high tower stops flapping he can hear the sirens of ambulances making their way to and from the hospital to pick up heart attacks and hips broken on slipped ice, and the stop-start sounds of cars that nudge their way from traffic light to pedestrian crossing to roundabout.

Up here, sound, like perspective, seems to elongate one moment and then shorten the next.

He is about to withdraw to return to work when something catches his eye over to the right far below. It is the tiny shapes of figures – of people, men – moving about an enclosed space. It is the exercise yard of Durham Prison. He sees the narrow lines that their footprints make in the snow, like an inverse version of the trails that the snails leave across the kitchen surfaces at home in the warmer months.

'Poor sods.'

Frankie is by his side, looking down. She shakes her head.

'The notorious HMP Durham,' she says. 'Built two hundred years ago. I'd take the icy breeze blowing in one ear and out the other any day. That place gives me the real shivers.'

Frankie takes off her gloves and rubs her hands together, and then replaces them.

'It's strange,' says Michael. 'Up here you can see for miles. It feels like total freedom, but down there they're like lab rats, trapped.'

'Hindley and Brady were in Durham, you know,' she says. 'One of the Krays too, I forget which. And some of the Richardson gang. It's a bloody long way from London; they must have felt like they were being sent to the Siberian Gulag. Rose West as well. She was in Durham for years. Yes, they've had all the greats here. It's like a *Who's Who* of English rotters, is Durham. And right next door to this great building dedicated to faith, generosity, goodness and charity. Cuddy's place. What a contrast.'

Michael thinks about this for moment and contemplates telling Frankie that he thinks his father used to live there too, and possibly still does, but he stays quiet. They stand like that for a moment, then he says, 'Well, best be going.'

'Yes. It'll nearly be time for our afternoon brew.'

🕯

Only when he has moved some sacks of refuse and rubble from the south presbytery gallery out to one of their skips and is halfway through clearing away a number of tools and unused scaffolding pipes that have been left in the corner of the Galilee Chapel, which is busy today with a variety of visiting tourists talking in a number of foreign tongues, does Michael realise he hasn't called his mother.

Lunch has passed and he is deep into the afternoon. He hurries past the Undercroft Restaurant and takes the exit that leads to the pleasant residential close, the college, which sits behind it. He walks over to an old octagonal stone tower called Conduit House that is set in the corner of the square, near to the entrance for the boys' private school. It is an unobtrusive, mysterious building with a small arched doorway and equally small rounded windows set too high up to see into. It gives away little of its past or purpose. Here Michael takes out his phone and calls his mother.

He listens to the dial tone and sees his breath before him. Leaning back, he looks up to the cathedral's central tower where The Bishop, Frankie and Harold and the other masons are working in their stone eyrie.

The phone keeps ringing until Michael hangs up. His throat is tight. It feels as if it is shrinking, contracting, as if he is breathing through a thin straw that runs through the centre of him. The first tingle of panic is in his toes.

He calls again. It rings and rings and rings, and there is no answer. He hangs up, counts to sixty, counts his breaths, then calls again and suddenly she is there, answering in a shallow faraway voice, and his panic retreats like an ebbing tide.

'Hello?'

'Mam?'

She does not reply.

'Mam, it's me,' he says, and then awkwardly adds, 'it's Michael. How are you feeling?'

'OK, love.'

'Better or worse than yesterday?'

'The same.'

'I tried ringing you.'

'Did you?'

'Yes, twice, just now.'

'I must have been dozing, pet.'

Their conversation continues much as it always does.

'Have you eaten?'

'A little.'

'The porridge?'

403

'A bit.'

'Did you put any treacle in it?'

'No, no treacle.'

'Sugar?'

'Perhaps.'

A pause.

'Have you had any biscuits?'

'I'm not sure.'

'Have a biscuit, Mam.'

'Maybe in a bit.'

'You need to keep your strength up. Or you could have an apple. There's bananas too.'

'Are you trying to fatten me up?'

Michael smiles to himself.

'I'm just looking after you, that's all.'

There is another pause and then his mother speaks.

'How is work?'

'It's good. I'm at the cathedral.'

'The cathedral?'

'Yes, remember I told you?'

'My son,' she says to herself as much to him, the pride rising in her voice. 'Working at *the cathedral*.'

'Has the cat been in?' asks Michael.

'Yes. He's curled up.'

She makes her usual noises to the cat – 'Puss, puss' – and then says, 'He doesn't like this cold. He's sensitive. And are you wrapped up?'

'Nice and warm.'

'Good.'

'Do you have your gloves?'

'Yes,' he lies.

They fall silent for a longer moment this time and he can hear his mother's breath.

'OK then,' says Michael.

'Before you go –'

Again, he already knows what she is going to ask. And he already knows he will play along.

'Describe the day for me, love. Tell me what you can see.'

'Well, the cathedral,' he says. 'It's towering over me.'

'Are you on the nice grass out the front?'

'No, I'm behind it in a square where the religious people and the academics live. The cathedral looks like a mountain that has burst from the earth. I know we've both seen it a million times but it's only now that I'm *really* seeing it. Maybe when something is on your doorstep for all that time you take it for granted. It's stunning, Mam.'

He pauses to hear her breathing, then continues.

'The towers are sculpted as if they have been hammered and shaped by the rain. I went up the main one this morning. I climbed to the top. The stonework is ornate and intricate and I met the men who are fixing it. There's a woman too, she's called Frankie. What a spectacle, Mam. It made me wonder what must it have been like here when they first dug the foundation pit ten centuries ago and all the people around it were living in hovels. It must have dwarfed everything, including the river too of course, down at the bottom of the gorge, looping around the headland.'

'You can see all that from where you're standing?'

'Yes,' he lies.

'You speak so beautifully, son. You're like a poet.'

'There's something else I learned: there's a saint buried here.'

'Is there now?'

'Yes, Saint Cuthbert.'

'Oh, yes, with the same name as us, Michael. Isn't that funny?'

'They made the cathedral just to bury him in it and people still come from all around the world to visit his tomb.'

'My dad always said we were descended from greatness. And I do believe Cuthbert's in you now, son.'

Michael blushes into the phone, squirms in his clothes.

'My son,' she says. 'The saint.'

405

Work continues this way all week. Michael rises in the dark and cleans and feeds his mother, and he tries to raise the subject of getting carers or nurses to come in, but she gently refuses to even discuss it. This conversation has almost become a daily ritual. Then he packs his lunch and sets off down the lanes and across the fields. He is alone with his worries and his hips and knees and ankles ache from all the walking, from the steep stone stairwells and the days spent almost entirely on his feet. Fatigue fills him as he crunches through the frozen crust created by another sub-zero night, but once he reaches the city and rises up through the winding medieval streets, taking back alleys that deliver him through darkened doorways, the cathedral appears so suddenly to entirely fill his vision as to be a surprise. The mass bulk of it strikes him as exciting and only then does he feel energised by the possibility of the day. He likes Edmund and the Bishop and the masons, and he especially likes the girl in the cafe. He likes the way they all accept him as part of the place already. They talk to him not as an inferior, like Chadwick or the various other site managers and people from the agency do, but as an equal. One of them. Part of the team.

And this thought makes him aware, perhaps for the first time, that he is part of history too, and that history is never-ending. He is one more link in a chain of people – of experience – that stretches deep into a past, a past where people spoke and ate and lived differently, but perhaps thought similar thoughts and desired similar things. A continuum, he thinks. Is that the right word here? We are all part of a continuum.

That evening, when he returns home dog-tired, his mother seems smaller than when he left her. She seems shrunken. She *is* shrunken.

It is not an illusion but a real physical deterioration. He is sure of it, yet staggered by the day's ability to diminish her so. Her face is a sallow mask around which her thin skin has tightened. For a moment it scares him, this reduced version of his mother. Her cheeks and brow seem to have been pulled inwards and her gums have receded in such a way that her teeth now look so much larger, especially the front two, which give a rabbit-like impression, but a rabbit that has been stricken by myxomatosis and left half-blind and stranded in the evening sun. He wants to turn away because mixed into the fear are burgeoning sensations of resentment and hatred that he dare not make real by acknowledging. Yet he knows that they are there nonetheless. The fear exists only for one fleeting moment during which he thinks – he *hopes* – he has managed not to show his true feelings, but the image of her is enough to be imprinted on his memory, perhaps forever. And guilt washes over him.

Is this how she looked this morning when he went through the routine of wiping and cleaning? Did the lack of light play devious tricks to obscure the true horror of disease, so that he was at least spared the haunting image of her drawn grimace until the working day was over?

Or perhaps he has somehow managed to censor the worst of it these past few weeks, until now, that is, when the veil has been lifted and he finds himself forced to accept her rapid decline.

Her neat tongue protrudes slightly to slowly encircle her dry lips. Her hair is matted; the auburn tinge that always gave it a radiant glow – natural when she was younger, and augmented with dye only in more recent years – is now the colour of ashes.

Yet still.

Yet still, even in freefall – even now as a passive and accepting host to a parasite of sorts – her eyes still show the spark of the young woman she once was, clinging to the moment.

In sleep, she swallows. Her mouth clicks with dryness and her tongue seeks a path around her lips once more. Like a kitten, Michael thinks. Like a tiny helpless kitten facing life rather than retreating from it. How similar, he thinks, the beginning and the end are.

But he has to remind himself that she is not an old woman. Forties is no age. Were she working she would still be twenty-something years away from being able to draw a pension. She should not be like this. This should not be happening.

'Mam,' he says, surprised to hear his voice breaking as he speaks. Michael clears his throat and tries again. 'Mam.'

Her eyes flutter faintly for a moment but still remain fully closed when she speaks.

'Michael?'

'It's me, Mam.'

'You're back, are you?'

'Yes.'

'How was work?'

'Work was good. Better.'

'You've always been a grafter.'

'They've got me up the cathedral.'

Her eyes finally open. They sparkle. He sees that the memory of the conversation earlier has already faded into a feverish fug of painkillers and time-slips.

'The cathedral. What a place to work.'

'It's an amazing building. It's so huge.'

She licks her lips but does not speak.

'I think you took me there once,' he says. 'Do you remember?'

His mother does not reply. His mother does not remember. Instead she closes her eyes again and nods a little white lie. She nods and she smiles. She smiles and she swallows. She swallows and she sighs, and he can almost hear the parasite shift position slightly as it tightens its grip within her.

Michael refills a plastic water bowl, and dips a small sponge, wrings it, then gently pats it around her mouth. Her lips instinctively find it and cling to it, then she takes it into her mouth entirely. He gently removes it.

'Mam,' he says. 'I really think you might need some extra help.'

Her response is dry and distant. Automatic, even. Her voice a coarse croak.

'Oh no, we don't need to bother with all that.'

She raises one hand an inch or two and brushes the comment aside.

'Let's at least think about it. It's no problem, you know. Dr Satori said that there are people who are paid to help. We just need to say the word.'

Her hand falls back down by her side, as if her arm is too weak to support it.

'We can't have strangers coming in,' she says.

'Why not?'

'The state of the place.'

This comment stings him. It is not intended to harm, but he takes the full force of the implied criticism nonetheless.

'They don't mind, they must see the inside of dozens of houses. Hundreds of them. They'll see far worse.'

'Still.'

'I'm trying my best.'

Her hand seeks his, and then falls upon it. Her palm is a cold glove.

'I know you are, son.'

'Well then.'

'I don't want to put anyone out.'

He wants to shake her then. He wants to shake his mother for being so nice, so selfless, even now, when she should be raging against the robbery of her existence. Even with the parasite's tendrils wrapped tightly around her slowing heart she is humble, when she should be treated like the angel that she is. Michael's eyes well and sting with anger – not with her, not with his mother, but instead with everyone else in the world, everyone there has ever been, and everyone who will come afterwards, for he knows that none of them will ever match her generosity, her kindness.

'I'm doing my best, Mam,' he says again, but she is asleep.

Michael's sleep is disturbed by a dream so vivid it shapes the day.

He sees a pallid man dressed in rags, his arms and eyes raised.

He is flanked by men, women. Serene, he knows him to be Cuddy.

That is all, a simple image. But the feeling it leaves is powerful.

The girl in the cafe is standing ready with the kettle before he has even reached the counter, her other hand extended to receive the Pot Noodle.

The sight of her makes something flex inside of Michael. His stomach is a flipped pancake.

He blushes, embarrassed to be seen in such a way. To be seen at all. For years he has always imagined he was invisible somehow, and assumed he rarely registered in most people's daily business. But now he has, and for the worst possible reason: scrounging something for free.

He almost turns right back around to walk out of the Undercroft again but it is too late for that. Instead he awkwardly peels back the foil lid, removes the sachet of sauce and passes the pot to her, while averting his eyes. Michael looks first to the floor and then across the room, and then to the display cabinet of the latest cakes and scones. He just hopes that she doesn't think he is taking advantage of her generosity, though is still glad that it is her who is working the till again.

The girl carefully pours the water into the pot but this time instead of passing it back to him she reaches into the glass cabinet with a pair of tongs and lifts out a huge fresh scone that is dusted in icy sugar. She gently places it on a plate, to which she adds a small side dish of butter, one of jam and a third full of clotted cream. She also puts a tub of fruit salad beside it.

'For the vitamins,' she says. 'To counterbalance whatever is in *that*.'

She nods to the Pot Noodle and then she slides the tray along the rack to the cash register.

'Oh,' says Michael. 'No, I—'

'I thought you might fancy something else. Pot Noodles are just dead calories.'

'Dead calories?'

'Yes, there's no nutrition. It's just MSG and various powders. I doubt there's any vitamins even in there.'

He looks at the plastic pot.

'But this one's got mushrooms in it. I think.'

She laughs. Michael's mouth suddenly feels useless and beyond his control.

'Are there vitamins in a scone then?'

She laughs again.

'Well, no, fair enough. But that's why I added the fruit salad. So as not to be a hypocrite.'

'Thanks. But I –'

She looks around conspiratorially and then, just as she did the other day, she leans towards Michael and lowers her voice. He likes the way it feels, being allowed into a shared secret such as this, even if it is one without meaning.

'Don't worry, it's on the house. We're allowed to give the odd thing away to friends. Staff perks for being good Christians.'

Friends. The word sends a surge through the centre of his body. Down his spine. She considers *him* a *friend*.

'It's also sort of an investment. I mean, I genuinely fear for the future of the cathedral if your work is fuelled solely by salt and dried noodles. I'm Evie, by the way.'

'Evie?'

'Short for Evelyn. Like Waugh.'

'War?'

'Yes, like Auberon. But a woman.'

'Right.'

'It could have been worse. I could have been an Arthur. That was Waugh's real name.'

Confused, Michael attempts a smile and the lie of it hurts his face.

In a lowered voice he says, 'To be honest, all I do is move tools about and take these flasks of tea to the masons. That sort of thing. A lot of sweeping up rubbish.'

'Still. It's rubbish of historical and theological significance.'

'So do you have to be a Christian to work here?' he asks.

'Not that I'm aware of, but it can't do any harm. Maybe we should get some T-shirts made up: YOU DON'T HAVE TO BE CHRISTIAN TO WORK HERE, BUT IT HELPS. We'd make a killing. Listen, if you come back tomorrow I can cut you in on some free soup action. The rumours are it's going to be mulligatawny. A real winter warmer. *And* as many croutons as you can eat. Just don't tell Trudy.'

'Who's Trudy?'

'The Undercroft's own battleaxe. I call her Gertrude the Unready. After Ethelred? She's alright, it's just she's worked here since the Reformation so she's a little stuck in her ways, that's all. She's actually the opposite of unready; she's freakishly organised, old Gertie. If she catches me out on the croutons she'll chop my hands off.'

'I don't want to get you in any trouble.'

'I think it's a calculated risk worth taking.'

'Well, OK, that sounds—'

'Like the greatest thing in the entire history of humanity?'

Michael finds himself grinning. He can't help it. He is aware of muscles in his cheeks he never knew he had.

'That's *exactly* what I was going to say.'

'I know,' she says, breezily. 'I'm a mind reader.'

I hope not, he thinks.

Michael is the happiest he has felt in a long time. So happy he treats himself to chocolate and a bus ride home through the December-dark evening as light snow falls across Durham county.

Today he does not even feel tired, more a kind of aching contentment. He is not exhausted like he is after a long shift on the building sites either. The smile from the girl – from Evelyn – sustained him right through the afternoon and the thought of seeing her again tomorrow to receive mulligatawny soup, will see him through the night too. Their interactions hint at new possibilities, and this emboldening thought makes him feel human, alive.

His mother is in her bed when he slips the key into the door. She is just a small shape in the half-light cast by the lamp-post outside now; in his haste this morning he had forgotten to leave any lights on for her.

'Mam, I'm so sorry,' he says, flicking the switch by the living room door.

She blinks back at him through sleep-struck glassy eyes, tinier still, and confused. Her face shows her mind racing towards something only distantly familiar: her son.

'Mam, it's alright, it's just me.'

'Michael?'

A small slug of snot flecked with blood sits on his mother's hand. It is the saddest thing he has ever seen. Her porridge pot is untouched, her cup full of cold tea.

He busies himself; it is the only thing he can do. He turns up the heating, boils the kettle, puts pie and chips in the oven, plumps his mother's pillows, empties her bedpan, checks her meds and does all the other chores that make him feel less guilty for feeling more alive than he has in a long time while she, a real-life living saint, is wading headlong into death's dark water.

He spends the night sleeping upright in the armchair next to her, dreaming of a smiling girl, dreaming of a saint beneath stone.

He does not mind waking up. For the first time in months, years even, it does not feel as if Michael is laid beneath concrete blankets and his mind is not endlessly accelerating around a circular track. He looks across and sees his mother's sleeping face turned towards him, placid in the morning gloom. The light is so dim that it softens the room, smoothing away all the edges and angles, until he opens the curtains and the December sun sharpens everything into focus once more.

He is glad to leave the house, and guilty too. But the thought of seeing Evelyn and Edmund and the stonemasons, and hearing more about St Cuthbert, propels him onwards into another still and frozen day. Walking in with a stomach full of porridge it is as if he is seeing the land through fresh eyes, for the first time, and when he enters the city he thinks of the past lives lived here. He takes the narrow backstreets where houses once stood so close together that their tenants could reach from their top windows and touch their opposite neighbours' hands were they to do the same, and would be privy to all aspect of their private lives when living in such close and cramped proximity, a time when the alleys must have been acrid with the stench of urine and shit, rotting fish and meat and discarded vegetables, and where belief in God was everything, and the love for Him – and the fear of Him – guided everyone's beliefs, decisions, desires and actions.

He breaks for lunch at midday and takes the steps down the tower two at a time, then heads straight to the Undercroft Restaurant, and she's there, Evelyn, wearing the day well, her hair tied back in another intricate plait, a touch of winter in her cheeks, at ease with her place in the world.

She is good to her word on the mulligatawny soup front, but there is a slight delay – 'We had a *situation*,' she says, pulling a comical face that melts his heart like a pat of butter left out in the sun. So while he waits for a second batch to heat up Michael stands to one side and tries not to look at her until she comes over and they have a snatched conversation while she transfers fresh sandwiches, slices of cake and fruit salads from trays into the display case.

'Sorry,' she says, wiping her arm across her brow. 'June Parnell turned her ankle and painted half the wall yellow; Sandy Fletcher's still picking bits of pepper out of her hairnet. Fortunately she liquidised it while it was cool otherwise it could have proven fatal. *Fatal*. Anyway, enough of our dramas, have you had much time to properly look around yet or have they got you working all hours?'

Michael shakes his head.

'That's a shame. If you get a minute I'd recommend the Chapel of the Nine Altars. Or maybe you've seen it?'

'I –'

His reply catches in his throat.

'I'm not sure.'

She smiles back at him.

'It's where Cuthbert's tomb is. It's my favourite part of the cathedral.'

414

Michael's face brightens for a moment.

'My name's Cuthbert too.'

'Is it really? That's *amazing*. I've never met a Cuthbert before.'

He blushes, and then attempts to backtrack.

'I mean, it's just my surname. My first name is actually Michael.'

'Well, if Cuthbert is your family name then that's even more impressive in a way as it suggests a possible lineage back to the saint himself. Also, in the Book of Revelation it is Michael who leads God's armies against Satan's forces. So you've got the double Christian whammy there.'

'Right.'

'Are you from here?' she asks. 'The city, I mean.'

'A few miles out.'

'So you could literally be a descendant of Cuthbert.'

'I don't really know much about him to be honest.'

Evie laughs and when she does Michael sees that her teeth might be the neatest he has ever seen, apart from one incisor that is crooked and pointing slightly outwards, an imperfection that he finds thrilling.

'Mind, Cuthbert didn't have children, did he?' she says. 'So how would that work? I mean, imagine the scandal. Then again, I doubt even the bishops and monks were impervious to indiscretion. They were, after all, mere mortal men. And not entirely what you would call "normal" ones at that. Even then, spending all that time alone on craggy outcrops in the sea was probably a bit peculiar. So let's just pretend you're a direct descendant of Cuddy.'

'Cuddy?'

'An affectionate nickname. And now it could be a nickname for you too. Either that or Daft Lad. I'm currently undecided.'

He beams back at her.

'So did he live here then?'

'Only in death.'

Michael looks puzzled, so Evie explains.

'He died on Lindisfarne, then he was transported here. I expect you've been there on a school trip or something?'

He shakes his head.

'Well, he actually died on a little island off Lindisfarne and was buried there, but then had to be dug up and moved when the Danes began their invasions. He was moved all around the north-east for a full century by an ever-changing community that was led by monks, until finally it was decided he should be buried here.'

'And they didn't mind, the owners of the cathedral?'

Evie laughs.

'Oh, the cathedral didn't exist then. In fact it was built entirely to house his corpse. Cuthbert is the reason this place exists. Every brick, every pew. And every scone too. It's all for him.'

Only now does it occur to Michael that Evie works in the cathedral's cafe not only for the income that must help finance her studies, but that she may actually be here for other reasons too. Religious reasons.

'All of this,' he says, 'just for his bones?'

'Mad, isn't it? Though it's said that when his coffin was opened – as it has been on several occasions over the centuries – more than his bones existed. The myth suggests that his body didn't decompose.'

For a moment Michael thinks of his mother withering away on the borrowed hospital bed in the front room of the house they will never own. He thinks of the decomposition that is already happening by way of a disease that he can only ever picture as a living parasite destroying her from within, as it eats away at her organs, her blood. But not, he thinks, her smile. Her smile still endures.

And he thinks of a dead saint, still alive, in a way, even in death.

'Why here though?' he asks. 'Why did they build it here?'

'That's another story.'

'I'd love to hear it.'

'And I'd love to tell you, and about the various exhumations too. But unfortunately –'

She cocks her head towards the growing queue of customers.

'You have work to do,' he says.

'And you do too.'

Michael hesitates for a moment.

'You'll tell me more though? About Cuthbert's corpse and the building of the cathedral and all of that?'

'I'd be happy to. Whenever you like.'

'Friday?'

He hears the word before he has even thought of it. It escapes his mouth like a butterfly and hovers there between them. Panic grips him but Evie does not seem to notice.

'OK. But I'm not working Friday. I have a meeting with my dissertation tutor.'

The panic subsides, but so does the excitement that he realises has been fuelling his side of the conversation.

'Oh.'

Evie eyes him with a look he cannot discern. Expectation, perhaps?

Then his face brightens as a thought occurs to him.

'Later on then?'

She nods and makes a noise, which he takes to be one of approval.

'Uh-hmmn.'

'When I finish work?'

'OK, yes. But not here – there'll be services on.'

'Where then?' he asks.

'I'll leave that up to you. But I'll meet you by Cuthbert's place in the chapel at six. OK?'

'Sounds good.'

'Well alright then,' she says. 'Peace be with you.'

Friday evening. The city wrapped tight, swaddled in ice.

Michael is ready and waiting in the Chapel of the Nine Altars at six on the dot.

He has washed his hands and face and even went to Superdrug during his lunch break to buy a new roll-on deodorant and a packet of mints.

He is not tired. Even after climbing the tower several times a day and constantly running endless errands, the pace is still slower and the job easier than any he has had. Full fatigue evades him. He feels fitter. Stronger. Unlike out on the demolition sites there is no violence in the labour here either, nor any simmering tensions or festering resentments amongst the workforce, or towards their superiors either. There are no racist jokes, no one calling him *mush* in a menacing manner and – obviously – no tacky porn mag pictures pinned to tea-room walls. Instead there is a quiet stoicism. An air of refinement.

Perhaps this is because the men and women are skilled. They have mastered their craft as an artist might, and they enjoy what they do. Their positions are not threatened and they are secure in their time-earned talents. In passing conversations Michael has detected a sense of pride here that was lacking amongst his former colleagues who were employed to either smash up failed municipal buildings that were hastily built in the 1960s – the failed dreams of arrogant architects or the results of contractors' backhanders and councilmen's bungs, perhaps – or hoist wet clay and broken rocks from the freshly dug foundations of the latest branch of Matalan or Dunelm to sprout from the soil like a tenacious weed, both of which he has done this past year.

Instead, on more than one occasion, he has heard the masons also remark upon being part of a lineage whose commonality is stone. Stone to be quarried and hewn, stone to be cut and dressed; stone to be turned and shaped and chiselled; stone to be placed and raised skywards, and then settled closer to the God whose people have chosen to honour it with an awesome spectacle that has stood for ten centuries, and should stand for ten more.

He has learned this week that all masons leave their mark somewhere – a shallow chiselled signature or perhaps a unique symbol or sigil. At lunchtime, after sandwiches and a bowl of soup, and with the sub-zero wind whipping around the four corners of the tower, Frankie had taken Michael onto the outer scaffold platform and explained this to him.

'Sometimes the marks were made to show who had paid for the stones – or the building – in the first place,' she said, running her hand over a new piece that had been hoisted into position. 'It was actually nothing to do with the mason; think of it more like a medieval barcode, a sign of ownership or transaction, if you like. Other times the stones were marked to help during their assembly, like the instructions that come with an Ikea flat-pack, or to identify their source, specifically the quarry they came from. And then there are the small and often secret markings made by us lot. Often they're hidden from view and set away on the tide of time like messages in bottles to be washed up on future foreign shores. I can't speak for the others but I get a kick out of the idea of conversing with my descendants this way, just as the voices of our ancestors speak through these old stones. I reckon this block here will outlast any computer on earth. Can you see the marking on it?'

Michael moved closer. He shook his head.

'Good, because that's deliberate. But it is there. Look —'

She hunkered down and pointed to the original cornerstone. 'See?'

He saw it.

'My favourite in the whole cathedral,' Frankie had continued, 'is the Cuddy stone.'

'Like Cuthbert?'

'Exactly.'

Michael smiled.

'Cuthbert's my surname.'

'Excellent, then maybe we should call you Mike Cuddy. He sounds like someone you could trust, doesn't he? "My pal Mike Cuddy." Yes, it has a nice ring to it.'

Frankie took out her phone and scrolled through some photos, then passed it to him. The picture was not of good quality on account of poor light and a lack of flash. The stone appeared small and tucked away somewhere discreet. Engraved on it in a very basic font he could just make out the word:

CVDDY

'The Cuv-dy Stone,' laughed Frankie. 'Not the work of the saint himself's hand obviously, but still a work to file alongside Graves's *I, Clavdivs*, eh? I'll give you a tenner if you can find it.'
'Yeah?'
'Yeah.'
'You're on.'

Now as he waits at the chapel he tips his head back and studies the ceiling, and while wondering if the Cuddy stone is up there, he also thinks about how perhaps it is this place that determines the mood and tone of all those who work within its walls. It is not just the stonemasons or the site manager or the conservation architect or Edmund but everyone – from the cathedral guides and the various other volunteers, to the dean, the deacons and the bishop. Whether the cleaners or the organists or the students like Evie who work in the cafe, all appear to Michael to conduct themselves with a quiet reserve and reverence that he now realises is shaped by the building and what it represents: an eternal sanctuary for this man called Cuthbert, and a devotion to a God whose existence Michael has always doubted, especially now as he has to sit by and watch as his mother is slowly erased. And even if God doesn't exist, the cathedral very much does.

History comes alive in here, he thinks, and the centuries overlap. The voices of the dead live on, they still speak today, just as they do in the masonry that adorns the top of the tower. It is almost as if he can hear them. And he is beginning to feel changed by the experience. Twice this week he has touched old stone and felt what he could only describe as a memory jolt, a fleeting photographic flash to a past time that he could never hope to explain or understand, but that he implicitly understands to be a glimpse of something buried deep inside him. Past experience, perhaps. All he can be certain of is that he has been here before, a young man, in the cathedral, in an entirely different age, and that he could never mention this to anyone.

All of this is on his mind when Evie appears at his elbow.

'Hiya, daft lad,' she says and again something pleasurably pops inside of him, like a bowstring being plucked.

The bones of the saint lie beneath a horizontal slab marked CVTHBERTVS. They stand at the foot of it, side by side. The cathedral is still and quiet now and the rows of candles that have been lit by tourists and pilgrims in Cuthbert's honour are short, smoking stubs, their flames flickering silently in an unseen draught.

'Cvth-bert-vus,' whispers Michael.

'What?' says Evie, leaning in closer, so close he can smell her, feel her warmth.

'Nothing. I was just saying "Cvth-bert-vus". Like *I, Clavdivs*.'

'Michael, that joke is almost as old as he is.'

He is glad to see she is smiling when she says this.

In a hushed voice Evie explains how Cuddy's remains were first kept in a simple timber structure somewhere nearby and then in a slightly larger building known as the White Church, before it was replaced by a building of stone, also known as the White Church, until that too was demolished. 'Then,' she elaborates, 'came the undertaking of a shrine on a scale beyond the comprehension of almost all who lived in its shadows. On August 11 1093 construction on Durham Cathedral began.'

Her voice drops to little more than a whisper, and though it is surely a story she has told many times before in her previous role as a volunteer cathedral guide, Evie shares it with the enthusiasm of the truly devoted. It is not merely a devotion to the building either, but to St Cuthbert, and to God. To the idea of faith itself.

'And he's been down there ever since?' Michael asks.

'Well, not entirely.'

'How do you mean?'

'Well, his corpse has been corrupted several times over the centuries.'

'Corrupted?'

'Yes, tampered with. Dug up. Remember how I was telling you about him being exhumed? The integrity of his supposedly perfectly preserved corpse has been spoiled by the nosiness of men – and isn't it always men?'

'What happened?'

'Well, his coffin has been raised and either moved or opened, or both, on several different occasions, at varying degrees of ineptitude and for various different reasons. His safety during invasions from first the Vikings and then the Normans being two of them, and then later it was down to the meddling of those wanting to either prove or disprove Cuddy's sainthood. His bones have been poked over and played with far too many times than is morally justifiable, though as a budding historian obviously I understand the allure.'

'Recently?' asks Michael.

'The last time his coffin was brought up was in the late Victorian era, around about 1900, I think, but that was only seventy years or so since the previous time, which was a far worse affair. At least since then history has been left to lie.'

'Why, what happened?'

'Well, when they brought Cuthbert up then – 1827, it was – his entire coffin collapsed and its contents fell out, with the saint's bones scattered amongst the dirt and the pulped wood. The last lot who had exhumed him – they were led by a librarian from the cathedral – had done such a heavy-handed and shoddy job that they had hastily put him in a new coffin and quickly reburied him out of fear that their lack of tact be discovered. An account was later recorded in the diaries of an Oxford historian that contradicts the one published by the librarian, though it's now widely accepted that they did a lot of damage. Either way, it presents a perennial dilemma faced by historians the world over: who to believe? I always think that history sits in the spaces between the differing accounts and, really, our job is to stop it falling through the cracks. Lucky for us the professor left his journal behind, which we got to see on our course. The *actual* diary. It was amazing. Reading it, he seemed like a man on the edge of insanity. Of everything. You can read it online if you're interested. Or I can send you a PDF if you like.'

'Thanks,' says Michael, keen to open up another line of communication with her.

'But we should get out of here though.'

'Oh yes. Right.'

'Have you eaten?'

Panic grips him again at the thought of having to eat with her. In front of her. Of having to spend money when he doesn't have any money.

'Yes,' he lies.

'You've eaten already?'

'Yes.'

'But you've just finished work.'

'I had a late lunch. A large, late lunch.'

'Right. But it was just soup, wasn't it?'

'I had some snacks this afternoon,' he lies, and then: 'Are you hungry?'

'Not especially,' says Evie. 'Working in the Undercroft is putting pounds on me. Or maybe it's this weather. It always makes me crave carbs. Last term I went rowing three times a week, but now there always seems to be something else to do.'

Unsure as to where to take the conversation, Michael hears himself taking the lead.

'Maybe we could go for a wander then? Burn off the scones.'

'OK then. That would be nice.'

🕯

Snow falls as they walk the perimeter of Palace Green, past the old buildings that once belonged to the city's Prince Bishops, including Moneyer's Garth, which is now used as the stonemason's yard, and then down onto Saddler Street.

As they walk Evie says, 'You look like a monk with that hood of yours.'

Beneath it he blushes, and pulls it down.

A fresh snowfall is stirring a childlike excitement amongst the Friday night drinkers, many of who have turned out early in short-sleeved shirts and tiny dresses.

Evie asks, 'So have you got any plans for Christmas?'

Though dimly aware of the background noise of advertising, and having passed the occasional party of men in Santa Claus hats already half-cut as they alighted at the bus station to continue drinking sessions that began back in their villages hours earlier, Michael has not given the festive season a moment's thought. He rarely does until a day or two before Christmas Day, when he takes the bus into the city to buy his mother a bottle of her favourite perfume, which she manages to make last exactly one year until she gladly receives the next one. While there he also buys the chicken and the vegetables, and the Christmas pudding that neither of them has had the courage to admit they don't like a great deal, and has been doing this ever since he has been allowed to get the bus alone, which he did for the first time aged seven. With just the two of them there has never been any need to get a turkey; his mother always said the white meat, dense like a thousand folded feathers, was difficult to digest anyway. He wonders whether he should buy the perfume this year, but dismisses the thought. He doesn't even know upon which day Christmas falls.

When he doesn't reply Evie says, 'Will you be with family?'

Michael thinks about the oversized hospital bed that dominates the living room, and he thinks about his mother in it. No chicken will pass her lips this year, not unless he purees it to a pulp with a bit of gravy stirred in. The cat, however, may yet enjoy the greatest feline feast of its long life.

'Yes,' he says, and it is not a lie.

'Are there many of you?'

'There's me, and there's my mam.'

'Oh?'

A look of surprise registers on Evie's face, but only very briefly. 'Is your dad not around?'

Michael shakes his head.

424

'You're not in touch with him? Sorry – tell me to shut up if I'm asking too many questions. It's the budding researcher in me, always probing.'

'It's OK. I've no idea where he is. The last I heard he was living very near here. About a minute's walk away actually.'

'Really? Wow. In the city centre?'

'Close, yeah.'

'Was he connected to the university then?'

Again Michael shakes his head, and turns away to suppress a smile at the thought.

'The prison.'

'Ah. He was a prison officer then. A – what do you call it? – a *screw*.'

'Not quite.'

Evie looks at him, then she understands.

'But that was years ago and I was just a kid,' says Michael. 'Don't you want to know what he was in for?'

'Well, yes. Obviously. But I thought it was rude to ask these things.'

'So did I,' he smiles. 'All I heard was that he was in and out several times, and graduated with flying colours in criminality, never to be seen again.'

'Do you miss him?'

'I never knew the bloke. Neither did my mam really. It's hard to miss something you never had.'

'I suppose it is. But does it not still leave a bit of a void, or unanswered questions?'

Michael shrugs.

'I've not thought about it,' he says, even though he has thought about it at some point during every day of his life. 'The way I see it, I had it better than a lot of kids growing up. There was no drunk dad slapping me about when he rolled in hammered and no stepfathers stepping in to do the same when the first one had buggered off. There was no drama, and no other kids to divide her attention. There was just me and my mam.'

'That sounds nice, the way you describe it. And it's a good outlook to have.'

'It's just the way it was – and still is. She had me at the age I am now, so we've always been more like mates really anyway. Best mates. What little I know I learned from her.'

'I bet she's proud of you.'

He feels his cheeks filling with heat.

'I don't know.'

'Of course she is. She sounds great.'

'Yes,' says Michael. And then after a long pause: 'Yes, she is.'

They walk and talk, Michael and Evelyn, and he sees parts of the small city that he never knew existed. This is collegiate-land, where wealth and education, or both, buys you a room in a campus building, or the medieval castle even, with many of the colleges named for saints. She takes him past several of them in a long, loping route, from the old colleges in the Bailey – St Chad's, St John's, St Cuthbert's ('Generally full of the worst kind of wankers,' she says of the latter, with a dismissive wave of the hand) – to those stretching up Elvet Hill to the south of the city, St Aiden's, St Mary's, Van Mildert, and all the way up to the new university buildings at Mount Oswald, out towards the crematorium where his mother's mother was turned to ash all those years ago. A distant memory now.

As they wander, time for Michael becomes a series of frozen moments that he hopes he will be able to remember forever, and if he could somehow preserve this night and all within it just as it is – the stars, their hot breaths pluming before them, even the way the small falling flakes settle on her woollen hat – then he would do exactly that. Already he knows he does not want tomorrow to exist because tomorrow he will not be here, with her, with Evie. Tomorrow at home with his mother, cleaning soiled sheets and scrubbings dishes, cannot possibly match tonight.

Evie continues to enthuse about Cuthbert, life on Lindisfarne and the *haliwerfolk*, and is surprised when he expresses ignorance about the sculpture of the famous wandering community down near the theatre on Millennium Square.

'But you must have seen it – it's six monks carrying a coffin?'

The way in which Evie says this, and the way in which her eyes search his face for recognition, makes Michael feels naked with shame and ignorance.

'*The Journey*?' she adds. 'It's called *The Journey*.'

There is almost a pleading in her voice, to which he responds "Oh that one, yes, of course, down on the square," but they both know that he is lying.

🕯

They walk in soft-footed silence until that silence become notably prolonged, a physical void, and Evie feels compelled to fill it.

'So how did you get on with school? Did you enjoy it?'

He shakes his head.

'It wasn't really my bag.'

'No?'

'No. I jacked it in around Christmas in the final year and never really went back.'

'You never went back?'

'No.'

'Isn't that technically illegal?'

Michael shrugs.

'No one missed me.'

'You mean you never sat your exams?'

'There didn't seem any point.'

'I'd say there's no point going to school for twelve years and then *not* doing your exams.'

'I'd had enough by then.'

'I think we all had, but still. All those hours in the classroom for nothing.'

'I was only there because it's what you're meant to do.'

Suddenly his face brightens.

'I do remember that spring and summer though. It was brilliant.'

'Brilliant – why?'

'Because it was the first time I felt completely free. The only time, actually. No school to go to and nowhere to be. My mam was out at work, so I had the house to myself or I was outside all day, every day. I just used to walk all the time, for five or six hours or more.'

'Where?'

They stop and sit on a wall to rest. The street is empty and the stone is bone-cold beneath them, but neither Michael nor Evie remark upon it.

'Everywhere. My village is surrounded by hills and woods and streams. It was great, just me and the birds and the animals and the weather. No people, no traffic, no noise. No teachers or other kids. It was like how I imagine the past might have been.'

'And you'd like to live in the past, would you?' says Evie, but before Michael can answer she adds, 'I know I would. I mean, I think deep down all historians do. Or maybe we do already. We find our preferred era and we occupy it, via books and lectures and essays, exams, field trips and societies.'

'And what's yours?'

'Anglo-Saxon England in the Middle Ages. I've got mates who are pure Jacobean fangirls and others who are total Tudor groupies but give me those centuries between the fall of the Roman Empire and the Norman invasion. It's such a vast field that I get overwhelmed.'

'Why then? Why that period?'

'Because so much happened after the Romans departed. You've got the rise of Christianity, tribal life in the seven main kingdoms, the increased frequency of Viking attacks, which was real blood-and-guts stuff, though the Norse colonisation wasn't entirely without certain benefits or advancements. Then you have the unification of England in the tenth century, and then not long afterwards that chapter ends with William the Conquerer coming over from France and turning the country on its head once again. 1066 and all that, as they say. It's probably a period best represented in its earlier years by the life and influence of Cuthbert and the beginning of the building

428

of Durham Cathedral at the end of that era and that which followed: Norman England.'

'Who's he?' says Michael, before smiling.

Evie rolls her eyes.

'Wow. Again, I've never heard that one before.'

'Sorry. You know so much.'

'I'd say I know about a tiny fraction of one per cent of what there is to know about that time. But perhaps that's the appeal: the enduring mystery of it, and the hunger to learn more. And where better than here, in the north-east, where so much of today's theological understanding began? Some of my non-historian pals back home thought I was nuts applying to come to Durham – they reckoned it was a second-rate Oxbridge – but what do they know? It's a hotbed of living history round here.'

'Is it?'

'Of course it is. Are you sure they didn't teach you *any* of this stuff – Cuthbert and the like?'

Michael pulls a face.

'Maybe. I don't know.'

'Anyway, it's the changing language of history that really bends my head.'

'How do you mean?'

'Well, it's a liquid entity, language, isn't it?' says Evie. 'Even fifty or a hundred or so years ago people spoke differently to how they do today. Seems like any historian who wants to get on has to be lyrical lexicon wiz who knows his or her diphthongs from their monophthongs too, and can exercise perfect control over the glottal stop.'

As she talks Michael studies the perfect angles of her face, her quizzical brow and her flawless skin, pale in the winter moonlight.

'Have things really changed that much then?'

'Over the centuries, of course, yes, language as much as anything. We're talking about a long period of time here, from the limitations of Anglo-Saxon with a sprinkling of Anglo-Frisian or Ingvaeonic and then on to the curious tones of Old Norse, Old Norman and Anglo-Norman, followed of course by

Middle English, which saw the great vowel shift that begat the Early Modern English that came next, alighting finally upon the fluid talk of contemporary times, from the sing-song poetics of the local Pitmatic of the past century or two to the flavour-some hybrid patois favoured by the young English of today. Also all these archaic texts that we're expected to get a handle on have significant regional dialectic differences, as well. If I gave you the opening gambit to, say, *The Voyages of Ohthere and Wulfstan* or *Ayenbite of Inwyt* in true Kentish dialect, or even perhaps that enduring favourite *Beowulf* unadorned and spoken as it was intended – "Hwæt. We Gardena in geardagum, þeodcyninga, þrym gefrunon" and so on – you would be left befuddled and consider me utterly pretentious, and that would be fair. You have very striking eyes, you know.'

At first Michael doesn't even hear this last part. He is caught off guard, overwhelmed by information and a conversation that he wants to be a part of but whose reference points and unfamiliar old words are too far-flung, too academic. She is looking right at him, her expression ambiguous. Snow is falling again.

'What? Do I?'

'Has no one told you that before? I've never seen a colour quite like it.'

'Brown?'

'No, not just brown. There's sparks of green and orange in there too. They're almost the colour of copper or rust. Sorry, that sounds weird and intensely personal. Don't take it the wrong way.'

What is the wrong way? Michael wonders. Is this a good or bad thing?

'Also,' Evie continues, 'they're big.'

'Thanks, they're all my own work.'

'Like a rabbit's or an owl's. But don't let it go to your head.'

'They're already there.'

'The observation, I mean.'

And then the moment presses pause on itself and Michael slowly finds himself leaning towards Evie. He can smell her scent. Their mouths are close, their eyes exploring each other.

He goes to kiss her, but at the last moment she turns away. She clears her throat and looks down the street. More flakes gather on her hat, the shoulders of her coat. Michael says nothing. He wants to die.

Seconds stretch to what feels like hours as Michael's empty stomach moils, troubled and sour. He looks at his boots, rimmed with snow. He looks at the footprints they have made, and which led to here.

Finally Evie turns back to him. The light of the moon is reflected by the snow so that even now, in deepest December, it does not feel fully dark. Her face is all he can see: the slightly upturned nose, her neat teeth. The strands of hair that have fallen loose from beneath her hat.

'Sorry,' she says. 'It's just that –'

Perhaps she expects him to interrupt her, or for him to apologise, but there is nothing to say. He only feels shame and embarrassment at ever thinking this might lead anywhere. She readjusts herself on the cold stone wall and tries again.

'My head's all over the place at the moment. I'm a bit of a mess. It wouldn't be fair.'

'Fair?'

He hears his voice rise slightly. There is a tremor in it which catches him by surprise.

'On you, I mean. Us getting involved, I mean.'

He looks back at his boots, then kicks them together. Strips of snow shaped by the soles fall away. But still he has no words to offer.

'You're a really nice guy, Michael.'

'But.'

'But I just have so much course work to get done, then I'm going home for Christmas and then the spring term is going to be insane.'

He clears his throat.

'I just thought I might – or you might – I mean—'

'I know, I know. I just don't want to lead you on.'

He looks at Evie. Looks at her eyes, the cheekbones. That nose. That skin.

'You're not,' he says. 'I mean, you haven't. I just like talking to you and being around you. I've not met anyone who's so bright and smart and funny too. Someone who sees me. I've not met anyone like you before.'

'And I've not met anyone like you either. You're much more fun than most of the blokes at this uni. Half of them are just so entitled, and have been since birth, and you just know they're going to waltz into positions of power by the time they're twenty-five and that sickens me. But you're different. You're more ... real.'

'Real?'

'No, not real. Sorry, that sounds like patronising town-and-gown bullshit, and that's not me, *at all*. I just mean, you're yourself. You're quiet and you're not trying to prove anything to anyone. You're not out thumping your chest on the rugby pitch or off on a pub crawl with the lads, wolf-whistling every passing woman. You're original. You're a good person. You're *you*.'

'But,' he says again.

She studies his face.

'But nothing really. I'm just not looking to get into anything with anyone. I'd rather be honest right now in this moment, than cause any uncertainty. I like you, Michael. I like hanging out. I hope we can do it again – as friends.'

He slowly nods.

'Friends, yes.'

They both look up as fat snowflakes fall upon them.

Michael sticks his tongue out and catches one.

'It tastes of the sky,' he says.

Laughing, Evie does the same.

It is late but Michael is not tired. The city echoes with voices and snatches of song and the scent of aftershave, lager, perfume and synthetic smoke; the scents of the intoxicated and the hopeful.

Doorways down to basement bars thump with the repetitive sound of beats, muted by their subterranean origins. Surly men guard the doors as if each building houses invaluable treasures or persons of huge importance. Their shirts are clean and pressed and strain to contain the valleys of muscles that flex beneath the starched polyester. Their small eyes give nothing away yet see everything; their feet are planted on the pavement, each stance a silent statement, each man as entitled to occupy their space as an ancient oak in a paddock.

Michael has an itch inside of him, a rattling sense of unease, so he walks and walks, away from the cut and thrust of the drink and drugs circuit, across the square and over the bridge, the cathedral leaning hard against the sour-milk moon.

He passes more pubs bubbling with music, the smokers gathered outside in roped-off pens. Bearded men rub their hands together and laugh, and women totter and cackle and sing in protest against tomorrow's sober reality, their goosebumps worn like medals. Some sport tans that defy the season and others offer quick and cutting verbal rebukes to the playful but witless suggestions of passing men whose hands are pressed snugly into their pockets.

Tonight the city is alive with potential; alive with the promise of sex and violence.

He climbs a hill, away from the hubbub, and he sees tombstones.

This city's old graveyard comes alive at night too. Here, amongst death, life blooms in the folded creases of darkness. Sometimes young couples lie on the cold flat headstones that have fallen from their soft soil beds, clinging half-naked to each other as if resisting the gravitational pull, while solitary men periodically shuffle singing into the shadows with beer bottle or phone in one hand, and spraying penis in the other. They shake off at the moon, and sometimes they howl too, domesticated creatures suddenly set free into the wild jungle of the weekend. At other times women go together, squatting precariously on dagger-like heels, hand in manicured hand, and they giggle as steaming trickles find the path of least resistance between the old uneven flagstones and fill the neat lines of the engraved names, the birth dates and the death dates.

433

Unseen, a well-fed fox skulks by, mean-eyed and cautious, almost glued to the cemetery wall. Tonight in the far corner there is a rough sleeper who makes a bed for himself in a sepulchral tomb, carefully sliding the heavy slab aside and climbing down onto a mattress of bone dust, moss and spiderwebs. The noise of the city fades first to a muted whisper and then an airless hush as he folds himself into this space as deep and immeasurable as England itself and then pulls the lid back into place, always careful to leave an inch of skylight overhead so that he does not become a corpse completely.

Michael passes on by, as stealthy and covert as the fox. His thighs feel the hill and his muscles carry memories of the many lost days of his adolescence tramping these same streets alone.

And, as if cut by the blade of the cold winter air, his lungs taste the metallic blood of the night.

He turns and walks slowly back downhill to the bus station.

It is late when he finally leaves the city, last-bus late. Something has been holding him back.

On the top deck Michael is surrounded by young and not-so-young drunks tipping polystyrene trays of gravy down their throats and vaping as if it is about to be outlawed. The lights in the bus are too bright and women adjust their skirts and slur their words, and the tinny beat of a bassline tune plays on a mobile phone for all to hear. It merges into the next one and the next one, each song much the same tempo as the last. Swaying in the aisle, one young man with his Friday night hair shaved so close on the sides that it's like a reverse haircut that the monks of old wore, steadily pisses into a pint glass while his friends roar with laughter. He sits holding it with one hand as it were a glass of expensive imported lager and then somewhere between the city and the first village he flings it through the open window, to more laughter and a short round of a song that Michael does not know.

Even though the bus is nearly empty now, he alights one stop early and walks the extra half mile to the village through the thickening snowfall rather than stay on the last bus any longer.

He slides his key into the lock and steps into the house.

'Mam,' he says. 'It's me. It's Michael. I'm back.'

There is a faint light from the one lamp that has been left on in the front room and the cat is at his legs now, winding in between them. It presses itself close, grateful for his return.

'Mam.'

He turns on the hallway light on the way through.

She is there, head to one side, mouth hanging open. It looks as if it is collapsing in on itself, her mouth, inverted somehow, like an old woman missing her dentures. Her skin appears a sallow green in the drained light of this December night.

'Mam.'

He touches her shoulder but she does not stir. He gently shakes her, the cat still at his legs, mewing. There is no reaction, so he feels her wrist but he doesn't know what he is feeling for exactly, so he pinches the loose skin on the back of her hand. He twists it, and it feels wet almost, greasy.

One eyelid flutters. He puts his ear to her mouth.

Her breath is there – just. It is hollow and shallow yet sounds as if it is coming from far away, like the slow drip of water deep in a dark and lonely cave in which no light ever penetrates.

Michael shakes her by the shoulder harder now and his mother's head is lolling. It moves a little on the pillow, but that is it. There is drool and he knows that death is in the room. Death has been in the house for a long time, but now it has crawled into bed with his mother and is intent on occupying her entirely.

He lifts her up, moves her forward, primps the pillows, and then removes the third one that she has by her side for support. He grips it with both hands and holds it to his chest, and as he does Michael Cuthbert feels a sob rise up from the dark and lonely cave that sits within him, that sits within everyone.

Oh Cuddy, can you hear me? Call out, Cuddy, if you can.

Michael, I am here.

Cuthbert? Is that really you?

It is me.

You're Saint Cuthbert?

On my life and on my death. I am he.

Are you in my mind?

I am in the minds of all who wish to receive me.

Am I losing it?

I don't know. We are each of us different, and our experiences are unique. That's what makes us human and defines us so.

At least tell me something so I know that it's you and not just a voice in my head.

But I am just a voice in your head.

But tell me something, just so I know I'm not making you up because of the things I've read and been told, or from standing on your tomb.

Maybe you are. Does it matter, Michael?

It does to me.

Do you believe in me?

I believe there once was a man called Cuthbert who they reckon tended sheep as a boy, and became a monk who lived on a rock, and his body was sometimes kept in a cave and then, when the Vikings came, carried all about the place. And then, later, when the folk who carried him got tired or saw a cow and received a sign, depending on what you believe, they built first a church to house his body, then a bigger church and then the cathedral, and Durham was born. And there his bones lie today, sealed beneath stone, where Japanese tourists kneel and the cafe sells scones the size of your fist. And he is you.

But what do you believe, Michael?

I don't know.

It's OK not to know. Only the arrogant and the ignorant are certain. Everything else is myth and mystery. Untold history.

Have you met God?

Have you?

No. Maybe. I don't know. But if he's about I could use him now.

Well, I'm here.

Are you?

Yes. Yes I am, Michael. I'm with you. You're not alone.

Show me a sign then.

A sign?

Yes. I just really need to know I'm not going insane.

Fine. Raise your right hand to heaven.

Like this?

Like that. There: I've made you move your arm as if I were a puppet master. Now look around you. Look to the sky and the trees. Have you seen any birds today?

Yes, of course.

Good. I put them there too.

I need to ask a question.

Ask me anything, son.

I want to know: in the eyes of God, is it a sin to want to end someone's suffering?

God does not judge.

Will I burn in hell?

That's not how it works.

But hell is real.

Perhaps. Perhaps not. Heaven and hell are merely each man's creation. Again, I say, we are all different.

But God—

God does not judge. We must only judge ourselves. That's all. Decisions are ours alone to be made. That's another thing that defines us as human: the choices we make in the moment. Mercy is not a sin. That is all you need to know, Michael. Mercy is not a sin.

But I'm scared, Saint Cuthbert.

Scared of what?

Scared of being alone.

That's understandable. Are you afraid of anything else?

Yes.

What?

Everything.

The snow falls all night and the silence is absolute.

Michael's eyes are heavy and thick with the sleep that lightly seals them shut. He forces himself awake and sits up in the chair. He is still gripping the pillow, but when he slowly stands he lets it fall from his lap.

His hands are shaking but when he clenches his fists they stop.

He feeds the cat and it exits by the back door, stealthily stalking the shadows of the garden, its form half-buried in the cold deep carpet of the fresh fall, and when it hops up on the fence, small clumps of snow that are too heavy to sit there fall and create a delightful flash of dusting that hovers and sparkles for the briefest moment, and then the night is still again. The garden settles back into itself.

It is still dark when he packs his bag and kisses his mother on her cold brow. As he does so he hears a small brave bird make the first call of the day.

He smells her hair. He breathes it in.

Turns the lights off.

Leaves.

Sources

Direct quotations from the following books, essays, articles, lectures and broadcasts were used in Book I: *Saint Cuddy*.

Two Lives of St Cuthbert by Anonymous Monk of Lindisfarne; *Life of Cuthbert* by Bede; *Lindisfarne Priory: English Heritage Guidebook*; *To the Island of Tides: A Journey to Lindisfarne* by Alistair Moffat; *St Aidan and St Cuthbert* by Henry Kelsey; *The Anglo-Saxon Chronicles* translated and collated by Anne Savage; *St Cuthbert's Corpse: A Life After Death* by David Willem; *St Cuthbert of Durham* by Philip Nixon; *The New Cambridge Medieval History I c.500–c.700* ed. Paul Fouracre; *A History of Britain: 1* by Simon Schama; *The Historical Works of Symeon of Durham*; *Vanished Kingdoms: The History of Half-Forgotten Europe* by Norman Davies; *Fire of the North* by David Adam; *The Edge of the World: How the North Sea Made Us Who We Are* by Michael Pye; *Journal of Ecclesiastical History* by S. Coupland; *From Holy Island to Durham: The Contexts and Meanings of the Lindisfarne Gospels* by Richard Gameson; *A Naturalist on Lindisfarne* by Richard Perry; *Marmion* by Walter Scott; *Building St Cuthbert's Shrine* by Lionel Green; 'Lindisfarne and the Origins of the Cult of St Cuthbert' by Alan Thacker (from *St Cuthbert, His Cult and His Community to AD 1200* ed. Gerald Bonner, David Rollason and Clare Stancliffe); *Chronicle of Symeon of Durham*; *St Cuthbert and Durham Cathedral: A Celebration* ed. Douglas Pocock; *Æthelstan: The Making of England* by Tom Holland; 'The Wanderings of Saint Cuthbert' by D. W. Rollason (from *Cuthbert: Saint and Patron* ed. D. W. Rollason); *The Oxford*

Illustrated History of Medieval England by Nigel Saul; *Anglo-Saxon Charters: An Annotated List and Biography* ed. Peter Sawyer; *The Age of Bede*; *Lindisfarne: The Cradle Island* by Magnus Magnusson; *Cuthbert and the Northumbrian Saints* by Paul Frodsham; *Saints Over the Border* by Margaret Gibbs; *Tales of English Minsters: Durham* by Elizabeth Grierson; 'The Spirituality of St Cuthbert' by Sister Benedicta Ward SLG (from *St Cuthbert, His Cult and His Community to AD 1200* ed. Gerald Bonner, David Rollason and Clare Stancliffe); 'Cuthbert, Pastor and Solitary' by Clare Stancliffe (from *St Cuthbert, His Cult and His Community to AD 1200* ed. Gerald Bonner, David Rollason and Clare Stancliffe); *Beasts and Saints* by Helen Waddell; *Lindisfarne Landscapes* by Sheila Mackay; *Outlandish* by Damian Le Bas, Jo Clement and W. John Hewitt; *100 Days on Holy Island: A Writer's Exile* by Peter Mortimer; *Monasteries in the Landscape* by Mick Aston; 'Elements in the Background to the Life of St Cuthbert and the Early Cult' by J. Campbell (from *St Cuthbert, His Cult and His Community to AD 1200* ed. Gerald Bonner, David Rollason and Clare Stancliffe); *The Anonymous Life of Cuthbert*; *Some Lovely Islands* by Leslie Thomas; 'Saint Cuthbert – Soul Friend' by Gerald Bonner (from *Cuthbert: Saint and Patron* ed. D. W. Rollason); 'Why Was Saint Cuthbert So Popular?' by D. W. Rollason (from *Cuthbert: Saint and Patron* ed. D. W. Rollason); *Newcastle Cathedral Saints* by George Miles; *Rites of Durham, being a description or brief declaration of all the ancient monuments, rites, & customs belonging or being within the monastical church of Durham before the suppression* by Anonymous (1593); *Leaders in the Northern Church: Sermons Preached in the Diocese of Durham* by Bishop Joseph Barber Lightfoot; *Northanhymbre Saga: The History of the Anglo-Saxon Kings of Northumbria* by John Marsden; *De clade Lindisfarnensis monasterii* ('On the destruction of the monastery of Lindisfarne') by Alcuin; 'The Treasures of St Cuthbert' by Dr Janina Ramirez; *A Brief History of the Anglo-Saxons* by Geoffrey Hindley; *The Anglo-Saxons* ed. James Campbell; *Byzantine and Romanesque Architecture* by T. G. Jackson; *The History of England Volume I: Foundation* by Peter Ackroyd; *Durham Cathedral* by C. J. Stranks; *Durham Cathedral* by Letitia Elizabeth Landon; *The Letters of*

Samuel Johnson by Samuel Johnson; *In Search of England* by H.V. Morton; *The Buildings of England: County Durham* by Nikolaus Pevsner; *Ecclesiastical History of the English People* by Bede.

Further titles that proved to be invaluable in the writing and research of *Cuddy* include: *King of Dust: Adventures in Forgotten Sculpture* by Alex Woodcock; *Briggflatts* by Basil Bunting; *Selected Poems* by Tony Harrison; *Place of Repose: St Cuthbert's Last Journey* by Katharine Tiernan; *Cuthbert's People: The Building of Durham Cathedral* by Ian Adams; *Lindisfarne Priory: English Heritage Guidebook*; *Finchale Priory: English Heritage Guidebook*; *Saint Cuthbert, with an Account of the State in which his Remains were found upon the opening of his Tomb in Durham Cathedral* by James Raine; *The Battle of Neville's Cross: The Whole Story* by Simon Webb; *The Prince Bishops of Durham* by Simon Webb; *The Expedition of Humphry Clinker* by Tobias Smollett; *The Abridged Life of St Godric and the Tragedy of Finchale Priory* by J. F. J. Smith; *Battles of the English Civil War* by Austin Woolrych; *The English Civil War* by Diane Purkiss; *To Catch a King: Charles II's Great Escape* by Charles Spencer; *The History of England Volume II* by Peter Ackroyd; *Cromwell's Convicts: The Death March from Dunbar 1650* by John Sadler and Rosie Serdiville; *Durham Cathedral: Pitkins Guides* by C. J. Stranks; *Lost Lives, New Voices: Unlocking the Stories of the Scottish Soldiers at the Battle of Dunbar 1650* by Christopher Gerard.

Notes & Acknowledgements

Cuddy was written on location on the island of Lindisfarne, Northumberland during two stays in the spring and summer of 2019. All sources cited are as accurate to the best of my knowledge. *The Mason's Mark* was written in Robin Hood's Bay, North Yorkshire and Mytholmroyd, West Yorkshire during the summer of 2020, and in the Lammermuir Hills of Berwickshire, on the Scottish side of the border, not far from St Cuthbert's birthplace of Melrose, in the autumn of 2020. The interlude section, *The Stone Speaks*, was written in Wensleydale, North Yorkshire in October 2021. *The Corpse in the Cathedral* was also written in the Lammermuir Hills of Berwickshire, Scotland, during the autumn/winter of 2019. It was loosely inspired by the real-life excavation of St Cuthbert's corpse in 1827, though names have been changed to differentiate between fact and fiction. *Daft Lad* was begun first and finished last. It was written in Mytholmroyd, West Yorkshire and Durham City, at various points between early 2018 and late 2021.

I share this information only because *Cuddy* began life as a bold (and possibly foolish) idea to write an alternative history of the north-east of England, a fictionalised account of true events. As the stories are tied so specifically to real locations, all of which proved to be inspirational, I thought them worthy of mention. So too readers might also note the dates coincide with a seismic global event out in the wider world – a reminder, perhaps, that history happens now. It is continuous.

Initial research for this novel was assisted by Arts Council England. With thanks and gratitude to them, and to Claire Malcolm and all at New Writing North for their continued support.

Thanks are due also to Pat Barker, Anna Barker and David Atkinson for their ideas and invaluable input, some of which came about during a podcast conversation recorded with Laura McKenzie of Durham University for Durham Book Festival 2019. Thanks also to my agents Jessica Woollard, Clare Israel, Alice Howe and all at David Higham Associates. At Bloomsbury, gratitude to my editor Allegra Le Fanu, who did a valiant job in shaping this work and also to Paul Baggaley, Terry Lee, Philippa Cotton, Emilie Chambeyron, Rachel Wilkie, Saba Ahmed, Francisco Vilhena and design wizard Greg Heinimann. Chloe Barton, font of all local Durham knowledge. Zaffar Kunial. Carol Gorner and everyone at the Gordon Burn Trust. Thanks to Kathryn Myers for her editorial input and continued assistance, my brother Richard Myers, and both their families

Special gratitude, as ever, to my family, friends and my wife Adelle Stripe.

A Note on the Type

The text of this book is set in Bembo, which was first used in 1495 by the Venetian printer Aldus Manutius for Cardinal Bembo's *De Aetna*. The original types were cut for Manutius by Francesco Griffo. Bembo was one of the types used by Claude Garamond (1480–1561) as a model for his Romain de l'Université, and so it was a forerunner of what became the standard European type for the following two centuries. Its modern form follows the original types and was designed for Monotype in 1929.